Eden Crossing

A MYSTERY THRILLER

David Stockar

Dedication

To my parents, Ivo and Helena Stockar, to whom I am forever indebted for all their love, guidance, and genuine kindness. They were my role models and I miss them every day.

In addition, I wish to pay a small tribute to the literary genius of Edgar Allan Poe, whose great works inspired select portions of this novel.

Contents

List of Characters

Major

- Bianca, Ariella - Leader of the Eden Sisterhood; Shaman known as The White Dove

- Cabot, James (The Inspector) - State Police Chief investigator, a seasoned detective

- Dvorak, Molly - Senior Detective, most senior member of Inspector Cabot's team

- Green, Gavin - Raven Inn employee, left Eden Valley as a boy but recently returned

- Hermit - Mysterious recluse who dwells in the vast North Woods

- Hughes, Sam - Innkeeper and widower, nicknamed The Raven, grew up in Eden Valley

- Lapp, Lenore - Young shunned Amish woman, oldest child in Lapp family

- Lee, Chen - Junior Detective and Data Analyst on Inspector Cabot's team

- Miller, Amos - Young widowed Amish farmer, Lenore's love interest

- Stevens, Kelly - Junior Detective, newest member of Inspector Cabot's team

- Walker, Alvin - Local Police Deputy, recently returned to Eden Valley

- White Witch - fabled Ghost of Evelyn Drake, who died 200 years ago

Minor

- Agnes - Young maid at The Raven Inn, joins Sisterhood

- Annabel Lee (Anna) - Member of Eden Sisterhood

- Davies, Hank - Assistant Coroner on Frank Dunn's staff

- Drake, Arthur - Historical figure in Eden Valley lore, a suspected former privateer

- Drake, Evelyn - Historical figure in Eden Valley lore, suspected of haunting the Valley

- Dunn, Frank - State Police Chief Coroner

- Fischer, Esther - Elderly Amish widow well-versed in medicine and lore

- Girard, Cheryl - Mysterious waitress at The Raven Inn

- Hazel - Young woman, member of Eden Sisterhood

- Kentahoe - Ariella's mentor, a powerful Sioux shaman

- Lapp, John - Amish farmer, Lenore's father

- Lapp, Josef - Amish youth in late teens, Lenore's younger brother, eldest Lapp son

- Lapp, Mary - Lenore's mother, Amish wife of John Lapp

- Marie - Young woman, member of Eden Sisterhood

- McAlester, Jerry - Cook at Raven Inn, high-school friend of Sam Hughes

- Miller, Linus - Amish community undertaker, older brother to Amos Miller

- Morgan, Gus - Local Police Chief, old friend of Inspector Cabot

- Myers, Jeremiah - Older Amish man

- Porter, Will - Bartender at The Raven Inn, grew up in the Eden Valley
- Rachel - Young woman, member of Eden Sisterhood
- Rebecca - Young woman, member of Eden Sisterhood
- Roberts, Elaine - Server at The Raven Inn, Sam's love interest
- Sarah - Young woman, member of Eden Sisterhood
- Schaffer, Harry - Childhood friend of Sam Hughes
- Snyder, Abel - Amish Bishop and leader of the local Amish community
- Stoltzfus, Ben - Young Amish farmer and Lenore's suitor
- Stone, Erin - Childhood friend of Sam Hughes
- Taylor, Andrew - Young man in blue pickup truck, married to Linda Taylor
- Taylor, Linda - Local young woman and Andrew Taylor's wife
- Walker, George - Alvin's older brother and Sam's childhood friend, now deceased

CHAPTER 1

Goddess of the Moon

$\mathcal{A}$ full moon danced on the pool at midnight, courting the subtle waves with a tranquil tempo, as a gentle breeze swept over the bare torso of a sole bather, creating a chill that aroused her. Ripples disturbed the serenity of the black water, full of mystery. The lone bather, intrepid, disappeared below the surface to emerge moments later in a spray of liquid pearls transformed by the moonlight. Silver rays like Luna moths played with her silken hair, turning her face into a reflection of the source itself. She was Diana the huntress, risen once more. Like the goddess of the moon, she frolicked with the milky rays that illuminated her royal bath. A deity resurrected that nothing could threaten—or could it?

At the base of the pool, a waterfall announced its presence. In harmony with the wind, it played a timeless tune while a cloud overtook the moon, plunging the magical scene into darkness. Rain clouds entered at the beckoning of the wind, which whipped the pool into a frenzy.

When the moon reappeared, the rain threat had passed but all had changed. The waterfall played in atonal apathy while the moon wondered what it had missed. The pool was empty. Only the dying wind and a lone black raven knew the secrets of the bather who had vanished, leaving only breadcrumbs of footsteps to her hidden throne.

Western Pennsylvania

CHAPTER 2

The Dove, the Devil, and the Raven

Beyond the roar of the Eden River, a mysterious woman stepped out of a log cabin to embrace the hazy morning. Wearing a white robe decorated in a mosaic of turquoise beads, her raven hair curled over her shoulders and flowed down her back. An ornate, white-feathered headband framed her perfect face, accenting her emerald eyes that possessed a tranquility bred of inner peace. Steeped in mystique, like the thick cloud of mist that covered the surrounding meadow, Ariella was her name. Finishing her cup of white tea, the enchantress descended the porch steps and crossed the foggy field, disappearing like a phantom. As she emerged on the far side against the tree line, a flock of crows climbed skyward, squawking in protest. Ariella ignored them, focusing elsewhere.

With a nimble gait, she entered the silver forest and disappeared. All fell silent. All was still. All expectantly awaited the coo of a white dove that now ascended from the shadowy woods like the spirit that defined them. Had the woman transformed from a witch to a dove or a woman to a witch? Which is which? Oh, these woods many secrets hold.

For within them, mystery and magic intertwined to weave a web so bizarre that to explain it doomed one to become entangled and risk losing one's reality. In deathly silence, this mystical land harbored the kingdom of the White Witch and the playground of the White Dove, whose powers far exceeded the imagination of their conservative neighbors, the Pennsylvania Amish.

* * * * *

A lone buggy made its way down the narrow, steep road toward the valley. On this late summer day, the smell of ripening corn foretold of the coming harvest. In the faint breeze, the worn horse found favor despite its heavy load of fruits and vegetables. Skillfully, an Amish youth in his late teens mastered the equine, pulling back on the reins to slow the cart's descent toward the Eden River.

Eden Valley had been patiently chiseled by the river that shared its name. In the ancient sea that covered all 300 million years ago swam strange creatures, most long forgotten and never to be revealed. Sole vestiges of that lost world were the layered rocks that resisted the insatiable appetite of the river, the persistent sculptor of the carved landscape. The steep valley was the masterpiece, and the rocks were the medium. Between them, the river and the rocks had witnessed countless dramas as either silent spectators or apathetic participants.

This part of Pennsylvania had been home to the Amish community since the time of the nation's birth. Living in harmony with the valley, securing their existence from the fertile soil, the "Plain People" changed slowly. Like the landscape, they found comfort, peace, and unity in the ways of the past and the values they fostered.

Mirroring the clear water of the patient river, the Amish youth driving the cart had no need for change and change had little control over him. He remained sealed in a cultural time capsule that, by any standard, seemed content to remain unaltered.

Nervous, the tired horse neighed and resisted as it neared the covered bridge that appeared as old as the original dirt path. The structure stood supported by massive, hand-hewn wooden beams made of mighty chestnut trees, giants that had dominated the native forests for millennia until the last century, when they were reduced to pathetic shrubs by a foreign blight. Like so many native species, they joined the growing number of victims sacrificed in the progress of "the English," as the Amish called outsiders. Such insatiable restlessness of these outsiders seemed to have no bounds. Even now, it threatened the old and tempted the young.

Suddenly, the horse reared and stopped, refusing to cross the bridge. With a crack of the whip, the young man urged it forward, to no avail. The animal refused to move, deciding to suffer the threat of a whip rather than enter that fearful crossing. Forced to traverse the red covered bridge twice every Thursday, it rebelled until the pain of the lashes outweighed the fear of crossing. Then, it would run across as if the devil, himself, was on its heels. The animal dreaded that bridge and for good reason.

Over its long history, the red covered bridge had been a place of numerous tragic events, gaining the moniker "Devils Bridge." The equine sensed its sinister energy. On this morning, no amount of whipping seemed to persuade the horse to cross.

"Cum on, ya! Cum on, ya!" the youth hollered at the old horse. "Ya makin' me late to market!" The Amish youth had to step out of the buggy.

"Whaz gotten in ya, Jake?" the youth complained in the old Germanic tongue of the Amish. As he tried to pull the horse forward by the reins, the animal began to rear, potentially upsetting the precious cargo. "Cum on ya, Jake!" He began to prod the stubborn creature. Clearly, nothing good would have transpired had not another Amish buggy arrived on the scene. It too had descended the steep hill to the bridge and now came up behind the youth and his charge.

"Josef, whaz the matt'r? Ya nev'r learn'd horsemanship, did ya?" An older man in the second buggy laughed. "Wait 'til yur *fader* hears how ya treatin' his horse," the jolly old man teased. "Here, let me show ya how it's done." Moving his one-horse buggy around Josef's, he took the lead, but as his mare reached the first plank of the covered bridge, she too froze in fear. Apparently, the two animals knew something the men had no power to perceive.

"Now, whaz with ya, Nellie? She nev'r stops like that. Oh, she don't like t'is bridge neither, mind ya, but she nev'r refuses to cross. Whaz the matter, girl?" The old man used a kind voice that showed his respect for the horse. He never used the whip. Normally, his voice and the reins were enough, but not this time. Just like old Jake, young Nellie refused to cross the bridge.

"T'is here's most odd. What'd ya do, Josef? Cum on there, Nellie girl. Nothin' but an ol' bridge. Nev'r bother'd ya before. Ya'd think the devil cursed the place and some sa'z he done jus' that. But there's been no bother 'ere for some twenty 'ears—not since them English drove in th' river with their fancy automobile. It waz right there." He pointed toward the river below. "That waz long before yur time, boy." Turning to Josef, he stepped out of his buggy, deciding to lead the horse on foot. With a firm and confident hand, he slowly coaxed the young mare across the bridge. Unhappy about her fate, she made the crossing at last.

At the sight of the other horse safely beyond Devils Bridge, old Jake finally found the courage to cross, although at a perilous speed, nearly upsetting the buggy and its contents. Josef had no choice but to race after him.

As he stared at the spooked horse, the old man laughed a hearty laugh. A sudden silence quelled his joy. Adjusting his round, wire-rim glasses, he spotted something near the middle of the river where the current pinned it against a half-sunken tree. A large raven sat on a branch next to it, waiting in silence.

"May th' good Lord save us!" old Jeremiah Myers proclaimed.

"Whaz gotten in ya, Jeremiah?" the youth asked, puzzled as he quieted old Jake.

"The devil's tak'n another in this hellish crossing!"

"What'r ya talk'n so, Jeremiah?" Josef asked as he followed the gaze of the old man. "Lord save us!" he echoed. "Get the police!"

"There's no time for that. She could be alive."

Leaving the horses hitched to the buggies, the two men ran toward the riverbank. Throwing down his hat while ripping off his shoes and outer garment, young Josef fearlessly dove into the river and fought the strong current, reaching the girl's body in seconds. Reluctantly, the large raven abandoned its perch and silently disappeared under the bridge. Working quickly, Josef freed the girl's body from the clutches of the dead tree and pulled her to the riverbank, careful not to allow her head to submerge.

"Help me pull her out, Jeremiah!" he exclaimed.

In no time, the two men extracted the girl's body onto the riverbank, laying her gently on the soft grass. Parting the long brown hair from her face, Josef froze.

"Whaz the matter, Josef?"

Josef did not answer but began trying to resuscitate the girl. Unsure what to do, he managed to rhythmically press on her chest in his singular determination to revive her.

Jeremiah looked on, suddenly realizing why the youth appeared so distressed. "Oh, my God!" he exclaimed. "The good Lord save her!"

* * * * *

A quarter-mile down river from Devils Bridge, toward Kamerynville, stood a colonial roadside inn constructed of native gray limestone. On this morning, the innkeeper, Sam Hughes, rose early. He was a large muscular man in his thirties with a silvering beard that contrasted with his jet-black ponytail.

Sam maintained a well-run establishment that included a bar, a restaurant, and nearly a dozen rooms on the upper floors. Until six years ago, he had embodied the typical upwardly-mobile professional, being a successful financial analyst at a large brokerage firm in Pittsburgh. A newlywed, he lived with his wife in a development destined to blossom with wave upon wave of newborns. Sam and Sandra had plans to contribute to that population boom. In fact, it was shortly after Sandra became pregnant with their first child that Sam's life changed overnight.

On New Year's Eve 2006, Sandra drove their new minivan, purchased weeks earlier with ambitions to fill every seat. She and Sam left her sister's house before the midnight celebration because Sandra felt too tired to stay up late. Sam let her drive, for he had downed more beers than the legal limit. They were discussing baby names when, without warning, a drunk driver crashed into their car, crushing Sandra. To Sam's horror, his beautiful young bride and their unborn child died in his arms. A large part of him died with them on that horrific night. The old Sam disappeared for good. With him went his home, his dreams of a family, and his faith in anything beyond the laws of basic survival.

Overnight, he quit his job to travel the world, becoming a wanderer with a quest far beyond the reaches of this sphere. He drank too much and swore even more, fighting everything and everyone, fueled by an anger that could not be tamed and a thirst for danger that could not be quelled. Death posed a meaningless threat—rather, it was a temptation at times. With little care whether he lived or died, Sam pushed the limit and cursed anyone who dared to stop him.

If anyone asked him how he ended up on the outskirts of the small Pennsylvania town of Kamerynville, Sam would probably say he could not recall. All he wished to remember of that transitional part of his life were the good times. Nothing else mattered. Or he might share stories of his adventures, but he would inevitably stop to silently reflect upon his lost wife and unborn child. At such times, he would walk away, unable to face that which still haunted him. If one was foolish enough to disrespect his sudden silence, he might get angry or he might say he won the bar in a duel. The simple truth was that he inherited it from his father, who had died of a massive heart attack.

The old gray-stone structure dated back two hundred years and had always been called The Eden Inn, after the nearby Eden River. But the first thing Sam did, after sobering up to accept his new role as proprietor, was to change the inn's name to The Raven Inn. Everyone simply called it "The Raven." Sam's inspiration for the name came to him as he slouched over the bar on the day he took ownership. His face buried in his right forearm, he stared at the all-too-familiar raven tattoo he had picked up in high school. "The Raven" had been Sam's nickname since he was sixteen, when his childhood friend Harry Schaffer called him that on account of his long black hair, strong nose, and mysterious dark side. His Raven nickname felt like the only thing Sam still possessed from a time that predated Sandra. He took that raven for a sign—of what, he was not sure to this day. But without hesitation, he changed the name of his newly begotten establishment and it had remained The Raven Inn ever since. That was three years ago.

On this fine, sunny morning, Sam had just unlocked the front door of the inn when a young man in a blue pickup sped into the parking lot, dust flying.

"Mister!" the young man yelled out of his truck window at Sam, who was standing on the large porch. "Have you seen a young woman, twenty-four, long brown hair?"

"Dozens, just last night. Why? You lookin' for a new girlfriend?" Sam replied in a gruff voice that matched his threatening appearance.

"No, I'm looking for my wife. She's been missing for two nights, and the only thing the cops can say is that they're doing all they can. But I don't believe 'em."

"Sorry to hear that, buddy. Hope ya find 'er. What's her name, in case I run into 'er?"

"Linda. Linda Taylor. Here's a picture of her." The young man stepped out of his truck and walked over to Sam. He showed him a torn photograph. "She's tall, brown hair, and blue eyes. Her smile's unforgettable," the young man reflected with pride.

"Pretty," Sam replied and handed back the picture. "Why'd she leave?" Sam was becoming intrigued. It was more interesting than mopping the sticky floor of the bar.

"I don't know. Two days ago, I got home and she was gone. Didn't leave a note. Just vanished."

"Kidnapped?"

"Doubt it. Not unless they made her pack her bags and her makeup."

"She left ya, mate. Clearly, she got a better offer." Sam was not one for sugarcoating his opinions.

The young man planted his feet firmly in a defiant stance, but Sam's size intimidated him. "Doubt it," he replied.

"Yeah. Well, mate, if I see your lovely wife, I may or may not call ya."

"That's not funny!" the youth shot back, glaring at Sam.

"Not being funny. Your old lady might not want to see ya. Did ya ever think of that? No wonder the police don't give a damn. She clearly left ya 'cause she wanted to. She could be in Georgia by now. Did ya think of that?"

"How'd you know her parents live in Georgia?" Andrew Taylor stepped forward two paces but his knees wobbled.

"I don't. Look. Face it. You didn't take the kind of care of 'er that she expected and probably deserved. The blame's on you, mate, and no amount of driving around and weeping over your loss's gonna fix it. If ya want 'er back, call 'er folks in Georgia or 'er best friend, and see if she'll talk to ya. She's bound to be with 'er mom or 'er girlfriend, if she ain't with a new guy. Don't you know anything about women?"

Sam was getting irritated and found no sympathy for this youth, driving around lamenting over what he had freely and willingly wasted. *Fool!* Sam concluded. "Look, I got work to do. Hope ya find her. But if ya ain't gonna treat her right, ya might as well stop lookin'." Sam's terse sense of justice rarely missed the mark.

Andrew Taylor clenched his fists but retreated from the burly man. It was not what he had expected or wished to hear. Slamming his car door in anger, he left without a word.

"Fool!" Sam proclaimed under his breath as the blue pickup disappeared down the road. He sighed, reflecting on his true love lost. "Nevermore," he muttered. "Nevermore."

CHAPTER 3

Lenore

"Oh, my God, it's Lenore!" old Jeremiah proclaimed as he stared down at the limp body Josef had ripped from the clutches of the hungry river.

Josef did not reply. He was determined to awaken life in his older sister who had disappeared months earlier.

"Oh, my God!" Jeremiah continued. "What'z she doin' here? She'z shunned."

To leave the Amish was to say farewell to everything and everyone, and to be as good as dead to your family and community. The punishment made most restless Amish youths reconsider their desire to live a modern lifestyle. Of course, there were a few whose desire to leave became so great that they chose to accept the high price. Lenore Lapp was one such curious, courageous youth. She had decided three months earlier to leave her family, including her younger brother, Josef, to pursue a life beyond the Amish ways. Her whereabouts had been unknown to her family and community, until now.

"Jeremiah, I don't care about no shunnin'. She'z my sister, und I'm gonna save 'er!" Josef proclaimed, as he returned to his task.

"How can I help?" Jeremiah replied.

"Find my *dat* und call an ambulance!"

Old Jeremiah jumped into his buggy and quickly crossed the bridge. His horse remained reluctant to cross, but the old man's determination easily persuaded the young mare. Before long, he disappeared on the far side of the river.

"Ya gotta live, Lenore. Please, God!" Josef prayed between rhythmic compressions.

Then, the seemingly impossible happened. Lenore spit out water and began to breathe. "Oh, thank God!" Josef exclaimed.

She simply stared at him in bewilderment.

"It's me, Lenore. Yur brother, Josef." Josef's ecstasy was replaced by confusion. Surely, it was Lenore. *How could she not remember?* he wondered.

Lenore sat up, frightened and confused, looking at him and the scene about her, genuinely perplexed. It felt as if she had stepped into this world for the first time.

"Lenore, I'm yur brother, Josef," he repeated slowly. "Ya're Lenore Lapp, my older sister," he explained. "Do ya remember?"

She sat there in silence, staring at him. There was no recognition in her eyes. Her tangled brown hair hung about her confused face, and her long white dress was wet and stained by the cuts on her arms and legs and a gash on the back of her head. The blood from the gash had stained the back of her dress in reddish ocher. Looking about, Lenore focused on the sincere face of her brother. Instinctively, she shrugged her shoulders before she spoke. "Where am I, and why am I wet?"

"Ya wer' in the river. Ya nearly drowned. What happen' to ya, Lenore?"

"Iz that my name? Iz 'Lenore' my name?"

"Yes."

"I can't remember. I can't remember anything. Did ya save me?"

"I guess."

"Thank you. Josef, iz it?"

"Yes. Josef, yur brother. I'm yur brother, Lenore! Please, remember that!"

"I'll try."

Seeing her shiver, Josef rushed to the buggy and returned with a worn blanket. "Here, cover up. Help's comin'," he added, as he spotted three black buggies rapidly descending the hill on the far side of the bridge. Jeremiah had alerted several of the Amish elders.

"Why're ya dressed like that?" she asked.

"I'm Amish, und so are..." he paused, recalling that she was shunned from the Amish community and no longer considered one of them. But, in his heart, she would always be his Amish sister. In his heart, nothing had changed.

"Am I Amish?" she asked, sensing his reservation.

He did not know how to answer this simple question. She wondered at his pause before looking across the bridge at the approaching buggies. "I'm not Amish, am I?"

"Ya were, but ya're not. It's complicated."

This answer simply added to her confusion, which began to overwhelm her fragile mind. Rather than return to the question, she simply smiled at him, adding, "Thank you. I don't care either way, as long as I can still be yur sister."

Josef was not a sentimental youth, but tears welled up in his eyes, for he had long wished to see her again and hear those words. He had grown up on an Amish farm as the oldest son of seven children. When not at school, he worked with his father, learning the Amish farming tradition. Like most Amish children, he attended a one-room schoolhouse until grade eight before ending his formal education and turning to farming full time and have his own farm—but first, he had to earn his way.

The unexpected departure of Lenore, the oldest of the Lapp siblings, had been a huge shock and a painful loss. Reluctantly, they had to release her, although they could not erase her memory or the love they had for one of their own.

A shunning was painful and embarrassing to the family that remained on the other side of its social wall. To leave the order was simply not allowed under the *Ordnung*, the strict traditional rules that govern behavior, dress, and attitude within the closely-knit Amish society. For one to leave the faith and to continue to freely associate with the community left behind was forbidden.

To allow an 'open gate' policy would slowly undermine the timeless, well-orchestrated, simple lifestyle that formed the heart of Amish tradition. It would contaminate the proven ways of the past, which were held up as the path to redemption, for they were based in the pious ways of the Bible and such timeless guidance as Christ's Sermon on the Mount. Tradition was proven and innovation was dangerous. There was communal and religious security in this conservative philosophy.

These traditional ways created unacceptable constraints for someone with Lenore's ambitions and natural curiosity, who could not accept the role of an Amish wife. She had struggled with the idea of leaving the faith because she loved her family and her friends. But something inside her could not rest and would not yield.

Although Amish women were treated with the utmost respect, they remained tied to traditional roles and were very limited in their opportunity to explore the world. The Amish culture had little or no violence and provided a loving, socially-secure environment until one tried to leave. It was not for a lack of love or respect that Lenore had left the Lapp family and the Amish tradition. Rather, it had become unfathomable for her to never experience the greater world beyond her religious borders.

To Lenore, it was not a question of right or wrong. Rather, it represented a difficult fork in the road, and Lenore had chosen her insatiable curiosity as her guiding light. Unfortunately, the price of the shunning had taken a heavy toll on everyone, including her, jarring her and forcing her to reach out to strangers for support. Some answered in love and grace, while others used her and discarded her. The latter had landed her in the river.

Now, the curse and blessing of amnesia ruled her mind, creating a clean slate. In this state of confusion and renewal, she reached out for stability to the one soul who had saved her from certain death, the one who claimed to be her brother Josef.

"Josef, what happened? Jeremiah told uz that….My God, it's true!" John Lapp stopped the buggy and stared at his first-born child as if she were a ghost. Since she announced her departure, he had been torn to the core between his sincere dedication to the ways of his religion and his community, and the love of a father for his child. He had spent the past several months quietly mourning the loss of Lenore, whom he treasured more than life itself. Her shunned state ripped at his heart, forcing him to doubt all that he knew and all that had meaning in his world. Spending countless hours praying to an all-forgiving God, he hoped to ensure that his dear Lenore would be protected and looked after now that he, as her father, had no power to fulfill that role.

"*Fader*, Lenore'z back. We must take 'er back. The good Lord has returned 'er to uz. We must take 'er back." Josef wasted no time in drilling home the key point.

John wisely ignored his son's statement, deferring to Abel. He simply offered to give the runaway girl shelter in his home but refused to refer to her by name. Abel pondered the situation before he spoke for all, recognizing that the issue would have to be resolved by the entire congregation at a future date.

"It'z Lenore, no doubt. But, of 'er own choosing, she'z no longer one of uz. However, the good Lord has mercy, und we're devout followers of the ever-loving Christ; so, let uz focus on 'er wellbeing first und foremost." Bishop Snyder's judgment conveyed his authority and his decisions carried much weight.

His words made John hopeful, but he dared not express his emotions. Abel Snyder could have difficulty guiding the flock through this potentially contentious case. Not only did it have little precedence, but Lenore was his niece. He, like John, had watched her grow up and his love for her remained strong and sincere. Yet he knew the rules, and to simply ignore her shunned state felt beyond his authority.

Thus, Abel wisely chose to focus on the young woman's health and safety before addressing any social and religious issues. That would be done in time, and time was of ample measure.

Also present was Linus Miller, who lived on the adjacent hill. When not farming, Linus held the position of community undertaker and informal medic. Given the physical state of the young woman, he too was summoned to the scene. Linus was surprised to see Lenore, but he quickly checked her wounds and began applying first aid. "Josef, run to The Raven Inn und call an ambulance!" he instructed the young man.

"Iz it life-threatening, Linus?" Abel asked.

"No, but she should get proper medical attention."

Abel feared the involvement of the English in Amish matters, especially potentially controversial ones such as a shunned youth. After confirming with Linus that the girl's injuries were primarily superficial, he decided not to call an ambulance and to investigate further rather than call the police. He reasoned that given Lenore's condition, involvement by the English authorities would not be warranted. Thus, he supported John's offer and Josef's plea to have Lenore return to the Lapp family so she could recover physically and mentally.

"Lenore, we're goin' home!" Josef said as John Lapp sighed in relief.

As they crossed Devils Bridge, the horses objected but with less insistence. Thus, Lenore Lapp returned home to the excitement of her family and to the new reality of her growing confusion.

* * * * *

Morning came with the sound of the birds chasing each other in the large oak tree outside Lenore's bedroom, a small room she shared with two of her younger sisters, neither of whom she now recognized. The family had let her rest while they tended to farm chores. Thus, on her first morning home, Lenore descended the old farmhouse stairs into an empty kitchen.

She felt frightened at first, as none of her surroundings seemed familiar and her deep sleep had robbed her of any sense of time. As she looked about the plain, worn kitchen, devoid of curtains, electrical appliances, and electrical lights, she had a flash of familiarity. *Maybe I'm just imagining this?* Walking toward the rear door of the house, she smiled at the sight of a calico cat perched on the windowsill, sunning itself in the warmth of the late morning rays. All was quiet, except for the cat, which purred at the sight of Lenore. Upon recognizing her owner, it jumped off the sill and began to rub against Lenore's legs.

"I wish I could remember you," Lenore whispered as she picked up the cat. *Even you seem to know me*, she reflected while caressing the grateful feline.

Returning to the sunny kitchen, she was surprised to see a complete breakfast waiting for her on the large oak table, along with a note written by her mother, whom she had met yesterday, seemingly for the first time.

How sweet, Lenore silently reflected. *What a perfect family. I'm lucky to have them if they are who they claim to be.* The breakfast consisted of two hard-boiled eggs, some homemade bread and jam, and a glass of fresh milk from the family's cows. Lenore read her mother's note, which welcomed her home as if she had been gone for a long time. *I wonder why I left.* No answer came to her, so she simply ate her breakfast while the grateful cat purred on her lap.

She had almost finished when the front door swung open and the lady of the house entered. For the first time, Lenore experienced an irrefutable recollection. There was something distinctly familiar about this woman who claimed to be her mother. Maybe it was the white apron and the dark blue dress she wore or her hair pulled into a bun. Something triggered her a brief memory that soon faded.

Since Amish women never cut their hair, not even when they were children, she covered it with a white prayer bonnet worn throughout the day since it was required for prayer and prayer was encouraged at all times. Her appearance resembled that of a European peasant from the eighteenth century.

She spoke in the native tongue of the Amish, a language that had its roots in Old German, also known as *Deutsch*. This gave rise to the misconception by many that the Amish were Pennsylvania Dutch, when, in fact, they had Swiss and German origins dating back to the late 1600s. Since they kept to their original European traditions, they maintained their own language, known as Pennsylvania German, on account of the fact that the first Amish immigrants settled in Lancaster, Pennsylvania, in 1737. It was this mother tongue that they spoke among themselves.

A more traditional form of *Deutsch*, known as High German, was used at all church services and in the singing of church hymns. Thus, to be Amish was to be bilingual in English and *Deutsch*.

To Lenore's amazement, she understood both languages. The sound of her mother's voice in her native tongue and the smell of molasses, which permeated the entire house, combined to form a strong memory trigger. Lenore recognized both, elevating her hopes that she would regain her memory.

"Ah, Lenore, my dear. It'z a blessin' to have ya back home." Her mother began in Pennsylvania German. Everything about this woman personified love and gentleness. Lenore could not imagine how she could have left such a mother. *What could have driven me away?*

"I see ya got yur appetite back, my dear. Let me have a look at ya. How're the bruises doin'? I need to redress that cut on your head." Her mother sat down next to her at the large oak table. "Ya look rested. Oh, what a blessin' to have ya back home. Lord be blessed!"

Unlike Lenore, her mother, or the woman claiming to be her mother, did not seem to have any interest as to what had transpired to bring Lenore home or what had made her leave in the first place. She seemed to simply rejoice in the fact that her daughter had returned to her alive.

"We'll get that memory back, but first ya must rest. Ya're not leaving uz this time. How about some shoo-fly pie? It'z about ready to come out of the oven. Just in time, too, 'cause before ya know it, everyone'll come in for lunch. It getz buzy around here, as ya might remember, my dear." The charming woman laughed. She was visibly pregnant and it suited her, possessing an energy that made Lenore smile.

"Can I call ya *'Mater'*?" Lenore asked, testing her reality and her native tongue.

"My dear, I am yur *mater!* Ya *fader* and I've been blessed with children, and yur my first blessing, my love. I'm yur *mater* and proud of it, regardless of what happened. We'll fix all that. It'z nothin' the good Lord can't fix. Right, Lenore? The Lord'z forgiving and so're the Amish. I trust in that for it iz so."

"If ya say so, *Mater.* But, what'z there to forgive?"

"Never ya mind. Yur *fader*'ll take care of all that."

"If ya say so, *Mater.*"

"Now, doesn't that word *'mater'* bring back some memories?"

Lenore shook her head from side to side. Except for the woman's voice and the smell of molasses from the four shoo-fly pies baking in the cast-iron stove, Lenore had no further recollection.

Their conversation was interrupted by several slams of the wooden screen door, as the rest of the Lapp family poured into the spacious kitchen, starting with the oldest son, Josef, right down to the youngest offspring, a four-year-old daughter named Ali. They all greeted their sister as if she had never left.

Only little Ali could not remain silent on the subject, despite previous parental coaching. "Lenore, did ya really get lost going to du market? That's not that far, ya know. I go with *Mem* all du time and never get lost. *Dat* told me ya got lost goin' to du market. Ya shouldn't go out by yurself if ya get lost. Okay? Next time, I'll take ya. That way *Mem* won't cry."

The little girl had an innocence unmatched by anyone else in the stark kitchen. At her age, all seemed simple. The idea of her oldest sister getting lost going to the market perplexed her sharp mind, but she had no reason to doubt her father's word. Ali lived in the present and reflected the love around her into a radiant joy that characterized her nature. She was the sunshine of the family. In her world, there was no reason to cry, except when one got hurt or when the animals mysteriously disappeared, such as the chickens or the turkeys. That awful fact perturbed her, as did the mystery of her oldest sister's disappearance three months earlier. But, like most great mysteries in life, the ones that really matter, no one seemed to provide an answer that truly satisfied.

"I'm sorry, Ali. I promise next time I go to the market, ya can show me the way," Lenore replied.

"Good, 'cause I know the way. Right, *Mem?*"

"Right, Ali. Your sister'z home again und the Lord be praised," Mary Lapp replied. She finally felt content, having all her children at home once more. The past three months had been an unbearable strain on her, having to face her community as a woman who had somehow failed them by losing her precious daughter at an insufferable price. But the shame was not what she loathed, for that she could bear; it was the loss of her child that had resulted in countless sleepless nights.

To understand the great shame that haunted the Lapp family since Lenore's departure, one must step into the world of the Amish. Although to the frequent tourist, the life of the Amish may appear to be nostalgic, or even romantic, that can be very deceiving.

It is a life full of hard work lived in a simple manner that is true to the strict *Ordnung*, the community rules that govern every aspect of Amish society and behavior. Although many of the Amish have some level of wealth, mostly because of their landholdings, they are expected to share with those who are less fortunate. Materialism is strongly discouraged and flaunting of wealth can result in being temporarily shunned by the community. People are discouraged to stand out.

Thus, the Amish do not stray outside of their plain ways. Some have beautiful and expensive horses, but they can only be solid black or solid brown in color, and all must pull the same plain black buggies. Some have large farms, barns, and houses, but none have wire hookup to the outside world. Therefore, none are connected to electrical and telephone lines or public water and sewer. They have no cars, tractors, rubber tires, air conditioning, television, computers, musical instruments, internet, or even curtains. Such frills are considered vain and unacceptable. Most are farmers. They grow and raise most of their own food on their own farms.

Besides farming, which is central to Amish culture, the other main occupations are carpentry, baking, and quilting, but many sell produce, flowers, baked goods, animals, crafts, quilts, and furniture.

The Amish life is like a time capsule that predates the industrial revolution. Their plain ways foster family, community, and teamwork. Since they have no insurance, if a neighbor's barn burns down, the community gets together and builds them a new one, often in one day.

They are very social and care for their young and the elderly, having no need for nurseries and retirement homes. Everything revolves around family and community, which provides for all that is needed. This sense of community is often extended to their English neighbors, for it not uncommon that they help build a new barn for them or help take care of their elderly.

"Well, let'z get ready for dinner." Mary referred to lunch as "dinner." It was the largest meal of the day. The evening meal, "supper," often consisted of lunch leftovers. "I made some piez for dessert, und there'z chicken, cabbage, und potatoez. Make sure ya all wash ya handz before ya sit down. Lenore, will ya help Kate and Eve set the table? It'll be like old timez. Yur sisters'll show ya how."

Mary Lapp had a plan that she had not had a chance to share with her husband. She would treat Lenore as if she had never left, and make her fall back into her old routine, hoping that Lenore might remember how it was before she decided to leave. The risk was that she would remember everything and resolve to leave once more. However, Mary opted to take that risk, for this time she would do things better.

After all, how often does the Lord give ya a second chance? she wisely concluded. Later that night, she shared her plan with her devoted husband and he agreed, for he rarely disagreed.

While Lenore began to embrace her life among the Lapps, several members of the community debated the *Ordnung* rules around allowing a shunned girl to return to their flock, given that she had not petitioned for forgiveness and formally repented. Some were upset, but most agreed that since Lenore had no seeming memory of having left her family and community, it would be unjust to punish her for it. If she remembered leaving, then the debate would surely resume, assuming she did not immediately petition for official forgiveness.

For now, all seemed well, except for two gnawing issues. One gnawed at Lenore and one at Abel Snyder, the Bishop and leader of the thirty-three families that made up the local Amish community. Neither seemed to have an answer. Lenore could not remember why she left the Amish, and Abel pondered what had happened to her at Devils Bridge.

In time both would be answered, but time has a way of revealing its truths on its own terms. For now, Lenore had returned to her life among the Amish and most of them accepted her without reservation.

The Amish Village of Eden Crossing, Pennsylvania

CHAPTER 4

Forgotten Love

Lenore readjusted to her Amish life faster than anyone expected. Although her memory had not returned, a deeper knowing seemed to guide her, and she found the Amish ways natural and subconsciously familiar.

Every other Sunday, the Lapp family, along with their community, attended an all-day church service held at alternating host homes throughout the region. The worship service almost always turns into a social gathering that often lasts until late afternoon or early evening. Then, the numerous horses and buggies disperse to the surrounding farms that dot the Pennsylvania landscape.

At one of these gatherings, held at Abel Snyder's farm, Lenore ran into Amos Miller. Amos, a young Amish farmer who lived alone, had been widowed for nearly three years. His young bride had died in a tragic accident: a drunk English driver drove his car into her buggy. As was often the case in such deadly collisions, the automobile driver sustained no injuries, while the young Amish woman and her horse paid with their lives.

In accordance with the ways of the Amish, Amos formally forgave the driver and neither pressed charges nor accepted a dime from the young man for the concept of suing someone did not exist in Amish culture. Nonetheless, the entire ordeal changed him forever.

The one healing grace that Amos had experienced since his wife's death had been the gentle kindness, selfless friendship, and magnetic charm of Lenore Lapp. Her sudden departure from the Amish community had left another hole in Amos's already tattered heart. He knew of her decision before anyone since she came to him for advice. Often he regretted that he had tried to remain unbiased in his counsel.

Amos possessed one of the most giving souls in the community. He showed his unconditional love for Lenore by not burdening her decision. Reluctantly and silently, he accepted it, and his heart had mourned her departure ever since. Now, he seemed tepid about her return, for he had heard of her memory loss and feared that she would not know him.

On this fine September Sunday, Amos Miller could no longer hide from the inevitable meeting. Purposely, he had avoided Lenore for over three weeks, even doing the unthinkable—missing a Sunday of worship, convincing himself that he had a stomachache.

His heart filled with angst and his stomach had butterflies as he spied her from afar. Lenore personified striking beauty inside and out. She had been his beacon and his muse, the one who inspired him to be more than just a widowed Amish farmer while respecting the love he would forever possess for his departed wife.

Her loss made Amos more rebellious, not unlike Sam Hughes. But unlike Sam, Amos remained subdued by his community, his religion, and his sense of duty. Nonetheless, he often tried to persuade his fellow Amish toward ways that were more modern than traditional. It was this rebellious nature that Lenore had found so attractive—a disposition that the two shared as he began to formerly court her late last year.

Since Lenore's mysterious return, the first meeting between them had been anticipated by many in the community. Would she recognize him? Would he talk to her? Many pondered such questions, although none knew the extent of the couple's close bond that stemmed from a modern relationship masked by a conservative culture.

The true character of their unique connection remained opaque to all outsiders under the guise of a traditional courtship. Its properly paced progress could be attributed to Lenore and her solid upbringing.

When she suddenly decided to leave the Amish and end her ties with Amos, the news shocked the entire community. In their collective perception, Lenore had lost her reason. After all, many eligible Amish girls, and more than one married woman, had a secret fancy for Amos Miller, the handsome and well-to-do widower.

Growing up, Amos knew Lenore, but the two did not seem destined for each other. The five years that separated them created an insurmountable gap for two children. However, as Lenore entered her mid-teens, her attraction for Amos grew into a hopeless girlish crush. The prospect of any relationship with Amos dwindled with his growing affection for Elizabeth Fischer, his neighbor and childhood sweetheart. Lenore's fantasies and hopes were dashed when Amos and Elizabeth married. On that fateful day, she cried herself to sleep and surrendered all hope for attaining true love.

One Sunday the previous fall, nearly two years after Elizabeth's tragic death, Amos re-entered Lenore's life. More precisely, she dropped into his life by landing in his lap after tripping over Linus Miller's left foot.

Amos had just seated himself at a foldout table next to his older brother to enjoy his lunch at the host farm. He waited for the Bishop to say grace, when young Lenore tripped and landed in his lap, spilling her pork and sauerkraut all over his Sunday best. Flustered, she tried to get up, she tripped again, repeating the maneuver. Startled, she sprang away, knocking over his lunch as well.

After he brushed off the remnant of two lost lunches, he found himself in the presence of an extremely embarrassed and striking young woman who had somehow grown up while he mourned Elizabeth. Apologizing profusely, she curtsying awkwardly before him. In her flustered state, she blushed and nearly knocked over the entire table.

After the laughter of the surrounding observers had settled, Amos invited Lenore to sit next to him and offered to get her a new plate of food. An instant spark of attraction began to ignite a deep, burning love within his sheltered heart. The two laughed and talked until the sun began to set and most of the buggies had departed.

Over the next few months, the strong mutual attraction blossomed into something more. Able to talk about anything, even subjects that were often forbidden or frowned upon, they fantasized about moving to Hawaii and laughed at the thought of having little idea of what they would do there. Pretending to be scientists, she explored the woods behind Amos's farm, studying plants, animals, and even lowly bugs. Mostly, they laughed and laughed, sometimes simply at the fact that they were so happy. Amos healed, becoming whole again—better than whole, for he had Lenore.

But Lenore became torn, with one foot in the Amish tradition and her love for Amos, and the other bound to her insatiable curiosity that grew stronger every day with every new discovery.

Within the eyes of the community, the pair seemed destined to marry. Even Lenore had to admit that her relationship with Amos seemed on an ideal track to that end, except for one critical hurdle—her fear of losing her identity by becoming an Amish wife. While he seemed to balance his own curiosity and the conservative ways of his religion, she saw them completely at odds.

Her growing inner tension finally surfaced on a fateful Sunday six months after they had formally begun their courtship. Lenore's fear of becoming an Amish wife had grown into a panic. She loved Amos, but she could not surrender her insatiable desire to experience a world beyond the Amish culture, beyond Pennsylvania. It was then that she approached him with the idea of leaving. He was shocked at first, but he had no desire to leave or to hold her prisoner in his Amish life. She had to choose him willingly. Thus, he hid his true feelings for her and voiced his support for her decision regardless of the outcome.

This had been their rise and fall. Now, four months after her departure, he was reluctant to see her again for fear of tearing the precarious sutures with which he had painstakingly tried to mend his broken heart. What if she did not remember him? What if she did not like him? What if he had to watch her fall in love with someone else, and in the process, die an emotional death worse than any that could physically befall him?

Lenore had returned, but had she brought him with her? That question he hesitated to explore. Wishing to avoid a potentially awkward public encounter, he had decided to leave right at the end of the morning service. As he walked toward his buggy, she came around the corner of the barn and the dreaded moment fell upon him, unrehearsed.

"Hello." He smiled his most sincere smile while his throat instantly dried up and his heart began to race.

"Hello," she replied and passed him as if he were a stranger.

His heart sank. The feared meeting had been anticlimactic. She made no struggle to remember him or even an attempt to reject him. Instead, the void filled with something worse—apathy—the kind that comes with a complete lack of association.

Just then, young Josef Lapp ran up to Amos. He had always been fond of his older sister's suitor and had hoped that she would marry him.

"Did ya see her? Isn't she pretty? Did ya talk to her?" Josef asked.

Amos sighed. He liked Lenore's oldest brother, and the three would often talk or play games in the backyard of whatever house hosted the biweekly service. Weather permitting, they would indulge in volleyball, badminton, or silly old games like tag or hide-'n'-seek. There was something unspoiled and simple about those times, and Josef had great memories that he wished would come alive once more.

"She's more than pretty. She's beautiful," Amos replied with another heavy sigh. "But she didn't recognize me. I don't exist to her."

"Oh, she didn't remember me either, but now we're great friends. She's the same old Lenore. Go talk to her."

"And say what? 'Hello, we were in love before ya left.' What do I say, Josef? I can't do this again. It's just too strange. I can't do it."

"But if ya don't, she may end up with someone else, und that'll be even stranger."

"That's what I'm afraid of und I ain't afraid of much these dayz. I can't stay here if she endz up falling for someone else. I'll be the one who has to leave."

"Let's go talk to her. I'll introduce ya." Josef pressed Amos.

"Ya know how strange that sounds—you introducing me to Lenore? We talked of marriage before she left. Now, ya need to introduce uz. It's ridiculous!"

"Yes, but that's the way it iz. Don't ya think she'z worth a second chance?"

"Of course. I just don't know if I can do it. That'z all."

"Ya can do it. Everyone'd love to see ya back together. Come on, I'll introduce ya."

"Okay," Amos sighed. He was not ready for this, nor would he ever be.

As the two came around the barn, they saw Lenore laughing with Ben Stoltzfus. They were having such a great time that Amos did not have the heart to interrupt. He decided to head home early, claiming that he felt sick in the stomach. This time, he was telling the truth.

CHAPTER 5

Gavin Green

To know Gavin Green was to question his stability, for there was little about him that seemed grounded. An example of a young man on a self-serving mission, he had arrived in Eden Valley six months earlier because his enormously wealthy father had an old family estate along the left bank of the river, adjacent to Devils Bridge.

This estate included an extensive parcel of land with an old stone farmhouse that lay in disrepair. A property surrounded by Amish farms, it predated many of them, for it had been in the Green family since 1753. It was this nostalgic obligation to the Green family roots that kept Cornelius Green, the Pittsburgh businessman and Gavin's father, from selling the land.

Having grown up in the lap of luxury, without a need unmet but in the shadow of a tyrannical patriarch, Gavin had rebelled soon after college. Nonetheless, the old man continued to fund his son's bohemian lifestyle that included extensive travel, a plethora of vices, and an insatiable narcissistic thirst for self-satisfaction.

His father had had enough of his son's behavior, and after paying damages to the latest victim of his son's endless revelry, he gave Gavin a choice. Either his son must maintain a steady, respectable position in the Green conglomerate of businesses or continue his galivanting ways without future access to the Green fortune.

Gavin chose the latter because the thought of holding a job terrified him. Besides, he prided himself on being a self-proclaimed playboy whose only quest focused on ever-increasing indulgence.

After months of living off his dwindling cash, Gavin returned to the old country house where he had spent his childhood summers. He knew that his father would never find him there, for it was now abandoned.

Gavin Green moved into the dilapidated old farmhouse near Devils Bridge in early April. He had hitchhiked his way to the Eden Valley with nothing more than a backpack and a sizable bundle of marijuana, all that remained of his once-bottomless supply. High most of the time, he lived off a small bag of provisions before he found The Raven Inn, a half-mile up the road from his front door. There, he hung out every night, running up a large bar tab on his last functioning credit card. Unfortunately, before long the card denied him further credit and Gavin faced the prospect of working or stealing.

Days later, Sam Hughes caught Gavin stealing from him. Being a large, formidable man, Sam made a convincing argument against stealing, and Gavin had to repay his theft and his growing tavern tab by scrubbing dishes in the inn's kitchen. It was the only job he had ever held in his twenty-seven years of existence.

At first, Gavin resented Sam and did anything and everything to be an annoyance. But Sam had little patience for spoiled brats and one more round of convincing, which included the threat of incarceration, had Gavin walking the straight and narrow, at least for a while.

Despite this seeming outwardly change in Gavin's character, little differed within him. He worked at The Raven Inn to earn his keep, but at night he transformed into a roaming predator. Several of the young women who frequented the tavern had complained about him to Sam, who refused to take on another burden. After threatening to fire Gavin, the complaints ceased for a while.

Like a Jekyll and Hyde, Gavin seemed to possess two distinct personalities—the often quiet, submissive dishwasher and bar hand by day, and the insatiable, self-indulgent partier by night. However, soon his antics would attract a more formidable force, one that called this valley home longer than Gavin could fathom.

CHAPTER 6

Two Suitors

Amos awoke early the next morning and tended to his animals. His heart felt heavy and his mind filled with Lenore. Everything seemed to scream her name or project her image. The porch swing reminded him of the day they began their courtship. And the meadow whispered her name for here he first held her hand. The barn had her image imprinted within the archway where they had first kissed.

The hardest memory of all sat in the kitchen, for there, she had shared her decision to leave. He remembered it like yesterday.

"Say somethin', Amos!" she demanded upon revealing the news.

His voice had vanished as did the strength in his legs. Had it not been for the nearby chair, he may have fallen to the floor.

"Please, Amos! Will ya come with me? I need ya with me."

"They'll shun uz, Lenore. We'll lose everyone, everything—this farm, everything. We can't live here und be shunned!"

Leaving the Amish in shame, like a thief in the night, and abandoning all his responsibility, like a coward, felt wrong and not in his nature.

"Amos, I love ya but to surrender my life to this—I can't! There iz so much more to the world than Eden Crossing und this life. But to leave ya—I can't! I can't stay und I can't leave! Amos, please come with me! Please!"

Lenore looked through Amos with her deep brown eyes, the eyes that meant the world to him, for they reflected her soul. Those eyes pleaded with him as they filled with tears. Then, she reached out to him to embrace him but he stepped away. Something inside him pushed her away. His reaction provided her the answer she sought but feared.

"I understand," she said in quiet resolve. "I should not have asked this of ya. Forgive me, Amos. Please forgive me but I can't be an Amish wife—not even to ya, my love."

"I know. I understand. I release ya!"

He embraced her one last time. Upon releasing her, her walked away to hide his swelling tears. When he looked back to find her, all he saw was the screen door of the kitchen swing shut with a bang.

She was free, but he was not. She found her wings and welcomed the wind, but he revered to the earth he had tilled since childhood. Her quest seemed grounded in naiveté that he had no desire to point out, for she would not have listened. That he knew as he knew her. Therefore, he simply caught himself on that kitchen chair because his legs finally gave out under the burden of his breaking heart.

There is no weight greater than a true love lost. If that love willingly walks out of your life, there is nothing that can mend the gaping hole. Even if time hides the gashes, such deep wounds never heal. At best, they simply drift away on the coattails of shattered dreams. For Amos, the time had been too short since his wife's passing, and with Lenore's parting the abyss in his heart reopened, ready to swallow him once more.

Now, four months later, as he walked alone with the memories of his beloved swirling in his head, Amos could not stay in that kitchen. That dreadful day when Lenore walked out, resurrected in that very room. Even now, he could still smell her natural fragrance as he rushed out to the porch for fresh air. There was no escape. She haunted his memory wherever he went—on the porch, in the garden, and most of all, that cursed kitchen.

As he looked away in panic, he encountered the recollection of her standing at the front gate the day she came to ask him to leave. All was Lenore. He could not escape the past any more than he could abandon this farm, which had become his pride and his curse.

Lenore, Lenore, my sweet Lenore! His mind would not rest for his heart would not let it. *What have I done? Why'd I let ya go? Why can't I let ya go? I love ya so.* His mind drifted. *I deserve this. I deserve this for not telling ya how much I loved ya when I had the chance. I deserve this for not going with ya when you begged me to go.*

"Was it right to hide my feelings und not burden 'er? Or was it my foolish pride disguised as honor that allowed me to let her go—my silence a lie?" He asked this of the two bovines as he entered the barn to start the evening milking. They answered him with apathy for anything and everything except the fresh hay in their trough.

A strong man in stature, Amos had his inner strength eroded by the two great losses in his life, Elizabeth and Lenore. One was dead and one was alive, but dead to their past. *Which is worse? Which is worse, to lose the one ya love, or to love the one ya lost? Josef's right—I need to see 'er. I need to remind 'er,* he concluded as he fed the chickens. *She needs to know. I need to help 'er remember. I can't lose 'er again.*

Soon, he finished his morning chores, having rushed through them, eager to make the trip to the Lapp farm. The thought of Lenore filled every moment and every thought. Quickly, he harnessed his best horse to his open buggy and headed down the dusty road with a determination to set things right. In the back of his mind, he wondered what had happened to her. *How had she ended up unconscious in the Eden River under Devils Bridge, of all the sinister places? Why is no one askin' that question? Why is there no investigation?*

Amos had separated himself from the situation long enough to question the wisdom of simply ignoring how Lenore reappeared nearly dead in the nearby river after having vanished for three months. It was as if the Amish community and the Lapp family wanted to erase her ordeal, starting with her decision to leave and ending with her mysterious return.

Why's that? Do they fear something terrible'll emerge? Are they unwilling to accept her rejection of the Amish ways and her rejection of them? Or is it hope that all will be as it was? Maybe it's a conscious decision that ignoring the unknown'll make it disappear? Amos headed to the Lapp farm pondering the obvious paradox—clearly everyone wanted to forget but only Lenore had truly done so.

As he stepped out of his buggy in front of the Lapp farmhouse, Amos shrank in confidence and determination. His outer stature remained the same, but inside he became unsure and fearful. No longer was he interested in why no one questioned Lenore's baffling return and battered state. No longer was he the unbiased critic and investigator. No longer was he fearless in his pursuit of truth and justice. All had dissipated as his buggy pulled up the long dusty road toward the white farmhouse.

His fate now flapped in the whimsical winds of fortune, like the monochrome laundry swinging on the long clotheslines strung between the house and the barn. His only thought focused on how she would receive him. Reconsidering his decision to visit Lenore, he wanted to step back into his buggy when the front door of the farmhouse let out a loud squeak that sent two dogs running toward it in their hope for breakfast leftovers.

"Amos! Good morning!" yelled John Lapp. "I saw ya comin' up the lane. What brings ya?" he asked, as he walked toward Amos. There was a twinkle in his eye for he had expected this visit.

John knew of Lenore's love for Amos for he knew his daughter well. In turn, he had observed Amos return her love in gentle kindness. He had felt sorrow for Amos when Lenore left. But then, he had enough sorrow for an army of men and could not accept more. Thus, he had avoided Lenore's former suitor, not because he did not like and respect him, but because he lacked the strength to weep over the loss of his daughter in the presence of another who loved her in kind.

However, now that she had returned, he embraced the anticipated visit, knowing the two were well matched. Before Amos had a chance to reply, a second open buggy pulled into the drive.

"Looks like we better put on another pot of coffee, Mary. We have visitors!" John Lapp shouted over his shoulder to his wife.

"Come on in, Amos. Looks like Ben Stoltzfus is right behind ya. I suspect neither one of ya is here to look at my old plow," John observed with a chuckle. "It's for sale, ya know."

"No, sir, but maybe 'tis a bad time," Amos replied, looking back at Ben's buggy, halfway up the drive. "'Tis a bad time," he repeated.

"Bad time for what, Amos? Come on in. Mary baked some pies this morning."

"I don't want to bother ya on a workday. I know it's harvest time und all."

"No bother, Amos. No bother at all," John replied, as he headed into the house to help Mary prepare for the influx of company. He did not care to stay and greet Ben. John preferred Amos over Lenore's other former suitor. Although Ben came from the richest family in the community, John wondered if his interest in Lenore stemmed from her beauty and little else.

Lenore, dressed in plain clothes and wearing no makeup, respecting the ways of the Amish, was nonetheless an indisputable beauty. Her classical good looks were accentuated by the fact that she cared little for her appearance and never considered herself anything other than plain. To her, physical beauty belonged to the flowers or the morning dew shimmering on the golden grass. Yet to a young man like Ben Stoltzfus, she represented a beautiful prize that could adorn his life and his marital bed. Despite religious and social constraints, most young men were the same the world over.

Although Amos recognized Lenore's radiance, he saw it simply as a natural extension of her inner beauty, and it was the latter that he truly loved. Wisely, he realized that only her inner beauty had permanence and formed the true window to her soul. John Lapp had sensed that about Amos. For this reason, above all, he would have preferred Amos over any of Lenore's other suitors, despite the young man's reputation as a non-conformist.

Ben was traditional but shallow, while Amos was radical but sincere. John could see why his daughter had chosen the latter. Deep down, he wondered why Amos had not influenced her to stay. Or had he influenced her to leave? The latter made no sense, so John dismissed it soon after losing his daughter to the world of the English.

Now, things were different, as if time had turned back. Once more, Lenore's two primary suitors converged upon her. The slate had been wiped clean, since Lenore had no recollection of a history with either. To her, the Lapp family felt new and Ben seemed even newer, while Amos did not exist at all. Before Amos could secure his horse, his old nemesis pulled up to the farmhouse.

"Well, if it ain't old dust bag Miller!" Ben emphasized the word "old," since he was four years younger than his competitor. "I should've known ya'd be here sniffin' about." Ben jumped out of his buggy and tied up his fancy horse to a post. "I suppose ya're here to look at John's plow. Ya know that's all that's here for ya, old man. I believe the plow's in the barn. If ya don't mind, I have a young lady to see." Ben pushed himself past Amos as he headed toward the front porch. "In case ya're wondering, Lenore invited me to visit with her today." He looked back at Amos and smiled as he stepped onto the porch.

John had wisely disappeared to avoid the clash of the two known rivals. It really did seem like time had been reset when it came to Lapp's oldest daughter. Before she and Amos had become a courting pair, Ben pursued her with vigor. Now, once again, Ben seized the moment first, wasting no time on a second attempt to win Lenore's affection. John looked out the window at the two young men and simply shook his head. Turning to Mary, he laughed and observed, "It's like ol' times, ain't it, my dear?"

Mary sighed. "I don't know if I want either courtin' our daughter. We know what Ben's after, und look what happened with Amos. Maybe he pushed her away. He's been trouble since he was a boy. I'd rather ya asked 'em both to leave. Lenore doesn't need either one of 'em—not now, not ever. She needs us. She needs love, support, und rest. Look at 'em! They're lickin' their wounded pride und fightin' for 'er like she'z a prize heifer at a county fair. Send 'em off, John! I'm done with the lot of 'em!"

"Oh, Mary, they're just young men acting like all young men do. Remember, I had some competition for your hand, too. A pretty, young woman attracts 'em like flies."

"Gnats, more like it. Our daughter can't even remember her own name, und these two're already sniffin' around like hungry dogs. If you don't get rid of 'em, I will! Last thing Lenore needs iz a couple of roosters paradin' about."

John knew that Mary would act on her threat, being a woman of her word. Theirs was a strong marriage in which Mary had equal say. The apple did not fall far from the tree, for Lenore exhibited the same defiant spirit as her mother. Unfortunately, she also possessed an insatiable curiosity like her father. Combined, the two traits were more than the traditional Amish culture could contain.

John walked out of the house and onto the porch with every intention of retracting his invitation to Amos and sending both suitors packing. As he searched for the right words, Lenore came around the corner of the house. At the sight of Ben, she smiled. Recalling his charm and kindness, she wished to spend more time with him. The other man she barely noticed, for she did not know him. Her attention focused on Ben, the handsome youth only a year her senior. He had flowing blond hair and piercing blue eyes, and best of all, he made her laugh.

"Lenore," Ben yelled out before John or Amos had a chance to take charge of the situation. "You asked me to come und visit you today, so here I am."

Lenore ran toward him, right past Amos. She acknowledged the latter with a simple nod, as she would acknowledge any other stranger who visited her father. Before Amos could accept what had happened, she ran up to Ben and beamed with joy. "I'm so glad you're here. *Fader*, can Ben come in for a cup of coffee?" she asked.

John looked panicked and was about to mutter "okay" when the strong voice of Mary Lapp bellowed through him. She stood in the doorway, drying her hands in her apron. "I'm afraid we can't host either of these gentlemen on this fine workday morning." Mary emphasized the words "can't" and "workday." "We've got too much to do. Come help me in the kitchen, Lenore!" she ordered before letting the slam of the screen door emphasize her resolve.

"But, *Dat*, can Ben stay for just a few minutes, please! Please, *Dat!*" Lenore turned to her father, instinctively knowing which parent was more likely to agree.

"I'm afraid not today, Lenore. You need to rest und we've got a lot to do. Your *mem's* doing the washin' und I need to mend the silos for the harvest. Go in the house und help your *mater*. Good day, gentlemen," John replied.

Lenore protested again, but by then a wilted Amos had steered his buggy down the long, dusty farm lane. His heart had shattered and pieces of it seemed to fall away, settling gently on the gravel beneath the wooden wheels. Fittingly, it began to rain, but he did not feel one sobering drop. He did not feel anything beyond complete loss. For beyond it, there was no feeling at all. The raw wound in his heart had opened again like a dark tunnel in which he lost himself once more.

Eden Valley, Pennsylvania

CHAPTER 7

The Old Stables

Gavin Green and Sam Hughes mixed like oil and water. One was slick and the other was erosive. Nonetheless, Sam felt an unexplainable obligation to continue to offer Gavin a means of livelihood. Although Sam acted firm and gruff at times, he had seen enough of the world to empathize with a young man down on his luck. After all, he had only recently fit that description.

On this particular afternoon, The Raven Inn was nearly empty. After the weekday lunch crowd dispersed, the staff fell into a routine that predated Sam's ownership. Agnes, the maid, would refresh the last of the rooms while the kitchen staff prepared the dinner menu. A server and the bartender would set tables in the dining room and restock the bar in the tavern. Sam would use this slow period to sort the daily mail, catch up on e-mails, and pay a few bills.

On this particular afternoon, Sam sorted mail at the front desk when he heard a piercing scream. The woman's scream sounded like it came from one of the rooms on the upper floors in the back of the large stone structure. Its high pitch betrayed desperation.

Sam instantly responded by leaping up the old stairwell three steps at a time. By the time he reached the first landing, the screaming had ceased. Disoriented, Sam yelled out, demanding a reply, but none materialized. A second time, Sam's bellowing voice resounded throughout the inn as he demanded a reply. The only reply was the sound of the staff rushing up the stairs.

"What's going on, Sam?" asked Will Porter, the bartender at the inn.

Will had worked the bar for the past three years. Like Sam, he grew up in the valley and two had been friends since childhood. A pensive fellow with an odd laugh that sounded like he was choking, he made an odd a bartender. Although he made a good income at the popular inn, an underlying jealousy grew in his heart toward his boss. It remained opaque to Sam but several of the other employees had noticed it. When not in Sam's company, Will often complained about him.

In addition, Will had a propensity for skimming the tip jar that was to be divided among him and the servers. He particularly disliked a young server named Elaine Roberts, who drew Sam's attention. The innkeeper's attraction to the young woman exacerbated Will's frustration. Thus, he began to associate with Gavin Green, the other disgruntled employee.

In the past, Will and Sam often spent their Saturday mornings fly fishing in the Eden River. However, since Elaine had entered the picture, Sam had abandoned this ritual. Clearly, the two old friends had grown apart. Even now, they rarely chatted in the lobby, as they had often done during slow periods.

"What's going on, Sam?" Will repeated.

"I don't know, Will. I heard an awful scream. Didn't you?"

"I did, but I thought it came from the backyard," Will replied. "Then, I heard you yelling, so I ran up here."

"I know it came from around here. Let's start checking the rooms. Where's Agnes?"

"She should be cleaning the rooms," Will replied.

Sam rushed to check the rooms on the second floor. All the unlocked rooms were empty with no sign of Agnes, the maid. Two of the rooms were occupied and locked. Sam knocked on one and then the other. There was no reply from either. Meanwhile, Will and Elaine headed upstairs to check the six unoccupied rooms on the third floor. The scramble did not yield any clues.

Panicked, Sam ran to the desk and grabbed the master key. Once again, he rushed up the stairs. Quickly, he opened both occupied rooms. Both were vacant. Their occupants were probably sightseeing, enjoying the fall foliage. The desperate search revealed nothing.

Most of the inn's afternoon staff, which consisted of Sam, Will, Elaine, Gavin, and two cooks, Johnny and Marco, gathered on the first-floor landing after searching every room to no avail. "Okay, maybe you're right, Will. Maybe the scream came from the backyard. I could be wrong, but I swear it came from somewhere up here. No matter. Let's search the entire property," Sam ordered.

"Hey, Sam, where's Gavin?" Elaine asked, realizing for the first time that young Gavin Green was missing.

"He came in about an hour ago. I thought he was in the kitchen."

"He was in the kitchen until twenty minutes ago, Johnny added. He said you asked him to help you. It's not like we'd miss him in the kitchen. The kid's useless. Jerry always says that and he's right." Jerry McAlester, another one of Sam's old friends, had the role of head cook at The Raven Inn. On most afternoons, Jerry arrived around two o'clock to prepare the dinner menu. This afternoon, he was late.

"I never asked him for help. Damn that guy! This proves I can't trust him. Okay, we need to look for Agnes and Gavin," Sam concluded.

Sam and Elaine decided to search the old stables behind the inn, while Will, Johnny, and Marco agreed to search the gardens and the large backyard. These stables were the last vestige of an early era. In its youth, 200 years ago, the inn served as the region's primary resting place for weary travelers and their equally weary mounts. Now, the large stone stables were in desperate need of repair.

A long, double row of twenty-two stalls served as a repository for nearly a hundred years of junk. As one entered the cobweb-covered space, one was struck by how the shadows and the light played tricks on the eyes. The structure and its half-collapsed roof were like a sieve and a prism for the sharp light emanating from the blazing sun.

There were old tires and a broken tractor in one stall, and another contained half-opened boxes of war rations. Still another had a ramshackle sleigh with a missing runner. A rusty 1928 Model T Ford with no wheels or axles shared space with gardening equipment and a history of lawnmowers. These were mixed with kitchen sinks and old cabinets, rusty old bed frames, and warped furniture that the rain had molded into twisted sculptures.

Mice ruled this time capsule, especially on nights when the stray cats were away. During the day, bats used it as a sanctuary to catch up on their slumber.

Thus, when Sam and Elaine barged into the old stables, they were greeted by a cloud of fluttering, confused bats that streamed out the old double doors. Elaine screamed and fell to the ground, while Sam waved his arms to keep the blinded creatures from getting entangled in his long hair. As the bats departed, Elaine continued to scream.

"Damn them bats!" Sam said as he calmed Elaine. "I haven't been in here in years. I forgot about the damn bats. You all right?"

Elaine remained seated on the ground in front of the old stable's doors. She had stopped screaming but refused to enter the building.

Will ran up. "What the heck was that? That scream sounded just like the first one," he observed. Soon, the entire staff of The Raven Inn was reunited once more, minus Agnes, Gavin, and Jerry. The latter had still not shown up for work.

"Okay, false alarm, gang," Sam said. "Let's resume the search. Elaine, you can go with Johnny and Marco. Will, how about you come with me to explore this lovely place?"

Elaine appeared visibly relieved, but Will was not pleased. He wanted to retreat due to his hatred for bats, but he did not wish to appear cowardly in front of his macho boss. Reluctantly, he followed Sam into the maze of shadows, lights, and rusting antiquity, while the others gladly departed. Sam and Will did not need flashlights, for the old stables possessed their own dim and haunting light.

As the two men made their way down the center of the structure, climbing over fallen timbers and various broken artifacts, they heard motion at the far end of the building. The stir came from the dark, dead end.

"Shhh…could be more bats or a stray cat," Sam whispered.

Will did not reply. He simply slowed his pace, allowing Sam to get farther ahead. He refused to run into another cloud of bats. By contrast, Sam, fearless and curious, accelerated his pace. As he reached the last pair of stalls at the far end of the stables, he heard a low moan coming from the last stall on the left, the one nearest the back door. Peering into the shadows, he spotted a body lying on the earthen floor.

Sam rushed to investigate and nearly tripped over a leather strap that appeared to be part of an old horse harness. Regaining his footing, he knelt next to the body just as Will entered the stall behind him.

"What is it, Sam?" Will asked, for he could not make out anything in the darkness of the stall except for the shadowy image of his boss kneeling on the ground.

"It's Agnes! Open that door! I need some light."

Will did as ordered, propping open the small rear door of the stable. The light illuminated the stall, revealing Agnes, the young maid. She sat up and her eyes were wide open, as if she had seen a ghost or something far worse. Her hands were bound behind her with another old leather harness, and she struggled to set herself free.

Unable to talk because of a cloth tied around her mouth, she shook her head from side to side. Quickly, Sam removed the rag. As Agnes gasped for air, he helped her untie her hands. Upon freeing her right hand, she pointed to the nearby door.

"Are you okay, Agnes?" She did not respond but reached for her neck. "Who was it? Who did this?" Sam asked.

She could not speak. She simply held her throat with her left hand. Then, in an attempt to answer, she reached for a nearby stone to carve the answer into the earthen floor. In the process, she released her neck to support herself, revealing dark markings that resembled two thumb prints over her windpipe.

"Who did this to you, Agnes? Who did this?" Sam asked once more.

Seeing Will standing behind Sam, she dropped the stone and froze in fear.

"What is it, Agnes? Who did this to you?" Sam repeated. She did not answer.

She lowered her eyes, stared at the ground, and shook her head slightly. Finally, she spoke in a strained voice. "I don't know. He had a mask. I didn't see his face," she replied without looking up.

Later that afternoon, Sam and Elaine tended to Agnes in one of the inn's vacant rooms. Recovering quickly, she refused to discuss the incident. Sam wanted to take her to the hospital and call the police, but she became uncontrollable at the suggestion.

Before dinner, when Sam went to check on her, he found the room empty. She had left a note that she resigned and did not wish to be bothered. Sam wanted to call the police, but Jerry, who arrived later that afternoon, talked him out of it. Apparently, Jerry had car trouble and ended up arriving an hour and a half late, missing the Agnes incident.

Thus, it came to be that Agnes left the inn for good and the mystery of her encounter left with her, except for one clue. Gavin Green walked into the inn soon after Agnes had been discovered in the stable. He was covered with dust and earth stains. When Sam interrogated him, the youth admitted he had heard the scream and ran to investigate, convinced the scream had come from the old hay silo, the only standing remnant of an old stone barn located beyond the old stables.

After Agnes disappeared, Sam questioned Gavin once more. Again, Gavin insisted he had not been near the stables, but admitted he had seen a shadowy form of a man fleeing into the thick growth of evergreens at the far end of the property. When questioned about his soiled appearance, he insisted he had pursued the mysterious man but never caught up to him. Asked to describe the man, he said, "He looked like a hobo."

Sam did not trust Gavin, but he had no proof that Gavin was lying. With Agnes gone, there was no victim to consult. To make things worse, there were no witnesses. The unidentified attacker had apparently tried to kill Agnes. Or was he simply trying to scare her? Whoever he was and whatever were his intentions, he controlled Agnes with a fear that seemed incomprehensible. Rather than expose the truth, the young maid had disappeared like the man who assaulted her. Unfortunately, the incident was a precursor to a more intricate mystery.

CHAPTER 8

The White Witch

That night, Gavin Green walked back to his dilapidated old farmhouse after ending a bizarre shift at The Raven Inn. Upon Jerry's insistence, he had to wash every dish and glass in the place. Despite this, he had managed numerous futile attempts at wooing Elaine Roberts, the young server. To his frustration, she completely shut him down.

Elaine hated Gavin, and the Agnes incident only increased her suspicions of him. Although Elaine was young, barely twenty, she had lived a fuller life than her years would suggest, or so she claimed. According to Elaine, her parents were poor, too poor to send her to college. Six weeks ago, she decided to leave her parents' home in Brennantown to find work and live on her own.

Two weeks ago, she ran into Sam while he shopped for office supplies in nearby Kamerynville. They started talking, and she reminded him so much of Sandra, his former wife, in her mannerisms, her blue eyes, and her wavy blonde hair, that he offered her a job at the inn. He even rented her a room upstairs for next to nothing.

On this night, Gavin seemed more predatory than ever. The investigation of the Agnes incident had fueled his anger toward Sam, and he wanted revenge. To make things worse, his libido skyrocketed now that he had run out of marijuana. In short, he was on an adrenaline- and testosterone-induced prowl, and Elaine remained his prime target, being not only attractive but also Sam's fancy. Despite her persistent rejections, Gavin would not take "no" for an answer. Several of the patrons noticed that his insistence had drifted into threats.

Finally, Elaine complained to Sam, who walked up to Gavin and demanded that he either stop and apologize to her or leave the tavern for good. Gavin was tempted to leave, but he needed the money. He decided to swallow his pride and walked up to Elaine, who was clearing one of the tables in the dining room. A few patrons overheard his poor attempt at an apology.

"You're a bitch, Elaine! I'll get you back for this. Consider that your apology," he said.

Given the Agnes incident earlier in the day, this threat scared the young server, who immediately informed Sam. The latter grew furious and countered by firing Gavin on the spot. Gavin glared at him, bellowing out several choice words, before throwing down his busboy apron and walking out. Sam was relieved for he had been looking for an excuse to dismiss the unruly youth, and this recent turn of events sealed his decision. The Agnes incident and the threat to Elaine were more than he could handle.

Besides, Sam had become very protective of Elaine, like he had been of her former body double, his deceased wife. At times, when he had too much to drink, he had nearly crossed the line and knocked on her bedroom door, which was down the hall from his living quarters on the second floor. So far, he had resisted, but every night made it harder to separate memories from present reality as the two blended into one young woman, named Elaine.

Gavin grew angrier. As he walked down the moonlit road, he cursed Elaine and Sam. "Damn them! He hired her so she could be his little screw. He's the dog, not me. I'll have my way with her. I always get what I want. My father taught me that much," he muttered.

The light rain that persisted throughout the day had ceased, and the cloudy sky parted to pay homage to the full moon. A light breeze swayed the row of evergreen trees that bordered the road leading up to Devils Bridge. Here, the old Green Estate butted up to the river's edge on the south side of the bridge. Even today, many believed that the Green family had erected the cursed bridge. Legend has it that one of the early proprietors of the vast Green Estate, Robert Green III, had been found robbed and stabbed at the crossing.

Gavin missed the small hole of an entrance within the overgrown, rusted iron fence that, along with the ominous evergreen hedgerow and large oak trees, completely sheltered the old farm from the road. Completely overgrown with ivy that had spread throughout the nearby trees, the gate was easy to miss. Gavin never bothered to clear it. He preferred to keep his presence at the old farm a mystery.

The farm had been abandoned for over two decades and the evidence of neglect showed everywhere. Fortunately, the old farm had never been vandalized. Rather, it simply decayed under the continuous onslaught of the elements.

As he reflected on Sam, Gavin cursed and spat venom before he realized that he had walked within fifty yards of Devils Bridge. Looking up the wet road, he could see the full moon partially disappear behind gray pillowy clouds, which seemed to bend the moonlight away from Gavin toward the bridge. He was about to turn around, cursing his stupidity, when out of the corner of his eye he spotted an eerie form. Focusing back on the bridge, he beheld the apparition of a woman in a white gown. The beams of moonlight made her seem translucent. She stood at the midspan of the bridge, looking down at the very spot where Lenore had nearly drowned.

As the specter become aware of Gavin's gaze, she turned to face him. At this distance, he could not see the details of her face, but he could tell she had long dark hair, her slender form enveloped by a flowing white dress that seemed to flutter behind her in an imaginary wind. She appeared to float on air as she moved toward him.

A chill filled his bones, enhanced by the breeze she seemed to summon as she approached. Even the moon hid behind the nearest cloud, immersing the scene in total darkness. Her form escaped the darkness, having its own ghostly white glow. Was she his imagination? Fear gripped Gavin and froze his feet to the wet pavement.

She continued to approach. He could almost make out her face, which replaced the moon in its paleness. She appeared to be not of this world. He could tell and the thought terrified him. Turning his back to her, he took flight as fast as his legs could carry him.

"Oh, my God!" Gavin muttered as he continued to run toward the overgrown front gate of the old Green estate. *It's the White Witch!* His mind raced faster than his feet, as he recalled the stories, told by several crusty Raven Inn patrons, of the White Witch who haunted the valley. Few had ever seen her, but those who had were sure they had seen a ghost.

She appeared only at night, most often during a full moon. One old drunk swore he had met her face to face one while staggering home from The Raven Inn. In his latest version, she snuck up behind him, her deathly breath chilling his neck. When he turned, she stood before him—beautiful yet pale, the moon reflecting in her demonic eyes. Overcome with fear, he dove into a ditch on the side of the road as she floated over him, never touching the ground.

That same crusty patron admitted he was so scared that he would not venture out alone anymore when the moon was full, not even to fulfill his endless craving for rum. He claimed that the only reason he survived the ordeal was that he had fallen into the ditch. Otherwise, she would have killed him with her satanic gaze.

"She's a she-devil, I tell ya. She's beautiful but evil. A ghost for sure, if I ever met one, and I never want to meet her again. If ya see her, pray and run as fast as you can—I tell ya," the old drunk proclaimed at the end of his story, which he told often to anyone who would listen.

Gavin had dismissed such tales, but they all came to life now, as he ran in sheer panic away from the covered bridge.

As he reached the overgrown gate of the old estate, the moon reappeared. Finally, he mustered the courage to look back down the road toward Devils Bridge. To his relief, he could no longer see the woman. Quickly, he snuck through the gap in the iron gate, disappearing down the overgrown lane toward the dilapidated farmhouse. Entering it as fast as he could, he shut and locked the rusty door.

The place was dark and damp. But he did not mind the darkness on most nights, yet on this night, it chilled his bones. Haunting, the moon reemerged to illuminate the sparsely furnished room, once a family room.

Gavin looked for matches and lit a candle, as the wires that led to the house were long torn down by fallen trees. By candlelight, he found his unmade bed in the adjacent room. Changing quickly, he dove into it, skipping his usual toilet. He was too frightened to sleep, as the pale, bluish-white moonlight continued to shine through the windows of the bedroom. His watch read midnight. Unable to sleep, he rose to draw the tattered curtains. As he faced the window, he froze.

Eden Valley, Pennsylvania

CHAPTER 9

A Nightmare

Nearly four weeks had passed since Lenore Lapp was found barely alive under Devils Bridge. Since that day, Abel Snyder, the Amish Bishop, could not get a good night's sleep. Something about that event had changed him. Something threatened the community whose safety was his charge.

Abel had made the final decision not to involve the police in an effort to protect his niece, Lenore, and the entire community from public invasion. After all, it seemed probable that Lenore had slipped in the creek, hit her head, and fell unconscious. Surely that was the explanation. At least, that was what most of the community believed. But why would she have been wandering about in a long white dress in the middle of Eden Valley like the rumored White Witch?

The legend of the White Witch preceded Lenore's disappearance by more than two centuries. Of late, the legend of the mysterious white figure had resurfaced with an increasing number of sightings. Several respectable members of the community swore that they had seen the specter on moonlit nights, walking near the river.

Was Lenore pretending to be that specter? If so, why? Had it been her revenge against a community that had shunned her? What about the gash on her head? Was it really due to a fall? It looked more linear, like a blow from a blunt object. *No, it was a fall,* he concluded to himself, as he lay awake in his bed. The mystery of Lenore Lapp and her potential secret identity as the legendary White Witch of Eden Valley kept him from getting his sleep.

In the predictable and consistent lifestyle of the Amish, Saturday, September 22, should not have been any different from Friday, September 21. Yet in this particular year, September 22 would change much, at least for a while.

It all started just after midnight with a nightmare that seemed to grow larger and larger until it engulfed the entire community of Eden Crossing. The actual nightmare occurred to none other than Abel, himself. With his wife sound asleep by his side, he awoke shivering with fright. As he jumped up in bed, he woke her.

"What iz it, Abel?" his wife asked, looking over at him. "Ya look like ya seen a ghost."

"Martha, was that pork properly smoked?" he asked, referring to the rich meal he had for dinner.

"Tonight's pork? Yes, of course."

"Was it fresh?"

"What's got into ya, Abel? Ya jump up in the middle of the night asking if the pork was fresh. Of course, it was fresh. I got it from Peter Miller. What does that have to do with anything?" She appeared visibly confused.

"Oh, nothing, I guess. I'm gonna go get some water." He got up and went to the kitchen. As he descended the creaky stairs, his nightmare returned, and he fell down the last two steps.

"Ya all right?" His wife yelled when she heard the crash. She went to the top of the stairs to investigate.

"I'm not sure."

"What'z goin' on, Abel?" she asked. Rushing down the stairs, she helped him to his feet.

The two sat down at the hand-hewn kitchen table. Abel, who seemed no worse for the fall, placed his head in his hands and looked down at the cracks in the wood. He closed his eyes. As he did so, he inhaled audibly, as in a fright, and immediately opened his eyes once more.

"Abel, what'z goin' on?" his wife repeated, as she looked across the table at him. They sat in the dark, except for the rays of bluish-white moonlight that illuminated them and their stark farmhouse.

Abel inhaled audibly once more before exhaling a long sigh. He looked up from the table at his wife. There was alarm in his eyes. "When I close my eyez," he began softly, looking straight into her eyes. "When I close my eyez," he repeated, "I see her. She's standing there. I see her lookin' at me as if she're still alive."

"Who, Abel? Who?"

"Why, the White Witch, of course. When I awoke, I had a nightmare that she was haunting the banks of the Eden River on this very night. She looked like a ghost in white, except she isn't a ghost at all. She'z a living person. I think she'z Lenore. Surely, Martha, the White Witch can't be Lenore. Please tell me it'z not so, for I'm not sure. When I first awoke, Martha, I heard a clear thought in my head, like a voice, but not like one," he paused.

"Oh, Abel! Ya must stop worrying so. Lenore had an accident. She'll get better," Martha reasoned.

"But what about the voice? I swear I'm losing my mind, Martha. I swear I heard her in my head. I haven't told anyone, not even you, but I heard her voice before. I heard it at that cursed bridge on the day we found Lenore."

"Abel, ya need some sleep."

"Don't ya wanna know?"

"Know what, Abel? Ya're scaring me."

"Don't you wanna know what she said then and now?"

"Not really, but ya wanna tell me, right? Okay, Abel, what'd she say? What'd this voice say?" Martha was a devoted and accepting wife, who loved her husband dearly. But this talk frightened her.

"This iz the strange part, as if the rest weren't strange enough. She said, 'Beware the Raven!' She kept repeating it. 'Beware the Raven und his lure!' That's what she said. Then she added, 'Know this, Theo's son, the White Witch und I're one.' Oh, Martha, the voice, that witch's voice, sounded like Lenore." He dropped his head and stared at the cracks in the wooden table. "Martha, I'm going crazy.

They say the specter of the White Witch iz the restless ghost of Evelyn Drake. Maybe I'm being haunted. I never believed that stuff, but this iz too much."

"Oh, Abel! Ya imagined it. It's a bad dream. Besides, she wouldn't know ya're Theo's son. And, who's the Raven, anyway? Ya're right about the legend. They say Evelyn Drake went mad when she began to practice witchcraft some two hundred years ago. They say she'z the White Witch, but it ain't Lenore, Abel. Ya had a bad dream. Come to bed. It'z the middle of the night."

"Maybe I ought to go see Esther Fischer?"

"Not tonight."

"No, of course not. Tomorrow."

"Fine, ya go see Esther in the mornin'. She'll give ya something for it. Now, let'z go back to sleep. It'z after midnight." Martha yawned and rose from her chair. "Come on, Abel," she urged.

Abel rose, while still staring at the wooden table in front of him. Carefully, he closed his eyes once more to see if the image of Lenore as the White Witch would appear before him. He was afraid at first, but then he quickly closed them again, taking the plunge. To his relief, he saw nothing but the backs of his eyelids. "Good," he muttered. "Let'z go to bed."

CHAPTER 10

The Tell-Tale Heart

Midnight struck and Gavin Green could not move. Fear had control of his mind and body. Outside his bedroom window, at about fifty feet, stood a white figure illuminated by the moonlight. With raven hair, she wore a draping white gown that seemed to press against her slim torso while flowing behind her in the strong night breeze.

Her face appeared pale, like the moon, which reflected upon it. It was difficult to make out her faint features, except that they appeared hauntingly beautiful. Gavin could not look upon her face for, like a mirror to the soul, she projected back one's true nature without distortion. Those unseen eyes did not lie, nor did they relinquish their hold on him for he could feel their piercing presence even at a distance.

In the spell of the White Witch, he felt powerlessly lost. "Please stop," he whimpered, still separated from her by the windowpane and the thick stone wall of the old farmhouse. "Please stop," he repeated, softer now.

She simply stood there, silent, and unmoved. He could not close the curtain. He could not extinguish her stare, or her power over him.

"Please stop," he said once more, petrified by fear. "I'll do anything. Just leave me alone." All stood still as the night fog rolled in from the eerie river.

In the deafening silence, Gavin became aware of a faint thumping on the door—or was it beneath the floor? He could not be sure. It startled him. Looking at his watch, he realized that midnight had come and gone.

Is she still there? The thought gnawed at his heart and churned his stomach. He feared her more than anything, yet he had never met her until this merciless night. She never touched him, but she had him still and would not let go.

"Please go away and leave me alone," he pleaded, crawling under his ragged covers.

The house steeped in darkness as he glanced at the window. To his relief, the White Witch had disappeared along with the moon, as if the two were one. As he dared to relax, he noticed a damp chill had permeated the room, pervaded his bones, and suffused his soul. Back under the safety of the covers, he buried his head in a musty pillow.

To Gavin's growing dismay, the soft thumping and rhythmic beating continued. All was silent, except the steady sound of the eager intruder upon his door. Now she knocked from beneath the floor, rattling his very core. As if immersed in her spell, he could not escape. Horror entered his heart. He pleaded for mercy to a God he had long forgotten or simply ignored.

Terrifying thumping upon the door, no the floor, but surely the door, he could not ignore.

Who was this woman, this specter of the night who would not leave him, who would not let him sleep? He tried to bury his head beneath the lumpy pillow, but that seemed to make the knocking louder. Although he wanted to scream, his voice refused and his throat choked with terror. His heart burst with fear, amplified by his mind, transforming him into a shadow of himself, into a ghost like the White Witch who terrorized him.

He feared the rhythmic rapping on the kitchen door,
By a frightful specter, the undying phantom of ancient lore.
Had she come to revenge the sins he bore,
By demanding entrance from death's distant shore?
Or was this karmic vengeance from days of yore?
The horrific thumping, never stopping, never ceasing, nevermore.

The eerie drumming shifted. Yes, it shifted 'neath the floor.
Gavin swallowed, drenched in sweat and terror to the core.
The sound grew nearer, no longer barred by the rusty door.
She beckoned, to remind him of their unsettled score.
Fear, his judgment clouded as the banging in his mind did soar.
The horrific thumping, never stopping, never ceasing, nevermore.

Gavin Green, terror stricken, saw her shadow on the floor.
The White Witch had come to claim him, passing through the futile door.
She leapt to ensnare him in the white robes she wore.
The deafening beating choked his breathing 'til his lungs were sore.
Yet nothing could stop the booming rapping beneath the bedroom floor.
The horrific thumping, never stopping, never ceasing, nevermore.

Blind with terror, he jumped up and crashed through the door,
To escape her and that satanic beating, panic-stricken to the core.
Toward the river he sprinted to stop the drumming of that ceaseless score.
The endless thumping still pursued him, louder now than before.
Fear, all consuming, embraced the shelter that the bridge now bore.
On the bridge, she stood bathed in moonlight, a frightening phantom forevermore.

She'd come to stop his fleeing, to settle a timeless score.
The river gave shelter and called him, sparkling through the old bridge floor.
Bathed in madness, he leapt to greet her, drenched in the moonlight she wore.
Pulling deeper, she embraced him, whispering what she had in store.
Among her rolling boulders, she released the terror that he bore.
The horrific thumping, finally stopping, finally ceasing, forevermore.

Was he dead or safe upon another shore?
All fell silent, except a woman's laughter grew into a screeching roar.
It rang the length of that devilish structure, filling crevices in its sinister core.
On the bridge, her haven, with her cackle she settled the score.
The thumping and laughing finally dying, finally drifting beyond the shore.
Was he dead or safe upon another shore? Hark, the Raven!

"Nevermore. No, nevermore."

CHAPTER 11

Linda

fter a long day, Sam prepared to close the tavern on schedule. At 1:45 a.m., he announced last call. He had had a tough night with a couple of unruly drunks plus the incident with Gavin, which had come on the heels of the Agnes attack. The series of events had Elaine so upset that she asked to leave early. She had headed up to her room soon after Gavin departed. Sam wished he could join her to console her but knew it would be as inappropriate as Gavin's forwardness earlier that night. Instead, he focused on closing the bar and getting some rest.

Unfortunately, last call resulted in a flurry of alcohol purchases for the patrons did not share Sam's eagerness to end their weekend merriment. Rather, the sudden spike in drink orders had the remaining servers busily running about the four-room tavern. To keep up with demand, Sam joined Will behind the bar. He was pouring drafts when he heard a soft feminine voice to his left. "Are you Sam Hughes?" inquired a young woman in a white dress.

"Yes." Turning to face her, he realized that although he had never seen her in the tavern before, she seemed familiar. Too busy to ponder his dilemma, he turned away to fill another last call request, this one for three shots of bourbon.

"Sam, let the place run long tonight," Jake Harris, a nightly regular, pleaded. "No one's keeping tabs on ya, and the crowd's not ready to call it a night."

"I can't, Jake. It's the law. You know that."

"But Sam, old Gus Morgan's here. He's the law. I'll go ask him if it's okay?"

Jake did not wait for an answer but ran over to Gus, who had been chatting up a curvaceous middle-aged widow named Polly. She gave him infinitely more attention than he had gotten from his wife in years, and he felt optimistic about the future of the evening. The idea of continuing this magical night was welcome news to the old police chief. So, without asking Sam, he proclaimed the bar open until four. He justified it as a special exception, the tenth anniversary of his tenure as police chief, which was not true, but which impressed Polly so much that she readjusted her wares in such a way as to ensure his full attention.

"Why, Chief, I'm so honored to be here with you on this special night," Polly said.

She knew the police chief had a reputation of straying on his wife. Anxious to rekindle a fire within her nearly extinguished embers, she decided the chief seemed like the right man for the job. All was good until Sam objected to the old chief's proposal, sending waves of booing and hissing throughout the tavern.

"Chief, with all due respect, I always close at two," Sam said. He did not want to remind the old chief about the state law, since that might cost him in the future, but he had no intention of remaining open. Despite the added revenue, he desired sleep. Sam's objection resulted in more boos and hisses from the thirsty patrons.

The chief walked over to Sam to straighten things out. "Look, Sam, do this for me and I'll owe you a favor. I need more time to settle things." He glanced over at Polly, who did her best to be pleasing to the eye, which included a staged sultry pose that she had practiced in front of her mirror for hours.

"Chief, not that it's any of my business, but you seem to have conquered your quarry. Why not cash out?" Sam asked, looking over at Polly, who was rearranging her push-up bra.

"Now, Sam, you know I'm a married man. That's not the point here, son. I'm celebrating my tenth anniversary in office, and you're cutting short my enjoyment. That makes me disappointed in you. You know what I mean," the chief replied.

"Let's split the difference. How about I close at three sharp?"

"You drive a tough bargain, Sam, but it's a deal."

"Okay," Sam replied and sighed. "You gonna announce it or should I?"

"You do it. It's your bar. Just don't say anything ya wouldn't want me to hear, if ya know what I mean?"

"Yeah, I get it."

The chief walked away and rejoined Polly, who seemed eager to have him back. Sam got up on a chair and made his announcement that the bar would remain open until three in the morning on account of the chief's tenth anniversary in office, and that draft beer was at half price. This took the sting out of the shorter-than-promised hours for the anxious patrons and left the chief feeling like a hero. Upon closing time, Polly gave him a hero's reward in the back seat of the squad car.

After the announcement, Sam kept busy tanking draft beer, when the familiar-looking young woman addressed him once more. "Sam Hughes, I have a favor to ask you. Would you be kind enough to help a woman in distress?"

"Depends on the woman and the dress," Sam replied, tanking more beer for one of the regulars. With the half-price drafts, his workload had increased dramatically.

"Not dress, distress," she replied and laughed, which made her even more attractive.

"Is this a business proposition?" he asked looking up at her over the edge of the bar as he washed additional pint glasses. "You're not a hooker, are ya? 'Cause I don't allow any solicitation in my bar. No exception." He stared at her, awaiting an answer.

"No, but how amusing. I'll try not to be insulted. I assure you I'm not a hooker."

"Good. 'Cause I'm not interested," Sam stepped over to the adjacent tap to fill more pint glasses with lager and ale. Business was booming with no sign of letting up.

"Actually, the favor I need is simply an answer to a question. That's all."

"Well, that doesn't seem that hard. What's your name anyway? You look familiar."

The final comment surprised the young woman, for she had never met Sam before. She would have remembered him. He was memorable, being rather handsome in a rugged way.

"Can't say we've ever met," she replied. "I must have a double. My name's Linda, Linda Taylor," she replied.

"Taylor?"

"Yeah."

"Hmmm…don't know ya. Must be somebody else," Sam replied, as he turned to clean more pint glasses. "I wish I hadn't suggested those half-price drafts," he muttered to himself.

"Let's just forget it. You seem busy, so I better get going." She downed her vodka drink.

"What was your question, Linda?" Sam wiped down the bar with a wet cloth. She had spurred his curiosity.

"I'm looking for Elaine. Is she here tonight?"

He stopped and looked her straight in the eyes, trying to place her. *What does she want with Elaine?*

"No, she went home early," he replied.

"You mean upstairs, don't you?"

"Yeah. How'd ya know that?" He looked at her with a perplexed stare.

"She told me where she lived. We're friends. Is that okay? You seem concerned." She matched his stare.

"No, not concerned. Just wondering."

"Wondering what, Sam?"

"Wondering why ya're looking for Elaine," he replied firmly. He had become suspicious of this new girl, who seemed to know too much.

"Long story. You'd have to be open 'til six. Elaine and I are friends, as I told you. No need to get jealous. We're both straight." She smiled her captivating smile.

"Very funny," Sam replied. He had to tank more drafts. "I'm not jealous—simply lookin' after my employees."

"Like ya did with Gavin?"

"You know Gavin, too?"

"I overheard two patrons talkin' about the little drama you had earlier," she replied.

Sam could not decide if he liked or disliked this forward young woman. She seemed pushy. "No drama. Gavin quit."

"If you say so."

"Look, I need to work. Elaine's not here, but I can give her a message," he offered, while washing more glasses.

"I know she's upstairs. How do I get there?"

"You can't."

"Never mind. I get it. You don't trust me, so you're protecting her. Well, let me assure you that she needs no protectin'. She acts innocent and naive, but she's got you fooled. Mark my words, she's got you fooled," Linda said with sudden anger.

"I don't like yar tone. Ya should leave."

"Are you kickin' me out, now? Why? 'Cause I dared to speak the truth about your little girlfriend? I bet she even told you that story about her parents being poor, and how she had to leave 'em to make money for the family. It's all a crock of crap, Sam."

"Ya better go," Sam insisted.

"She's got you right where she wants you. But, beware, 'cause she's a black widow with an angel's face."

"Leave!"

"Okay, I'll leave, but don't say I didn't warn you."

"What kind of a friend are ya to talk about her like that?"

"I lied. I hate her guts, and I bet you believe me, don't you? What's the real truth? Care to find out?"

"Ya're strange. Leave now, or I'll make ya leave," Sam threatened. He had had enough of this odd, aggressive girl.

"I'm strange? At least I'm not attracted to a home wrecker. Did you know she's the reason my husband left? If you don't believe me, ask 'im. I'm sure he'll be comin' around 'ere, sniffing after her 'cause she dumped 'im after she found you and your little gold mine, here."

"I don't believe ya," Sam replied, having concluded that the woman must be insane.

"Whatever you say. Whatever you say, Sam. Or should I call you 'Raven'?" She laughed once more.

Sam froze and stared at her. "How did ya know that?"

"I know all," she replied and disappeared into the crowd, leaving Sam baffled.

CHAPTER 12

Satan's a Trickster

Later that morning, Amish bishop Abel Snyder, fearing possession by demons, sought the help of his neighbor, Esther Fischer. Esther, an elderly Amish widow, was well versed in the ways of medicine and lore.

At ten past six that morning, he knocked on her door. She rose from her breakfast and answered the panicked rapping.

"What'z goin' on, Abel? Ya're visitin' mighty early t'is morn'."

"Sorry to bother ya, Esther, but I've got an emergency."

"Come on in, Abel. What sort of emergency ya got?"

He sat at her kitchen table and confessed his troubles. Upon hearing him out, she advised that he needed to determine if this voice in his head seemed good or evil, reminding him of one of the more famous bishops in the long history of the community, who had been audibly inspired by the Lord. That bishop happened to be Abel's great-great-grandfather. Finally, she warned that this voice could be the temptation of Satan.

"Satan's a trickster," she proclaimed in a knowing way. "Ya need to test 'im, Abel."

"How do I do that, Esther?" Abel asked, finding himself in a state of complete confusion. He had come in hope of comfort but received little from the old widow.

"Simple. Ya go back to where it first possess'd ya und…where'd ya say ya first picked up this voice?" She asked him as if he had found it lying in a cornfield.

Abel had been reluctant to share this, but she insisted. "At Devils Bridge," he confessed, softy.

"Oh, my Lord!" she proclaimed. "No need to test this. It'z Satan for sure."

"But it'z a woman's voice," Able objected, as if that made it more angelic.

"No matter. Like I said, Satan's a trickster. We need to get 'im out of ya und quick."

"How do ya do that, Esther?" Abel was extremely uncomfortable with the prognosis and the potential negative impact of this predicament upon his role as bishop.

"Ya pray to the good Lord at the very spot where it first possess'd ya. I'll need to cleanse ya with some dried sage, just in case. My grandmother swore by it, 'though it'z not our custom, ya know. So, keep it to yarself, Abel." Esther knew that the Amish officially frowned upon her unorthodox beliefs and practices.

"I will, but how does it work, Esther?"

"Ya light it und pray at the spot ya first picked up the demon. Ya should do it around the same hour it possess'd ya. When was that?" she asked, as she searched her pantry for dried white sage.

"Morning, around seven, the day we found Lenore Lapp under that cursed bridge. It started faint, but it scared me half to death. It disappeared for a while but came back a couple nights ago. Last night, it was unbearable."

"What'd it say?"

"It said, 'Beware the Raven und his lure!' I don't much remember the rest, but I remember this. It said, 'Know this, Theo's son, the White Witch und I're one.' It'z got me all knotted up inside, Esther."

Esther concluded with certainty that Abel had somehow managed to pick up a strong demon, if not Satan himself.

"Ya right about one thing, Abel. That White Witch is the ghost of Evelyn Drake. Merrill Schmitt saw 'er few weeks ago at dusk over at Drakes Plot—the very spot they buried 'er some two hundred years ago. Ya know the legend. She'z a ghost for sure. Evil don't sleep. But why she's about so much all of a sudden makes no sense to me. Must be that cursed bridge. They ought to knock it down or burn it," Esther concluded.

"What should I do? Am I possessed?"

"Sure looks like it. Hope we can get it out of ya. We better get down to that bridge in a hurry. It's six thirty already."

"We'll take my buggy," Abel offered.

The sun began to rise as Esther and Abel headed down the hill toward Devils Bridge. The river churned up a mist in the cold morning air, enveloping the red covered bridge in a mysterious shroud accented in pink and purple by the rising sun. As they reached the bridge, Abel had to crack the whip a few times to get his horse to make the crossing.

"This place ain't fit for man nor beast," Esther reflected under her breath.

"I agree, Esther. I agree. We ought to burn this thing down und replace it. But them foolish English keep repairing it. Let it fall down, I say."

Abel stopped the buggy at the far end of the bridge. He and Esther got out, and the two walked over to the riverbank. Esther carried a bundle of dried white sage and some matches in her apron pocket. When they reached the bank, they stopped to look down on the river.

"It was right here, Esther. Right here's where I first heard the voice." Able stopped four feet from the bank on the east side of the bridge, the side closest to the Green Estate and The Raven Inn.

"Are ya sure? It's gotta be the exact spot."

"I'm sure, Esther."

"Then, stay right there. Good. What time iz it?"

Abel checked his old pocket watch. "Five minutes 'til seven. It was about this time that voice started."

"Good," Esther said. "Then I'll light the sage und start the process. This smoke'll get rid of that devil. If it's Satan, himself, we may have to do it three times or more. Let's just hope it's one of them simple demons. Not sure I brought enough sage for Satan."

She lit the dry sage and swirled the white pungent smoke around Abel. "Start praying for salvation und for the voice to leave ya," she advised.

Esther was a curious old woman. Although she remained devoted to the ways of the Amish, she had inherited an interest in folklore traditions and medicines from her mother. Some of it had its roots in old European traditions and some in Native American rituals. It resulted in a curious hodgepodge of both with a little of Esther's improvisation for good measure. Many in the community sought her out when they had medical questions or simply issues with dreams, demons, or bad omens of any sort. Old Esther always had an answer and a solution, which was more than you could say of most anyone else.

Officially, no one would admit condoning or participating in her craft, nor did she advertise her skills. Being close friends with Abel Snyder, the bishop of the Amish community, gave her a certain level of protection, but she knew there were some who strongly disapproved. Thus, she maintained care not to advertise her ways for fear of negative repercussions. After all, she could be considered a pagan or even a witch, which she would not have been able to bear.

"Keep prayin', Abel, und I'll keep sagin'. Iz it workin'? Ya hear any voices?" Esther circled around poor Abel, who just kept on praying, keeping his eyes closed.

"No. I don't hear a thing, Esther. I think it'z workin'," he admitted, as he prayed for salvation.

"Now open ya eyes, Abel. I think we got rid of the demon. Ya're lucky it was just a junior demon, or we might be sagin' 'til noon." Esther snuffed out the bundle of smoldering herbs.

Abel stood dumbstruck, staring at the opposing riverbank. As the sage smoke cleared, he continued his gaze as if frozen in time and space.

"Ya all right, Abel? All good, right? What'z the matter with ya now?" Esther knitted her brows.

Finally, he spoke in a whisper. "The voice'z gone, but I see dead people," he confessed in horror, opening and closing his eyes to clear his vision.

"That Satan's a trickster. We need to do it again." She reached for her matches and her bundle of sage.

"Esther, the body's back. Lenore's body's back. I can see it as if it were real. It'z right over there." He pointed slowly to the opposing bank.

Esther was about to light the sage, but, before doing so, she looked in the direction of Abel's gaze. As she focused on the opposing bank, she gasped and exclaimed, "Lord, help us! I see Lenore's body, as well! Satan's got us both!"

As they tried to regain their composure, they were startled by Will Porter, who pulled up quietly in his truck, seemingly out of nowhere. "Y'all alright?" He asked the startled pair as he stepped out of his truck.

Abel was about to say that all was fine, but his eyes betrayed him. Esther spoke first. "Ya're William, Al Porter's son, right?"

"Yes, Ma'am."

"Well, tell me William, what do ya see over there?" Esther was about to point when Abel stopped her.

"Now, there'z no need to make a fuss. It'z nothing. Right, Esther?" Abel tried to coach her, but Esther would not have it.

She turned back toward the river and walked closer to the bank. "Look at the far bank, over in the thicket," she pointed to the spot. "What do ya see?"

Abel could not stop her. He feared that either way, he would have trouble. If there was a body, it would lead to a police investigation that could impact the Amish community. If there was no body, it would confirm that he was as crazy as old Esther. Either way, it spelled bad news.

Will walked up to the riverbank and stopped next to Esther. "What is it?" he asked. "Oh, God!" he exclaimed.

Without further delay, he hopped into his truck and rode across the bridge to the west bank. Once there, he pulled the truck to the side of the road and jumped out, barely shutting down the engine. He ran to the river and pushed through the thicket. As he reached the body, he shook his head in bewilderment.

Soon, Abel and Esther pulled up in the buggy behind Will's truck and stepped out.

"Who iz it? Iz it another girl?" Esther asked, as Abel's face went ashen.

"No. But, what do you mean by 'another girl'?" Will asked, knotting his brows.

CHAPTER 13

Dead and Barefoot

"**S**he said 'iz it an older girl', not another girl," Abel clarified. Will accepted the clarification since at times the Amish accent confused him. "No. It's not a girl. It's a man, and I know 'im. He works at The Raven Inn. His name's Gavin Green. I better call 911."

Soon, police and ambulance sirens were audible on the far side of the bridge. Abel's heart sank at the alarming sound that would certainly change his quiet world for the worse.

That morning, the investigation into the mysterious death at Devils Bridge found its way to Pennsylvania State Police Inspector James Cabot. Inspector Cabot was a seasoned detective in his mid-fifties. He possessed a keen deductive mind eclipsed solely by his paternal nature, which made him an exceptional mentor to his young investigative team. Often referred to as simply "Inspector," he and his team had a long list of solved cases and a growing reputation for tackling the seemingly unsolvable.

The Inspector shouted to Molly Dvorak in the adjacent office. "Molly, grab Chen and Kelly. We got a dead body near Kamerynville on the Eden River. The local police chief, Gus Morgan, an old friend of mine, called for help in solving the case. He suspects more than an accidental drowning but wouldn't tell me the details."

The most senior member of the Inspector's team was Molly. Although she had been with the force for only four years, she had already been promoted to senior detective for her contribution in several high-profile cases. Molly's deductive reasoning and resourceful nature, combined with her girl-next-door persona, made her the Inspector's ace investigator and infiltrator.

Next in seniority on this young team was Chen Lee. He had transferred into the unit from an FBI data analyst position to be near his wife while she completed her doctorate at McLaren University in Brennantown.

The final member, Kelly Stevens, had joined the team eight months earlier. Upon the departure of Bob Braxton, who had left the team to pursue a very successful music career, the Inspector backfilled the position with this young investigator who displayed a keen eye for details. She was twenty-four but looked barely eighteen. She had already made her mark with her astute observation skills, her photographic memory, and a nearly infallible intuition that even she could not explain.

Inspector Cabot and his team piled into an unmarked police car and headed southwest toward Kamerynville. Molly drove while the Inspector answered calls from the passenger seat. Kelly and Chen, being the most junior, sat in the back seat, like two mischievous children.

"What's with that town?" Chen observed. "That's where the Mary Collins case took place last year. Who can forget that one? Right, Molly? How's our old key suspect doing these days?" Chen asked with a smile, trying to unsettle Molly, a pastime he thoroughly enjoyed.

Molly glared at Chen through the rearview mirror. She had no intention of publicly exploring her relationship with Jack Fulton, the McLaren University graduate student who had been a key suspect in the Mary Collins case. They were still together, although their relationship strained under two busy careers.

Chen suspected trouble in paradise and could not pass up an opportunity to torment Molly. With Bob gone, he no longer had a partner in his favorite pursuit, although he managed to be very effective on his own.

The Inspector ignored the topic, not wishing to share his conviction that Jack would inevitably cheat on Molly, given Jack's track record as exposed during the Mary Collins case. He reasoned that it remained simply a matter of time before the relationship ended badly. To his surprise, a year had passed and his prediction had not come to fruition. But he took Molly's silence and glare to mean that he may soon be right, considering himself a fine judge of character. *Wonder if it happened?* he thought, hoping Molly would reply to Chen, but she did not.

It was an uneventful half-hour drive. Molly and Kelly remained silent while Chen and the Inspector discussed another case before falling back to their favorite topic—sports. By late morning, the team crossed Devils Bridge and entered the crime scene, which seemed uncharacteristically quiet, except for two local police cars, a coroner's truck, and a few remaining bystanders.

Most of the spectators who had materialized earlier in the day had withdrawn along with Will, Abel, and Esther. The three had been interviewed by the local police deputy, Sgt. Alvin Walker, who was the first responder to the 911 call. The latter had recently returned to the area from Austin, Texas, where he had spent a decade on the police force.

Alvin impressed Chief Morgan with his extensive knowledge of criminal justice, as well as his local stature. He had grown up in the Eden Valley and played football for Kamerynville High School before attending the University of Texas on a highly prized football scholarship. Being the biggest football star in the history of Kam High, his return warranted a certain level of fanfare in the local paper.

As Cabot's team entered the crime scene, Chief Morgan came to greet them.

"Great to see ya, Jim!" the chief said. "I had no idea ya'd bring such an entourage. I hope the trip's worth your while. We can handle a suicide or an accidental drowning, but I have a bad feeling about this one. It reminds me of the old Finley case we did together back in the dark ages. Remember that one? Ya'll will know what I mean when we get to the old house where the kid lived," he added.

Just then, a uniformed officer approached the group and stood next to the police chief. The chief smiled broadly as he introduced his new protégé. "This is my new deputy, Alvin Walker."

Alvin extended his hand to the Inspector. "Nice to meet you, Inspector, but I think you wasted a trip. We can handle it. It looks like a drug-induced suicide. The assistant coroner agrees with me." He had an arrogance about him that was hard to miss.

The Inspector ignored Alvin's comments and focused on Gus. He found the deputy's arrogance annoying. He had learned long ago to be careful with first impressions for they could be very deceiving, but he had also learned to trust his instincts.

"Who's the victim, Gus?" the Inspector asked.

Alvin answered for his boss, acting like he was in charge. "I identified him as Gavin Green—a local. The body's down by the river. The assistant coroner's still processing it." He pointed to the riverbank below. "We pulled it out of the water this morning. You can take a look, but, like I said, it's a clear-cut case."

The Inspector disregarded Alvin's comments and faced Gus once more. "Gus, as we discussed, we'll take over from here."

"Sure, Jim. Let me know what I can do to help," Gus replied. He was happy to unload the work and return to his quiet desk job.

"Any next of kin?"

"Father's alive, but his mother died long ago," Gus replied. "No one else turned up, so far. Last I heard, his rich father lives somewhere in Mexico. We haven't been able to locate 'im."

"Loner, then. Where's this house you mentioned?"

"Down the road on the other side of the bridge. You want us to take you there? Aren't you going to look at the body?" Gus was puzzled.

"Chen and I'll take a look. Molly, you and Kelly head over to the house. We'll meet you there once we're done."

"Will do, boss," Molly replied. "Will you take us over?" she asked the deputy.

"Gladly," Alvin said.

Attracted to Kelly, whom he perceived to be the shy one, he seemed more than willing to chaperone the two young female officers to Gavin Green's residence. Fancying himself a ladies' man, he hoped to get to know her better. The three drove off in Alvin's squad car before Chief Morgan had a chance to object.

"So, Gus, what do we have here?" the Inspector asked as they began to descend the riverbank.

When they arrived at the scene, the assistant coroner was hunched over the body, preparing it for transfer to the forensics laboratory in Brennantown. He rose at the sight of the three men approaching him and walked toward them. "Inspector Cabot. Good to see you, sir." He removed his latex gloves and reached out to shake the Inspector's hand. "Hank Davies at your service, sir. I'm the new guy on Coroner Dunn's staff," he added.

"Hank, it's a pleasure. Frank Dunn and I go way back. This is Chen Lee. So, what do we have here?" The Inspector did not waste time on cordialities.

"Male, late twenties, Caucasian. Time of death about eight to twelve hours ago. That's my best guess, but it's hard to tell with a floater. Cause of death appears to be head trauma with deep lacerations on the upper cranium. It's not clear if it was due to the fall or inflicted before the fall. History of drug abuse, including a probable heroin addiction, based on the recent injection markings on both arms."

"Did he overdose?"

"Not sure, yet. But, if he did, I'm pretty sure it was heroin-related. I'll submit the blood work as soon as I get back."

"Please have it rushed and copy me on the results."

"Of course."

"Anything else, Hank?"

"Tell the Inspector about the clothes," Gus reminded him.

"Oh, yes. Well, as you can see, the victim's wearing pajamas mono-gramed with 'GG.' Maybe he was sleepwalkin' and took a wrong turn," the coroner observed with a chuckle. In his line of work, he had to keep his quirky sense of humor for it helped make his job bearable.

"Interesting," the Inspector replied. "May I look at the body?"

"Of course." They turned to the body, which was lying on a white sheet along the grassy bank of the river. Chen took some pictures while the Inspector examined the deceased.

"Where was he found?" the Inspector asked.

"Right over there," Hank pointed to a thicket along the bank.

"Are these scratches from the thicket?"

"Some are, but not all. You can tell by the wounds," Hank replied.

He seems to know his craft, the Inspector silently concluded.

"What about these markings over here?" the Inspector pointed to what looked like deeper linear scratches on the victim's left arm.

"Those appear to predate his death, but it's hard to tell with floaters, even fresh ones," Hank answered. "The pattern's peculiar. There are more on the right arm." He pointed to additional symmetrical markings on the right arm. "I need to run more tests at the lab to see if I can extract anything out of the wounds," Hank added.

"Interesting. These linear patterns on both of his arms appear like fingernail scratches, as if he had a struggle with someone with sharp nails, which may or may not be associated with this event. Please take pictures of all this, Chen," the Inspector requested.

"Yes, sir."

"What about the head wound?" the Inspector asked the young assistant coroner.

"That appears to be the cause of death. It's certainly deep and the result of a forceful blow to the head. Based on the position of the wound, it may have been caused by a fall into the river, such as a leap from that bridge."

"Hmm…" The Inspector looked back at Devils Bridge. "Wouldn't it be closer to the front of the head, if that was the case?"

"Not necessarily. That would depend on the angle of impact with the shallow rocky riverbed. There appears to be some debris in the wound, but it could be post-mortem. I need to do a more thorough analysis back at the lab. One thing's for sure, it appears to have penetrated to the skull and possibly cracked it. That kind of impact's generally fatal."

"Chen, check the depth of the river below that bridge to see if that hypothesis holds up."

"Yes, sir."

"Hank, is it possible that the blow to the head occurred prior to the victim's submersion?"

"That's a possibility. It's unlikely though, since there are no blood stains on the victim's clothing, which one would expect if he was struck before submersion. I'll know more once I do a complete autopsy."

"Gus, I assume we know his identity since you searched his house. What was the means of ID?" the Inspector asked.

"One of the three folks who found him identified him and a second bystander verified it. He's Gavin Green, who worked part-time at

The Raven Inn up the road. It turns out it was the tavern's bartender who found him."

"Well, there's a curious coincidence," the Inspector opened his small notebook for the first time and began to take notes. "What's the bartender's name?"

"William Porter," Gus replied.

"Did you question him?"

"No. Alvin questioned him. He also questioned the Amish couple that discovered the body."

"So, who discovered the body, Porter or the Amish couple?"

"Not sure, but Alvin has it in his notes."

"I'll need a copy of those notes, and the names and contact information for the four people you mentioned. Anyone else who may have potentially tampered with the body before you got here?"

"No. Alvin arrived right after we got the 911 dispatch since he was in the area," Gus replied. "I was tied up in a meeting in Altoona, so I just got here right before you did. But Alvin's a great investigator. Comes highly recommended. I'm sure it's all in his notes."

"How long's he been working for you? I don't recall seeing him last time I visited."

"Three weeks. He moved up from Texas but grew up in the valley—a local kid come home. Best quarterback Kam High ever produced."

"I'll need a copy of his notes."

"You got it, Jim."

"Let's take a look at the place where the body was found. Before we do, is there anything else I should know?" The Inspector looked at the assistant coroner.

"No."

"No shoes?"

"Thank you for reminding me," Hank remarked. "The victim had no shoes and fresh lacerations on the bottom of his feet. See here." Hank pointed to the victim's bare feet.

"A barefoot heroin addict in a frightful hurry wearing nothing but monogrammed pajamas—curious, indeed. When did you say you can have the rushed lab results?"

"I can get some data by Monday and the rest by Tuesday."

"Okay. I'll need full copies of all the analyses, as well as the autopsy report. Did you take samples from beneath the fingernails?"

"Yes, sir."

"Good. Is this the spot where you found 'im?" The Inspector pointed at a nearby thicket that stretched into the river.

"Yes, sir. I helped Sgt. Walker move the body so I could analyze it. Apparently, the loose pajamas got caught in the thicket and held the body in place," Hank explained.

"I assume you took plenty of pictures before you moved 'im."

"Sgt. Walker did, sir."

"What's that in the thicket?" The Inspector pointed at a small piece of tattered white cloth caught on a thorny branch close to the riverbank.

"I hadn't noticed that earlier, but it may be part of his pajamas," Hank replied.

"It's white. His pajamas aren't white. It could be a clue," the Inspector observed. "Chen, please photograph and bag it."

"It seems like a random scrap of cloth that washed down the river, sir," Chen objected.

"Or it's a vital clue. If in doubt, we treat it as a vital clue."

"Yes, sir."

"Anything else we need to know about this scene and the body?" the Inspector asked the assistant coroner. He was frustrated that Sgt. Walker had disappeared with Kelly and Molly before he had had a chance to question him.

"No. That's it," Hank replied. "Can I take the body to the lab, now? We were waiting for you before we moved it."

"You're good to go." As the Inspector released the body to the assistant coroner for further testing, the latter returned to the body to finish prepping it for the trip to the forensics laboratory in Brennantown.

"Chen, what can you conclude from this case so far?" The Inspector began to teach his young pupil.

"It's probably a drug-induced suicide, like the deputy suggested. He seems to know what he's talking about," Chen replied, to the disappointment of his boss. Chen was a fantastic data analyst but his field skills needed work. He did not have the detective instinct that Molly and Kelly possessed. The Inspector often wondered if he would have kept Chen on the team if it were not for his data mining and analytical skills. When it came to obtaining and processing data, Chen came to life and his deductive skills were second to none. Even in interrogations, he was outstanding. But, in the field, he was a follower, as if he lacked confidence to step out on his own.

"I doubt Deputy Walker's correct. In fact, I'm certain that he's mistaken," the Inspector replied, studying the area around the thicket where the body was found.

"How can you tell?"

"It's not a suicide—bad drug trip, maybe, but not a contemplated suicide. Can you figure out why, Chen?"

"The pajamas."

"That's one piece of evidence. What else?"

"The scratches."

"What scratches in particular?"

"I don't know."

"Think. What scratches in particular support the hypothesis that this was not a planned suicide?"

"The ones on the face."

"No. Those could have been associated with just about anything, including the thicket that trapped the body. In fact, they're almost certainly the result of that, since one of them contained a thorn that is sure to match this thicket."

"Inspector, why are you quizzing me like this?"

"Chen, you need to get confident in your field deductive skills. You need to build working hypotheses on the go and prove or disprove them by collecting further evidence. What scratches, when taken with the tattered pajamas, imply that this was not a planned suicide?" the Inspector persisted.

"The feet."

"Right. Why?"

"Because the victim had no shoes on and must have been in a hurry to get the fresh, deep scratches on his feet. Maybe he panicked, and that's inconsistent with a planned suicide."

"Good."

"What other piece of evidence supports this?"

"I don't know, sir. The fresh, symmetrical scratch marks on both arms?"

"Perfect. See, you can do it. All you need to do is trust yourself. I know that Bob always excelled at the field work and you did the data analyses, but you can do both. To be a good detective, you need to be comfortable with both, especially the field work," the Inspector concluded. He was a caring father figure to his young team.

"Thank you, sir." Chen bowed his head in a gesture of respect.

"Glad to be of service. What seemed to be the oddest thing about that body?" The Inspector continued the lesson as they walked slowly toward the car.

"The pajamas."

"What about the pajamas?"

"The pajamas seemed too small," Chen replied.

The great thing about teaching is that everyone learns. The Inspector always held this belief, and this was one such occasion. He had not noticed that detail in the tattered pajamas.

"Look at this photo." Chen showed him one of his pictures. "See? They're way too small on the body."

The two returned to Hank and Gus, who were placing the victim in a body bag for transport. "Wait a second!" The Inspector stopped them.

"What is it?" Gus asked.

"I want to see something before you close him up." The Inspector walked up to the body bag. "Hank, you have gloves on. Can you please cut out that pajama label for me and place it in this bag, along with a small piece of the pajama pattern?"

"Sure." Hank did as asked without questioning the Inspector.

The Inspector was not used to such an immediate, unquestioned response, and briefly wondered what his old friend Coroner Frank Dunn was doing with his team to nurture such discipline.

"Thanks. By the way, I suggest you get a sample of that thicket over there. You may need to match it to the thorn fragment embedded in the facial scratches. That's all. Gus, can we follow you over to the victim's house?"

"Sure, once I help Hank load the body. By the way, why did you need the pajama label? I'm curious," the chief added.

"Just in case it's relevant," the Inspector replied, not wishing to open the door to useless speculation.

"Oh, okay." Gus shrugged his shoulders.

After they loaded the body into the coroner's truck, Hank left for the forensics lab. "He seems pretty good, no?" Gus asked Jim.

"Yeah. He does. Needs a little more attention to detail, but not bad," the Inspector replied. He wanted to add, *Better than your deputy*, but decided to keep that thought to himself.

The Inspector and Chen drove behind Gus to the dilapidated old farmhouse that had been Gavin Green's home for the past few months. Alvin had pried open the rusty, overgrown front gate, which provided a clear entrance for the police vehicles. Several had begun to congregate on the weed-infested front lawn of the stone structure.

"Shabby old place," Chen muttered under his breath, "and kind of spooky, too."

The Inspector did not reply. He got out of the car and followed Gus toward the rickety front door. The door must have been painted red at some time, as revealed by the peeling chips of brownish-red paint.

"You'll see what I mean about odd, Jim," Gus promised, as he led them through the front door into the small kitchen. Molly, Kelly, and Alvin were nowhere to be seen, as they were exploring the basement with flashlights.

"What a dump!" Chen exclaimed.

"Wait 'til you see this," Gus promised as he led them to a small bedroom located behind the kitchen.

Gus stopped at the door to the bedroom and let the Inspector enter first. As the Inspector entered, he stopped, taken aback by what awaited him.

CHAPTER 14

Hexes and Holes

The Inspector was awakened from his fixed stare by Chen, who entered the bedroom behind him.

"Damn! That's unbelievable!" Chen proclaimed, and began to take pictures of the shabby, smelly bedroom.

Gus smiled. "Now you know why I asked for your help, Jim."

"What do you make of this, Gus?" the Inspector continued to stare at a mural covering the wall in front of him. The bedroom had one small window, one dirty, disheveled bed, and some torn curtains. It had no closet, except for a warped wardrobe with one door missing. The latter was stuffed with disheveled clothes, few of which were hung. Two large walls were covered with yellowish, peeling wallpaper, and one wall remained the focus of the Inspector's complete attention. Slowly he walked toward it. Various hypotheses ran through his head, but none made any sense. Was this the work of a madman or a drug addict, or both?

"I don't know what to make of it, except that it's weird as hell," Gus concluded.

"I agree. Chen, take plenty of pictures. Much of this mural seems symbolic. We may need to get a specialist from Pittsburgh or Philly.

But first we need to get the forensic lab results. I don't want to send an expert out here on a wild goose chase. Let's just document it for now," the Inspector instructed as he studied the wall.

"Is that blood? That red color in the mural looks like blood," Chen reasoned, as he inspected the graphic mural without touching it.

"Could be, but that would be a lot of blood. The black looks like charcoal and the white looks like chalk, but we won't know for sure until we analyze it," the Inspector surmised.

"A wall-sized mural in blood and charcoal. That's bizarre," Chen concluded, as he continued to photographically document the finding.

"It looks like a story that starts right here." The Inspector pointed at the far side of the mural. "This part here seems so violent, but the rest seems almost religious. This guy had some major issues. Look at the black raven image dominating the top of the mural, while the large white image dominates the lower portion. The white figure seems to be either an angel or some sort of wizard with a white glow. Correction. It's female. So, it's an angel or a witch. By the way, the red is definitely not blood. It appears to be red pigment. I'm starting to think this entire affair's the work of a heroin addict who found a sorry end in the local river," the Inspector extrapolated.

"I'm with you, Jim, but it's the most bizarre case I've had in years," Gus confessed.

"And it gets more bizarre when you look further," Molly spoke up. She, Kelly, and Alvin had returned upstairs from the basement and stood in front of the bedroom door.

"This place's creepy," Kelly proclaimed. "With my luck, I'll remember everything and have nightmares for weeks. I knew I should've called out sick today."

"What else did you find?" the Inspector asked, looking at Molly.

"Boss, this room's just the opening act in this house of horrors."

Before she could explain, Alvin spoke up. "This place is clearly a drug den." He began to share his opinion without being asked. "I found a weird chapel in the adjacent bedroom, complete with a book on witchcraft and spells. It has some kind of a makeshift altar with burned candles, incense sticks, and pentagrams scribbled on the walls. It's like this guy had an obsession with witches. He didn't live here alone, either. He had company, including women's company. There's a lot of drug paraphernalia and used heroin needles everywhere, although I haven't found any measurable quantities of the opiate substance. The only thing I found was this bag of pot in the kitchen."

Alvin was on an unstoppable roll in an effort to prove his brilliance to his boss and to the visiting Inspector. Molly and Kelly couldn't get a word in edgewise.

"The basement's the weirdest part. There are dozens of large holes dug into the earthen floor. The patterns appear to be random, as if someone was burying things or looking for something buried. Weird. I found two old shovels in the far corner of the basement. I wonder if he buried anyone down there. Sicko!" Alvin finally came up for air.

It was clear that he liked to use the word "I" rather than "we." This confirmed the Inspector's initial impression that the deputy was not a team player, at least not when it came to police work.

"We took plenty of pictures, boss." Molly finally had a chance to comment. "As Alvin mentioned, we found a small amount of marijuana along with evidence of odd witch worship and of at least one other past occupant—apparently a woman."

"I'm telling you. Green had a bad heroin trip and ended up in the river," Alvin whined.

"What do you want us to do, boss? We clearly have a case of drug abuse but no evidence of a homicide. How far do we investigate?" Molly asked the practical question.

"We need to see what comes back from the autopsy. If this is a drug-induced or accidental death, regardless of how bizarre it may be, there's probably no need for us to stay involved. Like I said, the evidence should be in the blood work and the autopsy. If it's not, we decide at that point," the Inspector replied.

"I think Green's death is a closed case. It's clearly a drug-related suicide," Alvin reasoned.

"Except that in the upper right corner of the kitchen, above the cabinets, is a potential clue that may shed more light on the case," Kelly said softly, during a rare moment of silence.

"What?" Alvin turned toward her, knitted his brows, and addressed her in an irritated voice. "What are you talking about?"

"I just noticed it from here." She pointed at the warped wooden cabinets behind them. "I sense it's a vital clue."

"How could you know that? It's probably a useless scrap of paper," Alvin objected.

The Inspector and his team treated Kelly's intuition as if it were a request for a second cup of coffee, accepting it without question or any visible reaction. Gus remained silent, not sure what to make of this odd detective practice and the young woman who looked more like a teenager than a police investigator.

"Let's take a look," the Inspector suggested.

He had grown to respect Kelly's unorthodox intuitive skills. He understood the scientific premise of her photographic memory but could not explain her intuitive insights. More often than not, they proved to be correct. Thus, he had decided to simply accept them. Why question and fix something when it's working? he reasoned.

Alvin, who was by far the tallest one in the company, had the task of reaching up to the top of the dusty, shabby kitchen cabinet to retrieve the piece of paper. Kelly correctly observed that only a small corner of the paper remained visible from eye level. However, her deduction that it was a vital clue in the mysterious death of Gavin Green had yet to be proven.

The paper yielded a mysterious poem by an equally mysterious author. It made reference to witches, birds, devils, and a crossing to a nameless place. In short, it made little sense. As a result, it did not point the team in a meaningful direction. It simply raised more questions.

Nonetheless, just in case Kelly proved once more to be correct, the Inspector asked Chen to photograph and bag it as potential evidence. "Make sure you use gloves when you pick it up," he reminded Chen, while Alvin rolled his eyes and shook his head.

The following was written in a scribbled hand on the torn and well-worn piece of paper.

Beware the specter of the White Witch!
Beware the Raven of Devils Bridge!
The two are united under one,
But opposed like the moon and the sun.
To cross one is to cross them both,
But one I love and one I loathe.

The White Witch, whether woman or dove,
Is like a phantom from above.
She can haunt or she can free you,
But always she can see you.
Your soul is what she's after
Now and ever after.

There's a place you know but you've never seen.
She can take you there, back, and in between.
It's an odd crossing that's always even.
For it's been there since the days of Eden.
The price is high if you choose to go.
There's no freeloaders, that I know.

If you seek her as a guide,
Beware her power, beware your pride.
You may find her, the White Dove,
An arcane image of fear or love.
If you seek her as a foe,
You'll never catch her, that I know.

She's the princess of the moon and night.
She's the sorceress beneath the lunar light.
I know her well, and she knows me.
We are entwined in a bond of sorority.
She guards the passage, oaks in a row.
Don't ever cross her for she will know.

The passage is hidden, yet all have the key.
In time, all are invited. You will see.
Only the White Dove can truly deliver,
A two-way crossing over that mysterious river
That divides us all into form and soul.
In your heart, not mind, you will know.

Her light reveals all, high and low.
Ask the Raven, he's her foe.
One's the hunter, and one's the doe.
The heart of both, I finally know.
The Raven traps me, forevermore.
The White Dove frees me, nevermore.

I am lost. I, Lenore.

After Kelly read the poem through the transparent evidence bag, Alvin proclaimed, "This is a nonsensical hex. This just adds to the obvious conclusion that Gavin Green had gone mad before ending his life in the Eden River. It's clear cut."

"I think it's mysterious and beautiful. But, who's Lenore, and how's she associated with Gavin Green and his house of horrors? Maybe she's the other occupant?" Kelly reasoned.

"Good questions and a good hypothesis," the Inspector replied, "and one that we need to pursue, if this case isn't an accidental death."

"It's clearly a suicide and a drug-induced leap into the river by a madman. Look about you! He probably used 'Lenore' as a pen name and wrote that nonsense. It's clear cut," Alvin said.

The Inspector was less convinced but did not wish to start an argument with the arrogant deputy. Instead, he donned his manager's hat and gave his team clear directions.

"Molly and Kelly, you continue to dig deeper into this mystery. Chen, you and I need to get back and finish the Donnelly case. We can run the data if you find anything interesting. Gus, can you assure that no one gets into this place and disturbs the disturbing evidence?" he asked, while enjoying the play on words. Once more he ignored Alvin and addressed Gus.

"Molly, did you get pigment samples off of the murals?"

"Yes, sir. Here they are," she handed the Inspector the labeled sample bags.

"Great. Take a picture of the poem, and we will take it and the pigment samples with us back to the lab."

"Done."

"Good. We gotta go. Thanks again, Gus. We'll stay in touch."

"Thanks for your help, Jim" the chief replied, and he meant it, for he was glad to get back to what he understood—basic police work.

The Inspector and Chen said their goodbyes and departed.

"I have to get back to the office," Gus said. "Alvin, can you make sure we have this place locked down?"

"Will do."

"Ladies, the nearest place to stay is The Raven Inn, just up the road. It's clean, charming, and the food's excellent. Pleasure meeting you both. I'll see you back in the office, Alvin," the police chief said as he departed.

"I can give you ladies a lift to the inn," Alvin offered, suddenly becoming the perfect gentleman.

"Just give us a few minutes to take some more pictures," Molly replied. "By the way, Kelly, that poem might tie to the mural. Did you notice the white image depicted in the center of the mural and the raven at the top of it?"

"I did. The raven's large wings are like an umbrella over the entire mural. He seems to be in charge. Yet, the white female figure in the center of the wall painting appears to oppose him and push him back. She holds a long white staff, like a wizard's staff, which emanates white light. That could be a depiction of the White Witch and the Raven mentioned in the poem," Kelly replied, downloading exact images from her memory.

"What if the poem's a riddle that answers the mystery behind this case?" Molly asked.

"No way! It makes no sense," rebuked Alvin. "Besides, there's no one named Lenore in these parts."

Kelly remained silent. She was not impressed by Alvin, her latest suitor, although the latter tried his best to open doors, smile, and even make jokes whenever he had her attention. Molly was getting annoyed but had not said anything on the subject all afternoon. That would be reserved for girl talk later that night.

"By the way, may I take a picture of that poem?" Alvin asked. "I'll put it in the file we started for this case back at the office." The request puzzled both women, since only moments earlier he had refuted the poem's value as a clue.

"Sure," Molly responded, "but what file are you referring to, Alvin? Please make sure you're sharing all the information with us. Per your boss's request, we're running this investigation. By the way, we need your transcripts of the interviews you conducted with the Amish couple and the guy that found Gavin's body, as well as anyone else you talked to at the scene."

"Don't worry. I'm aware of that. You'll have everything by end of day tomorrow. I just need to type them up. Right now, they're scribbled in my notebook," Alvin replied. He liked Kelly but did not care for Molly. She seemed too stern.

"If you don't mind, we want the photocopies of the original notes, as well," Molly added. She did not trust Alvin. There was something about his behavior that felt suspicious, but she could not put her finger on it. She looked forward to comparing notes with Kelly over dinner.

After taking more pictures, checking for fingerprints, and carefully bagging additional evidence, such as samples from items on the makeshift altar, the two women were ready to leave. "Too bad the shovels had no prints on them. Odd, isn't it, since they seem new and recently used?" Molly concluded, as they closed the door behind them.

"You're not going to search the yard?" Alvin asked, seeing the two women headed toward his car.

It occurred to Molly that he had a point. They had focused on the house but had not searched the area around it. "You're right, Alvin. We need to look around the outside of the house."

"But make it quick. I need to get back home," Alvin replied, annoying Molly further.

Why does he suggest that we search the yard, and then tell us to hurry? Kelly wondered.

"Kelly, can you take a look around the back garden while I look around the front?" Molly asked her partner.

"What're we looking for?" Kelly asked naively.

"Anything out of the ordinary."

"Okay. Hey, where's Alvin?"

"Usually he's right behind you, staring at your butt."

"Very funny. I sense a streak of jealousy, Ms. Molly."

"Not! You can have him, ego and all."

"Thanks. Just what I always wanted, a pet deputy," Kelly replied and laughed. She walked toward the back of the old farmhouse. As she turned the corner, she saw Alvin carefully scurrying about the lawn. "What're you doing, Alvin?" she asked.

"Looking for clues," he replied, without glancing up at her. "Look, here's something."

Kelly ran over to him. "Don't pick it up!" she warned. "What is it?"

"Looks like a piece of a torn white garment," Alvin replied, while pointing to the ground.

"I better bag it," Kelly replied. She was tagging the small torn piece of cloth just as Molly came around the corner.

"Nothing interesting out front," Molly surmised. "What'd you find?"

"Alvin found it. It's a piece of white cloth. I took a picture and I'm bagging it just in case it's important."

"Odd." Molly crinkled her brows.

"What?" Kelly asked.

"What's a small, square tattered piece of white cloth doing out here, not far from Gavin's bedroom window?"

"Heck if I know, but I bagged it anyway."

"Might be a clue," Alvin offered.

"Might be. Let's take a final look around and then get out of here. It's getting too dark to see anything. I assume the patrol car coming up the drive's one of yours, Alvin?" Molly observed an old squad car slowly approaching them along the weed-covered, gravel road.

"Yeah. That's Joe comin' to watch the place on chief's orders. We'll have a round-the-clock presence to assure no one tampers with the evidence until you folks solve the case or until all this proves to be a wild goose chase," Alvin replied with a smirk.

"You make it sound like it's nothing, Alvin. Aren't you worried about the heroin? Looks like you've got a serious drug problem in this valley. It's certainly not a wild goose chase. That's an ignorant comment." Molly was annoyed with the arrogant deputy. "Let's get out of here. Ready, Kelly?" she added.

"Sure am, boss."

"I'm not your boss and you know it," Molly objected. She did not like that title. It made her feel old.

After they greeted Joe, the three piled into Alvin's police cruiser and headed down the drive. Little did they know that the entire time they were being carefully watched from beyond the line of trees at the far end of the property. The moon came out and the mysterious woman in white vanished into the shadows of the night.

CHAPTER 15

Washday

Earlier that afternoon, Mary Lapp tended to the family laundry she had hung on the clothesline that morning. "Lenore, please come help me take down this wash!" Mary shouted to her oldest daughter. She firmly believed that the best cure for Lenore's amnesia was an immersion into her previous Amish life. "Come child. I need to tend to the chickens. This washing needs folding."

Lenore walked up to her mother and smiled, happy to help. The past few days of rest were getting unbearable for the energetic youth. Although she had little recollection of her past, there were times when she remembered a smell, a sound, or a familiar object. To her frustration, none of these seemed to connect into meaningful memories.

Her initial panic of having no recollection of her past, or of her true identity, had been replaced by acceptance, as she enjoyed the company of this loving family. *Regardless of what happened in the past,* she thought, *I'm happy here.* It was in this mindset that she accepted the chore, projecting joyful gratitude in the process.

"Sure, *Mater,*" she replied. She still found it difficult to refer to Mary as her mother, but it was becoming easier every day. Besides, the woman made a perfect mother. *How could someone not want her as a mother?*

"Remember to fold it in the basket. Hurry, child. The breeze's kickin'" up und I don't wanna be lookin' for my clean laundry in d' henhouse," Mary said with a laugh. Her fear and anguish lifted; she had been a changed woman since the day her daughter returned. "Go on, then." After overseeing the folding of three pieces of clothing, she departed toward the henhouse, leaving Lenore alone.

Lenore was carefully removing the family's plain clothes from the line when suddenly she stopped and stared. There, on the line before her, hung a blue dress—her dress. For a mental image that lasted no more than a few seconds, she saw herself adjusting the dress in the presence of a young man. His face she could not recall, but she remembered the smell of black tea. In the same instant, she remembered that somehow this man was important in a way that differed from anyone in the Lapp family. The recollection frightened her, and it took her a while to resume taking down and folding the rest of the clothes. She left the dress on the line until all else was folded, in hopes that her memory would come back and fill the missing gaps. But it did not. Finally, she carefully folded the blue cotton dress, placing it on the top of the laundry basket.

After finishing the task, she sought out her mother, whom she found gathering the last of the eggs.

"*Mater?*"

"Yes, dear. Ya done already?"

"Yes, but I've got a question."

Mary paused, looking at her oldest child with complete focus. She sensed that the question would have something to do with the past, and she had mixed emotions. Part of her felt joyful that her daughter would remember, and part of her was fearful of what memories would surface and in what order.

"What iz it, dear?"

"Was I married?"

"No. Of course, not," Mary replied. *Odd question.* "Why would ya think that, my dear?" she asked.

"Oh, nothing. Here ya are. All folded. By the way, did ya make this blue dress for me?" She pointed to the top of the laundry basket.

Mary hesitated to answer, for she did not wish to lie. Yet to tell the truth might give way to the memories that she did not wish to encourage, at least not as Lenore's first memories. "No. I didn't. Ya got that from a family friend," she replied, deciding to be truthful without revealing the exact source of the gift.

But Lenore was clever, despite her amnesia, and sensed a revelation in the making. "What friend, *Mater*?"

Mary felt trapped. She knew that Amos Miller had given Lenore the blue dress not long before she disappeared. Lenore had worn it to her cousin's wedding. Lenore adored that dress but neglected to take it with her when she left her family. So, despite her daughter's sudden departure from the Amish, Mary could not part with it. It reminded her of Lenore's radiance on that day.

She had never seen Lenore happier—not since she was a little girl on the day that she got her puppy. That puppy was now the old dog that clung to Lenore's every step like a faithful friend who did not care whether she remembered him or not, only that he remembered her.

Mary could not lie. Never had she lied, not once. But, to reveal Amos and Lenore's relationship with him could cause her daughter to leave again. At a minimum, it would lead to many questions that Mary was not ready to answer. Torn, Mary desperately sought middle ground.

"Ya got that dress from one of the Miller boys. He has a sister and she's an excellent seamstress. Her name's June. She made it. I, too, have a fancy dress that she made. Fine seamstress, old June Miller. She's my age, as're most of the Miller children. That dress is really not that important, my dear."

Mary hoped that by way of her lengthy explanation she diverted Lenore's attention to the seamstress of the dress and stopped the sensitive questioning. Miraculously, she had managed not to lie and hoped that the conversation would end. Just in case, she decided to drop an egg from the egg basket to create a diversion.

"Oh my, look what I've done." Cody, Lenore's dog, quickly jumped on the opportunity for a treat. "I guess Cody enjoyed that. Well, we better head inside. I need to start dinner. Will ya help me?"

"Sure, *Mater*. But why does Cody always follow me?"

Mary was relieved that Lenore changed the topic to a more promising subject.

"Because he's yur dog, my dear. Father und I gave'im to ya on yur seventh birthday. My dear, ya should've seen how happy ya were that day."

Lenore loved how this woman, who claimed to be her mother, always called her "my dear" with such a heartfelt tone. It made her feel loved and safe. She could not imagine ever leaving such a wonderful woman. In a moment of genuine love and appreciation, Lenore uttered the words that her mother had yearned to hear for much too long. "I love you, *Mater*. I'd never leave ya, no matter what."

May God grant us that wish, Mary thought, but decided to simply reply, "I love you, too, my dear. There'll never be a reason to leave."

As the two women headed into the house, the older of the two reflected on the nightmare that had not so long ago been her reality. *No. Ya won't leave, again. Not if ya never find out the truth.*

The Sisterhood

A full moon appeared from behind the clouds, immersing all in haunting shades of white and blue. Its pale light illuminated the clearing, which was surrounded by large oak trees that stood in a row as if they had been carefully planted centuries earlier. These seemingly timeless guardians, like protective giants, formed a formidable wall beyond the flickering light of a large crackling fire.

Around the fire pit, made of rounded river stones, sat seven women. They sat on four hewn logs that formed a square around the blaze. The golden dancing light of the fire played with the contours of their young faces, turning them from beautiful to disfigured and back again. Somber, they listened to the woman with the white shawl around her shoulders. Although she spoke softly, her voice seemed to carry clearly across the silent meadow.

Her name was Ariella Bianca, the leader of this small enclave of young women, known as the Eden Sisterhood. Held her in high esteem by her small following, she offered them shelter, rest, protection, and wisdom that seemed beyond her years. On many evenings, weather permitting, they sat by this open fire talking and laughing. But on this night, the mood darkened as the subject turned to Lenore and the unsolved mystery that surrounded her disappearance.

Ariella had met Lenore, the runaway Amish girl, months earlier. After leaving Amos Miller and her Amish family, Lenore had wandered about the Eden Valley like a lost child. In her meandering, she had entered the vast, deep woods that stretched for thousands of acres north of Devils Bridge. These woods had a way of disorienting even the most seasoned traveler.

Lenore became lost for days until she stumbled upon Ariella, or, more precisely, until Ariella found her and brought her back to her cabin. Lenore stayed with Ariella and the sisterhood, quickly becoming a favorite among the girls, who persuaded her to join their informal sorority. Then, in mid-August, she disappeared.

A week later, Ariella had a dark premonition that Lenore was in trouble. She confided in Rebecca, Lenore's closest friend, and put her in charge of the sisterhood while she embarked on a mission to find Lenore. Rebecca wanted to join her, but Ariella insisted upon going alone. Unfortunately, Rebecca revealed Ariella's concerns to the other girls, and a panic ensued that had never fully abated.

Later that night the young women of the sisterhood got little sleep while awaiting news of Lenore. Early the next morning, Rebecca was sitting on the porch when Ariella came walking across the large meadow that surrounded the cabin. The scene looked surreal and haunting as the sun began to rise over the sea of tall grass, draping it in a magenta mist. The sight of the lone figure emerging out of the thick fog made Rebecca's heart sink, for Lenore did not accompany her.

As soon as Ariella reached the porch, Rebecca questioned her about Lenore and the events of the night, but her teacher did not wish to discuss either. Taking several items from the cabin, she disappeared back into the mist without explanation. That was the morning of August 26th, the day Josef found his sister, Lenore, left for dead in the Eden River beneath Devils Bridge.

That was four weeks ago, but the frightful impact of Lenore's disappearance on the young women of the sisterhood had lingered as a dark shadow of anxiety. Thus, it was not a surprise to Ariella that once again Lenore became the subject of their fireside discussion.

"Girls, as I've said before, Lenore's fine," Ariella stressed to the young women. At the age of thirty-seven, she was clearly the leader and matriarch of the Eden Sisterhood. By contrast, her charges were in their teens and early twenties.

"Ariella, you never told us the details of what happened to Lenore. Are you sure she's fine? How do you know? Where is she? Can we go see her?" asked one of the young women.

"Marie, I know she's fine because I've seen her. She's back with her Amish family and we shouldn't disturb her as she recovers." Suddenly, Ariella realized that she revealed too much. She had never shared with anyone, not even Rebecca, her full knowledge of the events of that night.

"Recovers? From what?" Marie picked up on the slip.

Ariella realized that she had to come clean. "I never told you this because I didn't want to frighten you, but Lenore was attacked at Devils Bridge. It was senseless evil, but I'll find the one who did it. The Amish got to her before I could, but I've been keeping an eye on her. She's fine. She's back with her family and she's fine."

"You've talked to her?" asked Marie.

"No, but I've seen her and she's okay. I don't want to disturb her now that she's back in her old life."

"Who attacked her and why?" Marie asked.

"I don't know, but I won't let this rest until I figure it out and make sure it never happens again."

"No offense, teacher, but how're you going to do that? You taught us to forgive and to love unconditionally. This sounds like revenge," another young woman observed. "Not that it's not deserved, 'cause it is," she added.

"Rachel, I'd never use evil against evil. The two combine to create something worse. But it's our duty to look out for each other and to assure we're not passive victims. I know some of you, coming from the Amish faith, were taught to be passive. I don't disagree that a life of passive resistance and peaceful balance is a worthy goal. But I believe that we shouldn't be willing victims of evil if it crosses our path," Ariella explained.

She taught forgiveness within the framework of passive resistance and active kindness. To Ariella, evil lurked in the twists and turns of the mind and was a potential weakness inherent to all humans. Thus, she preached love and the absence of hate, claiming that hell did not exist, except as the evil humans created in this physical world. Hell, as a place of eternal punishment, seemed to her a myth derived from vengeful thinking guised as justice. Ariella preferred to focus on the positive forces in life and an equally positive vision of an afterlife.

Her love, support and wisdom attracted this small following of young disciples. She was their muse and their chosen mother. They consisted of runaways and disenchanted girls of various backgrounds, each fleeing from her past and seeking a better future. Ariella never sought them out nor asked to be their teacher. They simply came.

One by one, they showed up on her doorstep or in the nearby woodlands, like strays. Always, she took them in and gave them shelter, unconditional love, and a faith in the pure positive spirit she tried to embody every day. Her caring nature and timeless wisdom kept them faithful to her. They would do anything for her in an unquestioned loyalty that she never requested or abused.

Hers were the ways of a servant leader who tried to follow in the challenging footsteps of the great servant leaders of the past.

"You should've gone to the police right away. They should be looking for Lenore's attacker. Instead, he's free to do it again," Anna objected.

Annabel Lee, known simply as Anna, was neither former Amish nor a runaway teen. Although barely eighteen, she seemed much wiser than her years. She had grown up with her paternal grandparents in neighboring Kamerynville after losing her father to a foreign war and her mother to a distant pursuit. Although she had no recollection of either parent, she had an unfulfilled longing for both.

Recently, her grandfather had died, which had created a huge void in her heart. That void, combined with the vacuum left by her missing parents, coalesced into a yearning that Anna could not quench. After a long discussion with her grandmother, she decided to seek her missing mother, who was presumably alive.

To make things worse, Anna began to remind her grandmother of the daughter-in-law that she disliked to this day. An odd dynamic was brewing, and both women grew weary of it. Now that her grandfather had passed away, Anna needed to leave, but she did not wish to run away. That was not her style. She had been told countless times by her grandmother that her mother had run away, and she had no desire to emulate her. Rather, an honest discussion with her grandmother convinced both women that it was time to part.

Unfortunately, her grandmother refused to share any information with Anna regarding her mother, except that she had returned to the area and was probably "haunting it." Clearly, she wished to forget her former daughter-in-law and any association she had with the son she lost in the Bosnian conflict.

Thus, Anna left her grandmother's home in search of her lost mother. Since she had never seen a picture of her mother, she had no idea of her appearance. She knew her mother's name, but little else had been revealed by either of her grandparents or anyone else. It seemed as if her mother had barely existed. A cone of silence and a shroud of secrecy surrounded her everywhere she searched. Yet Anna remained convinced that fortune would reunite them, if only she continued to believe.

Four months ago, fortune had brought her to the doorstep where Ariella welcomed her as if she were her own. Here, Anna felt truly at home and decided to postpone her quest.

"No police, Anna," Ariella replied. "They're useless. They'd break us apart and take all of you away from me. I know Lenore's fine and I'll discover her attacker soon. I'm working on it."

"What do you mean, 'you're working on it'?" Anna wanted clarity, always pushing for answers. She alone, of the young women gathered around the fire, refused to refer to Ariella as "Teacher." It simply didn't feel right.

"I have my ways," Ariella replied, looking at Anna across the yellow flames of the fire. "I have a strong feeling it'll soon be revealed."

A born scientist, Anna was a freethinker. It defined her as the openminded, pragmatic seeker of truth. To her, what Ariella accepted as faith or a deeper knowing seemed illogical. Her intellectual interest in this sisterhood stemmed primarily from her curiosity to explore Ariella's seemingly inexplicable premonitions. Ariella's answer did not satisfy, and she struggled as to whether she should push her generous host any further. She decided to try. "What're these 'ways' of yours?"

"As I've told all of you, when you find inner peace, the rest'll find you. Your heart'll guide you." Ariella felt tempted to reveal more but reconsidered, knowing it would only lead to more questions. Her students were simply not ready for more, not in this group setting, not now. Or were they? She decided to tread water.

"I have my morning ritual, as you all know. I simply meditate and quiet my mind and my fears. I attain peace and then I listen with my heart. It's in this quiet receptive state that I get insights. It's no different than inspiration. After all, in-spiration is being in one's spiritual state—shutting down one's fretting mind and listening to one's soul."

The young women listened but many did not understand. Once again, Anna wanted to probe this vagueness with scientific precision. Her powerful mind latched onto the idea that one could detect a spirit and use one's heart to do so, or, specifically, one's mind, since the heart was simply a living pump. To her, the entire premise sounded absurd, but she did not want to embarrass her host, nor did she wish to create a debate of science versus personal spirituality.

Reconsidering, she decided to cease her interrogation. This topic presented fertile ground for debate and discovery, for she had always been fascinated by the concept of a soul, a concept she was taught in her strict Catholic upbringing under her grandparents' supervision. But the time and company did not seem fitting for further inquiry.

Ariella knew that Anna was not satisfied with the explanation. She knew and smiled. *Who was the wiser disciple, Peter or Thomas? One accepted without question. The other sought to understand without hesitation,* she silently reflected. *Surely, in the end, it didn't matter—both virtues led to the same source if the practitioner remained receptive and the teacher remained true to the cause.*

To her, both defined a pure seeker. One trusted a higher power to achieve insights of wisdom and grace, while the other followed a trail of factual and insightful crumbs to the grace that created them. Thus, she admired Anna and her scientific mind no less than she admired the true shamans of the past. She viewed science as just another modern religion with the same objective as any other—to seek the truth and, ultimately, the higher purpose for all that surrounds us.

"Teacher, will we still take our walks by the river?" the youngest member of the group asked in childlike innocence, bringing the conversation back to simple relevance.

"Of course, Hazel. We can't allow fear to govern our actions. Fear and want are the two ugliest children of the human race." Ariella began to teach her pupils. "To succumb to either is to lose your noble self. Together, they account for the vast majority of man's evil, anger, prejudice, and hate. Beware of both, especially fear."

Anna wished to ask more questions but she chose silence. The silence continued as most of the participants accepted the response, except for Anna, who analyzed it. Her mind raced. She could not just accept without question. Her curiosity bubbled up once more.

"What does that mean? Isn't it smart to be cautious and to provide for yourself? Fear and self-preservation seem natural and heathy. What you just said doesn't make sense to me."

Ariella knew that when Anna appeared on the scene, her world had changed forever. No longer would she be the sage whose wisdoms were unquestionably accepted. Anna forced her to become a true teacher, whose truths were challenged, pressing her to explore them more deeply than ever before. In this way, Anna often taught Ariella, creating a full circle that benefited all.

"Anna, dear Anna, the wise do not gain wisdom through passive inaction. Only by seeking the horizon, does one see the rising sun," Ariella replied.

"That's not helping," Anna boldly replied.

"You should question when you don't understand or agree. You should all take an example from Anna." Ariella looked about at the remaining young women, inviting them to challenge her, so all could learn through the process.

"Anna, what I meant was that although fear and want are natural, they miss the mark. I'm not suggesting that any of us are free of them, or even that we can free ourselves of them by focusing on eliminating them. Such focus only keeps us struggling, making them front of mind and allowing them to grow within us.

"What I mean is that we must look beyond them at the path that is forgiveness, love, and joy. These are the mark. These are the beacons of light guiding our growth. But remember not to be too harsh on yourselves if you miss that mark and succumb to anger, to fear, or even to self-absorbed loathing. Just don't let that be your chosen state. Free yourself of such negative thoughts as soon as you recognize them, and, in time, you'll become more positive and more connected to your nobler self, which will lead to happiness, balance, and wisdom." She ceased her lesson. All was silent, except the crackling of the fire.

Anna concluded that although Ariella may not be all-knowing or always right, she possessed wisdom and insight beyond her years. Thus, Anna remained silent, pondering Ariella's answer while gazing at the leaping flames. The silence prevailed until Ariella suddenly perked up like a doe aware of a hunter.

"What is it?" asked the ever-cautious Sarah.

"We have a visitor," Ariella replied.

CHAPTER 17

Seek and Ye Shall Find

$\mathcal{M}$eanwhile, that same evening, Molly and Kelly sat at a small table at The Raven Inn restaurant, enveloped by a colonial setting complete with 200-year-old stone walls. Both were glad to be rid of Deputy Alvin Walker of the local police. His persistent advances toward Kelly were annoying and unprofessional. Although Kelly did not seem to mind, having grown accustomed to such attention after years of serving in restaurants in college, Molly remained visibly offended. She had a mind to complain to the police chief but knew that she had to try and keep peace with local law enforcement until the mysterious case of Gavin Green was solved. After that, she would file a complaint.

"I'm glad to get rid of that loser," Molly confessed aloud.

"He's just a typical guy, Molly. If I had a buck for each time I ran across a guy like that, I'd have a nice side income," Kelly replied and chuckled. She was much more composed and unemotional than her older colleague.

"Sounds like you need to start hanging out in better places."

"It's not the places. I need to get rid of this blonde hair." Kelly laughed and shook her long locks. She changed the subject. "What'd you think of the poem we found at Green's place?"

"It's weird. The entire place is creepy. I can't imagine how anyone could live there. I'd jump off a bridge too if I had to live there."

"Somehow I can't see you drawing disturbing murals on your bedroom wall. I can't see Jack taking kindly to that," Kelly replied, intentionally tapping the subject of Molly and Jack, hoping Molly would take the bait.

"Jack's a sweetheart and I'm lucky to have him. That case knocked some sense into him."

"Are you referring to when you met?" Kelly asked.

"Yes. The case Chen won't let me forget."

"Chen's a character but he'd do anything for you, Molly. He really looks up to you."

"He has his moments but I doubt that he looks up to me."

"I'm glad that you and Jack are happy."

"We are. Why're you fishing, Kelly? Did Chen put you up to this?" Molly did not like to discuss her private affairs.

"No, I was just curious. So, is this it? Is he the one?"

"Maybe. It feels like this could be it but I don't want to jinx it. The issue is that he wants a boatload of kids. I'm just not ready to give up my career to be a full-time mom. I'm a senior detective now and I like it. I worked hard for it."

"You wouldn't have to give it up, Molly. It's not like the 1950s."

"I know, but I'm not ready to go part-time even. Besides, how do you juggle two careers and four kids? He wants four kids, for God's sake! The man's crazy! Hell, he can carry and birth them, if he wants 'em that bad."

"Wow! You guys are serious if you're debating the kid count. Did he propose yet?"

"No, not yet. I'm scared that he might 'cause I'm not sure what I'd say." Molly finished her soup just as the main course arrived.

"Wait a minute! You're discussing the kid count, and you don't know if you want to marry him?"

"Well, he's smitten. What can I say," she said with a smug smile. "I mean...I love him, too, but I need to catch up."

"Did you tell 'im that?"

"I tried, but he doesn't want to hear it. I swear he's probably naming the four kids as we speak. It scares me to think about it."

"Uh, oh. You'd better talk to him like you're talking to me."

"You can talk to him 'til you're blue in the face, and he hears only what he wants to hear. That's the problem."

"Do you really love 'im?"

"Yes, of course. He's the kindest, most caring guy in the world. He always says I'm the one he's been looking for."

"That's so sweet. Sounds like he really loves you, Molly."

"He does, and I love him. But he's in a rosy world of infatuation and ten steps ahead of me. I'm not sure it's healthy. What if he wakes up one day, when I'm as big as a bus with our first kid and the rosy bubble pops. Then what? What's your reaction to a man who's smitten? I'm sure that's not foreign to you. Look at you…you're like every guy's blonde trophy."

"Thanks—I think."

"So what do you do with a smitten boyfriend?"

"Well, if he's smitten by you that's not a bad thing. But it would be better if you were smitten, as well."

"Would it? Then, we'd be like two blind fools. I'm a realist, not a crazed romantic like Jack."

"It's cute that he's so in love, but I guess you'd better talk to him if you don't feel the same way."

"How do I do that? He won't hear me. What do I do? Cut him off in bed?"

"If it works."

"There's an idea. Maybe then he'll come back to earth."

"It's a nice problem to have, Molly. I mean you've got a great guy who's smitten by you. I'm being hit on by anyone with testosterone and even some with estrogen."

"Do tell."

"Long story but nothing to tell. I'm sure it's happened to you."

Molly fell silent as she recalled Ms. Nightingale from the Mary Collin's case.

"I kind of like all the attention," Kelly added.

Molly sighed. "Just be careful not to attract the wrong people. From what I've noticed working with you, you seem to attract too much of the wrong attention. You're so cheery and friendly, and that attracts everyone. I don't want anything bad to happen to you."

"Oh, you're sweet. I didn't know you cared that much."

"Well, I do."

"It's sweet, but I can't be someone I'm not. I can't be pensive, like you. The joyful blonde is who I am. Not that pensive is bad, it's just not me."

"I'm not pensive," Molly objected.

"You define pensive. You're sweet, beautiful, and smart, but that mind of yours is always going, always evaluating, and always pondering. Come on, it's you!"

"I guess, but I can be fun. Ask Jack and his friends."

"What about your friends?"

"I have work, Jack, and Jack's friends."

"There's the problem."

"There's no problem, Kelly." Molly was getting defensive.

"I meant, there's the opportunity for reflection. Is that better?"

"No. You're still analyzing me."

"Sorry. I know I'm younger but I'm used to the big sister role. My mom and dad divorced when I was eleven, and although I still get to see them both, the divorce was not easy for anyone. Even though it was pretty civil and we were very well off, it still meant that mom raised us alone and I had to help her with my two younger brothers. I used to worry a lot, until I decided the best thing to do is let go and stay in the moment. So, that's what I try to do."

"I wish I could let go. I'm not the letting-go type."

"I know, but what I'm trying to tell you is that neither was I when I was younger. I had to learn it and work on it. It's all about attitude. Attitude's like a flag you're flying that everyone can see. So, the more joyful and positive that flag, the better. No?"

"Why's joyful better than pensive? Look at what you attract— Alvin. I like pensive," Molly replied.

"Pensive's great if it's not too dark. Like attracts like when it comes to attitude. That has been my experience. Unfortunately, it's hard to see through all the pretenses. I'm convinced the scariest thing for most people is to truly acknowledge who they really are and accept full ownership for all that they think, say, and do."

"I never thought of you as a philosopher, Kelly. You look and act like a bubbly blonde, but you sound like an old gray sage."

"I don't mean to. And what do you mean, gray? I have no gray," Kelly objected before continuing. "I simply think that a positive attitude's a worthy goal because it leads to letting go, which opens up the door to many great possibilities." Kelly finished her dinner, while Molly was still eating.

"By the way, eating too fast isn't healthy," Molly observed.

"It's a bad habit. I have a high metabolic rate. I eat a lot," Kelly confessed.

"Hollow legs and youth."

"I guess."

Their conversation was suddenly interrupted by a large man in his mid- to late thirties. He had a presence that was hard to ignore. "Hello, ladies. Is everything to your satisfaction?" He looked from one to the other, before focusing on Molly. She blushed, revealing her instant attraction to him.

"Yes, thank you," Kelly replied, realizing that Molly looked starstruck.

"If I can do anything for you, don't hesitate to ask," he replied, still looking solely at Molly.

"I won't," she managed to utter in a soft tone.

"How was your dinner?" he asked, looking over to Kelly and back to Molly. It was Molly who retained his focus.

As Molly was about to answer, a young server appeared out of nowhere and placed her arm around the man's waist. "I'm sorry to interrupt," she said, looking squarely at Molly, "but I need to steal him away." Turning to him, she added, "Tap three's kicked. Will's out and I've got three people requesting the IPA."

"My apologies, ladies, but duty calls," Sam Hughes looked from Molly to Kelly and back to Molly. He looked into her eyes a little too long before departing with the young waitress.

"Of course, if a hot guy gives you that kind of attention, that's a reason to celebrate and be joyful," Kelly observed.

"You think he's cute?"

"Yeah!"

"I guess. I didn't notice."

"Right. Is that why you turned beet red?"

"I did not! Besides, he and I are both taken. You saw the server. They're obviously together. I'm happy and not interested."

"Okay," Kelly replied. "That must be Samuel Hughes, the tavern owner. Gavin Green worked for him. We need to talk to him some more. You should talk to him."

"Why me?" Molly objected.

"He obviously likes you. Look, he's back at the bar and that server is nowhere in sight. Go for it."

Molly knew that Kelly was right. This presented a perfect opportunity to get closer to Sam. Reluctantly, she headed toward the bar, where Sam served drinks because Will Porter, the bartender, had called out sick. "Are you Sam Hughes?" she asked, as she reached the bar.

"Depends on why you're askin'."

"I'm with the State Police. Name's Molly Dvorak." She flashed her badge.

"In that case, Sam left an hour ago," he replied and resumed washing glasses.

"Too bad. I was looking forward to the interview."

He looked up and smiled. "So was Sam," he added and resumed washing glasses.

"Seriously, Mr. Hughes, I need to ask you a few questions regarding the death of Gavin Green."

"I figured as much. Do we need to do this right now?"

She nodded to the affirmative.

"The entire thing's a tragedy, but I've already told Alvin all that I know, which is very little. I guess he didn't share it with you. What I don't get is why he bothered to interview me in the first place, if I need to repeat myself to every cop that comes along? No offense, Molly, but I'm a little busy. I've got a hotel, a bar, and a restaurant to run, and I'm short-staffed tonight."

"I only have a few questions." She gave him her best smile.

"Fine. Give me a few minutes to get this done. I'll come to your table. Is your friend a cop, too?"

"Yes."

"It figures. I'll be over in a few minutes." He looked up at her.

"Okay. Oh, and can I get one Pinot Noir and one Sauvignon Blanc?"

"Sure. I'll bring 'em along."

Molly smiled once more before returning to an eager Kelly.

"That was short. What'd he say? Did ya get a date?"

"That's a cheap shot, Kelly. He's coming over for an official chat in a few minutes."

"He knows we're cops?"

"Yes. I told him."

"Was that wise?"

"I can't officially interview him and not tell him."

"I guess, but now our cover's blown."

"In a place this size, it was blown when we arrived."

They were interrupted by Sam, who was carrying two glasses of wine.

"That was quick," Molly noted.

"I've only got a few minutes," Sam replied. "Who's got the red, and who's got the white? Let me guess. You have the red, and you have the white. Right?" He gave Kelly the red wine and Molly the white.

"Not quite," Kelly replied with a chuckle as she switched glasses with Molly. "By the way, I'm Kelly."

"Pleased to meet you, Kelly. I'm Sam. The wine's on me."

"Thank you, but we can't accept that," Molly replied.

"Government employees. I get it," Sam concluded, as he sat down next to Molly. "So, what can I tell you officers, or is it detectives?"

"Either's fine," Molly replied. "Let me get right to it, Mr. Hughes. It's our understanding that Gavin Green was your employee and that the two of you had an argument last night here at the inn, after which time you fired him. Is that correct?"

"Yeah, although I assure you I had nothing to do with his death."

Molly took the lead, ignoring Sam's disclaimer. "Mr. Hughes, before the argument, how was your relationship with Mr. Green?"

"Call me 'Sam.' 'Mr. Hughes' sounds like you're referring to my dad. My relationship with Gavin was rocky. He was a rich kid, as you probably know, who had alienated his family."

"We know that. We've been trying to contact his father and stepmother."

"Then you probably know he came out here to run away from his father and took residence at the old Green Estate, which is still in the family. Soon after he got here, he started coming to my bar. That was late spring. I'd say—mid May. He drank a lot and ran up a hefty bill that he couldn't pay. So, out of the kindness of my heart, I gave 'im a dishwashing job. Not long after, he started harassing the servers. I thought I put a stop to it a few weeks ago, but I was wrong."

"How did you put a stop to it?" Molly asked.

"I told 'im if he did it again, I'd fire 'im. He fell in line 'cause he needed the money. He begged me 'cause he was cut off by his rich daddy. It's all kind of sad, really. I felt for the kid. My relationship with my old man was rocky at times, but he never cut me off."

"Was he working here last night, before he died?"

"Yeah. He was here until after eleven. Or it might've been closer to midnight. I'm not sure."

"Tell us about the argument you had with him. We heard about it from some of your staff when we interviewed them earlier."

Sam looked uncomfortable and paused for a while. "I hate to say it, but we had a pretty good squabble. Like I said, I had to fire him. He was out of control."

"Why did you argue?" Kelly was taking notes, while Molly conducted the interview.

"Gavin got off shift at eleven. The past few nights, he was working the crowd, looking for any woman that'd have 'im. He was starting to be a real nuisance. Last night, he decided to target Elaine, one of the servers. She was so upset she left and went upstairs. He was threatening her."

"Why?"

"He had a few drinks and wanted to…well, wanted her. I guess they had a fight. I stepped in to defend her—after all, she's my employee as well—and he got aggressive with me. It was the last straw. I'd been very patient with 'im, but he was a bad egg, especially when it came to women. He challenged me, so I finally decided to fire him, but I didn't hurt him or kill him."

"Does Elaine live upstairs?"

"Yes. She's a server here. You met her earlier tonight when I first stopped by."

"What's her last name?" Molly continued to ask the questions.

"Roberts. Elaine Roberts."

"Mr. Hughes…"

"Please call me Sam."

"I must ask this. What's your relationship with Ms. Roberts?"

"I don't have a relationship with her, except as her employer."

"Can we interview her?"

"Sure. I can call her over if you'd like."

"That'd be great."

"Okay. Let me get her."

"I still have a couple questions."

"Oh, sorry."

"Was there anything else unusual about last night?" Molly asked.

Sam thought of mentioning Linda Taylor but decided that it was not relevant. "No, just a normal, crazy Friday night, except for Gavin's death."

"You mentioned that Gavin had a fight with Elaine. Do you know the details?"

"All I know is that he threatened to harm her 'cause she wouldn't sleep with 'im. He was a real winner."

"I see. Is Will Porter back? I understand he's the bartender who found Gavin's body."

"He called out sick tonight, and that's why we're short-handed at the bar."

"Regarding the discovery of the body early this morning, can you tell us anything about that?"

"Not much, since I wasn't there. I know Will likes to go fly fishing on Saturday mornings. I used to go with 'im, but lately I've been too busy. The Eden's loaded with trout, and one of the best fishing spots is under the covered bridge. So I'm not surprised he was out there."

"Do you know anything about the Amish couple that was there when Will found the body?"

"Yeah, but they're not a couple. Abel's the local Amish bishop. He's married, and I believe widow Esther's his neighbor. I know 'em 'cause I grew up around here."

"What're their last names?"

"Abel Snyder and Esther Fischer.

"Is there anything else you can tell us regarding the discovery of the body?"

"No. You'll have to ask Will."

"Mr. Hughes, who's the White Witch?"

Sam laughed a hardy laugh and rolled his eyes. "I forgot you're new to these parts. Everyone around here knows the legend of the White Witch. Some say she's a ghost that haunts the valley. I've never seen no ghost, and I don't believe in one either. I figure it's just some people's imagination. Folks around here are so bored; they make up this crap. It's an old legend. This place's full of legends and superstitions. It's like another Sleepy Hollow. Next thing you know, we'll have our own headless horseman." He laughed.

"Can you tell us more about this legend?"

"You're askin' the wrong person. According to the legend, a brutal murder happened not far from here, near the Amish village of Eden Crossing. That was over two hundred years ago. Back then, this was the wild frontier. I don't know all the details, but apparently the victims were the Drake family, original white settlers in the valley. Many believe the White Witch is the restless ghost of the wife, Evelyn Drake. It's farfetched, I know, but like I said, folks around here are pretty superstitious. Some say her ghost has returned."

"What do you mean—returned?"

"Ahhh…it's all crazy, but more and more folks think they've seen her. I don't believe such crap. I gotta get back to the bar. It's been a pleasure, ladies. I'll send Elaine over once I get someone to cover her tables." Sam rose without waiting for a reply.

"Thank you, Mr. Hughes…I mean, Sam." Molly corrected herself and blushed.

"Pleasure's all mine. Hope it helped."

Once Sam departed, Kelly could not resist picking on Molly. There was something innocent about Molly that made her the favorite target for everyone on the team, even the Inspector. "The blush was a good touch."

"What're you talking about?"

"'Mr. Hughes…I mean, 'Sam,' followed by a big blush. Nice touch." Kelly laughed.

"Not you, too. It's enough I get it from Chen at every turn."

"I couldn't resist."

"Was it really that obvious?"

"Oh, no. You only turned beet red a half a dozen times. It was cute, in a schoolgirl sort of way."

"Shut up. At least, I don't let Alvin Walker run behind me staring at my rear end all afternoon like a lovestruck puppy."

"That, my dear, is strategy. It may come in very useful. Alvin's odd. I get the feeling he's hiding something."

"Maybe. What'd you think of this White Witch? She sounds like a hoax. This entire thing's getting bizarre," Molly concluded.

"We may be free of it. If the coroner's report on Green comes back as a drug overdose, the boss'll pull us out of here for sure. Oh, but you might not get a chance to say goodbye to Mr. Hughes…I mean, Sam."

"Shut up, Kelly. Seriously, be quiet. Here comes Elaine Roberts. Agh, she's way too young for him. Did you notice how she was staking her claim earlier with all the touchy stuff?" Molly whispered, so as not to be heard as Elaine approached.

"She probably smelled the pheromones coming off of you halfway across the room," Kelly replied with a chuckle.

Molly did not have a chance for a rebuttal. All she could do was give her partner an evil eye as Elaine reached the table.

"Sam said you're cops and wanna talk to me about Gavin. So, here I am. Funny, you don't look like cops," Elaine proclaimed, skipping the introductions.

And you don't look like a server but more like a high-end mistress, Molly thought.

"Please sit down, Ms. Roberts," Kelly replied. She could already sense the tension between Elaine and Molly.

Elaine Roberts exemplified the classic blonde with her Grace Kelly looks. She projected a blend of elegance mixed with street-smart worldliness; thus, it was difficult to assess her true nature based on a first impression. Molly could see why this blue-eyed beauty would be an instant magnet for most men, including Gavin and Sam. Yet there remained something suspicious about her. For one thing, she had trouble keeping eye contact and seemed nervous, continuously twirling her long blonde hair. And curiously, she chose to sit next to Kelly in the restaurant booth and opposite Molly, unlike Sam, who had done the exact opposite.

An uncomfortable pause followed as Kelly took out the notepad and Molly scrutinized the young woman before her. Finally, Elaine spoke, still twirling her hair. "Am I in trouble or something?" she asked.

"No. Not at all. We simply wish to ask you a few questions. Let's start with some introductions. My name's Molly Dvorak, and this is Kelly Stevens. We're detectives with the Pennsylvania State Police. We're here to investigate the death of Gavin Green and we would like to ask you a few questions." Molly spoke tersely, unlike her melodic tempo when interviewing Sam Hughes. Kelly picked up on this immediately and chuckled to herself. Molly's transparency often amused Kelly, but it remained a quality that she appreciated though never mimicked.

"Okay, but I need to get back to my tables soon," Elaine replied.

"Well, then, let's get to it."

"Sure. Whatever."

"Miss Roberts, could you tell us about your relationship with Mr. Green?" Molly asked.

"I never had a relationship with him," Elaine objected.

"But, you were friends, correct?"

"No. We worked together—that's it."

"You seem angry. Why is that?" Molly challenged the server. She detected a hostile vibe from Elaine. There appeared to be something deceitful about her.

"I'm not angry," Elaine replied, visibly annoyed. "But it's not every day you get treated like a suspect in a murder."

Kelly and Molly traded glances as if to say, "Did you just hear that?"

Molly returned to the interview, letting the comment rest for now. She would explore it later. Putting Elaine on the defensive this early in the interview could silence her. She decided to soften her approach. "My apologies, Ms. Roberts, we don't want to make you feel like a suspect. We're simply interested in knowing what happened last night. Mr. Hughes mentioned that Gavin Green threatened you. It's also our understanding that Mr. Hughes terminated Mr. Green's employment over the incident. Can you tell us more about that?"

"Gavin was evil. All he cared about was himself and any pleasure he could find." Elaine began to open up. "He deserved what he got. He bothered every girl in here, and Sam's been too nice for too long. He should've fired Gavin a long time ago. I don't know why he hired 'im. Sam's too naive." She twirled her blonde locks, then tossed them to her left with crescendo.

"Can you expand on that?" Molly tried to lock eyes with Elaine, but the latter kept breaking contact.

"Sam's just too nice and people like Gavin abuse that."

"How? What are some examples?"

"Gavin's the best example. He ran up a huge bar bill and Sam gave 'im a job. Come on! First, why did he let 'im run up the bar bill, and second, why would he hire a guy like that? I told Sam countless times the guy was trouble, and that he was bothering every girl in this place, yet Sam didn't do a thing. It was crazy. I don't know why, but Sam acted like he owed Gavin something. Sometimes, I think there was more to the story. I don't know."

"What do you suspect?"

"I don't know. They're either related somehow or Gavin had something on Sam. Heck, I don't know. Maybe Sam's just that nice of a guy. He's naive and nice, for sure. I'm not complaining. He's been wonderful to me. He got me this job and a place to stay upstairs at a great rate. He's really a big teddy bear."

"Do you and Sam have a relationship beyond a working one?"

Elaine continued to avoid eye contact as she replied. "What do you mean by that? We aren't a couple, if that's what you mean. That's ridiculous. He's fifteen years older than me. But it's really none of your business."

This blondie has spunk. She's not naive, either. I bet she can get whatever she wants from Sam, Molly concluded. She did not care for Elaine but did not want that bias to carry into the interview.

"Ms. Roberts, what exactly happened last night between you and Mr. Green?" Molly decided to get to the point.

"It's embarrassing, but Gavin tried to get me to have sex with 'im." She paused before adding, "The thought's so disgusting. Last night, he tried to force himself on me. I didn't tell Sam, and please don't tell him. He'd freak out. Gavin cornered me in the basement last night when I went down to get a rare bottle of wine for one of my customers. As I walked into the wine cellar, he closed the door behind me. I don't know how he got there, but he was there, waiting for me. All I can imagine is that somehow he overheard my customer ordering the wine and knew I'd have to go into the basement. Actually, I think I just figured it out." She paused to reflect.

"Mr. Gladstone—he's a regular here—always orders expensive wines when he brings his mistress, which he always does on Friday nights. Funny, he doesn't spend much on his wife when he brings her here on Saturday nights." Elaine chuckled at the thought. "Gavin must have seen me serving Mr. Gladstone. I always serve Mr. Gladstone. He always asks for me," Elaine said proudly. "That's how Gavin knew."

"Did he attack you in the basement?"

"Yes. He grabbed me, groped me, and tried to force himself on me. He was all hands. I managed to run up the stairs, bottle, and all. I was going to hit 'im with the bottle, but I remembered that it costs over $350, so I kneed 'im in the balls instead." She smiled before continuing. "Later, he followed me upstairs and threatened to hurt me. I got scared. I told Sam about the threats, but not about the attack. I told him Gavin threatened to harm me. If you want proof, ask Sam or some of the customers who overheard Gavin's threats. When I told Sam, he promised me he would get rid of Gavin and he finally did. It's about time. But I didn't see 'im get fired. I was too shaken up, so I went upstairs to my room."

"Why didn't you tell Sam about the attack?"

"I just didn't. I don't know. Sam and I are close, but not like you think. He's just a great guy. Besides, I'm a big girl. I can handle myself. I guess I didn't want to upset 'im even more. He's got enough going on."

"You should've called the police," Kelly added.

Elaine laughed at the suggestion. "No offense, but obviously, you're not from around here or you wouldn't've suggested that."

"What do you mean?" Kelly asked.

"Look, I don't need trouble. I've had enough trouble in my life already, and I have a good thing here. Sam's great to me and I'm happy here."

Molly began to feel sorry that she had ever suspected the young girl of potential wrongdoing. At twenty-three, Elaine had a tough exterior that appeared to mask a caring person.

"Look, Elaine, we promise to leave this out of the report, but we need to know what you mean by that comment about the local police," Kelly asked, locking eyes with Elaine for the first time during the interview.

"Let's just say I don't want to end up like Gavin. So I have no comment," Elaine replied and broke Kelly's gaze.

"Are you implying Gavin was murdered?" Molly asked.

"I know he was, but you'll never prove it. I need to go. I got tables to tend. Mr. Gladstone's here with his wife. He ordered the cheap merlot, as usual." She chuckled and departed before they could ask her any further questions.

CHAPTER 18

The Hermit

*E*arlier that morning, the golden sun's rays filtered through the mist that blanketed the banks of the Eden River, coloring them shades of pink and purple. A gray heron patrolled the small beach, silently focused on the darting minnows while the gentle flowing water added a sense of tranquility that seemed timeless. Along it, life flourished and faded in the natural rhythm of creation. Like a gateway between reality and eternity, the river nourished the secrets hidden below its hazy surface.

A soft white smoke rose from a nearby clearing. It mixed harmoniously with the river's mist as a strong smell of oak permeated the forest. The heron ignored it, for the smoke had long been a part of his morning ritual. When the smoke faded, the gray heron departed and a man of the same color appeared in his place.

Overgrown and mossy, the man looked like the woods around him. His hair matted in unruly tuffs of white that matched his long white beard. Together, they framed his furrowed face, which appeared gouged with deep wrinkles like a tilled field farmed by a life full of hardship.

With a name long forgotten, even to himself, he kept no company, except the misty river and the dark woods. He called himself "Captain" as he talked to himself for hours, his mind splintered in two by perpetual solitude.

Both the fearless Captain and the fearful Self personified him. Presently, he looked down at the darting minnows, and with the swiftness of the gray heron, used a makeshift net to fill his rusty, cast-iron frying pan with the shimmering quarry.

There was a time when he had a wife and a young child, but those times he could not recall, except in a rare dream. There was a time when he had served his country in a war not of his making, and in a place not to his liking. Those times he recalled too often in his vivid nightmares. The dreams and nightmares blended into fleeting recollections, each bearing more pain—a pain that crushed him, forcing him into this obscure, hollow existence.

He felt that he had no choice but to run, run away and disappear from all that remained of his life and his responsibilities. Disappear he did, into the wild North Woods Preserve that surrounded the Eden River for thousands of acres upstream of Devils Bridge.

He became one with the mysterious and ghostly nature of that land, blending with the Spirit that permeated it and owned it still. This was the Spirit that the Native Americans recognized for millennia. This was the Spirit that ruled the land, and to which all paid respect and homage until the white men came, disturbing and extinguishing everything.

After the first flood of trappers and explorers came the soldiers and early settlers. Finally, nearly two hundred years ago, the valley fell primarily under the stewardship of the religious farmers, the Amish.

These stewards brought their own rituals and rites, their own worship, and their own rules. They were more harmonious with the land than the previous transients, but, unlike the original natives, they did not fully recognize or accept the timeless Spirit that permeated this primeval forest.

On this particular morning, the Captain dominated the personality of the hermit, as his mossy form washed in the chilling water of the river. He was free of present society, but not of its grisly mark upon him. In this delusional freedom, he sought his salvation from a world that did not understand him—a world he no longer accepted.

After washing, the Captain disappeared on the left bank of the silent river. He walked quickly toward his home, invisible to the average man or woman for it was beneath the floor of the forest. The entrance to his subterranean network of limestone caverns rested at the base of an immense old oak tree, whose gnarly roots provided the perfect cover.

In front of the large oak, he had set up a small fire to cook his breakfast, which, on this particular morning, consisted of fried minnows and wild mushrooms. Late summer was bountiful, and he used the time to hunt and forage, storing as much food as he could for the harsh winter.

He had done this for over five years and was becoming well-versed in his hermit lifestyle. When not in his subterranean home, he would spend time wandering about the endless woods, seeking an escape from his haunted mind.

Today, he felt joyful—it being his birthday, or so he calculated using his primitive celestial calendar. Although he had forgotten his age, it did not matter. Today was his birthday and he was going to celebrate.

In a conversation with Self, he formulated a plan that included a night raid on the fields of the nearest farm, located several miles away. He would cut through Drakes Plot, the ruined former homestead and burial plot of the once prominent Drake family. The wealthiest of the early white settlers, they had pushed out the natives, and, in the process, squelched the Spirit. Then the Captain would descend a steep hill to Amos Miller's farm to steal fresh corn and maybe a chicken or two. After all, it was his birthday.

Self fearfully objected and tried to talk the Captain out of this dangerous mission. The two personalities of the old hermit fell into conflict, which was often the case, but the outcome never changed.

"Wha du ya know, ya coward?" the Captain questioned, while sitting under the old oak, finishing his breakfast. "If it 'ere up to ya, we'd all be dead," he added aloud with no one to hear, except his imaginary counter ego.

"But, but, but...Captain, sir...the enemy'll kill us if we try and raid their camp. There ain't no cloud cover, just the moon. It's too dangerous," the cautious Self objected.

"Soldier, ya're out'a line," the Captain threatened, with no one to hear but the hermit's splintered mind.

"No, sir. I just have a bad feelin', sir," the Self replied softly.

"At attention, Soldier! I'll 'ave no cowards in my ranks. We're doin' a raid and ya're gonna lead it. Is that clear?" the Captain ordered.

"Yes, sir," the deflated Self replied, subservient once more, the victim of a war he despised, a war that had stolen everything from him, even his identity and his sanity.

The Captain decided the plan. As happened to be the case on many a night, the Captain would insist that Self lead the infamous raid. Then, the Captain would die a violent death and Self would return from the enemy's camp with the stolen corn and a chicken or two. In this repeating scenario, the enemy's camp was most often Amos Miller's farm, but at times it became one of the other Amish farms in the area. Predictably, the reward of the raid would be a feast but the price would be reliving the violent death of the Captain, on yet another night. By morning, the Captain would return, and all would be as before until another nightly raid would extinguish him, once more.

This drama replayed itself in the poor hermit's delusional mind and had done so since his involvement in the war in Bosnia, a decade earlier. Although trapped in this illusion and doomed by his mind, he did not suffer pain, except during the weekly raids that reset the drama, like a replay button on an endless video. All around him were shifting shadows of the past mixed with the peace and tranquility of nature, which alone seemed to provide comfort to his shattered dreams and clouded mind.

CHAPTER 19

The Gold Coin

That same night, deep in the ancient forest north of Devils Bridge, a large campfire crackled as Ariella and the Eden Sisterhood turned toward the dark row of old oaks that bordered the meadow. A mysterious visitor emerged from the shadows into the flickering light. The figure appeared slight in form, shrouded in a hooded cape while fighting the urge to reveal itself. The members of the sisterhood pulled back toward the fire in fear of the apparition. Only Ariella remained unmoved.

"Welcome!" she proclaimed in a soft, strong voice to the approaching stranger. "Don't be afraid. You're welcome here. We know you come in peace."

All eyes were upon the mysterious figure, which stood at some distance from the fire, refusing to answer or to betray its identity.

"Come sit with us," Ariella offered to the dismay of all but Anna. The latter was governed by endless curiosity and an inherent faith. Within the light of both, fear seemed useless and uninviting despite her previous arguments to the contrary.

The mysterious figure crossed the last hundred feet of the meadow, which was illuminated by the haunting moon. This gray form seemed to be an extension of the row of ancient black oaks. Every slow step brought it closer to its revelation. Every cautious step brought it closer to its salvation. Until, finally, she stood within view, transformed into a woman.

"Come sit down with us, Sister. I've been expecting you. The oppressed are healed here and the lost are found. Release your burdens to which you are bound," Ariella proclaimed poetically.

At last, the young woman revealed herself before the others and stood within the light of the fire. The cloak no longer hid the visible bruises on her neck and face. She looked upon the many eyes that remained transfixed upon her. She had a sadness about her that was unquestionable.

At Ariella's request, she sat on one of the logs around the blazing fire. Without questioning, Ariella accepted her into the group. The silence that followed seemed accentuated by the cracking and popping of the wood that fed the flames. Finally, the visitor spoke. "How do you know me?" she asked Ariella, careful not to meet her eyes.

"I don't, but I've been expecting you since I saw you hiding in the woods this morning." Ariella smiled a disarming smile. "Let me introduce myself and our little group. I'm Ariella and these are my sisters." Each woman introduced herself in turn, ending with Anna, who sat next to the newcomer on the same hewn log.

Now, it was the visitor's turn to introduce herself. She looked at the fire as she spoke, before she moved her gaze to Ariella, clearly the leader of the group.

"My name's Agnes. Until yesterday, I worked at The Raven Inn as a maid until I had to leave."

"Why did you leave?" Rebecca asked. The young women around the fire were no longer alarmed. Their fears had been replaced by curiosity.

"I was attacked by someone who threatened me if I called the police, so I ran away as soon as I could. But I had no place to go. I was afraid to go home to my empty apartment. I didn't know what to do, so I came here. I sat at the edge of the meadow all day. I was afraid, but then I got hungry." She stopped and gazed at the tray of food sitting next to Marie.

"Oh, here. Please have some." Marie offered the food, passing the plate to Agnes. The latter ate ravenously. All paused to let her have her fill before resuming the questioning.

"Who attacked you?" Sarah asked.

"I never saw his face. But I know what he wanted. I'm sure he would have killed me had it not been for Sam Hughes. He's the owner of The Raven Inn. He saved me, but my attacker got away. Like I said, I never saw his face. He wore a mask. I'll never forget the mask. It had a laughing face on it, like a theatre mask. It was black and haunting. I was so scared. I'm still scared," Agnes confessed.

"You're safe here. I assure you of that. This is the safest place in the world," Ariella replied with a smile. "But you know more, don't you? You know more of this attacker than you told us."

Agnes looked down into the fire. There was an uncomfortable silence before she spoke once more. "When Sam Hughes found me, he was with the bartender that works at the inn. His name's Will Porter. My attacker was choking me, see?" She showed the large purple bruises on her neck. "When Sam found me, I couldn't talk. Sam wanted to know about my attacker, but I couldn't tell him. I couldn't talk! So, I picked up a rock and was about to draw the mask of the attacker, when I saw Will's face behind Sam. He had his right hand against his neck and made repeated gestures of slitting his throat. It's then that I remembered where I saw the mask. I dropped the rock. It was then that I knew I had to leave before they killed me." She paused, transfixed by the fire.

"Where had you seen the mask?" Sarah asked.

"Behind Will's bar." Agnes looked up at Sarah. "I think they're all in on it," she added.

"Who are 'they,' and what is 'it'?" Rebecca inquired.

Agnes had everyone's full attention as she looked about at their fixed stares. "All of them at the Raven Inn. I think it's a big conspiracy."

"Why? What's the conspiracy?" Anna asked, her curiosity fully awakened.

"I found a gold coin under the bed in Elaine's room when I was cleaning it. It looked old, really old. I was tempted to keep it, but that'd be stealing. So, I took it to Sam. When I handed it to him, he was flustered and wanted to know where I found it and how I got it.

When I told him, he seemed upset and told me not to tell anyone. He made me swear not to tell. It was later that morning that I got attacked." She stopped and gazed at the fire again.

"What happened when you got attacked? What did the attacker want?" Ariella asked. Agnes looked up at her, clearly uncomfortable with the question. "It's okay. You're safe here," Ariella added.

"You sure?"

"I'm sure."

"He was looking for the gold coin. He thought I still had it and threatened to kill me if I didn't give it to 'im. I started screaming for help, but then he silenced me and started choking me. I would've died if Sam hadn't shown up."

"Do you know anything more about this coin?" Anna asked.

"No," Agnes replied. "I didn't look at it much before I gave it to Sam."

There was reflective silence as the fire crackled. All were lost in thought, while one of Agnes's newfound friends fingered an old gold coin hidden in her pocket.

The Amish Village of Eden Crossing, Pennsylvania

CHAPTER 20

Drakes Plot

The full moon rose cautiously over Drakes Plot. The site had been a former homestead and burial ground of the Drake family, who first settled this land over two hundred years ago. According to legend, Arthur Drake, the son of a prominent London lawyer, and the youngest child in the Drake bloodline, abandoned his prospects of law school and his homeland for his love of the sea only to become a pirate. It is rumored that he came to the Eden Valley with a treasure of gold acquired through dubious means.

Before his arrival, he married a young English girl who was half his age. The two settled here in the uncharted frontier of the New World. They built a homestead at the site of Drakes Plot after receiving hundreds of square miles of virgin forest land on either side of the Eden River. These were once part of the vast holdings of William Penn granted to the Drakes in an effort to settle the wild western fringe of Pennsylvania.

William Penn, an English Quaker, had been granted 45,000 square miles of land in present Pennsylvania and Delaware by Charles II, the King of England. The large land grant to a previously obscure leader of a fringe religious group favored the king, for it would establish an English colony in a strategic part of the New World—specifically, the land between the British colony of Virginia and the Dutch claims to the north and their prominent port settlement of New Amsterdam (later known as New York City).

King Charles II could hardly foresee that Penn would become the founder of an important port at the head of Delaware Bay. Nor could he foretell that in one hundred years that port city of Philadelphia would become the first capitol of a new nation that would one day surpass his own in size and world prominence.

Thus in 1756, on the east bank of the Eden River, Arthur Drake erected a homestead of which only the stone foundations remain today. Some five or six years after Arthur Drake finished the barn and house, and soon after the birth of his third child, legend has it that tragedy struck the family. Arthur Drake and all his children were brutally murdered.

Only his young wife, Evelyn, survived after being repeatedly defiled by the merciless attackers. Tales abide that she lost her mind and took her own life by leaping to her death from the steep cliff that hangs over the west bank of the Eden River, near the site of present-day Devils Bridge.

At the time of the brutal attack on the Drake family, their farmhouse was burnt to the ground, leaving no trace of its grandeur or its reputed treasure. All that now remains is the legend, the stone foundation, and a small cemetery, where nearby settlers buried the bodies of the family. It is said that Evelyn's grave remains empty, since her body was never found.

Who committed the crimes remains a mystery to this day, but it is rumored that they were fellow pirates in search of the large treasure of gold that Arthur Drake had stolen from them. Legend also has it that the farmhouse ruins and the adjacent cemetery are haunted by Evelyn's ghost, who is endlessly seeking her lost children. Many believe that Evelyn's ghost and the White Witch are one, and that her spirit will never rest.

Drakes Plot is surrounded by Amish land, but no one owns the cemetery and the former homestead. No one dares to own it. It is still deeded to the Drake family. There are taxes due that far exceed the worth of the land, but the state will not seize it, given that it is a small cemetery plot on a landlocked grassy knoll. Some of the Amish believe and even perpetuate the rumors of Evelyn Drake's ghost and those of the White Witch, although most think these tales are simply stories propagated over countless generations.

Regardless, it is a frightening place at night. The old graveyard is surrounded by gnarly trees that appear sickly, covered with lumps and tumors, as if poisoned by the very soil that feeds them. A broken stone wall delineates the former homestead ruin and the adjacent cemetery, which together occupy less than an acre. Most of the old tombstones are weathered and barely legible, overgrown with weeds and small shrubs. Several are strewn about, probably vandalized by nameless hoodlums long dead or departed.

On this dreary moonlit night, in the waning hours of Sunday, a dark form took refuge in the shadows of the sickly trees that crouched about the east wall of the abandoned cemetery. He was digging a hole on the far side of the small graveyard. An owl screeched. This startled the man, as if he were expecting a ghost to materialize out of the very darkness that protected him from the curious moonlight. *I hate this place*, he thought and shivered, eager to get this dreaded task behind him. "This place gives me the creeps," he whispered.

Looking about, he pulled his black hood over his head and dug faster. With a clash and a spark, the shovel hit a large rock, splintering in the process. "Damn it!" he muttered, as he looked at the broken shovel handle. Only the upper part of the instrument had broken off. In desperation, the man continued to dig using the lower part of the shovel. Shovel full after shovel full of dirt finally revealed the top of a half-rotted, pitted pine box.

The night grew late and the moon had shifted in the sky. Sneaking around the gnarled trees, it began to shed light on the mysterious intruder. By the blue moonlight, the man could see that he had reached the object of his quest. Using the shovel, he began to break open the old wooden box, disturbing the ancient grave. As he splintered the rotting coffin, a large raven announced his presence from the menacing tree above him, as if it were the spirit of the dead disturbed from timeless slumber. It startled him, and he dropped the shovel, which fell to the base of the exhumed grave.

"Damn it! I hate this place!" he proclaimed aloud. Forced to retrieve the shovel, he bent down within the narrow, six-foot deep excavation. As he shifted his weight to the center of the pine box, the weathered wood gave way. Without warning, he broke through the coffin. In terror of being trapped, he let out a scream. Before he had a chance to recover his sanity, he thought he heard a groan, like that of a man disturbed from his sleep. The groan turned into a whisper that echoed within the tight confines of the excavation. He thought it was coming from the casket that had seized his feet. He panicked and kicked about, trying to free himself, imagining the grave's occupant as his captor.

Fear twisted reality. As he kicked about, he was horrified by what befell him. With his thrashing, the loose steep walls of the hole began to cave upon him. His legs were trapped. His heart raced, and he began to yell for help. In his desperation, he clawed at the walls of the hole, which only gave farther, and farther he sank into the cavernous grave that began to consume him. "HELP! HELP!" he screamed in terror.

To his surprise, his desperate pleas were answered much too soon, as a dark form peered over the edge of the hole. Its face was impossible to discern, for the moon had disappeared and darkness filled the void. All was pitch black, including the outline of the mysterious figure peering down at him. He was relieved, nonetheless, for rescue had materialized, as if out of thin air. "HELP! Please help me! Please get me out! My legs are trapped."

His pleas were answered by a disturbing silence. Then, his relief turned to horror. "Stop! What are you doing? Stop, for God's sakes! STOP!" The trapped soul screamed and pleaded.

To his horror, the deathly silence was finally broken by the sound of dirt falling upon him, upon his hair, upon his face, upon his open screaming mouth. With flailing arms, he struggled to free himself of this merciless quicksand. The dark form was emotionless as it picked up shovelful after shovelful of dirt.

In desperation, he tried to crawl out, but only one arm remained free. He pleaded for mercy, but none came, only more deadly dirt. Ten more shovelfuls and the screams were silenced. The struggle was over, replaced by the sound of additional digging. Earth filled the hole until all was restored. All was buried. All was still, except for a ghostly cry from the large raven, who had seen everything, even the secret beyond the grave.

As storm clouds gathered, the shadow blended into the curtain of early autumn corn. The wind began to howl as the great raven parted his enormous wings, taking leave of the sinister place, while a woman in white stood by the edge of the menacing woods, guarding the sacred ground of the Drakes.

CHAPTER 21

The Specter

The next morning, Amos Miller rose early to milk his cows. With is mind preoccupied by Lenore, he moved slowly, drowning in heart break. How could she forget him? How could she completely ignore him? How could she be falling in love with Ben Stoltzfus? Sure, Ben was young, well-to-do, and handsome, but to Ben, Lenore represented a prize, like a blue ribbon at a county fair. He did not love her for he loved only himself. It was so apparent. It was so apparent to Amos.

The old Lenore could see through this illusion. How could this Lenore be blind to it and to him who loved her? With his heart and sprit crushed, he moped about the farm for the next two hours in the mindless ritual of daily tasks and duties.

Amos was not sure how long his dog had been barking before he heard him. Having milked the last of the cows, he heard the irate barking from the top of the ridge. Ollie, a calm and faithful hunting dog, rarely barked or caused a ruckus. Most of the time, Amos barely noticed this faithful animal that shadowed him throughout his day. This time felt different as Ollie appeared audibly disturbed by something beyond the ridge.

Amos decided to investigate. As he neared the crest of the steep hill behind his farmhouse, he could see old Ollie barking at the sky.

"What'z the matt'r, boy?" Amos called to the dog.

At the sound of his master's voice, the animal calmed, his barking partially subsiding, as he ran toward Amos.

"What iz it, Ollie? A coon? A possum? What iz it? A fox? A wolf?" Recently, Amos had seen a large gray wolf on the ridge. Wolves were unknown in these parts. Coyotes had entered the area, but not wolves. "It's that gray wolf, isn't it?" As Amos reached the hillcrest, he could see the crumbling stone walls of Drakes Plot in the distance. Black, half-bare trees, whose aprons of fallen leaves swirled and danced on the nameless graves, accentuated the eerie setting.

"What'z got ya goin', boy?" he asked the dog, who barked louder while pointing at the old cemetery three-hundred yards away on the other side of an untilled meadow. The swaying, knee-high grass reflected the colors of the rising sun that peeked over the distant hills, turning shades of pink and lavender.

The dog urged Amos forward toward Drakes Plot but did so with a restraint defined by fear. His bark diminished to a submissive whimper as they crossed the field toward the old cemetery. They were halfway across the meadow when both man and beast froze in step and fell silent. There among the gray weathered tombstones stood the ghostly form of a woman, partially translucent in the low light of the awakening day. White was her form and white was her flowing gown—a ghostly white with touches of light gray that blended with the magenta light of the rising sun.

Amos rubbed his eyes to assure himself of reality. Old Ollie pressed against his master's side, looking for comfort in his protector while whimpering helplessly. Amos refocused on the white figure, who turned towards him, revealing a face that was hard to distinguish, except for a piercing gaze that made him shudder. Her gaze remained as she evaluated him from across the meadow.

Amos rubbed his eyes again, still doubting their perception. Upon opening them, he saw the white flowing dress disappear into the dark woods beyond Drakes Plot. In her place, a black raven descended into the old cemetery from the nearby trees, as if she had unleashed him. The bird made his presence known with a series of loud squawks, while setting himself down over the spot where the mysterious woman had stood moments earlier.

Ollie whimpered louder, having witnessed enough. Normally, he would chase a raven for sport, although he preferred squirrels, starlings, and crows. But he wanted nothing to do with this huge bird. Scratching at the boots of his master, he pleaded with him to leave. However, Amos was not one to be easily frightened. He possessed a natural curiosity, which at times put him at odds with his faith and community. Although Amish, in his heart, he exemplified a modern seeker of knowledge like the scientists of the English.

Despite Ollie's objections, Amos decided to investigate, which created visible panic in his faithful dog. The latter could not stand it any longer and remained crouched in the tall grass, unwilling to follow his master. As Amos neared the crumbled walls of the small cemetery, he could see the large bird perched atop a mound of fresh earth like a motionless sentry. The sun had risen now and the mist had nearly melted away. With every step, he came closer to the inevitable conclusion. The ominous black bird guarded a fresh grave.

Unaware of what had transpired the night before in this dreaded place, the recent grave made no sense to him. This burial plot had been long abandoned and inaccessible, except through Amish land—his land. *Why'd someone dig here?* he thought. To inter anyone in this cursed place seemed beyond reason to the young farmer. Now, the sight of the ghostly woman became less perplexing than the new grave. As he neared the small cemetery, he felt a cold, uncanny chill down his spine.

Still, the large black raven remained unmoved. It seemed to define the very nature of the mystery, ominous and callous, like the act that created its perch. But Amos was unfazed, determined to understand what had transpired. This curiosity brought boundless courage. With the sun on his back to illuminate his way, he walked straight toward the unearthly beast.

As he neared, he observed that the burial site was not new—rather, it was the old grave of Evelyn Drake, as marked by the barely legible, half-broken tombstone. He stopped to ponder this as the eerie bird blocked his passage. *No. That can't be. Are the ghost and grave related? No. I don't believe in such things. It's my mind playin' tricks on me,* he silently reasoned. Then he thought of the dog. *But Ollie saw 'er too.*

The raven remained unmoved as Amos reached the stone wall that surrounded the old Drake family plot. "Get! Off with ya, ya demon!" he yelled at the hellish bird, while waving his arms to frighten it. To his surprise, it did not frighten, nor did it look at him. It continued to look in the direction of the woods, at the spot where the white female specter disappeared minutes earlier.

With complete resolution, Amos continued to approach the grave while shouting and waving his arms. Finally, the mysterious creature turned toward the fearless farmer and their eyes met. Amos hesitated, for he had never seen such eyes on any living thing. They possessed an amber-yellow hue. *Ah, it's just the sun's reflection*, he reasoned.

He took another step as the eyes of the beastly bird gazed through him, through his soul. A shiver originated deep within him in response to the sinister bird's glare. One with a weaker disposition would have turned and run, but not Amos, who dismissed the chill as senseless fear. Composing himself, he resumed his stride, entering the walled graveyard. His intent was to challenge the black guardian and discover his morbid secret.

"Be gone, ya hellish bird!" he exclaimed.

The raven cared little for the likes of Amos. Once more, it glared ominously at the stout farmer, daring him to approach its domain.

"May the g'd Lord bless whatever ya guard, for I fear you not. Off with ya!" Amos yelled, clapping his hands.

Now, the demonic bird and the fearless farmer stood facing each other at twenty paces. Still, the black bird would not relinquish its perch, as if it held the soul of the departed in its talons.

Amos had no idea as to the origin of the words he now uttered. They seemed to come out of thin air, for he had no time to process them. "There's no devil that's not Man's demon. I fear ye not, hellish bird of apathy. I come in Divine Grace. Be gone!"

These words came like an inspired answer to a dark riddle. Upon their utterance, the ominous black bird rose in flight. With a defiant cry, it vanished into the nefarious shadows of the twisted trees.

Amos stood over the recently disturbed grave reluctantly vacated by the alien bird. Fresh dirt lay scattered everywhere, as if someone had tried to exhume the remains of Evelyn Drake and changed course, only to rebury them. A chill settled upon him, as if the spirit of this doomed, departed woman protested the intrusion.

A violent storm had passed through the area the night before, leaving the muddy mound marked with deep furrows. As he investigated further, Amos discovered that neither the mysterious white figure nor the large raven had left their prints in the muddy soil. Perplexed by that observation, he let it pass unexplained and pondered it no further.

Ollie had finally found the courage to join his master's side now that the frightful bird had vanished. He remained timid, sniffing the muddy earth while remaining close to the safety of his trusted owner. Being a seasoned hunting dog, he soon found a clue to the mystery that perplexed Amos. Digging into the side of the mound, Ollie extracted the broken end of an old shovel. Proudly, he presented it at the feet of his master, receiving a grateful pat on the head as his reward.

"What ya got there, Ollie?" Amos asked, as he picked up the splintered shovel handle. "Lukz like the end piece of a broken shovel." Amos looked at the milled wood. "No ghost owns a shovel. Not one like this," he added. Bewilderment flashed across his face as he recognized the carved initials near the top of the broken handle. "No. This can't be. This makes no sense," he muttered to himself. "Ollie, let'z find out what'z goin' on here." Amos shook his head while staring once more at the foot-long splintered handle. Then, he shook his head some more before departing with the shovel and his trusted dog.

CHAPTER 22

Golden Leaves

Amos wasted no time at the farm. The harvest of the western field would have to wait. He hooked up his horse to his black buggy and headed down the dirt lane, with Ollie eagerly running behind him. The lane connected to a large dirt road that led toward the center of the small Amish village of Eden Crossing. The village was located south of Devils Bridge, on the west side of the river. Kamerynville, the nearest larger town, was situated across the Eden River about six miles to the east. One had to go 28 miles northeast to reach Brennantown, a large college town and the home of McLaren University. The Amish never ventured that far and they rarely traveled to Kamerynville, except on Thursdays for the local farmer's market.

Eden Crossing consisted of a crossroads, as the name implied, of two old Amish cart paths that had been paved into roads in the 1960s by the English. The village, comprising a half-dozen old houses, a country store, a feed store, a one-room schoolhouse, and a four-way stop sign, had no utility poles or connections because such modern extravagances were forbidden, being viewed as direct links to the sinful ways of the English and their lavish possessions.

Amos passed through the quiet village and made a right turn, heading toward the Eden River to the west. Just outside of the village lay the first of several farms. Turning onto the long dirt path of this spacious property, Amos slowly proceeded toward the white, wood-shingled farmhouse. Ollie grew excited as he ran behind the buggy. He knew the farm well through countless visits. The buggy pulled up to the old farmhouse and Ollie greeted the three dogs, two of which were his siblings and the third, his mother. A joyous canine family reunion ensued. Unfortunately, the reunion between Amos and his older brother, Linus, shaped up to be less jovial.

Amos tied up his horse and headed toward the large wooden barn that stood across the muddy courtyard. He knew this farm well, for it had been his parents' farm. He had grown up here until he purchased his own farm. Both of his parents were deceased now, so his oldest brother, Linus, inherited the property as the new patriarch of the family. Amos, the youngest of seven children, arrived in the world much later than the rest, when his mother turned thirty-eight. Since most Amish women had children at a young age, such a large age gap between siblings was rare. In fact, Amos and Linus were nearly a generation apart. Linus often tried to act like a father to his much younger brother, who was merely three years older than Linus's oldest daughter. Most of Linus's eight children were married and living on neighboring farms. Only the youngest two remained at home to help their parents with the chores.

As Amos neared the large barn, he smelled the distinct, sweet aroma of drying tobacco. For the next six to eight weeks, the barn would be transformed into a spacious, tobacco leaf-drying shed as alternating side wallboards were pushed out from their base to create gaps in the barn's long walls. Countless clusters of large tobacco leaves hung inverted in parallel rows at various levels throughout the barn, completely filling its void with row upon row, and layer upon layer of the precious crop.

The Amish did not smoke, but they produced some of the finest longleaf tobacco on the market. Much of it would be used as the outer leaf in cigars and would fetch a premium price. It was a cash crop that was hard on the soil but farmers like Linus rotated their fields to allow at least one or two larger plots of tobacco per year. Amish farms were extremely fruitful, even though most relied solely on organic fertilizers. The secret to their abundance was the practice of crop rotation. A practice that the Amish had brought to the region centuries earlier. It served them well, especially when growing tobacco.

The tobacco plants looked like large green skunk cabbage until late summer, when they magically turned bright yellow, creating a tapestry of rich color across the rural landscape. These yellow leaves were harvested in the fall and hung upside down to air dry and to cure, assuring that the precious nicotine concentrated in their tips and not their stems.

It was an old process, unchanged for centuries. As the leaves dried, they turned to gold and then to the bronze-brown color familiar to cigar connoisseurs. This precious crop had to be well ventilated while it dried and cured. Since the Amish had no electricity, the gentle breeze blowing through the perforated barn did the work free of charge. If the drying was not properly performed, the crop could mold and become nothing more than nicotine-rich compost.

Linus and his youngest son, Isaac, were hanging tobacco leaves in the far corner of the barn when Amos entered.

"Hey, Amos. Haven't seen ya since Sunday service. What bringz ya this mornin'?" Linus asked. Isaac greeted his uncle with a silent smile and returned to hanging the green, sticky leaves. There was much to do before the rains came.

"Hey, Isaac. Good to see ya. Linus, I came to give ya this," Amos pulled out the broken shovel handle with the dark carved initials. They read 'LM'.

Linus instantly recognized the initials on the shovel handle. "Where'd ya find that?"

"Can we talk?" Amos asked and glanced at young Isaac.

"Sure," Linus replied and asked his son to tend to the mules. Isaac obeyed without question, as was the tradition of Amish father and son relationships.

Once the two brothers stood alone among the pungent leaves, Linus looked Amos square in the eyes before remarking, "Little brother, ya came all this way to return a broken shovel handle?"

"I came to get a straight answer. What'z goin' on?" Amos asked calmly, trying not to be too accusatory but failing in the process.

"What're ya talkin' about?"

"It's ya'r shovel, ain't it?"

"I don't have time for games, Amos. Why're ya here with this useless t'ing?" Linus asked, not breaking his gaze. He was the oldest brother and family patriarch and did not appreciate the tone of his younger sibling.

However, Amos possessed little respect for family hierarchy. Thus, he was not reserved in expressing his true feelings. "Linus, who'd ya bury in my backyard?"

"What?" objected Linus, genuinely puzzled.

"There'z a new grave in Drakes Plot, and ol' Ollie found this broken handle next to it. So, tell me what'z goin' on. How could ya bury someone there, of all placez? Who waz it?" Amos held a defiant posture, not breaking his brother's gaze. He simply assumed Linus performed the deed, given his initials on the shovel and his role as undertaker in the Amish community.

"Amos, I don't know what ya talkin' about. It's a broken shovel handle."

"With ya'r initials on it."

"Yeah, but it's one of my ol' shovels. That's what it iz." Linus inspected the handle. "I've got a lot of ol' shovels. I got rid of a few at Esther's yard sale. So, what?"

"Ya mean to say ya know nothing about this? How'z that?"

"I'm tellin' ya, I don't know anythin' about it. I haven't been at the Drakes Plot in yearz."

"So, what'z ya'r ol' shovel doin' at a new grave in that cursed place?

Eden Valley, Pennsylvania

CHAPTER 23

Balsam Wood

A morning mist enveloped the vast North Woods of the Eden Valley. As the sun still slumbered beyond the horizon, Ariella rose from her light sleep for she loved the early morning. It possessed a refreshing quality that she nurtured in her own self. Cherishing her daily ritual, she often ventured into the murky forest before the sun dawned and her young followers awakened. She knew the path to her sacred sanctuary by heart, having little need for the dawning light to guide her.

Today seemed no different as she stepped off her porch onto the worn path that led through the big meadow. Passing the warm ashes of the previous night's fire still smoldering in the open fire pit, she walked across the dew-drenched grass on her way to the dark woods. Once beyond the solid line of oak sentries, she disappeared into the thick haze of the dense forest. Some nights, she could not sleep. At such times, she would sit on the deck observing the stars and the haunting moon. She possessed a restless spirit with a depth that none could fathom and powers beyond her form.

Often, she recharged those powers at a spring-fed waterfall deep in the dark heart of the North Woods, a place that formed her private sanctuary. Here Ariella fostered her inner peace and connected with her inspiration. Natural splendor defined this tranquil site where the ancient groundwaters gushed out of the base of a steep rock face—a massive, moss-covered boulder protecting the artesian source. Upon its birth from the underworld, the pristine water cascaded down the gray limestone monolith forming a waterfall that fed a clear basin, surrounded by large ferns and native flora. Due to its deep source, the spring water and its pool remained at a warm temperature year-round. In the winter, its surface steamed in the cold air, while in the summer, it provided welcome relief from the heat. As autumn descended upon the western Pennsylvania woods, the pool filled with colored leaves, creating a mosaic in the dawn mist rising from its surface.

Ariella followed the well-worn path to the spring-fed pool—a path that she had kept clear with countless morning visits to her glorious sanctuary. Large maples and oaks provided multi-colored curtains around this magical place, while the songbirds chirped and rustled as they awakened deep within its protective splendor. Except for the birds and the melody of the waterfall, all was quiet as her footsteps fell silently upon the worn path.

Dressed in a flowing white robe held together by a belt woven in snaking ropes of gold and majestic blue, her raven hair framed her alabaster face and emerald eyes when she stood still, as she did now at the edge of her sacred place. Rays of the rising sun danced about the pristine sanctuary and illuminated the enchantress in white, who held a long staff carved of balsam, the symbol of her shamanic powers.

Ariella's story was as complex as her persona. As a child, her family had dissolved into an endless feud fueled by her father's drunken rages and her mother's shattered dreams. As the only child, she was often at the center of her father's mercurial mood swings—until one night, when it all ended in a tragedy that to this day remains unexplained. Her parents were dead—the victims of a fluke car accident. It happened in the spring of her senior year in high school, two days after her eighteenth birthday.

Her saving grace was her group of friends who included her boyfriend. The two were in love but destiny soon pulled them apart. She left for McLaren University, where she had already been accepted, and he went to trade school.

While at McLaren, she was courted by and soon engaged to a wealthy older man. It all happened so fast. The older man possessed a power of persuasion that she mistook for love and affection. Thus, in the spring of her first year at McLaren, Ariella became pregnant. Then, an odd thing occurred. Her fiancé became suspicious of the source of her pregnancy. Turning upon his promised bride, he publicly accused her of infidelity. A scandal ensued as he pinned a social scarlet letter upon the hapless girl, barely nineteen. Wedding plans were cancelled and the rich, spineless university patron found a new coed to woo.

The baby came the following winter, forcing the young single mother to postpone her education and seek humble employment.

Alone, her plight brought her back into the arms of her former boyfriend. He wanted to marry her, proclaiming his love and willingness to rear the child as his own. At first she questioned his sincerity, given what she had suffered, but his intentions proved genuine and she agreed to the marriage. They wed in secret and she never took his name, but true love had finally found her. The young couple and child set up residence in a small apartment over the man's parents' garage.

Initially, his parents resented their son's involvement with a publicly-accused harlot, especially when he confessed to the secret marriage. Despite their anger, they were kind to the young couple and child—at least for the most part. All would have settled into a tolerable balance had fate not intervened in the form of a horrible accident.

One day, the young bride was walking to her waitressing job at a local diner when a distracted driver crashed into her. Driving away, never to be identified, he left Ariella on the side of the road with head trauma and a broken leg.

But fate was not finished. Prior to the marriage, her young husband had joined the National Guard. Six weeks after her accident, he was called for duty in a foreign war.

Fortunately, Ariella's in-laws stepped in to help, raising her baby while she recovered. By the time she walked again, young Ariella had been transformed. Her head injury caused her anxiety, difficulty sleeping and frequent seizures. Fearing for her safety, Ariella's in-laws filed for custody of her nine-month-old daughter. Panicked, she thought of running away with her baby, but she had little hope for steady income given her condition, barely able to fend for herself. A losing battle ensued. In the end, she agreed to surrender the child, but something inside her died that day.

Then, came fate's final cruelty in the form of a telegram from the War Department. Her young husband had perished on a secret campaign and his body was never recovered. She felt like she was drowning, like she had died with him. To her troubled mind, she added a shattered heart.

No longer willing to be the victim of fate, she simply walked out of her life, reluctantly surrendering the child she could not parent. There and then she promised herself never to fall in love again. To her, such affection led to pain, suffering, loss, and resentment. All she desired was freedom. She was just shy of her twenty-first birthday.

The carved, balsam-wood staff she carried with her on her morning walk had been given to her by the one who had freed her from her emotional and physical suffering. He raised her from the ashes, like the embodiment of the mystical phoenix. The staff symbolized all she had suffered and all she had overcome. It represented the covenant between her and the source of her power, as well as a confirmation of all that lies within reach of any soul who sought to delve beyond the boundaries of the mind and body with unyielding perseverance, an open mind, and a caring heart.

Ariella had become a seeker, and, in the process, attained knowledge and abilities beyond her imagination. This balsam staff provided a daily reminder of her conscious shift; one inspirited by a dear friend, now gone. Every morning, she picked up the rod of sacred wood carved with symbols depicting the great shaman who had walked the earth long before white men set foot on the American continent. One such shaman, possibly the last of his kind, had been her savior and her teacher. A wise soul once said that when the student is ready the teacher will come. Ariella personified that wisdom.

Ariella's mentor came to her in a most unexpected way. It happened fourteen years before, almost to the day. Hitchhiking across the country after leaving her in-laws' house, she was barely twenty-three and two years into her journey of self-discovery, which included many positive encounters and several bouts with pure evil.

Until that point, the worst of these brushes with the dark side of humanity took the form of a wealthy man who gave her a ride near Chicago. He drove her to an abandoned parking lot, where he proceeded to molest her in the passenger seat of his large German luxury car. She barely fought him off. Distrusting of the police, she did not report her encounter. Nor did she report the time another man, posing as a trusted friend, tried to seduce her after secretly drugging her drink. That time, she managed to stagger away at an opportune moment. A stranger housed her. But this "kind" stranger snuck into her bed that very night. Kicking herself free, she escaped into the seedy alleys of St. Louis to resume her trek, no longer sure of what she was seeking.

Her seizures returned as she spent more time sleeping on the streets, transforming beyond recognition and beyond the desire of men. The harsh experiences did not anger her but did something worse—they slowly crushed her spirit.

Thus, after two years of a nomadic existence, her body, mind, and spirit were worn to the core. Her enthusiasm had withered to an illusion. She became a phantom of her own self, a reflection of society's apathy. Passion for the truth surrendered to a need to survive. Unfortunately, even that basic desire slowly drifted away. Her noble traits capitulated to basic instincts as her soul surrendered its lead to the needs of her form. To say that she had turned to a path of darkness would be grossly inaccurate. Rather, darkness now haunted her as if she were a foretold threat, slowly and patiently devouring her spirit. She had become a living shadow of her former self—a living specter of her once noble nature.

On a fateful October day in eastern Wyoming, Ariella Bianca was going to be tested to her limits. On a day that started like any other on the Great Prairie, she awakened to a spellbinding sunrise over the endless fields of golden grass. The rising sun and the gentle breeze had roused her from a dream she did not wish to abandon. With the opening of her eyes, the dream vanished along with the warmth it had provided her on that cold morning. Fall had arrived and the chill of winter crept into the wee hours. Night after night, its grip strengthened until the day too would surrender, transforming the prairie to a frosty white.

On this brisk morning, Ariella became aware of an inner sadness that surrounded her existence. She felt alone in the world. At some level, she had always been alone, even when in the company of her parents, her husband, and her child. Birth and death were lonely portals, and she felt that she neared the latter.

Love had not touched her in a lasting way. She had experienced moments of random kindness, but never did love germinate into the "happily ever after" of fables and fairy tales. Only one person, her departed husband, whom she missed with all her body, mind, and soul, had ever broken through her walls, but he was long gone, stolen from her by a foreign war in which she had no choice and no say.

After eating the last of the precious berries she had gathered the night before, she picked up her ragged backpack, which contained all her earthly possessions, and began walking along an abandoned fire road. A pervasive loneliness grew around her like never before. It seemed to take form and its depressive silhouette stalked her. She could not escape it. Like a growing shadow, her fears and her loneliness congealed into the thought of ending her existence by her own hand. Such thoughts had never penetrated her inner sanctum, the inherent source of her will to live. Later, she would explain what followed as if it were an illusion brought upon by her frail, starved body, and a mind robbed of its wit and will. But she knew it was more, dreadfully more.

As she walked westward, Ariella beheld a sight on the horizon, illuminated by the dawning light. There, shrouded in magenta mist, stood a striking natural feature. Like a giant black tooth or a sacrificial altar, this dark, flat-topped monolith beckoned her. It was a sacred place to the Native Americans who discovered it and made this prairie their home. Known as Bears Lodge or Ghost Mountain, it formed the unattainable seat of their timeless spirits and deities.

At this site, the Lakota received the White Buffalo Calf Pipe, the most sacred object of their people, from the White Buffalo Calf Woman, a legendary prophet of supernatural origin, who created the "Seven Sacred Rites" as the foundation of their faith and society. This was their Mecca, their Jerusalem, and their Rome. Here the Lakota held their sacred Sun Dance around the summer solstice when they celebrated and reconnected with their faith. Little wonder that the colonizing invaders renamed it as a place of evil.

Ariella did not know any of this history, but she immediately recognized Devils Tower, an imposing natural wonder, whether it be a seat of good or of evil, or simply the remnant of the once hot and fluid core of a now dormant basaltic volcano.

The ancient monolith drew Ariella toward it at a growing pace, as if connected by an invisible, indestructible thread. She could no more avoid being attracted to it than a moth can resist a blinding light on a dark summer night. As she approached, completely focused on her goal, her mood grew heavy, until her sense of despair became crushing. A starved stomach is a persistent persuader, but a starved heart can be an immobilizing deterrent. In desperation, her sole resolve became the black tower looming tall and powerful in the morning light.

Now, her subconscious feelings and conscious thoughts were at odds. The former pushed her away from the once sacred altar, while the latter pulled her toward it. As she struggled within her own self, another force entering the battle for Ariella's soul as it materialized at the foot of Devils Tower.

The opening sortie happened at 8:26 a.m. on September 26, 1997. Ariella turned to see a rusty old pickup approaching from behind her along the gravel fire road. Slowing to match her pace, the vehicle remained fifty yards behind her, like a mechanical stalker. At the sight of the lone dark figure behind the wheel, she felt a gut-wrenching fear. Oddly, she felt she knew the man; yet he was a stranger. It felt like the *déjà vu*. Ariella subconsciously recognized this soul, even at a distance.

Not waiting for his arrival, she began to run toward Devils Tower, hoping that the National Monument would have at least one park ranger on duty. For the first time since her journey began, Ariella was willing to sacrifice her present anonymity for security from an evil, the likes of which she had not encountered in this lifetime. Her conscious mind filled with fear, while her subconscious was terrified by the demon it recognized. Thus, finally aligned, the two propelled her at a reckless pace toward the tower.

The truck stopped yards away from her on the abandoned road and a burly man jumped out. Immediately, he began running toward her. Well before she could reach the security of the national park, he tackled her in the tall grass that flanked the fire road on both sides. Upon falling against the cold, hard earth, she lost sight of the horizon.

With her face against the ground, she could not see his identity as he pressed upon her, making it hard to breathe and impossible to scream. His weight was crushing, like the loneliness and apathy, her daily companions. He embodied both. From this nightmare there was no awakening. As she struggled against him, he struck her with a blow that numbed her. Like a cornered animal, she thrashed for freedom but to no avail. Freedom was not to be, as he forced her to look upon his horrid face, pockmarked with lust and apathy. A doe at the mercy of a starving cougar, she remained pinned and helpless.

This stranger possessed an unearthly evil channeled into the most primitive of man's desires. That juxtaposition of alien and human malice defined him and fueled her terror.

The drifter had stalked her since spying her on the fire road just after dawn. He had tracked her at a distance before making his move in the cover of the tall grass. A cowardly act was rarely performed in plain sight, and this was one of the most cowardly acts of all.

Those who claim there is no evil in the world have been spared its full encounter. Those who claim that there is no evil in the hearts of men do not know their own hearts.

Ariella tried to scream, but he covered her mouth with his filthy paw. She tried to pull away, but he pressed upon her further with his immense weight. As she desperately pushed him away, he struck her across the face once more to silence her. Not a person to him, her suffering added to his insatiable pleasure, that, once gone, needed yet another violent act to fulfill his sick addiction. He craved sexual satisfaction and the rest of her became a punching bag for his hate and aggression.

The blood from her lips entering her mouth as every new blow caused more stings on her body and face. Life was not hers any longer. Her body she occupied, only to suffer with it. Mentally, she had disengaged. Like a victim and an observer in one, she felt him rip at her clothes and grope her wilting body for his perverse pleasure.

He symbolized the empty shell of a man robbed of a soul. Forcing himself painfully and mercilessly, his evil entered her as she screamed for mercy that would not come. All seemed deaf to her crushing suffering. *Where is God now?* she wondered, as she felt herself pull away from her broken ravaged body. It was her last thought before he silenced her mind with one final blow that ended consciousness and existence as she had known it.

That singular question echoed across the empty prairie, rising higher into the vastness and emptiness of space itself. Where was the Almighty? Where were the fabled angels, those noble guardians of faith and lore, when she needed them most? Absent because they did not exist? Or too weak and callous if they did? Was all this simply an extension of a heartless universe that was nothing more than an expanding spectacle of indifference and personal survival, as science would have us believe with each new discovery woven of its own truths?

At that moment, these further questions no longer existed in Ariella's mind. She had finally released her form. It was dead to her, and she had gone back to her dream—the one that had consoled her the night before. The demon aggressor did his best to dehumanize and violate her body, while she lay unconscious, hidden in her subconscious, hidden in the tall grass of human apathy. Death, at that point, seemed a blessing within reach. Evil had gained a big victory in the battle for Ariella Bianca.

The mysterious demon in form, a mind so twisted in anger, hate, and lust that it no longer took orders from the remnants of soul within it, if such remnant still existed, had moved on, fulfilled for now. He had his will with her, until she was too lifeless to excite him to further pleasure. Like a soiled rag, he discarded her into the bloodied grass just beyond the edge of the abandoned fire road where he left her for dead. In fact, by most medical standards, she had reached that state of surrender. Ariella was gone, except for one spark of tenacity that refused to yield the battlefield in defeat. If unextinguished, one spark can a wildfire spawn. Would this be such a spark or would it simply die away with the mutilated unconscious form it still inhabited?

Night descended upon Devils Tower. As the sun abandoned the horizon, a chill followed and the dancing blades of tall grass took on a ghostly image. Covered with frost, they reflected the blue moonlight while swaying to the beat of the gentle breeze.

They say that heroes are not born but made. Well, perhaps both are true. The greatest heroes are born of great souls and made to fully embody them through their own will to fulfill their life's selfless mission, regardless of the odds and the cost to themselves. Few ever achieve such noble status, but such heroes have graced the history of our humble race. Let us hope for all our sake that they continue to emerge among us. Overcoming the seemingly impossible is a common trait of these souls. They are rare, but when one appears, nothing is ever again the same.

A wolf howled at the moon. Another answered. The hungry wolf pack descended from the base of the tower and began to scurry about the prairie for prey and carrion. Soon, pack scouts discovered the bleeding, dying girl. They howled in triumph as the remainder joined the anticipated feast. Some sniffed and some circled, but all waited for the arrival of the large gray alpha male. It was he who would feed first. It was he who governed them with order and fear despite their empty bellies. Slowly, he approached to investigate.

Most wild animals avoid people. The very scent of humans is a deterrent. Countless millennia of cohabitation have taught them to beware man's unpredictable and often merciless nature. These animals were no exception. But hunger has a way of dissipating caution, and the alpha male was hungry, as was the rest of the pack that counted on his leadership. He neared Ariella's torn and fallen body and sniffed her wounds, nudging her to see if she was alive. Once more, he nudged her. But this time, something in his primordial mind warned him not to strike. Despite his hunger, he pulled away without a bite.

As he did so, he encountered a threat from one of the young males in the pack. This particular male was more aggressive. Ravenous, he wanted to have his fill. Disagreeing with the alpha, he threatened his authority by approaching the body from another side. He was about to tear into his meal when he felt a sharp pain in his right hind leg. Inexplicably, the alpha male protected Ariella from his own pack. A battle between the two large wolves ensued, a ruthless struggle for dominance. The victor would be the alpha and the loser could be killed or banished from the pack.

This contender had the nimbleness of youth, while the alpha had size and experience, having repelled countless challengers over his long reign. But, after the hard-fought battle, the nobler beast won the field. Soon, the wolf pack moved on under the firm leadership of the large alpha male, who had spared the youth who challenged him, as he had spared Ariella's fallen form.

The scene proved once more that the struggle between good and evil goes far beyond the limits of man. But does it, really? Or is it simply our interpretation of the two extremes, which are as intertwined as the wiring of our own minds? Yet the gray alpha wolf held an answer to this riddle. Within an hour, he abandoned his pack and his role, returning to guard Ariella's body until dawn. Unnatural as the act appeared, it seemed completely normal to the one that came next.

As the day awakened to a crimson dawn to the looming black tower on the horizon, Ariella's body guarded by the huge lone wolf lay in its shadow. Several famished coyotes had challenged this guardianship but proved no match for his size and strength. Unexplainable, he sat there like a faithful dog until a greater master appeared.

An ancient man with a balsam-wood staff approached the seated wolf. The two gazed at each other as if to exchange a greeting. Once the gaze was broken, the wolf stepped aside from the body as if silently instructed to do so. Odd in appearance, the old man generated a presence far greater than the shadow he cast in the rising sun. Upon reaching Ariella's body, he fell to his knees and began a series of complex chants, while the wild gray wolf stood guard, deterring the growing number of circling vultures. Then the mysterious man pulled herbs out of his long white robe, which was embroidered with rings of beads of every color of the spectrum.

He wore a gray, weathered headband on which were symbols too ancient to have any meaning in this world except to him. The band appeared worn, like his brown face, which had furrows of wrinkles that betrayed his peaceful and joyful nature. As the great healer leaned over the seemingly lifeless girl, he asked the Spirit that he personified if she should live or die. Not passing judgment, he simply asked. He had been called here, but his mission was not clear. Suddenly, the Spirit answered with the call of a white mourning dove, whose clear, haunting cry echoed across the silent prairie.

"Very well," whispered the old man, looking up at the sacred white bird that appeared before him. "Let the two be united in this world as one." The old man, one of the last shamans of his people—yet one of the greatest—took an ointment, along with various herbs and other mysterious items, from a leather sash that hung over his right shoulder. He began to rub the mysterious ointment into Ariella's wounds. After applying several additional medications, he chanted and bowed over Ariella's body. As he chanted, his posture and stillness suggested that he had entered a deep trance. At one point, he appeared to rise slightly above the ground. Without a doubt, he was well-versed in his craft. All throughout this hours-long process, the wolf stood guard, acting more like a faithful companion than a wild beast. Then, miraculously, Ariella opened her eyes. Soon, she sat up to face the man and the beast before her.

At first, she felt alarmed and confused, not trusting her ability to distinguish reality from a dream. She had retracted into her deep subconscious throughout the horrific ordeal, only to emerge, like a crocus through the spring snow, at the coaxing of the mysterious old man. Seeing him and his odd companion, the wolf, she froze, lacking a logical explanation.

Her memory of the day prior returned, but, to her surprise, she felt no fear. As she looked upon her tattered clothes, she saw that in places where her flesh had been torn by the savage attack, there were bandages of mysterious leaves bound with thin straps of soft leather. She could feel the cooling ointment on her face, on her arms, on her legs, and on her loins. Reality sank in and with it came an abyss of sadness. Her body was no longer her own, or so it seemed. Until now, despite several aggressive attacks, she had managed to fend off the lustful demon of man's creation, but not this time. This time, the merciless drifter, like Satan himself, forced himself upon her, marking her with scars—some too deep to ever surface.

Violated, she felt exposed and defaced. At that moment, Ariella knew her rock bottom. At that moment, seated in the presence of this strange old man and his odd companion, she knew she had passed by the gates of hell and survived. At that moment, all the strength inherent in her soul poured into the shell of a human being that this violent act had left behind. On that morning, in the chill of the western prairie, a new force was forged—a force so powerful and so pure that no earthly foe could conquer it. From that moment, she would be feared by those of fear, loved by those of love, and hated by those of hate.

Although Ariella's transformation of inner will occurred literally overnight, her education as a shaman had just begun. The old man, a proud Sioux shaman, took her under his care and the two lived off the land, as was the way of the ancients. Those were happy years and times of wonder. During their journey together, she became his true daughter and his greatest student. By the end of their decade together, she had blossomed in her knowledge and power, both intensified by her steel will, endless curiosity, and patient perseverance. Like a sponge whose sole purpose was to learn, she mastered every task and every lesson. He taught her the forgotten ways of medicine, psychology and, yes, magic. Instructing her in the oneness of all and the sacred nature of existence, he tutored her in meditation and deep hypnosis, as well as the arts of transformation and illusion.

But she innately possessed a power he could not teach—a power attained by her miraculous return from the clutches of death. Ariella possessed an unearthly ability to push the boundaries of the ethereal plane that separated the living from the dead. All in all, she person-ified his greatest achievement. In the comfort of that attainment, he surrendered his form on a cold day in early December 2007 and the large gray wolf died the same day.

Upon the death of her beloved mentor, Ariella felt alone. A powerful shaman without a tribe, she decided to head east, back to her home. Before departing the land of the Sioux, a new companion emerged as mysteriously as the first. A lone, young gray wolf arrived two days after she had disposed of the old man's body and that of the old alpha wolf, returning both to ashes that she had spread in the wind across the prairie. Recognized the animal by his energy, she knew his origin and his purpose. He would guard her on her journey.

Along the way, she would help others, but she never stayed any-where for long. On a mission to return home. Her true purpose would remain known only to her, and, possibly, to the mysterious gray wolf. The latter accompanied her back to the Eden Valley and remained her companion for nearly three years before vanishing one cold winter morning as suddenly as he had first appeared.

Presently, as Ariella stood at the spring-fed pool located near her well-established home in Eden Valley, she reflected on the journey that had brought her full circle. She had often thought about her mentor and felt that he was always there to guide her, to give her strength and resolve. Her reflections fueled her determination, as did the tears she shed for him, the last of the great shamans of the plains. But the balsam staff in her hand provided assurance of strength and purpose, for it had been his and now it belonged to her, along with all the power and wisdom it symbolized. Thus she, her great teacher, the gray wolf, and the white dove were forever bound to one another—forevermore, one and the same.

Enjoying the sight of the pool as the sun's rays pierced the mist of the dark woods with pillars of light, she sat down under the great hollowed sycamore tree and crossed her legs into a meditative position. Thus began her morning ritual, tapping the source of her power just as he had taught her so long ago. Like the long and ancient lineage of aboriginal shaman that preceded her, she would connect to a higher dreamworld where magic was possible and miracles were routine. This connection sourced all that she learned and all that she borrowed, for all was borrowed and must be returned in time. To believe that one owned or achieved one's powers was to fall backwards into the limited shadows of one's ego. She knew better. Piously, she entered that holy place beyond her physical limitations and replenished her ethereal connection.

In this state of greater knowing, she suddenly became aware of an intruder within her sacred sanctuary.

CHAPTER 24

Mending Fences

Amos Miller was mending a fence around the large horse pasture when his older brother pulled up in a covered buggy.

"Looks good," Linus proclaimed while glancing at the mended fence.

Amos, preoccupied with the work, failed to look up.

"I came to see that grave at Drakes Plot. Can we drive up there from here?" Linus stepped out of his buggy and walked over to the fence.

Amos finally turned around. He was a tall, lean, handsome man. Standing there holding a large ax, he looked more like a Hollywood version of the Amish than a real Amish man.

"We better walk. The trail's bad. Hey, I need to apologize to ya," Amos replied sincerely. "I'm sorry I suspected ya of diggin' up there. I should've known better. But this Lenore thing's got me in knots." He was about to tell his brother about his White Witch sighting but decided against it. Even now, he suspected it was just his mind playing tricks on him for he had not been sleeping much.

"Ya're forgiven. It must be hard. I know the two of ya were close. I know ya loved her."

"Loved her? I still love her, Linus."

"I know."

"Can you keep a secret, brother of mine?"

"Yah, of course. Haven't I always been there for ya?"

Amos had to admit that his oldest brother always protected him, especially when he got in trouble with the rules, which happened a little too often. "Yah, ya have," he said with a sigh.

"What secret now, Amos? Please tell me ya're not in trouble with the Bishop, again," Linus replied, raising his brows.

"No. Not that. It's that Lenore came to me before she left. I had a chance to talk 'er out of it, but I didn't. I told her it waz okay to leave, if that waz what she really wanted to do. I helped 'er leave."

Linus sighed and looked away. "So, why're ya tellin' me this?"

"I don't know. I feel responsible for what happened to her, for what happened to us."

"What'z done's done."

"But there's more."

"Not sure I wanna know more."

Amos needed someone in whom he could confide his troubles. So in this moment of weakness, his older brother had no choice but to hear everything. "Lenore and I fell in love years ago."

"That's not a surprise. We all knew yuz were courtin'."

"No, ya don't understand. I waz attracted to Lenore WHILE I waz married to Elizabeth."

"What're ya sayin', Amos? Ya cheated on Elizabeth?"

"No! Of course, not! God, no! It waz just attraction to Lenore. I love Elizabeth, but she'z gone, und I love Lenore und now she'z…" Amos sighed. "I mean, Elizabeth und I had a great relationship, und I miss her terribly, but Lenore and I…well, we're….God, I'm ramblin'." He stopped.

"Amos, ya gotta let it go. Ya're drivin' ya'self crazy."

"But I can't let it go. I lost Elizabeth…I can't lose Lenore. I can't lose 'er, again. I didn't try und stop 'er. I let 'er go. Linus, I caused all this. I could've stopped 'er und I didn't." Amos felt on the verge of tears, a sight uncharacteristic of his strong persona. He turned to the fence and began to mend it once more, while wiping his eyes with his coarse dirty hands.

"Amos, I'm sorry." Linus did not know what else to say. He had not seen his brother like this since Elizabeth's funeral. It was as if everything had resurfaced.

"All this hurts on so many levels. I don't know what to do with it," Amos admitted, still mending the fence.

"I can't tell ya how to feel, Amos, but I can tell ya shouldn't 'old it in. Ya didn't cause what happen' to Lenore. Besides, ya know better than anyone there's no stoppin' that one if she makes her mind up about somethin'."

"Ya got that right," Amos replied, still mending the fence.

"Und if ya were attracted to Lenore before Elizabeth passed, it's no sin since ya didn't act on it. If it makes ya feel better, we all have secrets," Linus added. He regretted the last comment as soon as he said it.

Amos turned to face his brother, curious to hear. "I didn't know ya had secrets. Ya're always the righteous one."

Linus decided to confide in his brother. "Not always, Amos. None of us're always righteous. That honor belongs to the Lord, not to us."

"True," Amos reflected. Although he had a rebellious nature, Amos had one of the strongest faiths in the entire community. He simply felt that each person deserved to have free will and felt it in his heart—the same heart that rebelled when that free will was taken away. It had been a real struggle for Amos to remain Amish, for the rules were many and dated, dictating everything, even the clothes he wore. At times, it seemed too much to bear.

Amos yearned for freedom and free will. However, unlike Lenore, he did not have the courage to lose everything in exchange. He could not trade his greater family, his relationship with his brothers and sisters, nor his farm for that freedom. Envious of Lenore's strength, he could not stop her from leaving. To do so would have been hypocrisy. Deep down, he knew his support had tipped the scales. His lack of objection must have felt callous to her, forcing her to reconsider his love. For it was love that had kept her from leaving until that fateful day when he placed it in question. Now, he was dead to her, as if he were buried in that forsaken plot at the top of the hill, and he felt the blame.

"What secret could ya possibly have compared to the ones I carry?" Amos asked his older brother as he looked him straight in the eyes.

"How sturdy's that fence post, little brother?"

"What? It's sturdy, now t'at I mended it," Amos replied with a puzzled expression on his face.

"Then, ya may want to hold onto it," Linus answered, as his face fell ashen.

"Why? What iz it?"

"Ya can't tell a soul."

"I promise, I won't." Amos was completely confused by this dramatic preamble.

"Ok, ya got a hold of that post?"

"Yeah, but, if this iz a joke, it ain't funny."

"John Lapp's not Lenore's true *fader*," Linus replied.

As soon as Linus uttered the words, Amos dropped the heavy ax with a crash, just missing his foot. "Is it you?" he asked in disbelief.

CHAPTER 25

The Gray Wolf

Ariella concluded her meditation and walked to the edge of the spring-fed pool. She had learned to walk in silence. As she approached the pool, she could see that her premonition of the intruder had materialized. He was hard to discern, partially obscured by the thick morning mist created by the chilled air above the pool of warm water. Odd in appearance, he acted animal-like, as he crouched over the water and drank his fill.

Clothed in gray fur, he resembled a wolf, like the one that had accompanied her on her journey eastward. Recently, she had sensed his presence while in deep meditation, but only now had he materialized. Ariella knew much about illusion, so the duality of the apparition did not alarm her. Rather, she wondered at the identity of this half man, half beast. Lost in her thoughts, she refocused, only to realize that he was watching her. Their eyes met and remained fixed upon each other, neither breaking the silent stare.

Finally, the mysterious being looked down on his own reflection and cried out, in a wolf-like howl. The piercing sound startled her long enough to allow him to disappear into the morning shadows of the deep woods, seemingly without a trace. Ariella was used to being the one who startled others with her abilities. This was a role reversal.

As the sun began to dissolve the haze, her thoughts returned to her mentor, the Sioux shaman, who went by the name Kentahoe. He had taught her everything, even the nature of Spirit. "The wolf and the man are one," Kentahoe insisted. "I am this wolf, and he is I," he would proclaim, referring to the large gray wolf who had become his companion. The idea perplexed her, challenging her inherent beliefs. Rather, she preferred to explore other spiritual paths, ones more closely akin to science. She became a master at meditation and regression, not unlike a trained psychologist, and in herbal medicine she could rival any doctor or holistic healer.

But with all this knowledge, she was drawn back to the ancient ways that had been passed down for countless generations of Native American shaman. She explored the power of the dreamworld, in its capacity as a forum for connecting with spiritual guides. With time and practice, she surpassed her mentor in her abilities to connect with Spirit, and, at times, to be one with it. But the one thing she struggled to learn was the ability of transformational illusion. It had taken her nearly a decade to conquer, and she never surpassed her master in this craft. He truly was one with the wolf, and all creatures, for he knew no barrier between them.

For this reason, she stood staring at the vacated place of the strange visitor. Could it be her former master? *How could that be?* she wondered. *That was no apparition. That was a man,* she concluded to herself. Her deeper perception assured her of that. This being was of flesh and blood. Without further thought, she turned homeward, following the narrow, worn path back to her humble cabin. The girls would be awake, wondering why she had not returned from her daily walk by breakfast time.

As she entered the thick growth near the west edge of the North Woods, she froze at the sight of the vision that stood in her path. There, illuminated by the rising sun, stood the manwolf. He looked at her once more. This time, he disregarded her and slowly continued across the path into the deep woods. Clearly a man, no longer appeared as anything but a human.

Her curiosity aroused, she decided to give silent pursuit. Blending into the forest, as she had learned to do years ago, she followed him at a distance. If he was aware of her, he did not acknowledge it. Rather, he seemed to be in an argument with himself, often waving his hands about and screaming at times in his insanity. *That can't be the Master,* she reasoned. The thought saddened her but gave her incentive to reach out to this lost soul.

They passed deeper into the forest. He too seemed capable of becoming completely silent, as he plunged into a portion of the North Woods that Ariella had avoided. Here the energy was dark and the air felt heavy, thick with the smell of decay. The light played tricks with the mind and nothing seemed real.

In the darkness, the figure before her seemed to return to a wolflike form. She wondered if it was her imagination or something more. It was then that the manwolf approached a massive oak tree, the likes of which she had never seen. It stood against a solid wall of gray limestone. Reaching the tree, he stopped and looked about, as if he sensed her presence. Sniff at the air, he returned to an animal state. He looked toward her, but she managed to hide behind another large oak. She waited a minute before slowly peering around the edge of the tree. To her surprise, the strange manwolf was gone—vanished like the illusion that he resembled.

Carefully, she walked up to the massive oak. Looking around, she did not see anyone, but the smell of a wood fire permeated the morning air. Yet there was no fire. All was still. She could sense that she was alone. After carefully scouting the terrain for signs of the odd man, she sat down under the massive tree and began to laugh. For the first time since her transformation on the Wyoming prairie, she had been outwitted and outfoxed.

As she sat pondering the unexplainable, she heard a muted outcry. Had she not been completely quiet and alert, she would not have detected it. Holding her breath, she listened. To her surprise, the sound of shouting seemed to echo from within the earth. Ariella knew more about the supernatural world than just about anyone else in existence, but this illusion she could not explain. It was not unnatural, yet it seemed that some invisible being moved about her, unseen. She decided to remain still and simply perceive.

Soon, it became clear that no apparition haunted her. Rather, someone or something lived beneath the roots of the tree. So as not to lose her element of surprise, she rose in silence and explored the periphery of the massive tree. Soon she discovered a hidden passage behind it in the form of a vertical fissure within the gray limestone. The narrow opening had been purposely covered by thick vegetation. Slowly and carefully, she peered into the two-foot-wide crack that opened into a deeper cavernous passage. Examining the entrance, she froze in surprise. There in the damp earth around the camouflaged fissure were the tracks of a man and those of a large wolf. *How could this be?* she pondered. *Surely, this is no shapeshifter?*

Closer inspection of the fissure revealed a barely visible light emanating from the far end of the low and narrow cavity. Silently, she squeezed through the entrance and crawled down the tight tunnel toward the faint light that emanated from the well-trodden floor, twenty feet beyond the entranceway. As she reached the end of the small passage, she saw a two-foot diameter opening to a much larger cavern below ground level. Peeking into the hole, she could see a shadow cross the flickering beam of light. Clearly, this shadowy form had been the source of the outcry that had baffled her minutes earlier. Had the manwolf disappeared into a subterranean shelter? That seemed to be the logical explanation.

She had no reservations regarding the world of the supernatural, for she was well-versed in it, being a frequent guest. It was the world of men that perplexed her. For the first time in what seemed like eternity, Ariella felt anxiety, the precursor to fear. Her thoughts returned to that day beneath Devils Tower and the mysterious evil being that had attacked her without remorse. Surely, he was not the only pure evil in this world. Knowing the answer to that riddle, she wondered if she were at the doorstep of another such encounter. What she felt in her stomach was disturbingly familiar, although dormant for a decade. The one day she wished never to relive revisited her mind. Accepting her reservation, she silently crawled back out of the tight chamber and stepped into the daylight.

As she walked around the large girth of the old oak, something else in her took over and she stopped. *I vowed never again to let fear control me*, she silently reflected. With that thought, she mustered her courage and returned to her quest—once again silently creeping into the lair of the manwolf. After passing through the narrow passage and descending a rickety wooden ladder down the dimly-lit portal that minutes earlier gave her pause, she found herself in a surprisingly large subterranean room. It appeared to be a cave, half eroded out of the native limestone and half tunneled into the soil beneath the thick, gnarly roots of the supporting oak tree. The space, illuminated by a small fire that vented through a large fracture in the cave's ceiling, took her breath away in its primitive charm.

This was not the cold lair of an evil beast, but the charmingly peculiar home of a mysterious dweller. Before her eyes could fully adjust to the dim, flickering light, she felt a presence in the farthest corner of the room. Slowly, she looked upon him, seated on his makeshift throne of animal skins. As the firelight shifted to illuminate his face, she gasped. Although the walking dead were no strangers to her, she had never seen a specter like this one.

the Secret

Amos stared at his older brother, Linus Miller, in anticipation of his response. In the deathly silence, he repeated his question. "Linus, are ya Lenore's *fader*? Please tell me it ain't true."

Linus laughed a hearty laugh. "Why, little brother, my secret ain't absurd. Ya think I'd let ya court her if she were my daughter? Ya'd be her uncle, und that just wouldn't be right under any religion."

"Thank God!" Amos exclaimed and sighed in relief. "So, what'z the secret?"

"I told ya the secret. Lenore's adopted, but she don't know it. John und Mary decided not to tell 'er for they were afraid she might go lookin' for her real parents. Ya know John und I are close, so don't tell a soul I told ya—not even Lenore. "

"I won't, but who're 'er real parents?"

"No one knows, but she ain't born Amish."

"How'd she end up Amish, then?

"John found 'er on his front step, a year or so after he und Mary got married. Lenore was just a baby. She couldn't've been more than a few weeks old. Some English folk must've abandoned her, if ya can imagine that. Poor girl. That one's had a rough start. I guess it explains why it'z in 'er blood to leave," Linus concluded.

Amos wanted to dispute that reasoning, being born Amish and having a similar desire. But perhaps there was some logic to it. After all, Lenore was not like most Amish women. Amos sighed. His mind churned along with his stomach. It was then that he realized he had completely forgone breakfast. "Have ya eaten?" he asked his brother. "Ya want some breakfast?"

"I could go for another," Linus replied with a chuckle.

"Well, then, I'll make us some."

After the two brothers finished a hearty breakfast of eggs and bacon, the conversation turned toward the mysterious grave at Drakes Plot. Linus listened in disbelief as Amos retold the events of the previous morning. After he finished, silence filled the room. Linus could not process the information in a logical way.

"Ya sure ya saw her? Maybe it waz just the sun playing tricks on ya."

"I saw her as clear as I see ya sittin' here. I'm not one to buy into some old wives' tale. Ya know that. But I'm tellin' ya I saw the White Witch that all the talk's been about of late. I saw 'er in that curz'd place."

"Huh, not that I don't believe ya, but I just can't explain it. That raven sounded like the devil himself."

"One und the same, by the look of 'im. It had Ollie scared like I never seen 'im. I waz even a little scared. That bird didn't leave until I got right up to it. Boy, it had the strangest eyes, I tell ya. They were yellow."

"Like ya said earlier, it might've been the sun reflecting in 'em."

"That could be, but it still doesn't explain why that bird acted the way it did."

"Maybe it was rabid or something."

"I don't know, but it acted like it waz guarding that grave with its life, if it had one."

"Are ya pulling my leg? This sounds like one of yar campfire stories when my kids 'ere little."

"I ain't makin' this up. Ya wanna know why I got so upset with ya? After that strange bird disappeared, Ollie found yar broken shovel stickin' out of that new grave. When I saw that I nearly fainted. I guess I just figured ya buried someone up there on orders from our peculiar bishop. Ya know what I think of 'im. I thought it was cruel to bury someone up there. That's why I got mad at ya."

"Look, the Bishop may've got a lot of rules, but he und I don't go sneakin' about buryin' folks at Drakes Plot. How could ya think that?"

"I don't know. I saw ya broken shovel und ya bein' the undertaker und all, I guess I jumped to a conclusion. It didn't seem so far-fetched at the time."

"Well, ya're wrong. I don't know anything about this. But I wouldn't go around tellin' folks ya're seein' ghosts und devilish ravens with yellow eyes. Ya'll get in a lot of trouble. The entire thing's ridiculous. Ya pullin' my leg, ain't ya?"

"No, I'm not. I'm serious as death. I swear, I saw it like I told ya."

"Ya know drinkin' alcohol's against the rules, und could get ya shunn'd?"

"I've never drank a drop of alcohol in my life, und I ain't about to start. Ya don't believe me, do ya? Well, let's go look at that grave, then. For all I know 'em devilish ghosts're still up there, dancin' about or whatever they do with all their time."

"Ya're pullin' my leg, now. I know it. Well, ya nearly had me with this one, Amos. Why not add old Arthur Drake's ghost into the story? He could be floating around, too."

"Are ya comin' or not? I'm not pullin' yar leg."

"Ya're really serious, ain't ya?"

"Yah. Let's go. We'll have to walk. The road's too muddy und steep for the buggy."

"I guess we better bring a couple of shovels, und find out what's buried up there," Linus replied.

"Maybe someone's movin' in on ya job, Linus," Amos teased.

"If they are, they sure picked an odd place to start."

The two brothers ascended the hill toward Drakes Plot. Old Ollie led the way until the ruins of the old Drake home were in view. At that point, he fell behind Amos. This time he did not bark, for no apparition guarded the old cemetery.

As they approached, they were startled by a cloud of crows that ascended from the gnarly trees that surrounded Drakes Plot on three sides. They protested the presence of the intruders, while Ollie protested in return, letting out a sharp set of barks. After circling the cemetery for what seemed like an eternal minute, the loud birds departed towards the surrounding cornfields.

The sudden ascension of the black birds startled Linus and he dropped his shovel. At the sight of this, Amos laughed. "That's nothin'. Ya're lucky ya weren't 'ere yesterday. Ya'd've dropped more than a shovel."

Linus was not pleased. Although, as an undertaker, he was used to death and had little fear of it, he did not like being startled. Besides, he had no desire to see any ghosts or large ravens with yellow eyes. Luckily, he didn't have to suffer through either visitor, for they reached the grave site without any further disruption.

Looking down, Linus quickly assessed the situation. "Ya're right. It's fresh but very strange. This mound's an odd shape. It ain't long enough to be a new grave."

"What're you saying?"

"Well, if it were a real grave, it'd have to be longer for the coffin. This one's nearly square, or more like a circle. There ain't no grave like this that I know of, Amos. Someone or something dug up this old grave. See here!" He pointed at the broken tombstone. "It's Evelyn Drake's grave. You can barely read 'er name, but it's hers all right. Why would anyone mess with the dead? I don't like this, Amos. I really don't like it. We better just leave it alone."

"Ya're right. It ain't a new grave. Someone's been digging up Evelyn Drake's grave, but why? I wonder what they were lookin' for?"

"Whatever it waz, they either found it or it wasn't there. I say we leave it be," Linus suggested. He was eager to abandon the quest.

Unfortunately, his younger brother did not share his opinion. He was determined to take a look. "Well, I say we dig a little und find out."

"That'z a bad idea. I'm an undertaker, und I know to leave the dead in peace. Let's go!"

"Look, we got this far. I'll dig down two feet. If there's nothin', we leave. Okay?"

"Okay, but I say we leave as soon as we can. This place gives me the creeps, even in the daytime."

Amos began to dig at the center of the disturbed soil. The earth was loose and easy to remove, confirming that the area had been recently excavated. In fact, the digging was so easy that within minutes Amos reached two feet. "Okay, two feet und nothin'. Let's go!" Linus said.

His younger brother was silent, as if frozen. He simply stared down into the shallow hole as if he had seen the ghost of the White Witch staring back at him.

"What'z the matter with ya?" Linus asked.

Amos did not say a word. He simply pointed into the hole.

Linus looked into the middle of the small pit and exclaimed, "Lord have mercy!" and crossed himself. Amos also crossed himself, as he looked away from the stiff, ashen hand that protruded from the disturbed grave of Evelyn Drake.

CHAPTER 27

The Autopsy

That same Tuesday morning, Molly and Kelly were having a late breakfast on The Raven Inn's spacious porch, a large wooden structure decorated with hanging ferns and flower boxes. Old vines of wisteria in purple blossom were draped over its archways. White wicker furniture, arranged in clusters, created plush seating areas around wrought iron breakfast tables. The entire setting had a flavor of Cape May, the Victorian seaside resort in southern New Jersey.

Molly and Kelly had enjoyed their three-night stay but felt deflated in their quest. Countless interviews had yielded little additional information regarding the peculiar demise of Gavin Green. All interviewees agreed that Gavin was an odd young man with a temper and an eye for the ladies. Although he had been disliked by many, no clear motive for his death had materialized.

Further investigation of the old Green farmhouse yielded little additional evidence. The bizarre mural remained a dilemma, as did the odd poem penned by a mysterious author named Lenore. No one had heard of a Lenore, or if they had, they did not confess it to the police. All the questioning led to more dead ends. Alvin Walker's theory that

Gavin was propelled to suicide by a drug-induced, hallucinogenic high seemed to be the most plausible explanation.

The two young detectives were finishing their tea and coffee when Molly's cell phone rang to the tone of the Lone Ranger theme as the Inspector called with the results of Gavin Green's autopsy.

"Are you sure?" Molly repeated. "That makes sense."

"What is it?" asked Kelly.

"Okay, boss, if that's what you wish. Agreed." Molly hung up the phone.

"What was that about?" Kelly asked.

"Well, it appears that our work here is done. The autopsy came back and our mysterious Mr. Green appears to have overdosed on heroin."

"So, Alvin was right. More fuel for his insatiable ego."

"Furthermore, according to the autopsy, there's no clear evidence of foul play. Cabot wants us to get back to the office and considers this case closed."

"Hmmm…I still think Green was killed. Remember what Elaine Roberts said about the police?" Kelly whispered. "She was convinced that it was a conspiracy and that Gavin was murdered."

"Yeah, and she's also the one with the biggest grudge against him while sleeping with our stud innkeeper. I'm not sure she's reliable, Kelly. I agree with Cabot. This thing's odd, but not a murder case. Look at the facts. There's no evidence of foul play. There's no motive or weapon. There's no witnesses or even suspects. This entire case is about a drugged-up nut job overdosing and falling, or jumping, into the river."

"What about the pajamas and the scraped-up bare feet? What about that strange farmhouse with the murals and countless holes in the basement? And why are the local police acting so suspiciously? We couldn't even get an interview with the Amish couple who found the body. Why? Because the local police didn't think it was worth our while. This place's strange and my sixth sense is going crazy around here. It's a mecca for the bizarre and inexplicable. My instinct tells me there's more to this case. I don't buy the freak overdose as the entire explanation. Who runs around in the middle of the night barefoot in his pajamas and ends up jumping in the river?" Kelly objected.

"He was tripping on heroin, Kelly. He OD'd. Besides, this is the same weirdo that drew satanic murals on the walls and appeared to be into the occult, while digging countless, purposeless holes in his very creepy basement. This is a clear case of serious drug abuse. I hate to admit it, but Alvin's right, and the coroner's report confirms it."

"What about that poem? Why did Alvin, our favorite local cop, want to keep that poem so badly? What's in it that's so incriminating? Who's this White Witch who's in the poem? She appears to be a legend around here. Did you notice that several people acted suspiciously when the White Witch topic came up? It was as if they knew something of this legend but didn't want to say anything. Why? What is it that they're all hiding? And who's the feared Raven in the poem? Why's this place called The Raven Inn? Coincidence? Something isn't right here," Kelly reasoned.

"I agree this entire valley's a very bizarre place. I totally agree with that. But that doesn't mean Gavin Green was murdered. If you ask me, he belonged here. He was just as crazy as the rest of 'em. For all we know, jumping into rivers at night in your pajamas is a regular ritual in this place," Molly countered.

"Well, I don't buy it. I have a strong hunch Gavin Green didn't die intentionally."

"I agree it was probably an accidental overdose, but there's no evidence that it's murder. Based on the lab results, it's ruled an accidental death by heroin overdose. He had a bad trip and ended up dead. Drugs do that to you. Don't do drugs, Kelly! Take that as a lesson.

"Very funny, Molly, but I disagree about the OD theory. Something's not right. I wouldn't be surprised if another body turned up somewhere around here."

"You've been reading too many murder mysteries," Molly replied, alluding to one of Kelly's favorite pastimes.

"Whatever. Let's agree to disagree."

"Agreed, but orders are orders, and, as lovely as the beds are in this place, I'm ready to leave." Molly called for the check.

The two detectives were in the parking lot of the inn when Molly got a second call from Inspector Cabot. "What! No way! Okay, we'll stay here until you arrive. Right."

"Now what?" Kelly asked.

"Looks like we're staying in crazy valley for a while."

"Why? No, let me guess. I was right." Kelly smiled.

"I hate that you're always right."

"I'm not always right. I just follow my instinct."

"Well, then, I hate your instinct, 'cause a couple of Amish brothers just found a second body," Molly replied, as she turned to reenter the old inn.

CHAPTER 28

When Chance Strikes Twice

Ariella was frozen in disbelief. There, sitting before her, was the barely recognizable face of the one man permanently ingrained in her memory. Yet he ignored her, as if she did not exist. Turning towards her, he spoke aloud.

"Private Jennings! Don't just stand there! Sweep up this bunker!"

Looking at her, he did not see her—his mind preoccupied. She was simply a placeholder for a distant memory that haunted him. Confused, she did not know what to do or what to say, remaining frozen in disbelief.

"Jennings, if ya wanna make it home alive, ya'd better learn to follow orders. Ya hear me? Start sweepin' this hole!" He had a frightening expression as he ordered her to action.

Not wishing to upset him further, she pretended to sweep the floor. The act seemed ridiculous, especially given the setting and the lack of a broom. Although the cave was impressively large, the floor was nothing more than packed earth and stone. A small fire provided the only light, its smoke disappearing into a large fracture in the cave's smoke-tarnished ceiling.

The layout of the subterranean living space was rather ingenious. It contained makeshift furniture crafted out of rocks and wood. A cot made of dry straw and deerskins lay in the far side of the cavernous room while the center of the space contained the fire pit defined by round stones. Dried food hung from an old rope strung across the left side of the cave. It consisted of roots, edible leaves, and cured deer meat, as well as one gutted rabbit suspended by its hind legs. Tools consisted of several knives and forks, a rusted ax, and an old shovel. These were items apparently procured from nearby farms. The entire space had a Neanderthal semblance, accentuated by the prehistoric appearance of its occupant.

Ariella had seen many strange things in her adventurous lifetime, but this was one of the oddest. It broke her heart to see him like this. He was clearly delusional, yet seemingly content in his insanity. His mind had become his world, and all that existed around him was of its definition. She reflected on how reality was nothing more than mental perception and interpretation, as she pretended to sweep the floor of this peculiar abode with her imaginary broom.

"Private, ya're a dismal failure! This outfit's a pack of losers. At attention solder! It's time for inspection," the odd man ordered.

She was afraid to try and snap him to reality. For all she knew, that could make things worse. Wisely, she decided to comply with the adamant command. Ceasing her imaginary sweeping, she stood at attention, awaiting the inspection.

"Jennings, where's yar weapon? Yar weapon's yar life. Lose yar weapon, lose yar life! Do ya understand me, ya poor excuse for a soldier? Grab yar weapon right now! AT ATTENTION!!" The filthy, crazed being bellowed with conviction and rage.

She spotted a large stick near the fire pit and grabbed it. Holding the stick against her right shoulder, she pretended it was a rifle. Thus, she stood at attention, like a child playing soldier.

He walked up to her but did not see her. He saw the illusion that his mind portrayed. He saw a young, frightened soldier who had been torn to shreds over a decade ago in a war he could not forget.

"Soldier, yar weapon, please," he asked gently. It was the first time he showed any compassion. She handed him the large stick, and he inspected the narrower end and its gnarly length. "Pathetic. Is that how ya care for yar life? I dare say that ya don't deserve it. Yar weapon's yar life, soldier. DO YOU HEAR ME?" he bellowed once more.

"Yes, sir!" she heard herself say, as her heart was breaking.

"There're three things every soldier holds dear. Do ya know what they are, private?"

"No, sir," she replied, and a small tear streamed unchecked down her left cheek.

"Well, ya'll know 'em now. Ya'll live by 'em under my command, do ya understand?"

Their eyes were fixed on each other, and she could see the lunacy in his gaze. That confirmation made her stomach churn, and her heart broke in an instant. All her deepest desires fell to the earthen floor, along with her slow stream of tears.

"Are ya crying, soldier? What kind of a pack of cowards is this? Give me twenty!" he ordered.

She just stood there and wept.

"Twenty. RIGHT NOW!!"

Without thinking, she fell to the earthen ground and began her twenty pushups, still weeping. Every other pushup, she had to wipe her tears with her muddy right hand.

"As I was saying, there're three things every soldier must never forget, must always hold dear—Mission, Duty, and Brotherhood! DO I MAKE MYSELF CLEAR, SOLDIER?" he bellowed in his imaginary world.

Ariella lay on the earthen floor in defeat, her mind spinning and her heart crushed. The dream of happiness that she had held dear, seemingly beyond hope, ended here on this earthen floor within this insane tomb. Life was indeed stranger than any dream. As she lay there, she realized that all was silent. Her crazed nightmare had ceased. Struggling to contain her emotions, she sat up only to find herself alone. He was gone, but in her heart, he had never left.

"Harry?" she called out softly. "Harry, where are you?"

There was no reply. Walking toward the entrance of the cavernous hall, she climbed up the wooden makeshift ladder just in time to see him disappear through the tight entry fissure. Giving pursuit, she caught up with him at the edge of the small clearing, just beyond the massive oak tree.

"Harry! Stop! I need to talk to you!" she exclaimed, as he walked away, seemingly deaf to her pleas. "Harry!" She ran up to him and grabbed his shoulder, which was covered with tattered clothes and grayish skins. As she did so, he turned to face her. His eyes were sad, and the desperation in them was more painful than all she had just endured. "Harry, I'll help you. I can help you."

He stopped and looked at her for what seemed like an eternity. It was apparent that his mind was in a state of complete turmoil, as his memory tried to place the woman before him.

"Harry. It's me. Remember? We were once…" She paused, giving room for her emotions to swell in a second flood of tears. "I loved you. I've always loved you. Remember?"

Maintained eye contact, she thought. Something inside her acknowledged that to look away was to lose a precious chance. He looked at her in bewilderment that slowly changed to acceptance. This gave her the impetus to continue.

"Harry, before you went away, you told me you loved me. Remember? You said you'd come back for me. Please remember? I need you to remember 'cause I'm still here waiting for you. I've always been waiting for no one else but you."

She paused again as a second wave of emotions swelled from her heart and burst forth into the sobs she could not quell. "Please remember, Harry. Please!" Standing there, she held his gaze despite the river of tears for the broken man before her and the love that had been ripped away so long ago.

His look of acceptance slowly turned to awareness and then for a brief moment to recognition. A smile fell upon his furrowed, bearded face. "Where am I?" he asked and looked around as if for the first time. Before she could reply, his attention returned to her and he uttered the words that she had sought to hear for so long. "What're you doing here, my love?"

She had broken through his walls. In her excitement, she reached out to embrace him when he pulled back as if he had seen a ghost. In his fragmented memories, she seemed like a dream—like the White Witch herself. With a jerk, he fell back and lost his footing.

"Are you okay?" she asked and fell to her knees before him.

Whether it was the fall or his fright or both, she would never know. But Harry was gone and the Captain had returned, along with his merciless, endless war.

Jumping up, he bellowed at her, "Soldier, get up and get back to your post!"

"Harry, it's me!" she cried. As she rose to her feet, her heart sank at the sight of his eyes that gazed past her. Yet, there was a visible gentleness in him as if something had changed and the shroud had been torn.

He looked about in confusion while struggling with his dual reality. Turning back to face her, his previously hostile demeanor had changed and he spoke in a soft caring voice. "This war gets to all of us. I know. Woman, I understand your fears, but tomorrow we head to the front line. So, get it out of your system."

There was hope. He recognized her as a woman. But soon even that fragment of clarity drifted into confusion. "Get it together, son. Fear will kill you." The moment was lost as he walked away. She was Private Jennings once more.

Defeated, she turned away and wept profusely all the way back to the small meadow in front of her humble cabin. There, awaiting her, was her flock of lost girls eager for her return. As she neared her home, she regained control of her emotions and fell back to her duty. She had a responsibility to those who were alive and awake. The ones who were dead or asleep, she would revisit in her dreams. With that conclusion, she forced a smile on her face and entered her home.

"Where were you, Ariella? We were starting to get worried," Anna confessed.

"I met an old friend," she answered with a sigh.

"Who?" asked Rebecca, as she set the large table for a late breakfast. The young women had waited for her to return before eating.

"One of the finest souls I've ever had the pleasure to know."

"You should have invited 'im for breakfast."

"How'd you know it was a 'him'?"

"I don't know," Anna replied.

"You're right. He's an old friend, but he's too busy saving the world from itself, although I'm afraid he appears to have lost himself in the process."

"Too bad, 'cause Marie made her famous pancakes," Rebecca replied.

Ariella sighed, reflecting on the beauty of youthful innocence and the tragedy of its inevitable loss. "I'm sure he would've loved 'em."

"Well, there's always next time," Rebecca concluded, as she finished setting the table.

"Yes. There's always next time," Ariella answered with a sigh.

CHAPTER 29

A Bizarre Discovery

Inspector Cabot was on his way to Eden Valley when he called Molly and Kelly. Soon, the three met in front of The Raven Inn.

"What's going on?" Molly asked. The Inspector had given them very little information, insisting that they would discuss it once he got there.

"Get in the car and I'll fill you in."

Molly and Kelly got in the car.

"I got a call from our favorite police chief, Gus Morgan. It appears two Amish brothers were digging in an old graveyard and discovered a body."

"Dead bodies in graveyards doesn't seem that odd," Molly observed.

"Not if they belong there, but what if they're visiting?"

"Visiting?"

"The body they found is fresh and shouldn't've been there."

"Why were they digging in a graveyard, anyway? That's creepy," Kelly added.

"I'm not sure, but we shall find out. Gus is holding the two brothers 'til we get there. At least he's doing that right. I don't trust the sergeant that works for 'im," the Inspector observed.

Before Molly or Kelly could reply, they came into view of Amos Miller's property. The large farm was a juxtaposition of cultures. It was spacious but plain consisting of a clapboard house, two barns and double grain silos—all painted in a dull white. No electrical wires led to the facility, nor were there any curtains, trucks, or tractors. All the equipment seemed to be vintage nineteenth century, down to the wooden wagons and mule-drawn plows.

This humble lifestyle had been invaded by several police cruisers, lights still flashing, and an empty ambulance which pulled out of the gravel drive as the team arrived. Just ahead of Inspector Cabot's vehicle was the coroner's truck that had replaced the departing ambulance. The entire scene looked surreal, as if modern society had discovered a portal to the past and its presence threatened it. Foreign authority and native harmony mixed on the front yard of Amos Miller's farm.

At the center of this curious convergence was the Amish farmer, himself. He sat with his brother, Linus, on the front steps of his plain house. Gus Morgan and his deputy, Sgt. Alvin Walker, were in the process of questioning the two brothers. Several other officers were walking down the steep hill behind the farm, on their way back from Drakes Plot, not readily accessible to the rear-wheel drive police cruisers.

"You don't see this every day," the Inspector observed.

"Sir?" Kelly was confused.

"An Amish murder," he replied.

"I doubt they did it," Kelly protested.

"I didn't mean to imply they did. I meant the setting. This quiet little valley's become a dangerous place. I just hope we don't have a serial killer on our hands. If we do, the FBI will be pulled into this before you know it."

"But the Green death was ruled an accident, right?" Molly asked.

"Yes, based on the evidence, but now that may need to be reevaluated."

The Inspector pulled up behind the coroner's truck, which had just arrived. As he stepped out of his vehicle, he was greeted by Frank Dunn, the chief coroner, and by his assistant, Hank Davies. "Good to see ya, Jim," Frank greeted the Inspector.

"Frank, I see ya decided to come down yourself, this time."

"Two bodies in one week for a place this size's gettin' pretty unusual. As you know, we're still finishing up the Green autopsy, but it looks like an overdose. You read my preliminary report, right?"

"Sure did. Thanks for rushin' it."

"Of course."

"Hello, sir. Hello, ladies." Hank greeted the Inspector and his team. There was a mutual pressing of hands. It was then that Chief Gus Morgan walked up to the others.

"Hello, ya all…Frank, Jim, Hank, ladies. This's become all too familiar."

"So, what do we have, Gus?" The Inspector did not waste any more time on cordialities.

"I'm not sure what to make of it. The body's fresh. I guess you can confirm that." He looked at Frank. "Male, thirties is my guess. He looks like he dug his own grave, pardon the pun." Gus chuckled. "But by the expression frozen on his face, he must've changed his mind a little too late."

"Where's the body?" asked Frank. He did not care for Gus's speculations or his inappropriate attempt at humor.

"On top of that hill's an old, abandoned cemetery. It's up there," Gus replied.

"How do I get there?" asked Frank.

"Ya walk."

"We ain't carrying all this stuff up there. That's why we have four-wheel drive," Frank replied. He was a well-respected professional who knew his trade. As a former army doctor, he rarely encountered a situation that he could not easily overcome, nor did he take fools lightly. And based on his first impressions, the local police chief had all the makings of a fool. "Let's go, Hank. Anyone want a ride?"

The Inspector looked at Molly. With a motion of his head, he urged her to join Frank at the crime scene. She jumped in the back seat of Frank's truck cab.

"We'll see you up there," Frank announced to the others and departed without further comment. Soon, his heavy-duty, four-wheel drive truck dug a set of new tracks straight up the steep hill toward Drakes Plot.

"Don't mess with Frank," the Inspector chuckled. "I see your man's interviewing the witnesses," he added.

"Yeah. He does a nice job with that. If you all have any questions for 'em, now's the time to ask, before I have to let 'em go. We got nothing on 'em, except that they found the body," Gus began to explain, but the Inspector cut him off.

"I want to talk to them directly. Kelly, please take notes."

Gus led the Inspector and Kelly to the two Amish men seated on the front steps of the farmhouse. Sgt. Alvin Walker stood in front of them, asking questions and taking his own notes. The two Amish brothers seemed tired and overwhelmed by the intense police presence.

Alvin greeted the two newcomers. It was clear that he fancied Kelly. It was equally clear that the Inspector had little regard for the junior officer, as he did not bother to acknowledge him. He had not changed his opinion of the overly ambitious and arrogant sergeant. In the Inspector's mind, the man was useless or worse. Without touching Alvin, the Inspector managed to push the sergeant out of the way by taking visible charge of the witness interviews. After brief introductions, he began, "Gentleman, I see you've had a hard day. Would you be more comfortable elsewhere?"

The Miller brothers were uncertain of the Inspector's comments. "Elsewhere" could mean anything, even the local police station.

"Na, this'll do fine," Linus replied for both.

"Okay, do you mind if I sit next to you?" The Inspector wanted to befriend these two men. Standing over them asking insinuating questions, as he suspected had been the case until now, seemed to prevent that goal.

"Go right ahead. The stoop's wide enough," Linus replied, as Amos nodded his head.

"Do you both own this farm?" the Inspector asked, as he sat down next to Amos.

The question was followed by a chuckle from both men. "I own it," Amos replied, proudly.

"Beautiful place. What a setting. I live in a townhouse. What I'd give for this view." The Inspector looked around at the beautiful scenery.

Meanwhile, Alvin grew annoyed. The brashness of the intruder and his "take-charge" attitude did not sit kindly with the young officer. However, he feared the Inspector and wished to endear himself to this man of authority. Thus, he did not object verbally. His body language did that for him. Turning his back to the Inspector, he walked over to Gus, his boss. "That little guy's got gall. Did you see how he barged in on my interviews? Now, he's talking about the scenery. He'll be discussing the weather next," Alvin puffed. "Why'd you call him in here?"

"Look, Alvin, I know you're an ambitious guy, and that's good, but this is beyond us," Gus replied. Unlike Alvin, he had little ambition and liked his easy, quiet job. He hoped to push this off on the State Police and return to warming his chair at the station.

The animosity between Alvin and Gus was beginning to grow. At its root was this difference in ambitions and goals. Angry that his boss did not support him, Alvin walked away in disgust.

"Yeah. Fall's the nicest time of year," Linus replied. Amos remained silent.

"It's a great time of year. The weather's perfect," the Inspector added.

Overhearing the last comment, Alvin shook his head in frustration as he headed up the steep hill toward Drakes Plot.

After several more minutes of small talk, the Inspector finally came around to his intended purpose. By this time, he had both Miller brothers talking about farming, and the entire atmosphere had transformed from an official police interview to a friendly chat. "So, why were you guys digging up there?" he asked.

Linus decided to answer. He and the Inspector were closer in age and a trust was building between them. "Well, it'z like t'is. Amos'z dog waz all upset und barkin' at the top of the hill, so Amos went to have a look und discovered that someone'z been diggin' up Drakes Plot." He pointed in the direction of the steep hillside. "Like we told the other fella, Drakes Plot's abandoned. There ain't been a new grave up there in my lifetime. What'z more—" He was about to mention that his old tools were there, when he determined that this might not be wise. Therefore, he paused mid-sentence, which left everyone in anticipation.

Amos picked up on this and came to the rescue of his older brother. "What'z more's I saw strange going'z on up there. I saw a strange woman in white standin' over that grave."

"Tell me more about that," the Inspector inquired. Amos described what he saw, but he downplayed the apparitional aspects of the sighting, making the figure seem alive rather than the contrary. He started to doubt his own perception of the odd sightings. After all, real or unreal, describing ghost sightings was bound to sit poorly with the State Police. Besides, he did not believe in the White Witch, so to describe her as such would be hypocrisy.

"Interesting. This woman stood over the fresh grave and then simply ran off into the woods?" the Inspector asked, still baffled. *Do Amish folks lie?* he wondered. *They're humans, after all. Why wouldn't they lie?*

"Yes. She disappear'd in the woodz."

"Did you get a good look at her? Was she anyone you recognized?"

This was the question that Amos had dreaded. He was about to confess that it might be the White Witch, when he decided to repress his opinion. "No. I didn't," he replied.

"Was she the White Witch?" Kelly interjected. The sound of her voice and the nature of the question stunned Amos. In his shock, he muttered, "It might've been."

Furrowing his brows, the Inspector looked at Kelly before addressing the witnesses. "So, who's this White Witch?"

Amos had no desire to explore the subject. Linus, on the other hand, was fascinated by the topic. "She'z just an ol' legend in theze parts — just an ol' legend. Some sayz she'z a ghost of Evelyn Drake. I don't think much of it all, but it'z true that ol' Evelyn's got the very grave where that pur fella'z buried. It'z strange. Not the kind of stuff we're usez to 'round 'ere."

"Are you telling me that you saw a ghost over the grave in question, and that's why you both dug it up a day later?" The Inspector was starting to wonder about the two seemingly normal farmers.

"I'm the undertaker for our community," Linus began, "und that plot'z Amish land. I'z simply making sure no one'z disturbin' them graves. Amos waz helping me, given that it'z on his land. Our intentionz were to dig down a couple feet und stop. Which'z what we did, but we found the hand stickin' out. Crazy thing. So, we stopped und called the sheriff."

The Inspector understood that response, but the White Witch sighting was far more interesting.

"I see, Mr. Miller. You were simply following your duty as the local undertaker and helping your brother, here."

"Yez, zir," Linus replied. He had intentionally turned up the Amish accent during all his responses. It was a strategy that had often served him well when dealing with the English.

"Did you see this witch ghost, as well?" he asked Linus.

"No, zir. Never seen 'er in my life."

"I see. Very well. I assume we have your contact information." He looked about the Amish farm and its lack of electricity, and wondered how such a lifestyle was still possible, let alone desirable.

"Yez, zir. The other fella got all that," Linus replied.

"Thank you, Gentleman. I think we're done."

"Thank you," the Miller brothers said in unison.

They got up and were about to enter Amos's house, when the Inspector stopped them with one more question. "One last item. You mentioned that your dog found the grave. When was that?"

"Yesterday mornin' 'round seven," Amos replied, standing in his doorway.

"Prior to that, when's the last time you were at Drakes Plot? Either of you?"

"It'z been years for me," Linus replied.

"I waz there about five dayz ago," Amos answered.

"Did you see anything unusual five days ago?"

"No, zir. There'z no new grave up there five days ago. I'm certain of that 'cause I walked right through there on my way to…" Amos paused.

"On your way where, Mr. Miller?"

"To the woodz. I go huntin' there. It'z my property."

"I see. Thank you, Gentleman."

"Sure," Amos replied and closed the door. He was not in the house more than two minutes before he heard a knock. When he opened his front door, he saw the Inspector standing there once more. "Yez, Inspector."

"Do you know a woman named Lenore?"

Amos turned white and could not answer. Linus, standing behind him, answered for him. "No. We don't."

"Thank you. I always forget a question or two — age creepin' in." The Inspector chuckled and departed.

Amos closed the door and sat at the kitchen table. "Why'd you lie?" he asked.

"Last thin' we need'z the English police digging 'round lookin' for Lenore," Linus replied.

"He knew ya lied. I could tell on his face. Ya think this haz to do with Lenore?"

"I doubt it. It'z clear she just fell into the creek. This iz different."

"What 'bout that English fella Esther and Abel found dead in the creek? What if there'z a killer runnin' 'bout 'ere? He could've pushed 'er and wanted 'er dead. I need to protect 'er. We've gotta warn 'er. She needz to remember what happened to 'er. Linus, this iz seriouz."

Linus was silent. He simply sat down at the rustic kitchen table and sighed.

"What iz it?" Amos asked.

"I think I know who'z done t'iz."

CHAPTER 30

Spilled Milk

Lenore was beginning to settle into her Amish lifestyle. The pace and the setting seemed comfortable and deeply familiar, although her memory refused to release its secrets. Meticulously, she had begun to rebuild her history one question at a time. Fortunately, the Lapp family seemed infinitely patient with her, being content to have her back. Nonetheless, Lenore felt robbed of her identity, forced to rely on the people around her to define her. She felt like a blank slate that had previously held a detailed picture—now erased. Desperately, she tried to recall this lost picture, sensing its outlines below the surface of her mind. Frustratingly, every time she got close to recalling something of importance, it slipped back into the merciless void of amnesia.

Today would be different. It was the beginning of the slow process of healing and, more importantly, of remembering.

On this day, Mary asked Lenore to help with the milking. The idea of extracting milk out of a large creature seemed rather daunting to Lenore, but something inside her calmed her fears. "Sure, Mother. I'll give it a try, but ya'll have to teach me."

Mary wanted to respond, *Lenore, don't be silly. Ya've milked cows since ya were five,* but she refrained. Rather, she replied, "There'z nothin' to it. Just sit right here und grab two teats. I'll show ya."

Lenore did as instructed. At first, the feel of the large fleshy extensions of the bovine's swelled udder made her squeamish. When she finally attempted the task, a subconscious familiarity surfaced and she began to milk the cow like an old farm hand. "It'z easy," she observed.

A combination of all the familiar sensations associated with the daily task that was such a common part of her previous Amish life, awakened her memory. As she sat there, the feel of the teats, the sound of the rhythmic squirting into the stainless-steel pail, and the smell of the fresh milk worked their magic. For the first time since her accident, Lenore clearly remembered a part of her past. She was about to stop milking and rejoice in her success, when something deeper warned her to continue, undisturbed. Her memories kept coming as did the milk. The two seemed combined, filling both the empty milk bucket and Lenore's empty past.

By the time the cow was milked, Lenore no longer lacked an identity. She was Lenore Lapp, an Amish girl who had spent countless mornings milking the cows and doing her chores on the family farm. She remembered her family, for she was back at the age of seven. It was the day of her seventh birthday and she was so excited. There was one thing that she had always desired—a puppy. Any puppy would do if it was her puppy. For the past two years on her March birthday, she asked for a puppy. But until now the result had been the same—no puppy appeared.

But this year would be different. She could feel it. This would be the year and this would be the greatest day of her young life. Excited, she could hardly focus on the milking or on anything at all. Even her breath was short and fast, like the tempo with which she did her morning chores. There was a birthday ritual in her large Amish family that the one or two gifts that were exchanged on such a special day were exchanged after dinner. She could not wait for dinner. *Why can't this day go by faster? It takes forever. Everything takes so long,* she thought, as she moved to the next cow. It was hard to rush milking. It had its own pace that demanded adherence and respect. Even on this day, she had to relinquish her eagerness for the serenity of the process.

Now, sitting there, next to the cow, Lenore remembered that special seventh birthday. What a magical day that was! Later that day would come the greatest moment in her childhood, the day that she received her puppy. That puppy was old now. As she glanced at him, he stood up and licked her leg but she remained still, lost in the wonderful sensation of an actual memory. She savored every moment of that seventh birthday as if it were endless, and in her mind, it could be, for now she could recall it at will. The power was exhilarating.

"Lenore, what iz it? Are ya all right, my dear?" Mary asked, noticing that Lenore had stopped milking and sat motionless on the stool.

"Yes, *Mater!* You ARE my *mater!* I remembered!" she jumped up in joy, tipping over the full milking pail, which went unnoticed. "You ARE my *mater,* und this iz my home. Cody, I love you. You ARE my dog!" The dog appreciated the attention and jumped toward her, wagging his tail. "I love you, *Mater.*" Lenore embraced Mary.

Mary was speechless while embracing her daughter with all her heart as tears rolled down her cheeks. *Thank you, Lord!* she repeated silently over and over again. She held that embrace, unable to let go. "I'll never lose ya again. No, not ever again. No! No! No! Thank you, Lord," she whispered, while still embracing her precious child.

It was an overpowering reunion. The emotional embrace spurred further memories within Lenore's fragmented mind. Now, she remembered her mother holding her tight. In this memory, she was only six years old. Her mother kept whispering, "Thank you, Lord" repeatedly, as she did presently. Those early memories were flooding her mind now. Then, as now, she had been scared, finding safety in her mother's arms. In those arms, she was home. *Home was best! Of all places, home was best!* She remembered thinking that very thought at the age of six.

Now, it flooded her emotions once again. She remembered her father standing next to her mother. He too embraced his six-year-old girl. "Don't ya ever run up there again. It'z not safe. It'z not a place for a child. Ya had us so worried, Lenore. Thank the Lord, ya're okay." That memory seems so vivid, as if he were standing before her now.

Mary finally released her embrace. "Ya memory'z returnin'. Thank the Lord! He workz miracles. What'd ya remember, my dear? Come, tell me everything. The cowz can wait a little while, und don't worry about the spilled milk. We'll clean it up later. Ya *fader'll* be so excited. He loves ya so much. Ya brothers and sisters'll be relieved that ya remember them. Ya do remember 'em, don't ya?" Mary was so excited that she left all the milk in the barn, including the spilled pail, and walked away holding her daughter's hand.

"I remember you und *Dat* und Cody und Josef und Kate und Eve. I remember everyone!" Lenore exclaimed.

"What about Mathew, Melinda, und little Ali?" Mary asked eagerly.

Lenore crinkled her brow in confusion. She did not remember her past with the younger Lapp children. With seven children and one on the way, it was a sizable family to remember. "I don't remember them. I mean, I remember 'em from now, but not from before." She sounded apologetic.

Mary did not want Lenore to lose her new-found excitement. She quickly added, "My dear, this iz exciting. Ya remember. The rest'll come. I know it. Ya'll remember everything." But as soon as she made that prediction, a fear churned in Mary's stomach. *What if she does remember everything? What then?*

"I remember the day I got Cody," Lenore shared. The faithful dog heard his name and let out a bark, wagging his tail in triumph.

"That waz yar seventh birthday, my dear."

"Well, I remember it und all that happened before it, includin' when I got lost und came back. You und *Dat* were so happy to see me."

"Ah, yez, ya had uz so scared. Ya 'ere only six, und we couldn't find ya for hours. Finally, young Amos Miller..." she paused. She had not wanted to say that name.

"What happen'd, *Mater?* Why'd you stop?"

"Oh, nothin'. Nothin'. Ya'd run off und he brought ya back."

"He saved me? How romantic." Lenore chuckled. She was so pleased that her memory was returning.

"Hardly, ya 'ere a child. Anyway, he found ya und brought ya home. I'll always be grateful for that."

"Where'd he find me? I remembered a place wi't ruins und old headstones."

"Ah, it waz long ago und I'd rather not talk about it. Can we change the subject?"

"Please, *Mater!* I need to know my memory's real. Where waz it?"

"Let's not talk about it or old Amos Miller." Mary emphasized the word "old." She had no desire to help Lenore remember her relationship with Amos, for she feared that history would repeat itself.

"Please tell me, *Mater*. Waz it a place with ol' ruins und ol' creepy headstones? Is that why Papa told me never to go there again?"

"I don't know what he told ya, but it'z an evil place."

"What'z it called?"

"Oh, if ya must know, it'z called Drakes Plot. It'z an ol' cemetery. That'z all."

"I remember a spooky lady in a flowing white dress. Is there a spooky lady in white who lives there?"

The comment took Mary aback, for she had never believed the child at the time of her presumed sighting, and surely did not want to raise stories of specters at a joyous time like this, or any time for that matter. But she felt torn. If she negated the memory, it might trigger doubt in her daughter at a time when she needed her support. Yet if she agreed to the validity of the memory, more questions would arise about the legend of the White Witch, a topic she wished to avoid. Fortunately, she was saved from her dilemma by the lunch bell that her second-oldest daughter rang to call the family together upon hearing of Lenore's great news.

Within seconds the large kitchen filled with Lapp children, and Lenore's childhood encounter with the White Witch was soon forgotten—replaced by a jubilant celebration of Lenore's true return to the great Lapp clan.

CHAPTER 31

Elaine

The Raven Inn had finished serving lunch when Sam Hughes retired to his office on the second floor. Like a time capsule, his office was decorated exactly as his father had left it, being the one portion of the old inn that Sam had left completely unchanged. His relationship with his deceased father had always been a roller coaster of egos and emotions. The two men spent a significant amount of Sam's adult life estranged. Like the two alpha males that they personified, there never seemed to be enough room to house them both. Only after his father's death did Sam come to terms with the man he most resembled. What he could not express while his father was alive he sealed in this room, which became a memorial to the old man.

Covered with '70s wooden paneling and the decor to match, the office was peppered with plaques and hunting trophies on the walls, which included several large deer racks and the mounted head of an angry black bear. That same bear had rummaged through the trash for years, until the night old Conrad Hughes shot it from the window of his office—this office. His old rifle hung next to it, as if the two were forever linked.

The room had a stale smell of ancient tobacco that had permeated the worn brown shag carpet. A vintage stereo with a turntable and large boxed speakers sprawled across a tarnished shelf, along with eight-track tapes, countless country music cassettes, and dog-eared record albums. Yellowed baseball caps adorned the wall opposite the double window, which overlooked the rear parking lot and the trash containers. The entire place looked like a throwback to 1975, and Sam liked it that way because that was his birthyear.

Presently, Sam sat in the shabby office processing bills and restocking supplies, when he heard a soft knock on the door. He looked up at the small clock on his desk, the one with the numbers that flipped like plastic playing cards. Three of the numbers had just flipped simultaneously to reveal three o'clock in the afternoon.

"Who is it? It's open!" he yelled.

In response, the office door slowly opened, revealing a young woman.

Sam's stomach knotted at the sight of her. She had always had that effect on him. "Come in," he barely managed to utter.

"Sorry to disturb you, but we need to talk."

"Yeah, sure. Sit down. What's on your mind?" he offered.

She had a natural grace and elegance that seemed too innate to be the product of training. A sense of mystery permeated her very being. Nothing about her appeared normal or transparent, especially not her piercing blue eyes. Those eyes had him transfixed as she settled into the worn leather chair opposite his desk.

"What is it, Elaine?"

"I heard the details of Gavin's death. I hope he didn't suffer. I'm scared there's something out there. I know it sounds crazy, but all this talk of ghosts and witches has me worried."

"Oh, Elaine, they're just old wives' tales. They're nothin' but people's imaginations gone wild. Half the guys at the bar drink themselves nearly senseless, and then wonder why they're hearing and seeing things. I don't believe any of it and neither should you."

Elaine's eyes bore into his, leaving him helpless. "There's more to it. Gavin told me more." She shivered visibly at the thought.

Sam wanted to walk around the desk and comfort her, but he knew it was inappropriate. After all, she was his employee. Although he refrained, his interest in her showed in his eyes. He hoped she did not know, but she knew. Elaine, a highly desirable woman, was aware of her powers, sensing her boss's unspoken wish to be more than just her employer. But she had been down that road before and had np desire to risk a good job and cheap rent to satisfy another man's fantasies. She was too smart for that, despite her young age.

"What did he tell you?" Sam leaned over the desk, as if he wanted to leap over it to be closer to her. Ignoring his body language, she focused on her story.

"Two nights before he died, he told me 'bout the White Witch—he'd seen her twice near Devils Bridge. When he spoke, he sounded weird, like he was possessed or somethin'—he was so into 'er. The way he talked, he scared me. He said he knew her like she was real. He was infatuated with 'er. It was weird."

"Gavin was a strange guy, and the police say he was on drugs, which might explain it. God only knows what went on in his twisted head," Sam replied. Although he had taken pity on Gavin and provided him with a dishwasher job, he had begun to distrust him.

"But I heard rumors the White Witch killed 'im. The police won't allow anyone near the old Green place, but some kids got a good look anyway. They say the place's creepy. They say Gavin kept a mural of the White Witch on his bedroom wall. I guess they snuck a peek when the cops weren't watching. They say the place's like a temple to her. It's scary. We know people, and yet we don't really know 'em." She looked at him as if to ask him his secret.

He was uncomfortable with her probing eyes and broke eye contact.

So, he's got a secret or two, as well, she perceptively concluded. It was then that she decided not to have anything personal to do with her boss. Upon this conclusion, she brought her legs close together and pulled her skirt well over her knees.

"Like I said, Gavin was a weirdo. I wouldn't worry about any ghosts or witches, Elaine. That's ridiculous! Is that why you came to see me?" He seemed annoyed by the topic.

"I just wanted to know if you heard anything?" She resolved not to confide in him. Gavin Green's sexual attack on her in the restaurant wine cellar would remain her secret and no comforting from Sam would materialize. After all, if there was no future for them, why would she risk his pity? Her pride would not allow that kind of embarrassment. She would tough it out, like she did with everything and everyone in her life.

"No, I haven't," he replied and sat back in his worn leather chair, no longer exuding a yearning for her.

"Okay. Well, I gotta get back to work," she said in a terse tone, rising from her seat while lowering her skirt. Their conversation had transformed from words to body language.

Elaine's sudden emotional and physical withdrawal alarmed Sam. He recalled Linda Taylor's odd warning regarding this young woman. *Is she really who she seems to be, or is Linda's description true?* He wanted to ask her about Andrew Taylor, but decided that it was best to avoid the potentially controversial subject.

Thus, the two departed with a growing distance between them.

CHAPTER 32

Interred

$\mathcal{M}$olly walked up to the open grave at Drakes Plot and recoiled in horror. The partially unearthed victim seemed to scream out at her in the desperation frozen on his lifeless face. Most prominent was the partially outstretched right arm, with its fingers ripped raw by his futile attempt to reach oxygen—finding death instead.

"Was he buried alive?" she asked naively of Frank, the coroner.

"Apparently. Given the expression and the torn fingers, he certainly didn't enjoy his final moments," Frank replied callously. To him, death was job security. In his thirty years on the police force, he had seen it all. Looking beyond the grotesque, he was simply interested in clues to the cause of death. After exchanging some small talk with Gus Morgan, he and his assistant Hank got to work. Together, they carefully exhumed the body. With Alvin's help, they laid it on a stretcher. Then, they began the field forensic work and preparations for the body's transfer to their Brennantown laboratory.

Molly, fascinated by the process, asked many questions that softened Frank's stark demeanor. "When did he die?"

"I'd say it was probably two nights ago, given the lack of decomposition, except the decay in the eyes. That's why they seem so gray and bulging. It's also evidence of suffocation, suggesting that the likely cause of death was asphyxia due to interment," Frank replied. He liked the curious young detective.

"Who is he?" she asked.

"No idea. He's got no ID. We'll try prints since some are still intact."

"You think it's related to the Gavin Green death?"

"Honey, that's your job to figure out, but we'll do our best to help you. I'd say that either it is, or this is the unluckiest little village in Pennsylvania."

Kelly and the Inspector arrived on the scene. They had decided to walk up the hill, rather than risk getting the Inspector's car stuck in the ruts left by the coroner's truck. Hank was collecting lab samples, while Frank and Molly were talking to Gus. The Inspector joined the conversation, while Molly stepped out to talk to Kelly. Alvin had been curiously quiet the entire time. He hovered around Gus, acting bored, as if he had seen it all before. His behavior struck Molly as odd, but then Alvin was always odd.

"You won't believe it, Kelly. It looks like the guy was buried alive. It's awful." She led Kelly to the body.

As Kelly looked down at the victim, she fell back and covered her mouth. "Oh, my God! I know him."

CHAPTER 33

An Overactive Imagination

"What do ya mean ya know the killer?" Amos asked his brother in disbelief, as they sat facing each other across the small kitchen table.

"'Cause there's only one person it could be."

"Who? Certainly not one of us?"

"No, don't be foolish. We're pacifists. Did ya forget?" Linus replied.

"Never mind. But don't ya start with the White Witch stuff. I've had enough of that. For a while I believed it, und now that Inspector thinks I'm nuts," Amos objected.

"No. There's no witch. She's just in yar head."

"But I swear I saw a woman up there. She waz in a white dress und looked ghostly. Otto saw 'er too. He was barkin' at her und whimperin'. Someone was there."

"Dogs bark at shadows. Ya know that. Ya honestly think ya saw a woman up there in a white dress?"

"Und a bizarre raven, too. I swear he had yellow eyes, but that could've been just the sun reflecting from his eyes."

"Ya haven't been drinking, have ya? Ya know it's against the rules," Linus warned. He was beginning to worry about his brother's sanity.

"Ya ask'd me already und the answer's still 'No.' Ya und the rules. I'd never had a drink in my life. Look, either there's a woman up there in a white dress or…I don't know. But I'm sick of this White Witch nonsense, even though I may've seen her."

"Ya're making no sense, little brother."

"Ya think it's her? Ya think the White Witch's the killer, don't ya? I don't believe in that curse or the legend of a treasure buried up there. I don't know who made it up, but I don't believe it." Amos shook his head for emphasis.

"I don't believe it either. I don't think no witch did it. I think the hermit did it. I've seen 'im in these woods und he's a scary fellow. Nobody dares talk to 'im 'cause he's crazy as a loon. I hear he's got a war going on in his head. That's what they say, anyway." Linus focused on Amos as he revealed his suspicions.

"Is that who ya think did it?"

"Yaz. I'm certain of it."

Amos sighed and shook his head. "Ya don't have a clue. That ol' guy's harmless, except he steals my chickens und corn. I even leave 'im food to find. I know 'im 'cause he comes 'round here a lot, but he's as harmless as they come… crazy for sure, but harmless."

"Ya know 'im?"

"Yaz. He comes over here about every two weeks und grabs some-thin'. The first I saw 'im waz soon after I bought the place. He scared me half to death. It waz late one evening, und I was plowin' the north field when a man dressed in skins come creepin' out of the woods, talkin' as if he'd a band of men with 'im. He sounded like he was leadin' an ambush or something. I just watch'd 'im as he pretended my horse fence was covered with barbed wire. He crawled under it, shoutin' something about gunfire. I felt bad for 'im. He ended up attackin' my chicken house with a big stick.

"I went over to stop 'im, but he was like an overgrown, filthy kid. He had the stick in one hand und pinecones in the other. When I got near 'im, he pretended he waz shootin' at me with the stick. Then, he started throwin' pinecones at me pretendin' they's were hand grenades. Poor guy. He's insane al'right, but he's harmless. He scared some of the chickens from layin' the next mornin', but that was the worst of it.

"I felt sorry for 'im, so I let 'im have some eggs. I do that sometimes—let 'im have some eggs, or even one of the ol' hens that ain't layin' no more. He'z grateful too, if he'z not mumblin' of war. It'z sad what war can do to people. That'z one good reason to stay Amish—no fightin' in warz. He's harmless—crazy, but harmless."

"The friendz ya keep, Amos. No wonder Lenore left ya."

"That's a cheap shot, Linus."

"I'z kiddin'. That didn't come out right."

"Ya don't think she'z comin' back to me, do ya? Well, I'm gonna prove ya wrong, und if there'z somebody out there tryin' to harm Lenore, he'll have to get through me first. I'm gonna protect her."

"How're ya gonna do that? She doesn't seem to know ya."

"Oh, she will. Ya wait und see."

Linus sighed. He was starting to think that his brother was becoming delusional with grief. *He probably imagined everything he says he saw up at Drakes Plot.*

"Amos, come stay with us for a while. Ya need some rest und good food. The kidz'll love to see ya."

"Thanks, but I gotta stay here. Why, with them English digging up my farm, I ain't about to abandon it."

"Okay, but I'll be back to check on ya. I'd better head home und tell Melinda all about this."

The brothers parted. One wondered about the mental health of the other, while the other wondered about what he had seen. *Was it just my imagination?* Amos thought as he closed the front door.

CHAPTER 34

Evidence of Murder

"Kelly, who is it?" Molly appeared shocked at Kelly's apparent recognition of the victim.

"Don't you know?"

"No. I don't," Molly replied. "Am I supposed to?"

"He's the bartender at The Raven Inn."

"Oh, my God! You're right. We saw him there the first night. He served us drinks." Molly finally remembered. "Watered-down drinks, too."

"Maybe that's why someone killed 'im," Kelly replied. She was not squeamish around dead bodies, unlike Molly.

"That's not funny, Kelly. Look at the poor guy."

"He doesn't look happy, that's for sure. What'd you find out from Frank?"

"I'll tell you later. We'd better tell the boss who this guy is."

With Kelly's revelation, they all huddled around the body.

"You're right. I didn't recognize 'im covered with dirt and all, but that's Will Porter all right. What the hell's he doing up here dead?" Gus proclaimed.

Alvin remained oddly silent. Even the Inspector wondered why the arrogant deputy seemed so mousy. But he was glad not to have to suffer Alvin's deductions and proclamations.

"I hadn't looked at the body until now. When I got up here, only the one hand and the top of the head were showin'. You didn't catch it either, did ya, Alvin. You're slippin'," Gus teased.

"I hadn't examined the body until now," Alvin objected. There was visible tension between Alvin and his superior officer. Gus's teasing seemed like a cheap shot. The silence that followed spelled trouble between the two men. The Inspector and his team picked up on it but no one said a word. Molly and Kelly simply looked at each other and smiled. Neither liked the arrogant young deputy.

"Well, that's very interesting, isn't it Gus?" The Inspector walked around the open grave.

"What do you mean, Jim?" the police chief replied.

"Well, we've got ourselves a man interred alive in what appears to be a historical grave of one Evelyn Drake. He appeared to have been digging up the grave prior to his death, probably lookin' for something."

"How do you know he dug the grave?" Gus played Watson to the Inspector's Sherlock Holmes.

"Look at the shape of the hole. It's narrow and deep. In fact, it penetrates the rotted old casket. Frank told me that the victim had his left foot trapped in the rotted casket. He stepped through the top of it," the Inspector said.

"That still doesn't prove he was the one digging."

"He was digging because Frank found a broken shovel next to him, and because he had recent sores on his hands compatible with the task. The credit goes to Frank. He's very perceptive. He's done this a lot," the Inspector added. Molly and Kelly were fascinated by the Inspector's power of deduction. He decided to include them in his Socratic teaching.

"Molly, what's the one thing that strikes you the most about this homicide?"

"The fact that the victim was buried alive."

"How do we know this, Kelly?"

"I missed Frank's explanation," Kelly objected.

"Forget Frank's explanation or anyone else's. Trust only the scene and your power of observation," he insisted.

"Well, the expression on his face is one of horror, and I noticed that he had dirt in his mouth. I also noticed the hands were worn, as if he was fighting to dig himself out."

"Good. Very good. See, you don't need anyone else to tell you."

"The other piece of evidence is the bulging eyes, which suggest suffocation, per Frank's observations," Molly added.

Gus was bored. He found the discussion morbid and wished he could escape this makeshift class. Finally, he came up with an excuse. "It's all very fascinating. I'm glad it's in good hands. I'd better find Alvin. He seemed to have wandered off somewhere," he summarized, as if he were looking for a lost dog. "Jim, ladies, I'll see you at the station."

"Okay, Gus. We'll stop by after we're done here," the Inspector replied, aware of Gus's aversion to detective work.

Gus quickly walked away, happy to be returning to the comfort of his office.

"Strange fellow," Molly observed, when Gus was out of earshot.

"Yes, but that's for another time. Kelly, please take plenty of pictures. I want a close up of the body, including the hands, mouth and lacerations before Hank finishes preparing it for transport."

"Yes, sir."

"But first, let's finish our observation session. Molly, if in fact the victim was interred alive, was it accidental?"

"I guess it could be," Molly replied, shrugging her shoulders.

"Kelly, any thoughts?"

"Yeah, it could be that when he got his foot trapped in the rotted casket, he tried to free himself and panicked. In his panic, he disturbed the surrounding soil, and it all caved in on him."

"Molly is that theory feasible?" the Inspector asked, as he continued to look about the excavation.

"No. According to the two Amish brothers, the soil on the grave was mounded. If it were a cave-in, it would be sunken."

"Good. What else?"

"The walls of the excavation seem solid, except along the one side. That would suggest that a partial cave-in might have occurred, enough to trap the victim, but not enough to bury him."

"Very good. What else? Your turn, Kelly. Look around. Keep looking and see, not just look, but see." The Inspector loved to teach his team. He was well regarded as a teacher; he had taught many of the best detectives in the State Police.

"I see it!" she exclaimed in excitement and youthful energy. "The soil is backwards."

Molly looked at her with furrowed brows, as if to say, "What?"

"Go on," the Inspector encouraged.

"I mean that if you look at the soil that was dug out of the grave first, right here," she pointed to the pile that was dug by the two Miller brothers, "it's sandy white, like the soil in the bottom on the soil column, around the rotted casket. The reddish clay soil that's at the top of the undisturbed sides of the excavation appears to be much lower down in the fill within the pit."

"Why does that matter?" Molly asked.

"Because, if it was a simple cave-in, the soil would have settled in the same sequence as it appears naturally," Kelly explained.

"Not if the top caved in first?" Molly objected.

Kelly was stumped and had no clear answer.

"Go on, Kelly. You're on the right track," the Inspector urged her, but she ran out of ideas and remained silent.

"Your detective instinct was correct, but you overlooked one thing. You said it and saw it, but didn't register its significance. The soil around the casket is sandy, but the soil above it is clay rich. If a cave-in would've occurred, it would have been triggered by the loose sand around the casket caving into the void of the casket, and the walls would have settled or slid down maintaining the natural soil column sequence. That happened partially, right here." He pointed at part of the excavation.

"Here's the partial cave-in that trapped the victim. But, as you correctly observed, Kelly, the soil that killed the victim started the sequence again. Thus, a second layer of white, sandy soil appears much higher in the fill than in the original undisturbed soil column. Thus, it must have come from the previously excavated soil pile that was subsequently deposited on top of the victim. Based on the evidence at the scene, we can deduce that Mr. Will Parker was murdered."

"Porter, not Parker," Molly corrected.

"That's what I meant. But something still bothers me. The shovel buried in the grave is broken. The upper handle's missing. Where is it? Also, where's the shovel used to bury him? And why did Will Parker…I mean Porter…dig here in the first place? For that matter, why did the two Amish brothers dig here? Given that I don't buy the White Witch story, something made all of them dig here. Why Evelyn Drake's grave? Why now? What're they looking for and what're they hiding?" the Inspector questioned.

"You suspect the brothers? They're Amish," Molly objected.

"I suspect everyone — Amish or not," he replied.

"I suspected someone else," Molly countered.

"Who?" the Inspector asked.

"The one person who looked straight at the victim's face multiple times and didn't recognize him—except that he did recognize him but wasn't about to admit it."

"I agree that he's increasingly more suspicious and suspiciously absent, but he has no motive and a clean record," the Inspector objected.

"Alvin Walker, I presume," Kelly added.

Eden Valley, Pennsylvania

CHAPTER 35

Who Are You?

Midnight had come and gone as Amos lay awake. The coroner and the police had long since departed, taking the victim's body and volumes of documentation with them. Gone were the lights, the police dogs, the countless vehicles, and the uniformed personnel. All fell silent, except a persistent owl. It proclaimed the loss of innocence, for Amos's farm seemed permanently violated. This uneasy feeling left him wondering and wandering about the empty house in the wee hours of morning. His misery and his faithful dog, Otto, followed him about like silent shadows until two o'clock when he finally fell asleep.

As the moon floated peacefully above the quiet Amish fields, the owl gazed down upon a dark figure holding a long shovel. Fall was in the air and some of the eager leaves were already parting from the limbs of the gnarly trees. A chilling breeze foretold of winter, carrying the sweet smell of oak burning in the farmhouses below the haunted hill.

The man with the shovel seemed at ease with the excavated grave of Evelyn Drake and the yellow caution tape that surrounded it. He did not step near it; he knew what he would find there, or rather what was no longer there. A cloud covered the moon and darkness poured in behind it. The owl questioned the foreign figure with an unanswered "Who?" Who dares come out there in the middle of the night to dig in a cursed cemetery? Who?

A dog barked at the nearby farmhouse. It was Amos's dog, Otto, but his master slept soundly. In answer, another dog barked from across the valley. All else fell silent, except the slow, steady sound of the shovel and the occasional inquiry of the owl. "Who dares disturb the dead?" questioned the solemn night bird. "Hoo? Hoo? Who?"

As if in answer, the dark form pulled a hood over his head to hide the face he wished to conceal. The digging continued with little pause, as if time were critical to the disturbing task. It continued until it stopped.

Minutes later, the dark figure fell to his knees as he probed the hole. Rising, he looked about in confusion, doubting his location—or did he doubt his task? He looked up at the old headstone, illuminating it with a small flashlight. Barely visible on the weathered headstone was the name of its occupant. "This is the spot," he muttered to himself, and began to shovel further, while the owl continued to question him. "Who? Who dares disturb the dead? Hoo? Hoo? Who?"

As the hole grew in depth, the digging slowed. Once more the mysterious figure stopped and prodded the bottom of the hole with the end of the long shovel handle as if he had lost something or someone. "Who?" asked the lone bird. "Who?"

Turned in the direction of the curious bird, he finally acknowledged the question. "Not 'who' but 'what,' you cursed bird! Satan, what have you done with it?" He questioned the owl as if it were the Evil One, himself. In his head echoed a disturbing thought. *You'll never find it 'cause the Satan is you.*

As if on cue, the owl rose out of the tree, circled the dark form, and disappeared into the haunting, misty woods. The mysterious figure probed some more, but in vain. Later that night, when the moon came out from behind the clouds, it illuminated a newly dug hole over the ancient grave of Arthur Drake, the once murdered pirate and Evelyn's husband. Next to the excavation, lay a small, tattered remnant of a fine white cloth, along with a discarded shovel that bore the initials "LM."

CHAPTER 36

Cheryl

At six o'clock that morning, Inspector Cabot, Molly, and Kelly met in the breakfast room of The Raven Inn. For the time being, the Inspector had decided to set up field headquarters at the inn. He anticipated continuing the investigation over the next several days or weeks.

A server in her mid-twenties entered behind them and quickly began to set tables with silverware and napkins.

"Are we too early?" the Inspector asked, checking his watch.

"No. Sit down anywhere you like. I've got coffee brewing," she replied.

The Inspector selected a table in the rear of the room. It had a view of the meadow, west of the inn. As they sat down, the waitress ran up with the place settings. "Sorry about that. I haven't gotten back here, yet. Here're the menus. My name's Cheryl. Would you like some coffee?"

"Sure. I'll take a cup. Black," the Inspector replied.

"I'll take one, as well. Cream, no sugar," Kelly requested. "Thank you, Cheryl."

"I'll have a cup of Earl Grey tea," Molly said, locking eyes with the server.

The latter quickly turned away. The reaction surprised Kelly. "Cheryl, do you work here most mornings?" She decided to dig deeper.

Cheryl was taken aback by the question. She looked at Kelly, but quickly turned away once more, as if she were hiding something. "I fill in at times," she replied, departing quickly.

"What was that about, Kelly? Why'd you ask her that?" Molly inquired.

"I've seen her before, but I can't place her. She wasn't a server, then. I'm pretty sure of that. There's something suspicious about her. She doesn't maintain eye contact."

"Maybe she's just shy," Molly suggested.

"Let's compare notes on this case," the Inspector began. "By the way, Chen's pulling together data on both victims. For the time being, we're treating the Green case and the Parker...I mean Porter...case as related. Based on the evidence we already observed, it's obvious that Porter's death wasn't an accident."

"But the Green autopsy confirms a heroin overdose," Molly added.

"Yes, but we can't rule out that the two aren't connected. The timing's suspicious."

The waitress returned with the coffee and tea, before disappearing once more. Kelly still wondered where she had seen Cheryl before, while the young woman's face remained imprinted in her memory.

"I began a suspect list for the Porter homicide. I know it's not officially a homicide until we get the autopsy results, but I'm treating it as such." The Inspector paused to sip his coffee before resuming. "This coffee's awfully cold. Anyway, here's my suspect list." He handed a small torn piece of paper to Molly, who sat next to Kelly. The two women looked at the list together.

"Why Sam Hughes?" Molly objected. "He seems to be a genuinely nice guy."

"Nice or not, he is linked to both victims," he replied.

"You have some odd suspects on this list, boss," Kelly said and chuckled.

"Obviously, we don't know the identity of the rumored White Witch, if she exists at all. We know even less about the Black Raven, referenced in the mysterious Lenore poem, but they're potential suspects, as is the elusive Lenore, if she exists. The rest are obvious. We have Hughes, the Miller brothers, and, possibly, Sgt. Alvin Walker. Unfortunately, we lack any clear motive. This one's going to be a challenge," the Inspector concluded.

"Sure, boss. It's a great start. We've got no motive and a solid list of suspects: a legendary ghost, a sinister bird, two Amish pacifists, an unidentified poet, a respected innkeeper, and the local deputy. It's a fine list of suspects," Molly replied, tongue-in-cheek. "Maybe we should let the media run with it and see what happens."

"Very funny, Molly. Do you have a better list?"

"No. Let's face it. We've got nothing. White Witches and Black Ravens? Come on! We need a motive."

"I agree. That's why we need to dig deeper into this White Witch legend and the entire Drake family history. I've got Chen searching the internet, but so far he hasn't found anything of value. This means we need to get back to old fashioned detective work and look under every rock.

"Molly, you focus on this place. Sam Hughes is linked to both mysterious deaths. The name of this inn is The Black Raven, which is the very reference in the mysterious poem. Kelly, I need you to dig deeper into the White Witch legend and Green's link to it. Also, I need you to get closer to Alvin Walker. Maybe you can combine the two. Chen should be here later this morning, and he and I will oversee the investigation into the Will Porter death and explore a possible Amish connection.

"Finally, we all need to ask about Lenore. We need to find out if she exists or if she's a cover for someone else. If so, we need to find out who's hiding behind the pen name. I made a copy of that poem and sent it to our handwriting experts. They believe it's written by a left-handed woman. That means Gavin Green didn't write it." The Inspector paused. "Ladies, enjoy your breakfast, 'cause we've got a lot of work to do."

"I like the plan. I'll stay around here today and start investigating the inn," Molly replied. Deep down she liked the idea of getting to know Sam Hughes. Her relationship with Jack Fulton seemed to be at a crossroads. They'd probably either get engaged or break up. In her mind, there were no other options. Lately, she had been leaning toward the latter.

"I'm not sure where to start," Kelly confessed.

"It's your call. But I suggest you take a second look at the old Green estate for clues we may've missed. Let's treat the Green death as a homicide for now," the Inspector instructed.

"Okay, I'll head over to the Green place right after we're done here. What're you gonna do, boss?"

"I'm heading over to see Mr. Linus Miller. He seemed the more cooperative and less suspicious of the two Amish brothers," the Inspector replied.

"I know where I've seen her!" Kelly exclaimed unexpectedly.

"What?" Molly and the Inspector said in unison, looking at Kelly in confusion.

"She was there when we found Gavin Green. I never forget a face. This server was at the river when we investigated the Green death. She was one of the by-standers. I'm also pretty sure I saw her in the lobby talking to Will Porter the day before he died."

"So, that doesn't mean anything," Molly objected.

"It's an odd coincidence, if you ask me."

Just then, Cheryl approached the table and all fell silent. "Can I get your orders?" Her southern accent suddenly revealed itself. They gave her their orders. "More coffee or tea?" she asked.

"I'll have some more coffee but can I have it hot this time?" the Inspector asked.

"Oh, I'm so sorry. We've been having problems with the coffee maker in here. I'll get ya a fresh cup from the kitchen. I'll be right back. Would ya like some more tea, Miss?" she asked Molly.

"Sure," Molly said, focusing on the young woman, trying to recall her face.

"Can I ask you something?" Cheryl said, looking at the Inspector.

"Absolutely."

"Are ya all detectives?"

"Yes, we are," the Inspector looked at her earnestly.

"Well, there's somethin' ya all should know." The young woman paused and looked about to see if anyone was watching. Then, she stepped closer to the Inspector and continued in a whisper. "Gavin

Green was murdered. You'll see. When he first got 'ere, he had a girlfriend. She was an odd girl. I've no idea what happened to 'er. Her name was Lenore, I think. She just disappeared—moved out of town, I think.

"After Lenore left, Gavin was interested in Elaine, until Sam, the owner, got angry. They had a big fight the night Gavin was killed. I think he was involved. Don't trust 'im. Sam's a liar. But, most of all, don't trust Elaine. She's a manipulatin', lyin' man-eater. I think she killed Gavin and old Hughes is coverin' up for 'er.

"It's scary 'round 'ere. I don't trust either of 'em. I think he's in on it, along with Jerry, the cook. The only trustworthy one was Will, the bartender, and look what happened to 'im. He probably knew too much. I heard he got buried alive up at Drakes Plot. It's all over town. Poor guy. I'm lookin' for another job. I'm afraid to work 'ere. I'm leavin' as soon as I can and ya all should, too."

"Cheryl, right?"

"Yes, sir."

"Did you say Gavin Green's girlfriend was named Lenore?" All eyes were on the young waitress. The Inspector had so many questions for her that he did not know where to start.

"Yes, sir. I'm pretty sure. I only met her one time. Odd girl. Moved out of town, I think. Got scared, I figure." She stopped and looked about in fear.

"You think Gavin was murdered? By whom?" Kelly was intrigued and had completely forgotten the protocol for questioning potential witnesses.

"I'm sure he was murdered, and I think Elaine and Sam did it, and that cook, Jerry's, coverin' for 'em. She's a smart snake with a mean streak. They killed Gavin, and probably Will, as well. Something's not right here. This is my last day. I'm gonna quit today 'cause I'm scared to work 'ere." She looked about suspiciously.

"Before you go, we need to get an official statement from you. Can you spend some time with Molly, here? She has a lot of questions for you," the Inspector asked, looking over at Molly.

"I could get in trouble talkin' to ya all—y'all bein' detectives and all." Her southern accent thickened, as she looked about nervously.

"In trouble with whom?"

"Why, Mr. Hughes, of course."

The Inspector looked at Molly and smiled, as if to say, "I told ya so."

"We'll protect you, Cheryl."

"Okay, I'll talk to ya, but give me a minute." She disappeared toward the kitchen.

"Do you still think that Sam Hughes is innocent?" the Inspector asked Molly.

"Hell, I don't know what to think. This place's too bizarre."

"She's lying," Kelly replied, while calmly finishing her coffee. "She's lying about something. I can tell."

"How do you know that?" Molly replied.

"Well, for one thing, she kept looking down at her note pad, so as to make sure she said everything as scripted."

"Are you sure?" Molly asked.

"I was watching her. She did exactly that," Kelly replied.

"Well, let's confront her with that." The Inspector looked across the room toward the kitchen doors.

"Good idea. She must be in the kitchen. I'll check." Molly got up and disappeared into the kitchen.

"This place is odd. I'm getting some bad vibes here," Kelly looked about uncomfortably.

"I don't know about that. But maybe we better check on her." The Inspector looked toward the kitchen door. Five minutes had passed and Molly had not surfaced. The breakfast room remained empty, and there was no sign of Cheryl. As Kelly and the Inspector got up, Molly reappeared through the kitchen door and walked over to them. She seemed disturbed.

"Did you find her?" the Inspector inquired.

"No. I never found her. What's more, no one in the kitchen ever heard of a Cheryl, nor does a woman that fits her description work here."

"What! That's preposterous. She served us coffee," the Inspector replied.

"Apparently, the place doesn't even open for another thirty minutes. It seems that she got the coffee and tea over there, at the employee coffee station. Who the hell was that, and who scripted her?" Molly asked, still bewildered.

CHAPTER 37

The Morning Fog

Ariella awakened that morning from a bad dream. She wondered if her encounter with Harry had been real, for there was nothing sane about it. Like every morning, she rose before the others, quietly sneaking by several of the girls sleeping in her small living room. Silently, she opened the front door and disappeared into the thick mist. No one witnessed her departure, except for Annabel Lee, who was awakened by Ariella's exit. Curious, Anna followed her mentor into the morning fog.

The morning chill signaled that autumn had arrived. A dense fog covered the meadow that surrounded the cabin. Anna could not see Ariella but thought that she heard her in the distance. On faith, and with a sense of adventure, she plunged into the milky obscurity.

As she pushed through the tall grass of the meadow, Anna realized that the fog had grown so thick that she could not see her own outstretched hand. Blind to her next step, she pushed on. Soon, the only sound came from the dry grass breaking under her feet. All else remained wrapped in defining silence. Having lost track of Ariella, she soon lost track of time. Wandering about in the dense curtain of fog, she felt alone and uneasy. It was an odd realization to be completely blind, surrounded by opaque white. She stopped and listened, but heard her own heartbeat and nothing more.

Then, it happened. As if out of nowhere, she felt a gentle tap on her left shoulder. The sensation sent shivers of fear and paralysis through her entire body. Wanting to scream, she calmed herself. "Ariella?" she asked, certain that her mentor was playing a trick. Slowly, she turned. But no one was there, and no one answered, only the impenetrable fog remained. An urge to scream surfaced once more as her heart raced faster, louder. Unable to contain it, her heart pounded like a steady drum within the surrounding silence.

With her senses acutely alert, she felt another gentle touch on her left shoulder. What ghostly foolery was this? She turned faster now, but, once more, encountered nothing. Surely, she was alone. Or was she in the presence of some mysterious, stealth entity that would not reveal itself? *It must be my imagination*, she thought, calming herself. She was about to move on, only to realize that she had become hopelessly disoriented by the white obscurity that consumed her.

"Damn this fog!" Walking quickly in the direction that she perceived to lead back to the house, she soon realized that the vast field had become an endless maze. No closer to reaching its terminus, she was lost.

If I walk in one direction, I'll reach the end of the meadow, her logical mind reasoned. Again she stopped, exhausted now. Listening with the keen perception of a hunter, she heard nothing and relaxed. *It's my imagination*, she concluded and began to walk slowly in one direction.

She got about thirty yards, when, once again, a gentle touch grazed her shoulder. It was then that she realized she was not the hunter but the hunted. Or was she being haunted? It felt like both. In desperation, she swung her arms at the invisible intruder—nothing, except dense air.

"Who are you? Show yourself! If it's you, Ariella, please stop! This isn't funny!" she yelled into the dampening fog. Her words were swallowed by the thick silence. She wanted to scream for help but felt silly. What if this was simply her imagination?

Desperate, she started to run. Recklessly, she tore through the blinding fog, no longer thinking, no longer conscious of anything but her fear. Suddenly she stopped, trying to listen for the footsteps of a pursuer. There were none. Only the foggy silence greeted her senses; only the frightening silence kept her company. Yet there was more. Once again, as she stood listening to her intense heartbeat, she felt the touch, that haunting gentle touch. This time she felt it on her right arm. It felt cold. She spun around and tried to punch the invisible intruder, only to see her arm disappear into the thick fog, finding no resistance by mist.

"Who are you? Tell me. I'm not afraid." She stood her ground, unmoved, like the stagnant air. Something inside her grew, a confidence built of despair. No being would challenge her now. "Come and show yourself, you coward!" she yelled at the fog. As expected, there was no answer, only deathly silence.

She stood, defiant, challenged by the unknown. What haunted her remained shrouded in obscurity. Was it real or was it her fear? No longer sure, her logical mind began to betray her, replaced by distressed confidence. Or was it confident distress? She was not sure. She was not sure of anything as panic crept into her mind, quietly but rapidly.

As the fading confidence wrestled her growing panic, the two numbed her senses. No longer able to stand the torturous cage that the misty field had become, her brief defiant stance had crumbled and her sanity followed. Anna began to run and scream like a child fleeing its unyielding nightmare. It was in this frenzied state that she ran straight into another being. The encounter sent terror through her mind and her veins. Overwhelmed, her terrified mind shut down, her exhausted legs buckled, and she fainted at the feet of a dark stranger with a raven tattoo.

CHAPTER 38

Kindred Spirits

Prior to Anna's collapse, Ariella had reached the spring-fed waterfall and warm pool that gave birth to the lively stream running through the center of the dark misty woods. She knew the way by heart, so the thick fog had been a feeble challenge. It was still early morning and the rising sun created a backdrop of magenta against the thick steam rising from the thermal pool. In the silence of the morning, the falling water seemed to sing a melody as old as time. There was a welcoming, eternal assurance in its song, an assurance that all transformation, regardless of its nature, was simply an extension of an eternal evolution and an infinite connection. Time became inconsequential, as Ariella entered her morning ritual of deep meditation.

The secret to her power was this ritual. In her ability to reach a transformation consistently and rapidly, Ariella walked nearly synonymously in two distinct worlds. To her, reality was not framed by the limitations of her senses or her physical mind and body. She had discovered the secret of the sages and of the greatest spiritual leaders of the ages, a sustained ethereal crossing that even her shamanic master had struggled to achieve. He knew the way but could only pass so far.

Gradually, Ariella had pushed further and reached an ability that few had ever achieved. For longer and longer periods of time, she was able to coexist in form and outside of it, simultaneously. This ability brought her great power. Yet all such power had a dark shadow that she could not escape, for it was inherent to the very mind and body that allowed her physical existence.

On this particular morning, Ariella, the White Dove, went further than ever before into the unknown through the "Portal of Eden," as she called it. This time she dared to drift so deeply that she seemed to lose her way in the complete stillness. Free, in this unrestrained and receptive state, her clarity reached well beyond her mental barriers into an uncharted realm. Here, she could see the struggle of good and evil, not as something right or wrong, but as a continuum, natural and inherent to the unnatural state of souls in physical form. Her clarity revealed what she had long suspected, that no soul was truly at home in the limitations of the body and the mind. She realized that this arrangement had only one purpose—for a soul to learn from the experience and grow in its vibrancy, knowing that some souls struggle more than others with this temporary, avatar-like arrangement called "life."

As she looked deeper, Ariella could see that even now, in this sheltered Amish valley, an evil was rising that had its source in fear, greed, and a need for dominance. Likewise, she understood that this need for gratification and power was partially inherent to a mind and body designed by a cruel, merciless process known as "natural selection." All this she glimpsed and all this she inherently knew.

Through this inner vision, she recognized that this "earthly school," as it was revealed, was about a soul's increased purity, defined as "growth", confirming to herself that "evil" had one singular definition—anything that harmed the "growth" of other souls. It simply "missed the mark" of learning. She realized that "missing the mark" was the true and original definition of "sin" in the old Greek texts of the early Christians.

Now she saw it clearly unveiled. In this oracle state, she saw that the evil entering the gentle harmony of the Eden Valley was nothing more than the oppressive actions of an uncontrolled mind—a very sick mind. She could see that in the grander picture each evil act harmed the predator, as well as the victim. Both were victims. Despite this, it was revealed to her that she must stop this evil whenever and wherever she encountered it because it was not the "true way."

On this particular morning, she dared to enter deeper still. What she sensed next horrified her to the core.

Suddenly, Ariella realized that she too was part of the growing evil entering the sanctity of this innocent Amish valley, having drawn it here and opened the flood gates. In her vision, she could see the dark side of the mysterious white figure that seemed to haunt the valley. The lines between good and evil were becoming blurred like the ghostly image of the White Witch. Ariella seemed to straddle them both. Like every soul in the valley, she possessed both. But, unlike any other, she had been shown a way to reach across the ethereal plane that divided the living from the dead.

The White Dove and the White Witch, in her frightening vision, were one and the same in their connection. Desperately, she tried to know more, before the vision became obscure through her own fears. Fear, the impenetrable fog, began to shroud all. Evil stood silently hidden in this fog of fear. There—waiting, like a merciless spider. It was then that she heard a familiar voice in the thickening fear, a scream for help and a faint outline of a female figure blindly searching in the dense fog. In her trance, she tried to reach that helpless figure, who seemed so familiar. Ariella tried to catch her to warn her of the evil that hid in the merciless mist. Trying to gently touch her, she seemed to pass through the frightened form. Every time she tried to catch her, she passed through her. Frustrated, she focused harder on touching the frightened girl trapped in the blinding fog. This time, the girl felt her, for she reacted but her fear grew in the process.

Evil, the merciless fog thickened and Ariella lost control, lost her way. Who was that frightened figure fading into obscurity? What was the evil waiting for its next victim? Suddenly, the frightened girl sounded like Anna. Her heart told her so. Desperate, she tried to touch her, to catch her, to warn her, to save her from the evil foe whose presence grew ever nearer. Once again, Anna seemed to feel her gentle touch, but they were worlds apart. In her deep trance, Ariella had willfully separated a portion of her energy into a form-less state. That state was no different than that of the ghostly White

Witch — the splintered, fearful fragment of Evelyn Drake, a shadow hopelessly imprinted onto this mystical land. At that moment, the two blended into one.

Was she controlling the rumored specter and simply energizing it in her recent ventures through the Portal of Eden? The idea seemed preposterous. In this altered state could the White Witch and White Dove become one?

Ariella's haunting realization quickly led to doubt, which began to erode her trance. She could not help Anna, nor could she warn her. The portal began to close as, to her horror, she sensed the evil nearing Anna before everything faded into white. Was she that invisible evil? Was she the specter? She no longer knew. In the disorienting fog, she could not tell. Feeling her power weakening, she would have to go. The transformation was nearly over as the portal collapsed. Her energy oscillated between planes. She became more and more enveloped by the blinding fog of doubt and fear. As everything around her became obscure in a ghostly white, she had one final reflection of the mysterious White Witch that seemed to belong to this ethereal place. In a blurry vision, deep within the recesses of her transformation, she saw the face of the White Witch, the face that no one had clearly seen before and lived to tell the tale. This revelation broke her concentration, propelling her back into physical and mental reality. Awakened from her deep meditation, she gasped for air. Running to the pool at the base of the waterfall, she desperately splashed water on her face, as if to cleanse it from the truth that had horrified her moments earlier.

How was it possible? How was it possible that she, the noble shaman, was linked to the one that haunted this valley? Looking into the pool, she saw a pale face, her face, the face of the shaman known as the White Dove. To her horror, it was the same face, the face of the White Witch. "How is that possible?" she pleaded for an answer. Falling to her knees, she wept in despair. Her tears of horror and disillusionment fell into the crystal-clear waters that on prior mornings had cleansed her soul. There were no longer any boundaries. She had plunged too far into the portal and got lost. All was lost. Falling to the ground, she felt defeat, except for one thought that sprung her to action:

Where was Anna and was she safe?

CHAPTER 39

A Barn Raising

A grassy field behind the white wooden farmhouse sparkled with morning dew. The plain farm dwelling was newly constructed for Jacob and Elizabeth Miller, a young Amish couple who had recently married. Jacob was Linus Miller's second son. He had started a farm of his own on land he purchased from his father's holdings. It was a festive time for the young newlyweds with many family visits and endless support from their Amish community. One of the most visible forms of family and community unity would take place today in the open field behind the farmhouse. Here, the young Miller couple would soon possess a spacious barn of their own. By nightfall, it would be there, as if magically erected from the barren earth. This was the miracle of an Amish barn raising.

Before dawn, the young Millers were already preparing for the invasion of neighbors, friends, and family members. By the time they finished the preparations, the sun peered over the horizon and the first of many Amish buggies pulled up the long, newly-created drive that was no more than two parallel sets of buggy tracks. Within half an hour, over twenty buggies had pulled into the open fields of Jacob

Miller's farm. In the next hour, the number had swelled to sixty-three horse-drawn buggies, many of which were flatbeds carrying lumber and other building supplies.

A sea of tables sprang up like mushrooms after a warm autumn rain. Dozens of women created makeshift kitchens that produced volumes of food, as men of all ages began laying out building material in well-organized stacks. Young children ran everywhere. For them, this was a long-awaited gathering of all their cousins, many three or four times removed.

Morning prayers were provided by Bishop Abel Snyder. After the good Lord was praised, the work of laying out the dimensions of the barn and sinking the key posts would begin in earnest. John Lapp had the honor to oversee the massive, rapid construction. Known as the finest carpenter and barn builder within the greater Amish community, it was a great privilege to have a barn built under the experienced eye of John Lapp.

The women cooked oatmeal and scrambled countless dozens of eggs while toasting a mountain of sliced homemade bread. To complement this grand breakfast, they heated over eighty pounds of bacon and over two hundred links of sausage for a feast that would be served at eight o'clock sharp. Meanwhile, the men began the laborious process of sinking the barn posts in the precise locations designated by John Lapp. The great posts were placed in holes dug by hand to a depth below the frost line. These massive timbers, brought to the site days before the event, would form the structural shell of the large barn and bear its weight. John Lapp was a traditionalist, who did not believe in the use of nails in barn construction, so everything was jointed with hand-hewn, tongue-and-groove seams, like fine furniture, and locked in place by large wooden pegs.

Amish barns were built to stand for centuries and most did just that. A "Lapp Barn," as these barns were known in the area, for the carpenter tradition was passed from generation to generation in the Lapp family, lasted the test of time better than any other structure. A few of the originals were nearly 200 years old and looked as good as when they first appeared on the picturesque landscape. Linus Miller and his family had three such barns already in their possession. After all, John Lapp's wife was the first cousin of Linus Miller's wife. They were family.

Eight o'clock finally arrived with the clatter of the breakfast bell. The men welcomed the break from the grueling work of post digging. This strenuous construction process was a marvel as no modern tools were used. Rather, everything was done by hand with simple tools, such as shovels, hammers, handsaws, ropes, wooden pulleys, wooden mallets, chisels, and hand drills.

Unfortunately, the congregation spent little time enjoying the feast or the company. After all, the barn had to be built in a day, and presently only the sixteen vertical posts were in place, buried within the deep hand-dug holes. They stood like ancient roman pillars or the massive ribs of a colossal creature time had forgotten. It was hard to believe that before sunset these posts would transform into a fully functional barn. Next would come the task of connecting these posts with horizontal beams that would support the upper layer of construction, the beams and cross beams of the roof and hayloft. All the basic framing had to be completed by lunchtime for the construction to stay on schedule.

John Lapp, as the master builder, was constantly in demand; he was endlessly engaged in supervision and problem solving. Men were divided into teams, each run by a master carpenter and craftsman who had barn-raising experience. The entire feat was a well-orchestrated symphony of construction and craftsmanship.

As soon as the men finished eating, they fell back into their work teams and pushed forward in accordance with John Lapp's instructions. Meanwhile, the women fed the endless multitude of hungry children, before eating the leftovers as their own meal. As soon as breakfast was over, the preparations for lunch began, and the second of the three meal cycles started anew.

During this communal undertaking, Lenore helped her mother prepare the meals. She was still a little uncertain of her role, but Mary made sure her daughter had plenty of instruction. If in doubt, she would team her up with her two teenage daughters, Kate and Eve. Although Lenore was beginning to recall her Amish past, she could not recall anything after her seventh birthday. That period, between the day she turned seven and the present, remained a complete void. It would take time but it was frustrating, nonetheless.

Also frustrating were some people's reactions to her disappearance and odd return to the community. Although most were extremely receptive, a few treated her with reservation and resentment, as if she had committed some kind of a crime that she had no recollection of owning. One or two even avoided her, as if she carried an infectious disease. When Lenore asked her mother about this, she got no answer. Nor did her father or her siblings discuss her departure, as if it was a secret. Usually, she dismissed it, but today, in the presence of the entire community, it was hard for her not to ponder what horrible secret her family refused to reveal.

It was during lunch preparations that Lenore encountered Emma Fischer, a young woman of eighteen. Emma snarled at Lenore when the latter asked if Emma could help peel the mountain of potatoes that would become part of the dinner meal. Lenore was about to walk away, when she decided to inquire into the meaning behind the hostile reaction.

"Why'd ya do that?" she asked.

"Do what?" Emma snarled again.

"That."

"What?"

"The snarl. Why'd ya snarl at me?"

"I didn't snarl at ya. I'm just tryin' to shun ya."

"What's that?"

"What's what?"

"What does 'shun' mean?"

"I shouldn't be talkin' to ya," Emma replied and turned away.

"Why?" Lenore insisted.

"'Cause ya ought to be shunned. Ya know—ignored, as if ya don't exist."

"That's awful! Why would ya do that?"

"If ya leave the Amish, ya get shunned—ya exist no more. No one's to talk to ya, of ya, or anything. Ya're worse than dead. It's like ya never lived."

"Why?"

"I don't know. It's always been that way. I guess if ya leave, it's yar own fault. My *dat* says we can't have people comin' und goin' as they please, 'cause there'd be no Amish left. He say it's so we can live this way. I don't understand it, I just know I should shun ya 'cause ya left. He sayz ya're not Amish no more und he don't understand why ya got to come back like nothing happened without askin' the community to take ya back. He thinks it's 'cause yar uncle Abel Snyder's the bishop. I've gotta stop talkin' to ya before he sees me und I get in a heap a trouble." Emma looked away. "Go away, please," she added, not looking at Lenore.

"Do ya know why I left?" Lenore asked naively.

"I don't know. Ya tell me. My *dat* sayz ya can remember und this is just an act. So, why'd ya leave, anyway?" Emma was curious, so she whispered to Lenore while looking away, pretending to focus on her potato peeling.

"Ya papa's wrong. I really can't remember. I wish I could, but I can't."

"Papa say ya left on account of Amos Miller. *Dat* sayz he's trouble, but I think he's handsome. Some of the girls think ya slept with 'im, which is a sin 'cause ya weren't married. Did ya sleep with 'im?"

"What! No! I'm sure I didn't, und who is he, anyway?"

"Don't you know anything? Every girl wants 'im, und ya had 'im und left." Emma shook her head and glanced at Lenore. "Ya had 'im, und left the Amish und 'im. Most girls our age think ya nuts. Ya sure ya ain't pretending?" Emma looked back toward the potatoes. "Ya better leave. I shouldn't be talkin' to ya. *Dat* sayz ya're shunned no matter what Abel Snyder says."

"Emma. It's Emma, right?"

"Go away!"

"Emma, besides yar *dat*, what do others say about why I left?" Lenore decided to absorb the young woman's negativity and focus on enlightening the black void that masked her recent past.

Emma couldn't resist this juicy subject of recent gossip. "Most think ya went crazy. Some think Amos threw ya out. Some think ya got pregnant with Amos, und somehow lost the baby after ya left."

"Oh, my. That's all so horrible."

"I think ya're a big fool to leave Amos, no matter what happened. Now, go away before *Dat* sees us talkin'."

"One last question — which one's Amos Miller?" She looked up at the hoard of men working on the barn.

"Are ya kiddin'? Ya really don't know?" Emma looked up in disbelief. "Ya're weirder than I thought."

"Which one is he?" Lenore repeated.

"He's the handsome one workin' with yar father — hewing the beams. Ya remember yar father, don't ya?"

"Only recently."

"Just go away. I need to shun ya, okay?"

"Shun away, Emma. Shun away," Lenore replied and looked toward the young man working next to her father. She could not get a good look at him from that distance, so she decided to approach her father with the intent to discover the identity of this mysterious man in her past life.

Lenore had nearly reached her father when Ben Stoltzfus intercepted her. "There ya are. We finally get to talk. I missed ya," Ben confessed.

"Hello, Ben. It's nice to see ya, too," she replied, while keeping one eye on the man working with her father.

"Did ya miss me?" Ben asked.

Lenore looked past Ben, trying to make out the identity of Amos Miller. He had his back to her, so she was unable to see his face. Although she liked Ben, the story that Emma had relayed made her curious about Amos. Why was he such a desired husband, and what was her past with him? What happened between them? These urgent questions filled her mind, while Ben Stoltzfus filled her field of vision— trying to keep her attention.

"Ya don't have to answer that. I'z just kiddin'. I heard ya memory's comin' back. Do ya remember me before yar accident?" Ben asked eagerly. In his self-serving purpose, he barely noticed that Lenore's attention had been diverted elsewhere.

"Suddenly, Lenore switched her complete attention to Ben. "What'd ya say?"

"I said I heard ya memory's come back. That's great. Right?"

"Yes, but what'd ya say about an accident? What accident?"

"Why, the one ya had before ya come back."

"What accident? Is that why I left?" She completely focused on him, hanging on his every word. She forgot about Amos. Right now, she simply needed to find out the truth about her controversial past.

"Lenore, I don't think we should talk about that."

"Why? Ya just said ya care for me. If ya do, why ya keepin' secrets from me?"

"I'm not, Lenore. It's just—I don't wanna upset ya given yar fragile state und all."

"My fragile state? Is that what I am to you—fragile?"

"No, of course not. I just don't wanna get in trouble with..." he paused.

"With whom? Who's controlling what is und isn't said to me?"

"It's not that, Lenore. What's gotten into ya, anyway? Ya're not yourself, today."

"Ya mean I'm not naively passive."

"I better go and help. I'm supposed to be measurin' them crossbeams."

"Ben, please tell me one thing — why'd I leave the Amish?"

"I honestly don't know, Lenore. I don't."

"Okay, I believe ya but, please, tell me about the accident. What happened?"

"I don't know that either. All I know's yar brother found ya nearly dead in the Eden River under Devils Bridge. Ya must've fallen in head first, or jumped, but no one knows, except you, und ya can't remember. Until ya remember, it's a mystery," Ben replied earnestly.

"Where's Devils Bridge?"

"What does that matter?"

"I want to know. Where is it?"

"It's the red covered bridge down the road from the village of Eden Crossin'."

Ben disappeared toward the worksite. As she looked after him, she could see that her father was no longer in the same spot as before, nor was Amos Miller. Unfortunately, she couldn't recognize Amos since she never saw his face. Most of the men looked the same from where she stood, since they all wore plain clothes and round straw hats. As she was about to resume her search, she heard her mother calling. Her chance had come and gone. Amos Miller would have to wait, as would the mystery that surrounded her recent past with him.

By the time the sun began to set, the new barn was completely built. The miracle of the Amish barn raising had happened, as it had time and time again over the centuries. As the friends and family parted, young Jacob Miller's farm rapidly returned to a peaceful homestead. Buggy after buggy rolled back down the long lane until all was quiet.

On her way home, Lenore was left to ponder the mysteries of her own making. It would take a miracle greater than a barn raising to unlock those secrets.

236

CHAPTER 40

Dirty Little Secrets

That morning, Kelly and the Inspector arrived at Amos's Farm as the sun rose over the tree line. Amos Miller had completed half of his morning chores by the time they pulled into his driveway. He did not seem eager to speak with them and disappeared into the barn before they had a chance to intercept him.

"He sure acts suspiciously," the Inspector observed.

"The Amish are extremely peaceful people. Do you really suspect them?" Kelly questioned.

"Experience has taught me not to trust anyone, regardless of reputation or appearance. Amos Miller acts suspiciously. He's hiding something, but I'm not sure what," the Inspector concluded.

"I'm sure he is, but it's not murder. I noticed his older brother coaching him during our interviews. They were using hand signals. You know I notice everything," she replied and laughed.

"That you do, but are you sure?"

"Yes. They were simple signals, but Linus was making the signals and Amos was adjusting accordingly. They're hiding something, but Amos isn't a murderer."

"How can you be so sure?"

"First of all, it's completely against Amish beliefs of nonviolence. Second, why would he and his brother call the police when they found the body? The Amish don't like conflict. Why start a potential one by contacting the authorities? They're innocent of the murder, but they're hiding something...or someone," she added.

Just then, a police cruiser entered Amos Miller's driveway and pulled up behind the Inspector's car. Sgt. Alvin Walker stepped out of the vehicle.

"There's your boy." The Inspector nudged Kelly. "Wonder what he's doing here this early. With the body at the coroner's, there's not much to see."

Before Kelly could respond, Alvin walked up to them. "You're up early," Alvin addressed Kelly with a smile. He nodded to the Inspector, but the two did not exchange a word. It was clear that they did not care for each other.

"We just got here," Kelly replied. "We wanted to take another look around. What're you doing here this early?"

"Same thing," Alvin replied.

The coincidental early morning appearance of Alvin Walker perplexed the Inspector, but he remained silent. A cloudburst of heavy rain had passed through the area in the early morning hours, and the parallel ruts that led through the harvested cornfield to Drakes Plot had turned to mud. The three had to proceed up the hill on foot. Amos's dog, Otto, barked at them as they passed the barn, but neither he nor Amos came out to meet them. Ten minutes later, the detectives came into view of the small cemetery and the old stone foundations of the Drake family farmhouse. Piles of gray stones and the cemetery were all that remained of the early homestead.

A large black raven greeted them. It was sitting atop one of the weathered headstones. As the three neared, it took flight, protesting their intrusion with a loud squawk. There was something sinister about the large, dark bird, and Kelly could not help but reflect on Lenore's mysterious poem. In the low light of dawn, the old cemetery looked as ominous as it had the night before. The gray dawning light, under thick cloud cover, seemed to accentuate the twisted trees whose bare branches clawed at the weathered headstones which leaned in every direction, as if kicked around by an irreverent intruder. Kelly shivered, as she detected a menacing energy that seemed to mock them. It appeared to emanate from the dark bird that had settled in a tree beyond the dilapidated walls of the ancient graveyard.

"This place gives me the creeps," Kelly shared with the Inspector, who was walking next to her. He did not respond.

She noticed that Alvin seemed nervous. Earlier, when they first met in Amos Miller's driveway, Alvin voiced his desire to proceed to Drakes Plot alone. His wishes were quickly silenced by the Inspector's stern stare, followed by his only comment to the officer. "Why?" Alvin had no response. Now, the sergeant raced ahead of them, as if he needed to reach the cemetery first.

"What's with him?" the Inspector asked Kelly.

"He's an odd one. He seems eager to beat us to the crime scene, like it matters. Your guess is as good as mine," Kelly responded, shrugging her shoulders.

Alvin was twenty yards ahead of them, now. As he reached the cemetery, he ran toward the grave of Arthur Drake and reached down. It was not clear if he had deposited or removed something. "We'd better catch up to him," the Inspector observed, not trusting the sergeant.

When Kelly and Inspector Cabot reached the small graveyard, they were surprised to see a second disturbed grave site. The Arthur Drake grave, adjacent to Evelyn Drake's, was clearly excavated and backfilled overnight. "What the heck's this?" the Inspector asked Alvin.

"I have no idea, sir. It seems like someone's been digging up here last night. I hope we don't find another body. Look, it's another broken shovel, like the one we found yesterday, but this one has both parts including the broken handle. Interesting—the initials 'LM' are engraved on it. See?" Alvin proudly showed the Inspector the broken shovel handle with the worn, carved initials.

"Walker, why the hell would the perpetrator leave a shovel handle behind with his initials? That makes no sense," the Inspector protested. "It'd be like leaving a calling card."

"Maybe he was in a hurry," Alvin speculated. "Wonder what 'LM' stands for? Wasn't that Amish undertaker named Linus Miller? It could be his. Maybe he was digging up here last night," Alvin concluded with a winning smile.

"You sure are a good detective, Sergeant," the Inspector said in a sarcastic tone. "'LM' could also stand for 'lying moron,'" he mumbled under his breath.

Kelly overheard it and wanted to laugh but curbed herself.

"What was that?" Alvin planted his feet firmly and stared at the Inspector.

"Nothing of relevance, Sergeant. Although I wonder about the likelihood of our Amish friend, Mr. Miller, digging up graves last night and leaving his monogrammed shovel behind to inform us of his actions. It seems more likely that this was planted here as a poor attempt to throw us off. Of course, it failed to do so—right, Sergeant?" The Inspector stared at the young police officer. "By the way, why were you in such a hurry to find this clue?"

"I take offense to your attitude and questioning, sir," Alvin replied.

"Why? I'm simply asking why you wanted to come up here alone, and why you were in such a hurry to get up here?"

"Are you implying something, sir?"

"Should I be, Sergeant?"

Kelly stood back. She purposely wanted to stay out of the encounter. The Inspector had planned to use some excuse to unnerve Alvin, but he never suspected that he would have such an easy opportunity. Earlier, he shared this plan with Kelly. Her role was to show empathy and support for Alvin. In the process, she would begin to win his trust.

As the Inspector began to document the newly excavated grave, Kelly walked over to Alvin and whispered in his ear. "He's this rude to everyone. I hate it, but he's a very powerful man. I wouldn't take him on. I suspect he's jealous that you were right about the Gavin Green death and he was wrong."

"He's a bastard and I'm gonna get even with 'im. He's got no right to attack me like that. You watch—this shovel belongs to that Amish undertaker. I bet it does and I'll be right again," Alvin replied.

The Inspector had purposely given Kelly space, using the opportunity to investigate the newly disturbed grave on his own. *Why another excavation?* he wondered. *Who dug it, and what were they after?* The only thing he could conclude was that someone sought something buried at Drakes Plot—something worthy of a murder.

He wasted no time calling Chen Lee, the information technology-savvy member of his team.

"Yes, sir. I'll get right on it," Chen replied.

"This is top priority, Chen. I'm starting to wonder if Green's death was really an accident. We could have two murders, and I need a motive," the Inspector clarified.

"I'm on it, as soon as I get my coffee."

"Good. Did we track down Gavin's father or anyone related to 'im? Also, does Porter have any next of kin?"

"Negative on both counts, boss. No leads on Gavin's father or anyone else related to him, and Porter was a loner. Parents died years ago of natural causes, and he did not have a wife, ex-wife, or girlfriend."

"Okay. Keep digging. Also, check in with Molly. She's investigating The Raven Inn. My sense tells me that the inn's connected to all this. We need to move on this before another body shows up. Also, I need you to find out anything and everything regarding Sam Hughes, William Porter, and Alvin Walker…Yes, Sgt. Walker of the local police. He's probably clean, but he's acting peculiar, so I'm covering all my bases. I suspect you won't find anything on the two Amish brothers, Amos and Linus Miller, but run them anyway. Finally, I need to know all about Gavin Green's history and connections. Look for any references to a woman named Lenore, last name unknown. That's all. Call me when you get something."

The Inspector had decided to keep Chen in the office a little longer to conduct an exhaustive database and web search. He had a hunch but did not want to speculate, hoping that Chen would find a clue to a motive.

Meanwhile, Kelly charmed Alvin Walker. It was an easy task, since the young sergeant clearly fancied her. However, before she had a chance to get any new information out of him, Gus Morgan showed up with two additional police officers. The latter two dug into the fresh soil atop Arthur Drake's grave. Fortunately, no new victim surfaced, but it became clear that whoever disturbed the resting place dug down to the old wooden casket that housed Drake's remains. If something had been removed from the grave, its nature remained a mystery. A detailed search of both excavations followed but did not yield anything of interest.

The Inspector grew frustrated. After taking additional photographs and measurements, he decided to approach the local police chief, whom he had known for over a decade.

"Gus, what's your take on this?"

"Crazy, I tell ya."

"What's with the White Witch?"

"Ahhh, it's nonsense, if you ask me. People got nothin' to do, so they let their imaginations run wild."

"What do you know about it? I'm curious."

Gus shook his head. "If you ask me, it's nothin' but local folklore. I believe it started with the Amish but I'm not sure. Legend has it that the Drake family was brutally murdered over 200 years ago on this very spot. Some swear the ghost of old Evelyn Drake still haunts these grounds and this valley. I don't believe it. It's an old wives' tale and fodder for quilting circles and bar stories."

"I figured as much, but why would anyone want to dig up these old graves for no apparent reason, and even die in the process? There's got to be a strong motive here. What is it?"

"The same folks that spread these rumors of ghosts spread rumors of treasure. Why not? If you're creating one rumor, why not two? Don't waste your time on the rumors, Jim," Gus advised.

"Sometimes there's some truth to a rumor. What treasure?"

"Hell, I don't know. Ask the Amish. They probably started all these rumors. It's all crap."

"Sounds like a couple of other folks believed in it."

"What do you mean?"

"Well, someone may have killed Porter for it," the Inspector suggested.

"Not for that kind of treasure."

"What do you mean?"

"Jim, I just learned this mornin' that the Feds've been after Porter for goin' on a year. He worked at The Raven Inn but lived in Kamerynville. Apparently, they've suspected for months now that he'd been pushing drugs at both locations—heroin, to be specific. That's what I came here to tell you. I bet he crossed the wrong person and ended up paying for it. That's your motive. The rest is probably a crazy cover-up."

The Inspector was about to ask more questions when his cell phone rang. "Chen, that was quick. What'd you find?"

"So far, there isn't much, except a few references to the old legend of the Drake family. According to folklore, they were murdered 200 years ago and the old lady's thought to be…get this…a ghost." Chen laughed.

"I know. Is there anything about a treasure?"

"You know?"

"Yeah. Anything about a treasure?"

"No. Nothing about a treasure, but the same legend claims old Drake was a privateer."

"What's that?"

"A pirate."

"What? What was he, a land pirate? We're hundreds of miles from the ocean out here," the Inspector protested. *This entire thing's getting ridiculous.* He was starting to side with the local police chief.

"There isn't much, but it seems Arthur Drake took his family from Philadelphia to the frontier of western Pennsylvania and bought a sizable estate from William Penn's holdings along both sides of the Eden River. According to one reference, the old Drake Estate encompassed the entire Eden Crossing area. That's all I could discover in under an hour, but I'll keep digging. I'll find out about the treasure."

"You did great. Anything about a White Witch?"

"Apparently, she's the ghost of Evelyn Drake. So far, I found only one reference that mentions her. It was a short paper by Professor Albert Murray of McLaren University's History Department."

"Interesting." The Inspector rubbed his mustache. "See if you can track him down and get an interview."

"Yes, sir. Anything else?"

"Yes. Can you look into William Porter's record? Apparently, he's suspected of drug dealing, according to Gus. See what you can find on 'im. Thanks, Chen. Call me if you find something interestin'."

"Yes, sir," Chen replied. Prior to his role on Inspector Cabot's team, Chen worked for the FBI in data intelligence. Prior, he received his computer science degree on an ROTC scholarship at the University of Connecticut, before serving four years in the Army and now the National Guard. He had a military style and the Inspector liked it, always addressing the Inspector as "sir." By contrast, the two young women on his team were much less formal. Molly was more like a daughter to him, and the two had a very informal and taunting communication style. Kelly was still new, but it was clear that her approach had little reverence for authority.

Thank God at least Chen shows some respect, the Inspector thought as he hung up the phone. Looking up, he saw Kelly walking toward him. *Here comes Chen's opposite*, he concluded silently. "Anything new, Kelly?" he said aloud as she reached him.

"Alvin's definitely hiding something," she whispered. "He thinks that Porter was high on drugs and his death was a drug hit. When I asked him why he's so sure when we're still waiting for the autopsy results, he had no reply, except, 'because I know these things.' He's an odd one."

"That alone doesn't make him suspicious, Kelly. Arrogant, maybe, but not suspicious," the Inspector objected. "Unfortunately, he may be right about the drugs as a motive. Gus just told me that the Feds confirmed that Porter was suspected of dealing heroin and has been on their watchlist for the past year."

"Interesting. But when I asked Alvin if he knew Porter, he said no. I could tell he was lying."

"How could you tell?"

"He wouldn't look at me, and he pinched his nostrils together right after he said it."

The Inspector laughed out loud. *She's a unique one*, he thought. "And the nostrils are the key clue here, I take it," he responded, trying to regain a serious appearance.

"You laugh, but people always give themselves away when they lie. You simply need to know what to watch for in their expressions or mannerisms. Alvin Walker's nostrils don't lie, even when he does," she explained.

"I can see it now. We're in court and the judge asks why we have a well-respected police officer on trial for murder. At that point the prosecutor brings out the condemning evidence. 'Your honor, Officer Walker's guilty of murder because his nostrils don't lie, even when he does.'"

"You poke fun. But I know he's lying. Every time Alvin Walker lies, his nostrils pinch together. I have tested it several times. That correlation has always held. Test it yourself. I tell you that he's hiding something. What? I don't know. But I'll tell you one thing, he knew Porter, and he knew him well."

"Did you find out if he killed Porter?"

"Now who's unrealistic? I can't simply ask him, 'Oh, by the way, did you kill Porter?' while staring at his nostrils," she replied.

The Inspector laughed and played along. "True, but you can begin to find out what he knows, assuming your nostril test is accurate. I can't believe we're having a conversation about Alvin Walker's nostrils. Only you, Kelly. Only you."

* * * * *

Later that morning, the Inspector received a second call from Chen. "Hello, Chen. What'd you find?"

"I investigated Alvin Walker's background like you asked me. He appears clean, based on records from the police force in Austin, Texas. The captain there seemed reluctant to share much about him. After I pushed him for information, he admitted that Alvin was not a team player and liked to party on his days off. I guess you already know that he's originally from the Eden Valley. Both of his parents are deceased due to natural causes. He had one older brother, who died in a car accident a couple years ago. He studied criminal justice at the University of Texas. He may be odd, but he doesn't seem to have a criminal record except for a DUI that was later dropped."

"Why was the DUI dropped?"

"Apparently the officer who pulled him over changed his mind and dismissed the charge three days later, claiming the breathalyzer malfunctioned."

"Interesting. What about Sam Hughes? He's my odds-on favorite."

"He's got an interesting past. Like Walker, he was born and raised in the area. In fact, he grew up in the house that's now The Raven Inn. It was known as The Eden Inn until he renamed it upon taking it over after his father's death. I don't have anything on his childhood, yet, but when he went to nearby McLaren University, he was suspected of cheating on his final exam in English Literature during his freshman year. The fellow student who accused him withdrew the accusation, and he passed with an B. I had to get into old McLaren records to get this level of detail. I'm good, huh?"

"Yes, go on."

"Seemingly, this wasn't all that Mr. Hughes managed to accomplish at McLaren. Later that year, he was involved in a scandal that got the attention of the provost. Hughes and a young woman, named Erin Stone, appear to have been romantically involved," Chen revealed.

"Why is that such a scandal?"

"Because at the time she was engaged to a very wealthy university trustee, who happens to be…hold on to your hat, Chief!" Chen stopped for effect.

"Are you there? I lost you."

"You didn't lose me. Take a guess at the identity of Stone's sugar-daddy fiancé?"

"I have no idea. The mayor of Brennantown."

"No, but a good guess. He happens to be Cornelius Green, the powerful businessman."

"Any relation to Gavin Green?"

"He's his father."

"Was the affair legitimate?"

"I don't know."

"Interesting. Great work!"

"There's more. Cornelius Green's first wife, Janet, died a mysterious death, falling down a long set of stairs. Guess who found her body?"

"I don't know. Cornelius."

"No. It was her son, Gavin Green. He was eight at the time. Janet's death was ruled an accident. I got all that from the local papers and police reports. A few months later, Ms. Stone and old Cornelius got engaged. The suspected Hughes affair seems to have occurred shortly after Stone's engagement to Green. But that's not all. Six months after the affair scandal surfaced, Ms. Stone gave birth to a baby girl. When the scandal first broke, Cornelius broke off the engagement and went on record to proclaim that the child was not his, claiming Hughes had fathered it. Crazy, huh?" Chen paused.

"Yeah. What happened to Stone and the child?"

"She remained publicly silent throughout the scandal, dropping out of school shortly after it surfaced. It's not clear what happened to her and her daughter after that. When she delivered the baby, she listed an address that never existed."

"What happened to her? She and her daughter couldn't have disappeared. Did she get back with Hughes? I knew I didn't like that guy for a reason."

"I don't know. I've got three web searches going at the same time. Based on what I could find in the past hour, it appears that she vanished from the public record like a ghost. Things weren't electronic back then, so I don't know what happened…I just got this—Cornelius Green remarried and had two children with his second wife. They're still married. Her name's Gloria Green. The kids are a boy and a girl, eighteen and sixteen, respectively and they live in Puerto Vallarta, Mexico."

"Wow! Some family. Well, Hughes is officially a suspect. Tell me about Will Porter. You have anything on him?"

"I'm just starting on him, but he's very shady."

"I gathered that from what Gus Morgan told me."

"As best as I can tell, Porter was not only suspected of dealing drugs, but he had been arrested twice on possession of marijuana. Both times he was bailed out by guess who?"

"I don't know," the Inspector replied.

"Sam Hughes. In addition, Porter has been interviewed several times in recent months by our federal drug enforcement friends at the DEA. I've got them looking through their files. It appears they didn't have enough evidence to convict him. He always managed to slip away."

"Okay, keep digging."

"By the way, I just found more on Hughes. Apparently, he cleaned up his act after college and became a high-powered financial analyst in Pittsburgh. According to this Pittsburgh paper, he got married to one of his coworkers, named Sandra Shea…Wow! That's awful. She died tragically in a car accident on New Year's Eve 2006. This article says she was six months pregnant with their first child when she died." Chen was reading information off one of his many computer screens. He could conduct database searches faster than the Inspector could process the information.

"All the women in Hughes' life seem to be disappearing or dying. We need to get more out of him. Molly's got to come through on this one."

"Looking at his Facebook pictures, he's totally Molly's type," Chen chuckled. *Jack Fulton better watch out*, he thought, but decided not to say anything. He knew that Molly and the Inspector were close, and that the Inspector still disliked Jack.

"Anything else?" the Inspector asked, ignoring Chen's last comment. He too could see Molly's attraction to Sam and decided to try and use it to his advantage. It was risky, but it was just the kind of risky move that often paid off in the past.

"Nothing on the Amish brothers, as you predicted," Chen replied, "and nothing more on the Drake history and legend. I've got a call in to Professor Murray's office, but no reply."

"Anything on Lenore?"

"No Lenore anywhere, except the one associated with Edgar Allan Poe's poem "The Raven." You think that's significant?"

"Are you trying to make me lose my mind, Chen?"

"No, sir. Just curious."

"Wait a minute! You may be onto something. Maybe Lenore's not a real person at all, but a code for someone associated with Gavin Green. Check into that. Thanks. Great work!" The Inspector was impressed with Chen's data mining abilities. *Thank God I have him on the team.*

"Okay. You're welcome, sir. I'll call you if I find anything earth shatterin'."

"Do that. Thanks again." They hung up, and the Inspector looked around for Kelly. She was talking to Amos Miller, who had come up the hill from his neighboring farm. *Now there's a bit of fortune*, the Inspector thought, as he approached the two.

"Mr. Miller, how are you, sir? Anything new?" the Inspector asked.

Amos stopped talking to Kelly and faced the Inspector in silence. His only reply was a barely audible "No."

"Seems like we had another disturbed grave overnight." The Inspector pointed at the fresh excavation of Arthur Drake's grave. "Did you happen to see or hear anything suspicious last night?"

Amos Miller was cautious around the inquisitive little man with the dark mustache. There was something about the Inspector that he did not trust. "He seems shady," he had told his brother Linus the night before. Thus, when the Inspector appeared, Amos put his guard up and remained silent.

Kelly filled the uncomfortable conversation gap in an attempt to answer the Inspector's question. "Mr. Miller and I discussed that while you were on the phone. He didn't hear or see anything peculiar. His dog was quiet all night, as well. He doesn't believe that any intruder crossed his property to get here. Right, Mr. Miller?" She looked to him for a response.

Amos simply nodded in agreement but did not say a word. Kelly could clearly read his discomfort and wondered at its origin. She was about to add to the conversation when the Inspector spoke. "I see. Mr. Miller, do you have any idea who may have done this?"

There was complete silence once more. Amos felt that any conversation with this shrewd inquisitor could lead to a growing suspicion about his involvement and that of his brother, Linus. Finally, he looked up at the Inspector and replied, "No."

"Mr. Miller, we found a broken shovel handle at this excavation. It has all the makings of Amish woodwork and happens to have initials carved into it. Are you interested in what those might be?" The Inspector was baiting the potential suspect.

Once again, prolonged silence prevailed. Kelly was uncomfortable and wanted to clarify. She was about to speak when the Inspector glared at her, inciting her to suffer the uncomfortable quiet.

Finally, Amos looked at the Inspector and replied, "No."

"I see. Well, it just so happens that the initials are 'LM'. Do you know anyone with those initials?" the Inspector asked. *I better get a 'yes' out of him on this one. If I didn't know better, I'd think he lawyered up,* the Inspector silently reflected and nearly chuckled at the thought.

The ritual repeated itself once more, and once more Kelly had to bite her tongue while Amos used up the prolonged silence in seeming reflection. Finally, he looked up at the Inspector and replied, "No."

What? Why, you lying pilgrim! the Inspector silently screamed in his head. Amos was starting to annoy him. However, he regained his composure. "I see. Well, it just so happens that your brother, Linus Miller, is an undertaker, and his initials are 'LM.' Isn't it interesting that an old grave was dug up by a mysterious someone in your backyard, and that someone used an Amish-made shovel with the same initials as those of your brother, the undertaker? I find it very intriguing, don't you?" A long silence followed.

Kelly was about to scream. She and prolonged silence were sworn enemies. This was like Chinese water torture for her. The silence between the two men continued longer than ever this time, and her lower lip was sore from her continued biting. *Please, someone say something!* she pleaded in her own flustered mind. Nothing was said for another whole minute. Then, Amos looked up at the Inspector and replied, "No."

The Inspector's annoyance with the uncooperative Amish man was staring to boil over. He was about to release his anger, when he saw Kelly standing slightly behind the man, making the universal sign of "shut up" by simulating the cutting of her own throat with her right hand. The Inspector understood the gesture and decided to walk away without further comment.

Once he was gone, Amos resumed his conversation with Kelly. No longer holding back, he explained to her in detail how he and Linus discovered the body of Will Porter. He even shared his odd encounter with the mysterious White Witch but downplayed her as a specter. When Kelly questioned him about the monogrammed shovel handle, he lied and did not betray that it had once belonged to his brother. After all, he wanted to believe that Linus was innocent. *Surely, my brother would not be mixed up in this. God, please forgive me for the lie but I had to protect Linus,* he silently prayed.

He was unaware that Kelly sensed his reservation to tell the truth. Furthermore, he was completely oblivious that his body language had betrayed to her his suspicions that Linus was somehow involved in what had transpired at Drakes Plot.

CHAPTER 41

Sam Hughes

It was ten o'clock in the morning. The breakfast rush at The Raven Inn had ended, and Sam Hughes headed to his office when Molly Dvorak stepped into his path. "Mr. Hughes, good morning. Can I talk to you for a few minutes?" Molly asked, flashing a winning smile.

"Good morning, Molly. Sure, we can talk. You want to sit here or in my office?" he asked, pointing to the deserted front lobby of the inn, which boasted the rugged style. Inspired by local hunting lodges, the lobby decor included numerous trophies of large bucks, a moose head and two large bear heads. These were only a small portion of the extensive taxidermic collection that Sam inherited from his father, an avid hunter. The trophies, along with the hand-hewn pine beams, the fieldstone fireplace, the brown, worn leather furniture and hunter green curtains, left no doubt in the minds of the guests that they were in rural western Pennsylvania.

"The lobby's fine," Molly replied. Once again, she could feel her attraction toward Sam as her heart rate increased and her palms began to sweat. *Damn this!* she thought, as she felt her cheeks redden with a blush.

Her reaction did not go unnoticed by the rugged innkeeper. He too felt an attraction, but unlike Molly, his body did not betray him. "Let's sit in the back corner near the fireplace." Sam pointed to the large hearth, where a small wood fire crackled. "It sets the mood," he added, to see if the young detective would blush once more.

She did, and he silently chuckled. *Wonder what's her story?*

Damn the blushing, she thought as she followed him toward the fireplace and sat in one of two large leather recliners that faced the fire.

"Can I get you a cup of tea or a glass of water?" he asked, before sitting down.

"No, thanks. All good," she replied with a shy smile. *God, I'm acting like a schoolgirl in front of this guy. How embarrassing.* With that thought in her head, she blushed once more, feeling the red heat of her cheeks.

He found the blushing irresistible. Molly had a girl-next-door beauty seamlessly blended with a professional air that juxtaposed strength and determination with vulnerability and charm. The entire package, accented by her long legs, large brown eyes, and flowing chestnut hair, was irresistible to most men. Likewise, her indisputable sincerity easily befriended most women. If the Inspector had a secret interrogation weapon, it was Molly Dvorak.

Sam's attraction to Elaine had quickly drifted into recent history as he sat beside the appealing detective. If their thoughts had materialized into words, Molly and Sam would probably be looking upstairs for a vacant bedroom. The subconscious weakness passed, and Molly regained control of the moment, while leaving Sam appropriately prepped to answer whatever question she desired to ask. His mind raced across dreamy images of the young woman whose doe eyes seemed to own him.

"Mr. Hughes," Molly began the informal interrogation with a professional air, "are you aware that another one of your employees, Will Porter, was found dead yesterday morning?"

"I heard. I still can't believe it," Sam replied, shaking his head. "Do you know what happened? I heard he was buried in a grave at Drakes Plot. Is that true? That's ridiculous! Rumors spread like wildfire in this valley. Was it linked to Gavin's death? What's going on around here?" Sam spoke in an emotional tone, visibly flustered.

If this guy's guilty, he sure is a good actor, Molly thought.

"I heard Gavin's death was an accident. Is that true?" he continued.

"I'm not privileged to discuss that."

"I understand, but what about Will's death?" he asked. "Was he really buried alive? There are crazy rumors circulating."

"Sorry, I really can't discuss details since it's an open investigation. But I need to ask you a few questions," Molly replied.

"Sure. Glad to help." He smiled, causing Molly to blush once more.

"Let's start with what you know about Mr. Porter. Can I record our discussion?" Molly asked.

"Yeah. I've got nothing to hide."

"Very well."

Molly set her smartphone to record mode and placed it on the rustic side table that was positioned between the two leather recliners that she and Sam occupied. The fire within the hearth grew, as if fueled by the subject at hand.

"Mr. Hughes, please be aware that what you are about to say can be used in a court of law as official evidence and testimony. Are you aware of this, and may I proceed?"

"Yes, and yes."

"Okay. Can you tell me about your relationship with Mr. William Porter?"

"He was a bartender here at the inn."

"How long has he worked here?"

"For about a year."

"Did you know him well?"

"Yes, as an employee."

"Were you aware that he was suspected of dealing drugs, even at work?"

Sam turned white in apparent shock, but quickly recovered. Molly picked up on this and made a mental note. "Are you referring to this inn?"

"Yes."

"No." Sam had regained his composure. "No, of course not."

I don't believe you. "Yet, you bailed him out twice when he was arrested on possession of marijuana in the past. Isn't that right?" she probed.

"It was one joint each time and that was a long time ago. Will liked to smoke a little, but he was harmless."

"So, you did know him on a personal basis?"

"We grew up in the valley. Here, everyone knows each other. We used to fly fish together, but…" He paused to weigh his words. "We are just work friends, now."

"What happened?"

"People change. Will pulled away. I don't know why."

"I see. On another topic, how did you come up with the name for this inn? I believe it was called The Eden Inn prior to you taking it over."

"Sounds like you already know a lot about me, Molly. Did you know that my dad was a stern SOB, and that I didn't want to have anything to do with this place? It was his baby, not mine, but life has a strange way of twisting your ambitions into its own reality, doesn't it? Sometimes you end up with the most unexpected bedfellows." Sam stared straight into her eyes, maintaining eye contact until she broke it.

Molly felt exposed and naked. *Does he know about me and Jack? That's impossible,* she concluded silently. "Yes, it does. So, how did you come up with the name, Mr. Hughes?" she asked remaining unflustered. She was in interrogation mode, so the blushing had ceased.

"Sam, Molly. It's Sam. Mr. Hughes was my old man."

She ignored the correction, having no desire for informality in what was shaping up to be a potential piece of court evidence. "If you don't mind, I prefer Mr. Hughes," she added with a smile.

"Suit yourself," he replied, with a hint of disappointment.

"Mr. Hughes, you didn't answer my question."

"What question? You have too many questions!" He raised his voice.

She knew she was nearing a sensitive point. Pausing for effect, she repeated the question in her best monotone, "Why did you rename this inn The Raven Inn?"

"Well, 'The Raven' was my nickname in high school. I guess it was my black hair and strong nose. Happy?"

She glanced at his handsome face, which did not look raven-like in the least, nose or otherwise, but accepted the answer without further question. She returned to the subject of Will Porter. "Can you tell me more about Mr. Porter?"

"There isn't much to tell. We were friends in high school. Like I said, we used to fish together but drifted apart. I got too busy, I guess. But there's no way Will was a drug dealer. I can tell you that much. I'm just horrified at his death and don't know what to make of it. There's no reason for it. Everyone liked him. The patrons loved him. He knew every drink in the book yet did not drink himself. He was the perfect bartender."

"Was there anything suspicious about him?"

"No. He was a perfectly normal guy's kind of a guy. I'm deeply saddened by his loss. Why was he digging at the old Drake grave, anyway?"

"How did you know that?"

"What?"

"About Drake's grave."

"I told you the rumor mill's been busy around here."

"I see. Do you have any idea what he was doing there?" Molly looked Sam straight in the eye and held her gaze.

He too held the gaze until she finally became uncomfortable with it and looked away. She was attracted to him yet scared of him at the same time. There were obviously many facets to Sam Hughes.

"I have no idea, but I need to get back to the business of running this inn," he replied. "It'll soon be lunchtime. The restaurant's crazy busy this week. Are we done, Miss Dvorak?" He decided to respect her insistence on formality. The fire had died down to cooling embers, mimicking his feelings for the intriguing detective.

"Yes, thank you. We're done for now," she replied. *In more ways than one,* she wanted to add but refrained. Somehow he had lost his appeal, but she did not know why.

"Good," he replied and quickly rose from his chair. To him, the encounter had been disappointing. As he was leaving, he turned to ask, "How long are you staying here? I have you, the Inspector, and Kelly booked through Sunday."

"I'm not sure, but Sunday's good."

"Fine, but I'll need to know by tomorrow if you need to extend the stay. I need to open the rooms up in advance, given it's leaf season."

"In that case, extend it through next Wednesday for all of us, including Inspector Cabot. Oh, one last question—where were you last night?"

"I was here, as always."

"'Til when?"
"'Til closing, why?"
"When's closing?"
"Two, why?"
"Nothing."
He raised his forearms in frustration. As he did so, his right sleeve slipped down to his elbow, exposing a Black Raven tattoo. Molly noticed it just as he quickly pulled his sleeve over it. Before she could ask about it, he was gone.

I'm not sure if he's telling the truth or lying, Molly concluded. She was unaware that a pair of eyes was watching her from the far corner of the lobby. The figure remained hidden as Molly ascended the stairs to her room. After she disappeared, Elaine emerged from the shadows before heading to the dining room.

CHAPTER 42

Jerry McAlester

"What the hell's this, Marco? I told ya never to make that crap in my kitchen! I'll be damned if we start servin' up that slop!" Jerry McAlester yelled at his kitchen help. "Where's Johnny? How the hell're we gonna get lunch ready?"

Jerry was a man who wore his temper on his sleeve. His heart was another matter. It did not seem to surface much at all, lately. The inn staff knew that Jerry and Sam were high-school friends, but the two men could not be more different. Sam was quiet and reflective, even brooding at times. Large in stature, he resembled a pensive bear. His friend, Jerry McAlester, head chef at The Raven Inn, was a small, wiry, red-headed Irishman who seemed to perpetually oscillate between irritated and flamboyant. With a brashness that often rubbed others the wrong way, including some clientele, he could transform, minutes later, into a gala spectacle of exuberance.

Despite this unnerving imbalance, he was a natural at cooking. A large part of the inn's success was tied to Jerry's culinary bravado. He was making a name for himself in local restaurant circles, which added to the growing popularity of The Raven Inn. However, Jerry had a deep, dark side that few dared to explore. Those who inadvertently wandered there were certain to never venture there again. It was as if two different people were wrapped into one.

Tension had grown between the two figureheads of the popular inn. Sam, the owner, was often visibly annoyed by Jerry's antics and mood swings. Jerry was increasingly jealous of his boss's growing financial success, which he felt was exclusively due to his under-appreciated and underpaid talents. Most patrons had witnessed the strain between the two, as it often erupted in quick, heated skirmishes. It seemed only a matter of time before Jerry would quit or Sam would fire him. The fact that they were high-school friends made things even more bizarre. Then, about three months ago, just when it seemed the anticipated parting was at hand, the seas calmed and the two men became visibly close. This sudden peace was inexplicable to all.

Both men were staunch bachelors. Although Sam had been married in the past, he appeared to have no desire to reenter the straits of matrimony. Despite his bachelor reputation, he clearly fancied Elaine, the young restaurant server who had become a boarder at the inn. Speculation was rampant that the two were having a secret romance, despite their fifteen-year age difference, but no concrete evidence ever materialized, not even a public kiss.

Jerry seemed uninterested in women, preferring drink instead. His culinary talents seemed to drain him, as if creativity had a price that needed recharge from a bottle of bourbon. Sam allowed him three free drinks a night, but Jerry often exceeded the limit. For that reason, he had become close with the lead bartender, Will Porter. However, in recent months, that friendship was under a growing strain, for Sam had begun to track alcohol consumption more closely and docked Will's pay for gross, mysterious overruns. Sam suspected Jerry's growing fondness for whiskey and decided to cut off the source. As a result, Will stopped serving Jerry free drinks beyond the three drinks per night limit. Jerry blamed Will. He dared not start another feud with Sam. Despite Jerry's outer brashness, he had grown careful around Sam and for good reason. Sam, like the bear he resembled, was not one to anger easily, but he was the one force at the inn that Jerry seemed to fear. The history of that fear remained a mystery.

On this particular morning, Johnny arrived thirty minutes late to work and Jerry laid into him. "Ya want this job or not? I'll make ya the dishwasher. Ya can have Gavin's job. Ya want that? Damned thankless kid! One more late day, and you're my new dishwasher! Ya hear?" Jerry raged.

With breakfast over, it was time to prepare for lunch. But Jerry remained irritated with his two cooks. He was chopping pork, swinging a meat cleaver in formidable fashion, when he decided it was time for a trip to the pantry. "Take over. I want these chops thick. You understand?" Jerry instructed Johnny. The two changed places without looking at each other. Johnny did not care for Jerry, but he needed the money. Although he was only twenty, he had a three-year-old son and another baby on the way.

"Bastard," Johnny whispered under his breath as he picked up the meat cleaver.

"What'd ya say?"

"Nothin'."

"Ya better start kissin' up to me, boy!"

Silence followed.

"Marco, aren't you done with the onions? I haven't got all day. I'll be right back. I need to get some spices from the pantry."

Both kitchen hands knew that this was a code word for a drink of whiskey. On an average day, Jerry started drinking before eleven and didn't stop until he fell into bed late at night. It was his routine. But, of late, he had been taking time off from work, and the sous-chef had to run the kitchen.

The sous-chef had just walked in the door as Jerry disappeared into the pantry. "Where's Jerry?" he asked. His name was Harold, which was a rather formal name for a very informal young man.

"He's in the pantry."

"Already?" Harold replied.

"He's startin' early this morning 'cause Johnny was late again," Marco replied.

"It's 'cause Marco was makin' refried beans just to piss 'im off," Johnny replied.

"It worked, too," Marco answered and laughed. None of the kitchen staff cared for Jerry McAlester. He was a difficult boss who insisted on strict discipline.

"Did ya hear about Will?" Harold asked the others as he donned his work clothes.

"Yeah. That's crazy. What the hell was he doin' up at the old Drake place, anyway? I wouldn't go up there if ya paid me. That place's creepy," Johnny observed.

"I have no idea what he was up to, but I heard he was buried alive," Harold said, while changing into his kitchen whites.

"Get out!"

"I ain't screwin' with ya. I heard it from a reliable source."

"Who?" Johnny asked, looking up from chopping the pork.

"Phyllis Preachy."

"Phyllis Preachy's full of shit!" Johnny proclaimed, emphasizing his case with a crash of the cleaver against the chopping block.

"She heard it from one of the cops."

"I don't believe anything Phyllis Preachy says. Not now, not ever."

"I wouldn't be surprised if she was right," Marco chimed in. "That Drake place's haunted. I heard the Amish say so. They don't lie, like you, Johnny. And, just the other day, old Stanley Houser claimed he saw the White Witch when he was huntin'."

"You two're both nuts!" Johnny proclaimed. "Believin' Phyllis Preachy and Stan Houser. Huh! Why don't you get that drunk, Finley, to swear that he saw Will's ghost and the White Witch dancin' at midnight. If ya suggest it, ten minutes later he'll swear it happened. You guys're killin' me."

"Speakin' of drunks, here comes our fearless leader. Pantry party's over," Marco observed.

"I heard that, Marco. Watch your step! For what it's worth to you clowns, I've given it up. So, mind your own business and focus on gettin' lunch ready. Harold, it's about time ya got your sorry ass in here!" Jerry exclaimed. "It's almost lunchtime and the prima donna rolls in late again. I'm dockin' your pay, boy!"

"Screw you, Jerry!"

"What did you say to me?"

"I said, 'Screw you'!"

"Get the hell out of my kitchen, right now!"

"You sure you want that, Jerry? With you hittin' the sauce, who's goin' to cook up those famous dishes ya take credit for every time I create one?" Harold asked. He had no fear of Jerry for he knew the real boss was Sam Hughes, who had brought him in to shore up his unpredictable chef. Harold was starting to outshine Jerry with his creativity, and the latter was getting jealous.

At this point, Jerry could not run the kitchen without Harold. Despite his culinary talents, he had become too dependent on him, as he seemed to spend more and more time outside the inn. Where he spent that away time was not certain. Most speculated that he simply got drunk in the barn or the backyard, but none bothered to confirm it or complain. It would not make any difference. Sam would surely side with Jerry. If Jerry did sneak away with his whiskey, he seemed to be getting better at holding his alcohol, reappearing from his mysterious lapses seemingly sober. He was becoming more and more of an enigma, but no one dared to step between Sam and Jerry. That would be career suicide. Even Harold knew that he could only push Jerry so far.

"Watch yourself, punk! I need to run out for some fresh herbs. By the time I get back, I want to see lunch ready," Jerry growled, resetting the power in the kitchen before disappearing out the back door.

"Sam ought to make you the head chef, Harold. You're the real chef, anyway," Marco said, after Jerry disappeared.

"They're high school buddies—that counts for a lot. They've been very chummy lately. Not like a few months ago. Back then, I was sure Sam would can 'im," Johnny said.

"Too bad he didn't," Marco replied.

"Wonder what changed?" Harold piped up.

As they pondered this while preparing lunch, Jerry had decided to bypass the herb garden and seek out Sam, who manned the front desk at the inn. He got there just as Molly left the lobby. The night before, Jerry had noticed that Sam fancied the tall, young woman, and could not resist poking a little fun at his boss and long-time friend.

"Ya new girlfriend just left, ey? I hear she's a cop. Is that true? If so, ya better watch yourself, ol' dog," Jerry said with a sly sneer.

"Shut up, Mac! Shouldn't you be in the kitchen cookin' lunch?" Sam looked at his watch to emphasize his point. His nickname for Jerry had always been "Mac." Jerry hated the name but Sam was the boss, so he put up with it.

"I can tell ya fancy 'er. But we don't need 'er to complicate things around here. They're screwed up enough."

"The only thing screwed up is you, Mac."

"What've ya been up to, Sam? I can tell you're hidin' something." Jerry looked Sam in the eyes. The latter broke the gaze.

"Mind your own business, Jerry, and get back in that kitchen, or I may decide to can you, yet."

"Ya wouldn't dare 'cause I know all about Will and Gavin, and what went down."

CHAPTER 43

Where is Anna?

ater that same morning, Ariella awakened by the side of the woodland pool to the sound of the gentle waterfall. The fog had lifted and the forest was filled with sunbeams that penetrated between the massive trees. These rays of light made the dew sparkle before it disappeared, evaporating like Ariella's noble image of herself. She no longer felt like the savior of lost souls or the protector of innocence. Her confidence as teacher guiding troubled youth to harmony and self-worth vaporized with the fleeting dew.

Damn it! Why did I go that deep? She lamented her choice to callously push beyond her previous boundaries. *I saw too much this time. I saw too much!* She buried her face into her palms and sighed in disbelief. *Surely, good's good and evil's evil, and the two can't live in me in seeming harmony. What've I done that I'm unaware of? I must be losing my mind. Maybe all that's happening is part of my descent into insanity. Damn, why did I push so far? The Master made me promise not to go there. He warned me when he taught me that there's a dark side to every eternal truth, like the dark backing of a mirror or the shadow created by the light. He warned me that the ultimate "Mirror of Truth" is the most frightenin' thing of all.*

I reached it and now I know too much. Damn my foolishness! She pressed her face back into her palms, hiding it from the rays of sun that illuminated her in her despair.

Ariella's unbreakable spirit seemed crushed by her recent revelation. How could she, the White Dove, the loving, caring shaman, be linked to the unsettled spirit that haunted this valley? How could she be so directly connected to the White Witch, somehow energizing the specter's recent increase in activity? Surely, if the ghost existed, it was that of Evelyn Drake, as legend had it. *Maybe, the whole thing's nothin' but a bad dream?* she concluded. *How am I to face the girls, now?*

The thought of her girls made her heart sink, as she remembered feeling Anna's presence in her dream, or whatever it was that she had encountered in her deep trance. *I need to find Anna!* With that thought, all her self-loathing and self-analysis dissipated. She rose and rushed toward her cabin in search of Anna.

When she reached the house, she found several of the girls eating breakfast. Only Sarah and Marie were still asleep. The two were night owls; no morning routine ever fit their natural rhythm.

"Is Anna here?" Ariella asked as she burst through the cabin door. It was unlike her to be flustered, especially after her morning meditation. This change in her character took everyone by surprise.

"I haven't seen her this morning," replied Rachel. "She might be sleeping. Sarah and Marie aren't down yet, either."

Although Anna's two roommates, Sarah and Marie, were late risers, Anna was the opposite. Ariella hoped that Rachel was right.

"Are you all right, Ariella?" asked Rebecca. She and Anna were the most forward of the half-dozen young women that comprised the group.

Ariella did not answer. Instead, she rushed up the worn, pine stairs to the small room shared by Anna, Sarah, and Marie. Knocking softly and hearing no reply, she entered. Sarah and Marie were sprawled out on the double bed, hugging pillows. They were fast asleep, but Anna's cot was empty.

"Marie, Sarah, wake up!" Ariella nudged at the sleeping youths.

"What's the matter?" Marie muttered.

"Sorry to wake you, but have you seen Anna?"

"Isn't she in her bed?" Marie replied, while Sarah continued to slumber.

"No. Did you see her get up this morning?"

"No." Marie rolled over and went back to sleep.

Ariella rushed back downstairs. "Has anyone seen Anna this morning?"

The girls all shook their heads. "I was the first one up after you left and I haven't seen her. I awoke when I heard the screen door slam as you went out this morning," Rebecca replied.

"Maybe she disappeared, like Lenore," Hazel speculated in a frightened voice.

Ariella betrayed a rare moment of panic. Her fear became contagious, and soon the entire house was in an uproar. "We need to search the grounds," Rebecca suggested.

Agnes, the former maid at The Raven Inn and the newest member of the sisterhood, feared the worst, recalling her own recent attack. "I hope that masked guy who attacked me didn't find 'er," she whispered.

Ariella had not been this frazzled since she became a shaman. She had always prided herself on her composure, regardless of the situation. Somehow the combination of her horrific revelation while in her deep meditation, combined with Anna's disappearance, had triggered a fearful panic that had blindly taken over her mind and blocked her perceptive powers. Presently, she found herself lost in a fog of fear, not unlike the thick layer that had surrounded the cabin earlier that morning. Except now the vast meadow in front of the cabin glowed in the bright sunlight that accentuated the tall, golden grass. "We need to search the grounds. Everyone, search the grounds for Anna!" Ariella exclaimed.

The girls, most of whom were half-dressed or in their sleeping attire, raced about the cabin grounds and the neighboring meadow like alarmed mice spurred by a prowling cat. Fear led to panic, which transformed into mania, that died back to despair, ending in gut-wrenching emptiness. Collective fear filled the void. Ariella had doubted herself, her powers and her worth. In that doubt, she opened the door to fear, which spread through her followers like wildfire through the golden meadow, in the center of which the disturbed and disheveled group now coalesced.

"She's gone, just like Lenore!" Hazel proclaimed through her tears.

"She wouldn't leave without saying goodbye to us. Something happened to her," Rachel said.

"Ariella, you know something. What is it?" Rebecca asked their leader.

"I don't know anything, Rebecca. I sense nothing. That's what scares me. I sense nothing." Ariella decided not to share her disturbing meditative trip, or its revelations about her and Anna's potential fate. She did not want to panic the young women any further. Regaining some control over her fears, she added, "But, I'm sure Anna's fine. She's a strong woman. Besides, there's nothing to fear in these woods."

"What about the masked guy that tried to rape me? That's something. What if he got her? He was scary," Agnes reflected, increasing the group's panic.

"Agnes, no such evil can touch Anna."

"How do ya know? How do ya know he doesn't have 'er already? If he does, God help 'er!" Agnes replied.

"She's fine. Don't panic. She's out for a mornin' walk." Ariella tried to console herself and her little makeshift family. Inside, she harbored a growing fear. Her powers, as well as her confidence, had disappeared. *What's going on here?* she thought, while trying to maintain her composure. She had to be strong for the others, even though inside she was nothing more than a shell for her fears. These fears, which seemed to have taken over her stomach, began attacking her heart.

"He had a black raven tattoo on his arm. That's all I saw," Agnes muttered softly.

"Who?" asked Rachel, naively.

"The monster who attacked me."

CHAPTER 44

Dead End

It was nearly eleven o'clock in the morning when Kelly and the Inspector decided to leave the crime scene at Drakes Plot. They headed along the Eden River to the small neighboring town of Glen Ryan in search of lunch. On the way, they picked up Molly at The Raven Inn before proceeding south, through the heart of Eden Valley. The day was sunny and the splendor of autumn transformed the landscape into a colorful masterpiece. A gentle breeze harvested a bountiful crop of leaves from the tired trees. There was a sense of closure in the air that foreshadowed the deep slumber of another cold, snowy winter in these rolling hills that were the last eroded remnants of the once tall and mighty Appalachians.

The Appalachians had reached their apex about 300 million years before, attaining a grandeur well beyond that of their much younger siblings, the present-day Rocky Mountains and Sierra Nevada. One of the oldest existing mountains on the planet, they had witnessed the evolution of life from primitive sea creatures to the age of man.

In comparison, the primary sculptor of this picturesque valley was a mere youngster. That sculptor, the now tranquil Eden River, had carved her way through strata dating back half a billion years. These rocks, some pulled, crushed, and twisted by the unimaginable forces that are still active within our unique planet, were a reminder of a slower, mightier change, whose time scale made the daily actions of humans seem like dew drops in the river's vast watershed.

The village of Glen Ryan was slightly larger than Eden Crossing. It contained a supermarket, a hardware and feed store, and an old restaurant that claimed to serve the finest cheesesteaks outside of Philadelphia. That restaurant was called The Dead End, referencing the fact that the old railroad track that ran through the heart of Eden Valley ended in Glen Ryan—its southernmost stop. This popular eatery sat atop a steep bank overlooking a set of cascading falls, the most spectacular waterfalls on the Eden River. At the rear of the restaurant was a large, covered deck with a breathtaking view of the terraced cascades. This view and the legendary cheesesteaks were the main draw to this rural gem.

"How'd you know about this place, boss?" Molly asked the Inspector.

"Gus recommended it. I didn't want to meet at The Raven Inn. There're too many ears in that place. Too bad it's the only hotel around; otherwise, I'd move us out of there," the Inspector reflected. He pulled into the small parking lot adjacent to The Dead End restaurant. "Let's get some lunch, ladies. This one's on me. After that, we'll call Chen and have our team meeting."

After ordering their lunch on the spacious deck, the Inspector called Chen and put him on speakerphone. The police team had the seating area all to themselves. The main lunch crowd had not yet materialized, and the other early birds sat inside due to the chill in the air. Nonetheless, the team discussed the case in a low tone, often using their own code according to a set of rules that the Inspector had developed over decades of detective work. The Inspector's code seemed silly to the younger team members, but, since he invented it, he often insisted on using it.

The Inspector began. "Chen, how are you? I'm here with Molly and Kelly. We're at a small local restaurant. You open to talk?" The term "open," which the Inspector emphasized, was the word triggering Code #3. The Inspector had three codes. The most restrictive was Code #1. Code #3 was the least restrictive. It simply meant use caution and minimize use of names.

"Sure. No problem. Open to talk," Chen replied in a drab voice, realizing he would have to be careful about what he said. By replying "open to talk," he confirmed that he would use Code #3 during the entire discussion.

"Great. Any news? I informed the ladies about what we discussed earlier. Remember you're on speaker."

"Hello, Molly. Hello, Kelly."

They got through the cordialities and Chen replied to the Inspector's question. "Sir, as I dig deeper, another person appears as a potential player." According to the code, he also avoided words such as "suspect," "investigation," "victim," "killer," and others that might spur the attention of anyone eavesdropping on the conversation.

"Who? You can talk freely. Coast is clear," the Inspector advised. He did not see a reason to code the name, which was a cumbersome process.

"Jerry McAlester, the cook at the inn."

"Interesting. Why?"

"Ya wanna use #3 or not?"

"Drop it. Darn this," the Inspector muttered, adding, "We'll warn you if there's an issue." Molly and Kelly looked at each other and smiled. Kelly almost burst into laughter, but quickly turned away to control herself.

"Okay, that makes it easier. McAlester, like Hughes, has an odd past."

"Say more."

"A native of the Eden Valley, he grew up on a nearby farm and attended the same high school with Hughes and Porter. They graduated together. I couldn't find anything else from the high school years, except for the yearbook picture I just e-mailed Molly. It's a picture of Porter, Hughes, McAlester, and a couple classmates."

"So far, I don't see anything odd about McAlester," the Inspector interjected.

"That was background. The odd part's coming up," Chen replied and chuckled. He, too, liked to tease the Inspector at times.

"Chen, can you get to it before our lunch arrives?" The Inspector was getting impatient.

"Okay, okay, the odd part is that McAlester, Porter, and Hughes, along with two other classmates, seemed to have a club called 'The Black Ravens.' I got that off the yearbook picture I just sent Molly. The purpose of the club is unclear. But I did find out that both Porter and McAlester were arrested for marijuana possession shortly after high school graduation. Hughes bailed them out. By the way, the two other young men in the photo I sent you are Harry Schaffer and George Walker."

"What's the story on those two?" the Inspector asked.

"Seems they're both dead. Schaffer disappeared in Bosnia and was officially presumed dead, and Walker died in a mysterious car accident four years ago. His car plunged into the Eden River at Glen Ryan."

"We're in Glen Ryan right now. Where was the accident?" Molly asked.

"It was off of a bridge."

"That must be the bridge just past here. The one that's closed."

"Walker? Any relation to our friend Alvin Walker?" the Inspector asked.

"Brothers. George was his older brother."

"The plot thickens," Kelly said in a hushed voice.

"Dig up what you can on George Walker's death. Also, dig into Schaffer's past. I know he's dead, but this Black Raven Club could be significant," the Inspector instructed Chen.

"I'm on it, sir."

"Good work. Anything else on McAlester?"

"Nothing. There's so little on this guy that it's odd. It's as if he didn't exist between high school graduation and when he took over as chef at the Hughes' restaurant, three years ago."

"Who's the young lady in the high school group pic?" Molly asked, as she looked at the photo that Chen had texted to her.

"I'm not sure. I'm looking into it. I'll know soon."

"Thanks, Chen. Good work. Call me if you find anything else of value," the Inspector added before ending the call.

"Interesting history," Molly observed.

"I have a feeling this picture's key." Kelly pointed to the photo that Molly displayed on her smart phone. "Could all this be drug related?"

"Could be. That would tie into Green's deadly overdose. But exactly how are they linked? That's the question. Or are they not linked at all? That seems improbable. This one's got me stumped," the Inspector lamented. "Molly, how was your interview with Hughes?"

"Fine. He seems like a nice guy. Unfortunately, I didn't get anything significant out of him regarding Will Porter or any drug dealing. He swore Porter was clean."

"He's a smart one, that Hughes. Reminds me of…eh, never mind." The Inspector thought of Molly's current boyfriend, Jack Fulton, and decided to refrain from aggravating her. He never liked Fulton, and he certainly disliked Sam Hughes. *Guys like that think they're invincible, but they're not. Eventually, it all catches up to them.* His reflections were interrupted by the server, who finally appeared with a large tray of food.

The deck at The Dead End restaurant sat fifty feet above the cascading river. With a view of the tiered waterfall, framed by the yellow, orange, and red foliage, it provided a setting that could have been cut out of a travel brochure. Sound of the churning water added to the ambiance.

"Why is the place so empty?" the Inspector asked the server.

"Usually we're closed on Wednesdays. But, with the foliage, the owner decided to stay open today. Unfortunately, the word didn't get out, so it's been slow. Where ya folks from?" asked the server. Although in her early fifties, she did not look the part.

"We're from Brennantown. Can I get some ketchup?" the Inspector replied.

"Sure. I'll be right back."

The woman returned with the ketchup. "And here's some more water." "So, what brings you and your two daughters to Glen Ryan?" she asked the Inspector.

Kelly and Molly looked at each other and tried not to burst into laughter.

"The leaves," the Inspector replied.

"I knew it. It's beautiful, isn't it? It's nice to visit, but there's not much to do here, ya know. What do ya do?" she asked the Inspector, while completely ignoring the two women.

"I'm a cop."

"Oh, wow! I guess even the police deserve a holiday. Nice of ya to bring your daughters out. They're pretty. Their mother must be, as well?" The recently-divorced waitress was fishing.

Molly and Kelly could barely keep from laughing. Molly was staring away at the river, as Kelly responded, "Yes, she is. Thank you so much."

Annoyed, the Inspector had no desire to prolong the conversation by correcting the woman. The exchange continued for several minutes before the friendly waitress got the hint and disappeared into the restaurant.

"You're still a chick magnet, boss, and we're proud to be your daughters," Molly replied with a laugh.

"As your younger daughter," Kelly began, giving Molly a quick glance to see if she would react, "I can't fathom why such a hunk as yourself isn't married." The two women laughed some more.

The Inspector brushed them off with a wave of his right hand. "You're lucky I raised two daughters of my own. Otherwise, I'd have both of you written up for insubordination."

"Oh, admit it—you'd be lost without us. Who'd solve all the cases for ya?" Molly replied.

"Yeah, without us, you'd have nothing but Chen and his computer," Kelly added. "By the way, I promise never to call you a 'hunk' again."

Molly was laughing so hard that she spit out her French fries, which caused Kelly to laugh hysterically. Finally, the Inspector joined in the fun. He loved his team, and although he missed big Bob Braxton, Kelly was a fine replacement. Ironically, these two young women were like daughters to him.

After more laughter and some serious eating, it was time to head back to Eden Crossing and resume the investigation. Upon settling the bill, the three headed toward the car. On the way, Kelly made an observation. "I just got a weird feeling."

"What?" Molly asked.

"I think we were followed here."

"Why would you think that?"

"Don't look now, but that car hiding in the driveway across the street looks like Alvin's."

"You're imagining things, Kelly." The Inspector looked at the black sedan, nearly hidden by the trees.

"Am I? Look over there."

Molly and the Inspector looked back toward the front door of the restaurant. They noticed Alvin just before he disappeared into the building.

"Interesting. I never had a case where the local cops were spying on me," the Inspector replied. "I'm going to ask old Alvin what he's up to." He returned to the restaurant. Molly and Kelly quickly followed. They did not want to miss the fireworks.

"This should be good," Molly whispered. She did not like Alvin Walker either.

When they reentered the restaurant, they found no sign of Alvin. Instead, they ran into the friendly server. She had not seen a man fitting his description.

Just as they were about to leave once more, they heard a car race down the road. Running outside, they saw Alvin's sedan disappear down the dead-end road, which was marked as such.

"I thought that bridge was out and the road's a dead end?" Kelly looked over at Molly.

"Obviously not!"

"This case keeps gettin' weirder," the Inspector concluded.

"Daddy, you got that right," Molly replied, before she and Kelly burst out laughing.

CHAPTER 45

The Portal

Ariella fell into a panic. Anna had vanished, just as Lenore had before her. But this time there was a difference. When Lenore disappeared, Ariella had full control of her powers. The insights and intuition they provided gave her a sense of peace. She knew that Lenore was alive. Anna was a different story.

"Rebecca, please come here," Ariella requested.

"What is it?"

"I need to leave for the afternoon. Can you look after the girls until I return?"

"Sure. Are you goin' to look for Anna?"

"Yes, but I'll be back by nightfall. If anything changes, I'll call you."

"Do you know where she is? The girls are worried. First Lenore disappeared, and now Anna. What's going on?"

"The two aren't related. Lenore's fine. She's back with her family. I'm sure Anna's fine, as well. She's been talking about leaving." She lied to try and pacify her little flock.

"She has? Funny, she never said anything to me. So, you know where she is?"

"I think so."

"I'll come with you. She's my best friend," Rebecca insisted.

"You're the oldest. I need you to stay here. I'll be back by dinner time."

"With Anna?"

Ariella hesitated for a second before replying. "Yes, with Anna."

"You're amazing. Thank you. Should I tell the girls?"

"Tell them after I leave. I need to go now," Ariella replied and disappeared out the back door. She had no idea where Anna could be, but she knew that until she regained her composure, any search for Anna would be of little use. Quickly, she crossed the meadow and entered the thick woods. Determined, she headed to the sanctuary of her beloved waterfall and thermal pool.

As she approached the site, she could see it transformed by the rays of the afternoon sun peeking through the high canopy of oak and beech trees. The fog had disappeared, as did the magenta hue of dawn. Both were replaced by beams of gold, creating a warm and inviting setting. As she entered her place of refuge, her panic subsided, replaced by fatigue—a peaceful fatigue.

I need to center myself, she thought. *I need to cleanse this fear.* With that idea freshly implanted in her mind, she looked about the glen. All seemed quiet with no intruders. She disrobed and plunged into the warm water of the pool. The water invigorated her body as she finally relaxed. *Ah, better, but I'll need to enter the cave,* she thought.

The small cave formed her deep sanctuary. It was well hidden behind the waterfall, accessible through a short underwater passage. Presently, she entered it by diving beneath the churning water, swimming through the flooded cave opening, and emerging in a small pool located in the floor of the cavernous chamber. This submerged route provided the only viable entrance into the grotto, part of which was open to the back of the waterfall such that air and a faint light entered it through the cascading water. But this rocky window into the back of the cataract was too small to be an entryway.

Once inside, she was greeted by a greenish glow that emanated from the small pool through which she had entered. The result looked eerie, yet incredibly beautiful. She called this chamber and its reflective pool "The Portal," for here she received her greatest insights.

Yet this time felt different. She had never entered here in a more fragile state of mind than she did today. Knowing that doubt and fear were the arch enemies of the very connection she now sought to regain, she had to relinquish both. *I hope this works,* she thought. *It has to work. I need to find Anna.*

Getting out of the water, Ariella shivered in the cold air as she wrung out her wet hair and knelt before the pool. The water looked crystal clear, revealing the shallow bottom covered with river rock and green algae. To anyone else, this unique place would be a natural wonder and nothing more. But, to her, it represented a sacred place, as it had been to the Native Americans centuries earlier.

Gazing into the turquoise pool, she began her chant. Closing her eyes, she cleared her mind, receptive to all. Her shaman mentor had taught her how to reach a state beyond the mind. Usually, she could do so without retreating into this sacred sanctuary, but today she would need all the help she could muster. The revelation in which she saw herself as the mysterious White Witch still haunted her mind, the very mind she now tried to clear.

Love is a powerful force, especially when combined with perseverance. Ariella loved Anna, and it was that love which drove her determination. In its presence, she finally shed her fear. In her deep trance, she no longer cared if she were the White Witch. If find Anna, she had to use the mysterious scepter or her phantom energy to do so—so be it.

With this single focus, she fell into a deep hypnotic state. The small pool appeared to transform into a mirror that transcended time and space. Ariella felt free—free of all that was of the mind and of her own reality. Deeper she dove until the portal fully opened, and by entering, she lost herself completely. She seemed to cross over to a plane that may or may not have been of her own creation; it did not seem to matter. Free of fear and doubt, she floated in a receptive state that few could ever attain. It was here that she "saw" Anna at last.

The revelation appeared briefly, for her power remained weak, but it divulged enough to fuel her search. What she saw reassured her and frightened her in one brief instant. Anna was alive, but at the mercy of an evil that seemed much too familiar. Although she could not distinguish the identity of Anna's captor, she could see, in her receptive mind, the image of the Black Raven, her dark nemesis.

As in Lenore's prophetic poem, Ariella accepted her dual identity, that of the White Witch and the White Dove. After all, like everyone else, she owned the darkness and the light of her existence. She refocused, trying to identify Anna's captor. A deeper darkness crept into her receptive state. Once again, this darkness took the form of the dark raven. It appeared clear that he held Anna's life in his merciless talons. Despite her best efforts, his name and physical identity remained a mystery that she could not unravel—not today, not in her weakened state. He was too powerful. It became obvious that he, too, had access to this portal between reality and illusion, between life and what lay beyond. How he got it, she did not know.

Who are you? she thought, and the thought took on a voice in her dreamlike state. There was no answer. She asked the dark raven once more, *Who are you?* Once more, there was no answer, only the fear clearly portrayed in the face of her beloved Anna.

A third time, she asked *Who are you? I fear you not. Reveal yourself, you cowardly evil.* Her thoughts echoed through the timeless portal, as if she had shouted them from a mountaintop. Finally, the evil bird awakened. In a screeching sound, half-beast, half-man, it answered. *Your shadow! The price of your power.* This voice was familiar. She knew this dark presence. She knew the Black Raven. He had been with her before on more than one occasion. *Show yourself! I command you to show yourself!* she thought. The command echoed like thunder beyond the portal.

In response, she heard laugh, so evil it sent chills back to her highly receptive mind. *Now I hold the power over you, for I control the one you love the most. She will die and you cannot stop me. Lenore was a warning and the rest is a game—a game of revenge—a game of cat and mouse. Surprise! You, Ariella, are the mouse, ha, ha, ha, ha, ha.*

She shuddered at the voice and the threat, but she knew that to accept fear would mean losing the connection. *You're a coward. Show yourself,* she demanded in her thoughts that bellowed in this alternate reality. Was she insane or enchanted? She was not sure anymore, nor did she care. It did not matter. All that mattered in this charade was Anna. *Show yourself, you coward!* she screamed in her mind and through the portal beyond time.

Here, you foolish woman. Behold this, the evil answered.

Now, she recognized the one who had betrayed her, so long ago. She knew the Black Raven from her youth. *How could this be?* she thought, while the portal amplified it into a haunting question.

Opposites attract, my dear, and you and I are opposites. Or are we an extension of the same frail force that you call 'yourself'? The beast laughed in her receptive mind. *Your powers led you to me because you and I are one. We are kindred spirits made of the same mold.* He laughed an evil laugh that echoed through her mind, targeting her heart.

No! she screamed. *That can't be. We are NOT one! Do you hear ME? I'm your enemy, now and forevermore!* There was silence once more. She was getting weak. She could not sustain this alternate reality for much longer. *Where's Anna? Where are you keeping her?* she demanded.

No answer materialized. The image was obscured by the dark wings of a massive raven that took flight beyond her dream state. Shaken, Ariella awoke to find herself lying on her back, pressed against the cold rocky floor, just beyond reach of the small pool—naked, like the memory of what she had "seen" and "heard." Quickly, she tried to remember it before it faded into obscurity, for the two "realities" could not coexist for long. Unlike the revelation of the morning, this knowledge did not frighten her. It made her stronger and empowered her determination to crush the very oppressive force that haunted this valley, that haunted her.

Yet, deep down, the experience had a disturbing effect. *Am I really the source of this evil or have I gone completely mad?* she silently wondered as she reentered the turquoise pool.

CHAPTER 46

Lenore's Dream

That night, Lenore Lapp lay safely in her bed. Being Amish, her family had no electricity; they utilized only candles and lanterns. Bedtime was early, for the morning milking would come before dawn. Within the small farmhouse, Lenore shared a bedroom with her two younger sisters, Kate and Eve. Her sisters slept in one bed, while Lenore slept on a cot under the double window. According to Amish rules, none of the windows contained curtains. Such decorations were deemed frivolous. Thus, on clear nights like this one, Lenore had a beautiful view of the stars and the moon as she lay on her cot. And tonight, the waning moon illuminated her bed in a ghostly white light.

At ten past eleven, Lenore awakened from a vivid dream that startled her in its seeming familiarity. Unfortunately, her persistent amnesia did not allow her to judge it as a genuine memory. It felt familiar, even though it presented a reality beyond her belief.

In her dream, she sat around a fire pit, surrounded by young women like herself. At the head of the circle was a woman in her thirties, dressed in a white robe and Native American attire. She appeared to be in a trance, which inspired her small flock to imitation. Some seemed to have achieved their own version of a mental nirvana, but not Lenore. Instead, Lenore was the silent observer, no different than the large gray wolf that sat just outside the light of the fire, such that only the occasional burst in flames briefly illuminated his pale face and knowing eyes. The entire scene felt like a page from a Native American legend. All seemed silent, except the soft chanting of the shamanic woman, a chanting that Lenore could not understand for it utilized the native language of the Sioux.

This dream seemed so vivid that she still remembered it as she sat up in her simple cot at the Lapp homestead. Physically exhausted from the day's farm chores, she closed her eyes and fell back to sleep. As she reached the early phase of slumber, the dream returned as if it were a dual reality.

In this half-dream, Lenore was once more a member of the circle around the bonfire. The chanting had stopped, the wolf had disappeared, and all the participants seemed deep in a meditative state. All was silent until the shamanic woman awakened and floated, not walked, toward Lenore. As she approached, she seemed ghost-like, as if she had left part of her form seated at the far end of the circle of participants. When Lenore looked back to where the shamanic figure had originally sat, she still saw her there, seated as before, yet here she was, an apparition advancing toward her.

This dream differed from Lenore's usual dreams in that it seemed so real. Lenore felt frightened, but the dream would not release her. Despite a subconscious effort to awaken, she could not. She was trapped. The white apparition, with the flowing white gown, approached slowly, as if time was of little value and had little control over her actions. It was simply another extension of space and just as easily transgressed.

In her odd dream, Lenore's fear turned to wonder. Within the deep, dark eyes of the specter, she could see herself. Those eyes grew until they were like a mirror that did not reflect her form but her very soul, with all its fears, joys, strengths, and weaknesses. There was no escaping this haunting phantom that seemed capable of crossing to a formless state.

Now, the white specter reached Lenore and took her hand. This being possessed an energy and a force, such that Lenore could not let go. Yet there was something extremely familiar about this act and about what followed. The world around Lenore seemed to diminish as she took flight over it, effortlessly formless. Time was like space to this phantom; there seemed to be no difference as she carried Lenore beyond the world of reality. In this bizarre dream, Lenore simply saw an outline of her previous form, as if only a distant memory.

This flight ended in a place of incredible beauty that seemed earth-like, yet foreign. Her guide did not speak but all was clear. She had crossed into "Eden," a place of innocence unknown to the human mind. Was this heaven? Was she dead? Surely, it was nothing more than a very strange dream. Deep inside, something seemed to answer, "Welcome home."

Then fear took over, and she pulled away from her guide, who appeared surrounded by a bright white light. As she pulled away, she started spinning and all became blurry, as if she were in an endless vortex…falling…spinning. Startled, she awoke in her bed at last. Reality had returned, and she exhaled in relief. Part of her was happy to have shed this odd experience, and part of her felt alien in this place, the Lapp family home. The waning moon illuminated her in ghostly white as she looked at it through her window. *Strange dream,* she thought. *I wonder if supper didn't agree with me.*

It was just before midnight. At the beckoning of the wind, a few clouds drifted toward the white moon. Lenore sat at her window, staring into the adjacent field and the tree line beyond. Then, in the waning moonlight, she saw the very object of her bizarre dream. At the edge of the field, illuminated by the moon, stood a white phantom, staring up at her—its energy focused on the Lapp house and on her very window. Shaken, she hid her face. When she finally looked up, the white apparition had moved closer. She knew it was the White Witch; they had met before. *She found me,* she thought in despair and hid under her covers, as if these would shield her. For what seemed like twenty minutes, she stayed hidden.

Finally, her curiosity overcame her fears. Slowly, she shed the security of her blanket and looked out the window. The scene had changed for the moon had disappeared behind a thick wall of clouds taking the white specter with it. As Lenore relaxed once more, she heard a faint tapping on the window at the other end of the wall. It grew stronger with every rhythmic beat, persistent, eager to enter. Peering over, she fell back in fear.

A black raven sat of her outside windowsill, knocking on her bedroom window. Then, it stopped and whispered, "Oh, my Lenore—nevermore."

It was then that she finally awoke, gasping for air, a twisted sheet wrapped around her neck. The room was dark, all was silent, and the light of the waning moon had disappeared like the specters in her haunting dreams.

CHAPTER 47

Midnight Visitor

The hour was late as the small group of young women huddled around the stone fireplace in Ariella's cabin, their frightened faces illuminated by the wood fire. They did not dare to venture out for fear of encountering the evil that had robbed them of their ranks.

A deathly silence mixed with the crackle of the fire. Hazel, the youngest, broke the silence with a soft stream of sobs. Her crying spoke for all the remaining girls, who were the sentries of secrets they themselves did not fully comprehend. On this dreadful, endless night, they huddled together for support.

To date, they had lost Lenore, and nearly lost Agnes. Now, they had lost Anna, the brave one, while Ariella, their mentor, had not come home. Petrified, the six remaining women, Rebecca, Rachel, Marie, Sarah, Agnes, and Hazel, waited for Ariella's promised return. It was nearly midnight, yet she had promised to return by suppertime.

"What should we do?" Marie asked Rebecca, the Amish runaway who had become the leader of the small group.

"We go to bed, I suppose. It's getting late," Rebecca replied, looking at the clock on the old wooden mantel of the gray fieldstone fireplace.

"What if she doesn't come back tonight?" Rachel asked.

Rebecca shushed her charges. "She'll be back. She's stronger than anyone I've ever met. She'll be back."

Sarah joined her positive outlook. "Rebecca's right. Ariella'll be back with Anna. They're both very brave. If they ain't back tonight, they'll be here by mornin'."

Sarah was often the quiet one. Of all the young women, she tended to be the most positive and very curious, second only to Anna in that regard. Unlike Rebecca and Lenore's Amish roots, Sarah, like Marie, was an urban runaway. After a taste of the hard life on the streets of Philadelphia, she simply started hitchhiking west ending up on Ariella's doorstep nearly a year ago. This was now home to Sarah.

She and Marie were best friends. They were both abandoned at a young age and grew up on the streets of poverty as minorities in a landscape of little opportunity. Sarah was African-American and Marie was Puerto Rican. Both were forced into prostitution at a young age but managed to escape that fate through sheer determination. So, although they feared for Anna and for Ariella, both were strong young women who had risen beyond the social cesspools that tried to drown them.

Marie echoed her inseparable soul sister's words. "Sarah's right. They'll be back in the morning. I'm going to sleep. You comin', Sarah?" She rose and looked over at her roommate.

"I'm coming, but I need to give Hazel a hug." Sarah walked over to Hazel and embraced her. "You want to crash in our room?"

"Can I?"

"Sure, but Marie snores."

"I do not, Sarah!"

The lightheartedness had returned to the group, and soon they were all kidding one another as they prepared for bed. Hazel usually slept on the couch in the living room, a room she shared with Ariella, who slept on the other couch. Tonight, she appreciated the company of her older and braver "sisters." At twelve, she was the youngest member of the group—the baby in this family that everyone protected.

Ariella unofficially homeschooled her. The possible loss of Ariella frightened Hazel the most for she viewed her mentor as a mother figure. To make things worse, Anna had become the older sister that

Hazel had always wanted. Anna often looked after her, helping her with homework. Losing her two protectors terrified the youngster.

Hazel grew up with her grandparents, but when they died in an automobile accident, she was left orphaned, having never known her parents. After the accident, she ended up in a foster home. There, the father figure often beat her. Then came the night that he crawled into her bed and cornered her. Despite the frantic screams, her foster mother did not come to her aid. Desperate, she fought off her attacker, managing to poke him in the eyes. Seizing the opportunity, she ran out of the house in her pajamas and kept on running.

In Kamerynville, she ran into Ariella and Rebecca, who had gone to the Amish Market to get food and supplies. That is how she found her way here, and she had never felt more secure, until now. She was scared again, but at least she had her sisters, two of whom had just stuck her in between them on their large, old mattress.

"Remember, Hazel, if Marie starts to snore, just nudge her. It always works," Sarah instructed.

"I don't snore," Marie objected.

Hazel simply chuckled. She felt secure again, at least for now.

After all the other girls went to bed, Rebecca sat in front of the waning fire and could not sleep. She had been Ariella's first student, and Ariella was her rock. Anna was the brave, insatiable seeker. Sarah was the quiet thinker. Marie was the passionate warrior, Agnes the shy newcomer. Hazel personified childish innocence and acceptance. Rachel was the scientist and nature girl. And Rebecca was the loyal and brave rock. Lenore had been the storyteller and the poetic romantic. They all missed her and her stories.

Each young woman had struggled for freedom to be herself on her own terms. Each was different, and each was special. Ariella knew this, and her entire chosen purpose in life had become to raise and guide such young, promising women as these. Fortune had not sent any young men her way, but, had it, she would not have turned them down. It would have complicated things a little, but so far this was a sisterhood by the choice of Providence.

It was midnight when Rebecca heard the noise. All were asleep. She sat by the fireplace in the small living room, keeping guard over what she loved most—her sisters. Ariella was right to put her in charge.

Only she, Anna, and Rachel got that responsibility. One of the three older girls was always there for the rest.

The noise seemed subtle, like water dripping. With each drop, it grew into a tapping. Soft at first, the tapping became knocking—a steady knocking on the wooden door. Rebecca was braver than most, but this midnight knocking had her flustered. She wanted to awaken Sarah and Marie, but she remembered that Hazel shared their bed, and she did not want to awaken Hazel. She wanted to rouse Rachel, but she did not want to scare Agnes, her easily frightened roommate.

Deciding to investigate on her own, she grabbed the long iron poker from the fireplace and silently rose from the wooden rocking chair. The room had fallen into darkness, except for the glow of the embers in the dying fire. Their red radiance turned the log timbers of the cabin walls into ominous backdrops for the drama that unfolded.

The knocking ceased. Rebecca stopped in her tracks and tried not to breathe. She listened intently for the next sound. No sound came. Waiting, barely breathing, for what seemed like eternity, but no sound was audible. All was quiet, except the soft sound of Marie's snoring. This made Rebecca smile. Then, the noise returned. It sounded like a flailing bird trapped against the entryway—scratching and tapping on the wooden door.

Silently, Rebecca approached the doorway, while holding the iron poker. The tapping turned to rapping as the creature grew desperate, demanding to enter. Rebecca's senses became keen as adrenaline entered her veins. She heard the wind kick up and a passing shower brought the tin roof to life with the beat of a thousand keystrokes, peppering all, including the mysterious visitor at the front door.

"Ariella, is that you?"

No answer materials except the sound of the rain on the roof and the wind in the eaves.

"Ariella, is that you?" Rebecca repeated, louder this time. *She has a key. Why would she knock?* she thought as she reached the front door.

No word was spoken, but as the rain stopped, the rapping on the front door began in earnest. Whatever or whoever was at the door was forcefully trying to enter. Rebecca's hand touched the handle, which vibrated with the forceful energy of the intruder. Or were her shaken nerves making the handle dance in her hand? She was not sure. Holding the poker, she prepared to strike. As she was about to open the door to challenge the mysterious visitor, a voice behind her shouted, "STOP!"

Eden Valley, Pennsylvania

CHAPTER 48

The Raven Tattoo

Turning quickly, Rebecca saw Rachel standing at the far side of the room.

"Don't open that door, Becky!" Rachel instructed in a firm voice.

"What if it's Ariella and she's hurt?"

"Ariella has a key and she'd speak out. You let that evil in here and God help us. I know you're brave, but that'd be foolish."

Rebecca backed away and lowered the iron poker. She looked back at the door, which shook with the force of something or someone trying to enter. Rebecca pointed to the back of the house.

"I checked. It's locked," Rachel replied, referring to the back door. "The curtains are all drawn, and the windows are all locked. I checked them all this evening. I had a feeling, a bad feeling, but I didn't want to frighten the others."

The pounding stopped, giving way to the sound of the rain and the howling wind.

"What if it's someone who needs help?" Rebecca asked.

"It's not. Think about it. Use your head, Becky. If they needed help, they would have called for help or answered you. This is someone or something trying to get in. Why? I don't know, but I know it's evil. I sense it. I'm sure of it."

"You're right, Rachel. I felt it too, but I also felt this urge to help. Wonder who or what's out there? It's quiet but it's probably still out there. It could be at the windows. It could break in."

"If it could, it would've entered already. It hasn't 'cause it can't. It has to be allowed to enter. I wish we had a gun, but Ariella's so against guns. Back on the farm, I had a gun. Wish I had it now," Rachel replied.

"Guns breed violence. You know that."

"Yeah, but in this case, one would be very useful, wouldn't it?" Rachel replied with a chuckle. She had the curious ability to draw on humor in dire situations. This was part of her innate power that had helped her survive a hellish childhood.

The knocking started on the window next to the door. It was a tapping, and then, a slight rapping. "Let's go see who or what it is?" Rebecca suggested.

"You're brave beyond reason, girlfriend. Are you serious?" Rachel looked at her sister.

"Yeah. I think what you said's true. Whatever it is, it can't get in unless we let it. So let's see who or what it is."

"I wish I had that gun," Rachel mumbled. "I can't believe I'm doing this. What if I'm wrong, and it's some lunatic that'll break the window and grab you? He could easily break it."

"Like you said, he would've already. I'm going to greet our visitor at the window."

Just as Rebecca approached the window, the rapping stopped. But she did not. The room was dark. The embers of the fire had died away. There was a flashlight on the coffee table and Rebecca grabbed it. In what seemed like one quick motion, she pulled back the curtain, turned on the flashlight, and illuminated the visitor at the window. At the sight, she screamed and dropped to the floor, leaving the bright flashlight on the windowsill.

"Are you all right?" Rachel ran to her.

Rebecca sat on the ground staring at the window, whose curtain remained open. Rachel ran to the window and grabbed the flashlight. Shining it out the window, she could not see anything. Quickly, she drew closed the curtain and turned toward Rebecca. "What was it, Becky?"

"It was a man. I've never seen him before. He had an evil stare and wore a dark wet cloak. He looked like a homeless man. But the thing I remember most is that when he tried to block the bright beam from the flashlight, he raised his right arm. On that arm was a large tattoo," Rebecca paused at the recollection.

Rebecca's scream had awakened the entire house. The rest of the girls quickly filtered into the living room, illuminated solely by the flashlight on the floor. This low light gave their faces an eerie appearance.

"Was it a black raven tattoo?" Agnes asked in a frightened voice. All she had seen of her recent attacker at the old stables was a black raven tattoo.

Rebecca turned toward her and nodded to the affirmative. "Yes. The very same."

Agnes whispered, "God save us all."

CHAPTER 49

A Morning Jog

That morning, Molly woke up early. The case of the two Eden Valley deaths, those of Gavin Green and Will Porter, was no closer to being solved than when the team had first arrived in the valley. Reality, legend, and random acts of odd behavior created an indiscernible web of tangled clues, plots, and subplots. It made Molly's logical mind spin, and she could not sleep.

It was 6:35 in the morning when she stepped out of The Raven Inn to go for a morning run along the Eden River to relieve the strain of the case. The Inspector had added to the stress by proclaiming if the two deaths were linked and began to appear as serial killings, the FBI would take over the case, displacing him and his team. Time was of the essence, and no one felt this more than Molly, as she jogged toward Devils Bridge past the overgrown hemlock trees that shielded the Green estate and farmhouse from the road.

As she neared the covered bridge, she entered a low-lying mist emanating from the river as the cold morning air mixed with water evaporating from the warmer river water. It was a common scene during this time of year, as the nights grew progressively colder while the river still held the heat of late summer.

Molly entered the mist, which appeared thicker than she had anticipated. Now, the bridge took on an ominous gray image as she neared its gaping entrance. Silence seemed to increase with the thickening fog. Soon, the wooden planks of the old, covered bridge creaked under her feet, each step resonating through the wooden structure as she quickened her pace. The river was invisible, as everything disappeared in the curtain of white.

As she approached the midspan of Devils Bridge, Molly was startled by what appeared like the black devil himself, complete with hoofs and horns. She nearly fell back in fright. Here, the impossible seemed possible in this mystical valley complete with rumored ghosts and witches. Despite her strong, logical mind and her well-grounded sense of reality, this devilish vision completely startled the veteran detective. Molly stared as the figure approached through the far opening of the satanic bridge. Her heart racing, she heard the sound of hooves hitting the wooden planks of the structure. Calming herself, she chuckled at her own fears as the suspected devil turned into a black horse pulling an open buggy laden with fruit.

* * * * *

Thursdays were market days in nearby Kamerynville, and young Josef Lapp had undertaken his weekly journey to the Amish market in the early hours of the morning. As he spotted the frightened jogger, he pulled the buggy to a stop.

"Sorry to scare ya. The fog sure's thick t'is mornin'. Lenore und I didn't see ya," he said as he gestured toward the slender Amish girl seated next to him. "Ya better be careful on the hill back there," he pointed behind him. "Gets pretty slick."

Startled, Molly stared at the Amish youth and his sister. The Amish girl looked straight at her as if she were silently looking through her. The sensation made her uncomfortable, but Molly brushed it off.

"Well, we'd better get goin' or we'll be late to market. Ya enjoy yur run," the friendly young Amish lad waved at Molly. He beckoned his horse forward, but the animal kept neighing and shaking his head in protest at having to cross Devils Bridge.

"Wait!" Molly finally regained her composure. "Your name's Lenore?" she asked the young woman. The latter remained silent and simply shook her head in the affirmative. "This may sound strange, but is Lenore a common Amish name?"

The girl remained silent, but her brother answered on her behalf. He seemed very protective of her. "No. As far as I know my sister's the only Lenore in these parts. Why?"

"May I ask your name?" she looked at the Amish youth.

"Josef Lapp." The boy was becoming a little weary of the inquisitive stranger.

"I'm Molly Dvorak. I'm with the State Police. May I ask you and your sister a few questions?"

At the sound of the word "police" Josef became guarded. "No. Sorry. We're late to market," he objected.

"Just a few questions. Please," Molly pleaded.

The gentle youth finally agreed to allow her questioning, while his sister maintained her silence.

"Do you live here, at Eden Crossing?"

"We live on a farm just up the hill, near the village." He pointed behind him, while his horse continued to be nervous and wanted to leave this dreadful place.

"Lenore, did you know Gavin Green?" Molly went right to the heart of the mystery.

The girl shook her head in the negative.

As Molly looked closer at Lenore, she noticed a nearly healed cut on her forehead, at the hairline. It looked like it had been a deep cut.

"How'd you get that cut?" Molly pointed at the girl's forehead. She knew she was getting personal with her questioning, but she needed to seize the opportunity.

The girl did not answer but seemed nervous. The boy, unlike his horse, was eager to cross the bridge.

Josef had no desire to disclose anything further to the police. He did not trust the English and their rules, especially the police who enforced them. Fearing that his sister and the entire Lapp family would be dragged into an English investigation, he cut the interview short.

"We really need to leave now. We're late to market," he replied and signaled the horse forward. The beast, which had been impatiently waiting to distance himself from this horrid place, had changed his mind and shot out as soon as Josef allowed. Almost instantly, the Amish buggy disappeared into the thick fog, leaving Molly standing alone in the middle of Devils Bridge.

That must be THE Lenore, she thought. *Lenore Lapp. This may be the break we needed. I need to get back and tell the boss*, she reasoned and quickly returned to The Raven Inn.

She found Kelly sitting at breakfast with the Inspector. "There you are. We were starting to wonder if you slept in," the Inspector observed, looking at his watch. It was nearly 7:30 in the morning. "We need a break in this case, ladies. Otherwise, we'll lose it to another agency, probably the FBI."

"I think I just found one," Molly said, as she sat down next to Kelly. "I was jogging across the old covered bridged when I ran into two Amish youths, a brother and sister. He was friendly and she was reserved, but you wouldn't believe who they were?" Molly was so excited that she ignored the server, who was standing next to her, asking if she wanted a cup of coffee.

"You want tea or coffee?" the Inspector interjected, feeling empathy toward the busy server.

"Tea, thanks." Molly brushed off the young woman.

"We don't know, Molly. Other than the Miller brothers, we don't know any Amish," Kelly replied on behalf of herself and the Inspector.

"I found Lenore. She's an Amish girl," Molly whispered excitedly.

"Lenore, as in the poem? She really exists? I thought it was some bizarre take on Edgar Allan Poe," Kelly replied.

"She exists, and she's Amish."

"That's impossible, Molly. Green would not have had an Amish girl living with him at his house," the Inspector objected.

"Maybe they were friends. Maybe she just came over, or somehow he got the poem from her. But I'm sure it's the Lenore we've been trying to find. How many Lenore's can there be?"

Molly's tea arrived, but she was too excited to drink it or to order breakfast.

"Where's this Lenore, now?" the Inspector asked.

"At the Amish Market in Kamerynville with her brother. Can I borrow your car and go talk to her? She's away from her family, except for her brother. I may get more out of her there."

"Chen should be here soon. You can go right after we have a quick team meeting," the Inspector replied.

"Shouldn't we have it somewhere besides here?" Kelly looked about the restaurant.

"Good idea. We'll have it at Amos Miller's farm. Are you getting anything to eat, Molly?" the Inspector asked.

"I'll just grab something in the lobby. I need to get upstairs to shower and change. I'll be quick."

"Okay, we'll meet you in the lobby in ten minutes," the Inspector replied.

"There's no way you'll be ready in ten minutes," Kelly protested, seeing this as an impossible task in her repertoire.

"No problem, girl. Unlike some people, I don't take long."

The two co-workers had initially started as competitive over-achievers. Molly was the older and more senior, which Kelly initially perceived as an unfair advantage. However, that had not kept her from trying to outdo Molly whenever she could, especially when the Inspector was involved. Annoyed by the continued competitive pressure, Molly finally spoke up. That was about four months ago. Kelly took offense.

For two weeks, the two women barely acknowledged each other. It was not until a subsequent team-building dinner that the two made peace after Kelly broke the ice and apologized. Late that night, they bonded over a pitcher of strawberry margaritas, long after Chen and the Inspector had gone home to bed. That changed the relationship, such that now the two women were becoming close friends.

As Kelly had predicted, Molly was not known for her timeliness and her ten-minute promise was no different. The Inspector had long accepted this trait in his second-in-command, so he too arrived late, although not as late as Molly. Only Kelly showed up in the lobby on time. Thus, when Molly finally descended the main staircase into the spacious lobby of the inn, Kelly was waiting for her with a snide remark. "Molly, you surprised me. You're only eighteen minutes late."

"Look, Princess, I'd like to see you do all that under thirty minutes while spending half the time on the phone with Chen. He got lost but should be here any minute," she added, looking at the Inspector.

"Kelly, my dear, don't lose your punctuality. It's a trait I admire. Molly'd be late to her own wedding. Right, Molly?"

Molly sneered at her boss, who managed to hit on two touchy subjects in one sentence. She was about to make a snide counter remark when Chen walked into the lobby.

"This place's impossible to find. My GPS failed me. Thanks for the directions, Molly. If I'd asked Kelly, I'd still be circling Kamerynville."

"No worries, Chen, but you made me late," Molly replied.

"Sorry, but you're here now; so, how're you late?" Chen asked in a confused tone.

"Never mind," Molly answered.

"Hey, Chen, at least I'm not the one who can't find my car in the parking garage at least once a week, like someone else I know," Kelly huffed.

After the banter subsided, the team left the inn and drove to Amos Miller's farm. Molly went with Chen to show him the way, and the Inspector and Kelly followed them in the Inspector's car. Once there, the team was greeted by Gus and Alvin of the local police.

"Sleepin' in today, Jim?" teased Gus. "Ya missed the action. I see ya have the entire crew with ya. Well, there might not be much for ya to do. I'm going to call in the FBI. It's clear to me the two cases are linked."

The Inspector had barely enough time to get out of the car before he had to process the news. "Can I talk to you in private, Gus?" he asked.

"Sure, Jim. No problem. What's up?"

Soon, the two men walked away from the cars toward Amos Miller's barn. The farm of the young Amish man had become a staging ground for the investigation into the mysterious death of Will Porter, since the actual crime scene, Drakes Plot, was only accessible through Miller's land.

As was the way of the Amish, their peaceful nature did not lend itself to complaints about the official police intrusion. Therefore, although Amos was perturbed by the disruption of the authorities, he did not make it known, Rather, he went about his daily business, despite the interruptions and continued traffic along his lane. He had no other choice. Besides, his concerns were elsewhere, focused on one individual, Lenore.

"Look, Gus. I understand this is your district, and I respect that. And I'm glad you turned this over to us. But it's up to my discretion when we call in the Feds." The Inspector sounded perturbed.

"That's all fine, Jim. But it's lookin' like the two deaths are linked. I don't know about you, but it feels like we may be dealing with a serial killer, which means we need to call in the FBI," Gus reasoned.

"What makes you think we've got a serial killer?"

"This!" Gus finally revealed what he had been holding the entire time. It was a piece of white cotton cloth in a labeled evidence bag. "We found it this morning."

"Who found it and where? My team and the CSI folks were all over that crime scene and never saw anything like that." The Inspector was puzzled. He knew the significance of the torn white cloth. It was the same as the two other pieces of cloth found associated with Gavin Green's death. One had been found near Green's body, in a thicket by the bank of the Eden River, and the other had been discovered in the backyard of Green's farmhouse. All were unsoiled and recently discarded. This one was no different. The Inspector looked at it closely while awaiting the police chief's reply.

"Alvin found it near the woods, about ten yards from the grave," Gus replied.

"I see, and you're sure this is genuine evidence?"

"What are ya implying, Jim?"

"I'm simply questioning the probability that the same torn white cotton cloth should show up at every location relevant to the two bodies. Doesn't that seem a little odd to you?" He was going to add, "And every time it's discovered, it's found by your deputy," but he decided to reserve that remark for another time.

"What're ya thinkin', Jim?" Gus Morgan was liked in the community because he tended to interpret the law in favor of most of the locals, but he lacked the deductive powers of his old friend, James Cabot. Thus, he eagerly deferred to the latter whenever investigative logic entered the equation.

"Gus, I'm not sure what to think, but I believe it's premature to conclude that the two deaths are related based on this evidence alone." The Inspector raised the plastic bag with the white cloth to emphasize his point. "Nor is it clear that Green's death was a homicide. I believe Porter's death to be a homicide, but Green's death seems an unfortunate overdose. I have no idea what to make of these torn fragments of white cloth, except they seem highly suspicious."

"Ya think someone planted them?"

"They seem too regular and too easy a clue. So, yes, someone may have planted them."

The Inspector looked over at his team. He noticed that Kelly and Alvin were strolling together up the hill towards Drakes Plot, deep in conversation. Molly and Chen were patiently waiting for the Inspector to finish his private conversation. *That Kelly's a pain at times. I told her we were going to have a team meeting, and she takes off,* the Inspector thought. He wanted to end his conversation with Gus, for it did not add any value and had derailed his team meeting. Chen had told him that he had more information and he was eager to hear it. Trying to clue in Gus to the case seemed fruitless.

"Who would have planted them and why, Jim?"

"Let's take this one step at a time, Gus. Any other new developments since yesterday evening?" Gus had one of his men, Fred, at the crime scene overnight to ensure that it was not disturbed again.

"Ah, Fred thinks the place's haunted. I think everyone's getting scared and the White Witch rumors are spreading. He swore he saw a large gray wolf last night at the edge of the woods at Drakes Plot. Can you imagine a wolf in these parts?"

"Unlikely, but it might have been a large coyote. I heard they're entering the area." The Inspector excused himself and walked back to Molly and Chen.

"Kelly decided to keep working on Alvin. I hope you don't mind," Molly pointed out.

"I do mind. We need to have a meeting. Can you get her down here?"

"Sure." Molly stepped aside to call Kelly, who had disappeared over the top of the hill.

"It's like herding cats with those two," the Inspector complained to Chen. "You're the only one that follows orders around here. Keep it up. I can't wait to hear what you dug up in the data search, but I want all of us together before we get into it. I doubt our Amish friend'll care if we use his gazebo for our meeting."

Soon, Kelly returned and the entire team retreated to Amos Miller's gazebo. Out of courtesy, they asked his permission to use it, but Miller did not care. He simply wanted peace. If this helped achieve it, he was supportive.

"Okay, let's pull together what we know," the Inspector began. "Molly, you can go first."

Molly described her encounter with Lenore for Chen's benefit. "She's at the Amish Market in Kamerynville this morning, and I'd like to go there and talk to her," she concluded.

"I think it's a far shot, Molly, but if you have a strong hunch, go for it," the Inspector replied. "What about your interview with Sam Hughes? He's still one of our key suspects. Anything to share?"

"He's hiding something, but I can't get it out of him. Also, he has a black raven tattoo on his right arm. I have yet to question him about that."

"Same as Porter's tattoo?"

"Yes."

"Interesting. Keep at it, Molly. We need to get the truth out of him," the Inspector advised. "I'd rather you pursued him than your Lenore idea, but if you can do both, great. Anything else?"

"No."

"Okay, your turn, Kelly. What do you have on Alvin Walker? He's an odd one."

"He sure is. I did manage to get him to confess why he was follow-ing us in Glen Ryan. He claimed that the police chief put him up to it."

"What?" the Inspector replied angrily. "Heck, I forgot to raise that with Gus."

"He said Gus Morgan wanted to make sure we saw him. That's why he drove out in front of us."

"That makes no sense. I'll check with Morgan. Why would Morgan spy on us, and then want Walker to be seen?"

"Walker said his boss was feeling left out and was sending you a message."

"He could've talked to me. He didn't say anything to me just now." The Inspector seemed visibly annoyed. "Where did Walker disappear to after we saw him? He couldn't have crossed that closed bridge."

"He said there's a little alley before the bridge, and, if you know your way around, it takes you back out of town along the same road we came in on. The entire thing seems far-fetched."

"Because it is. Walker found another clue up there at the Porter site. It's this." The Inspector pulled out the plastic evidence bag that contained the torn white cotton cloth. "Seems like the same clue as the ones we found near Green's body and below Green's window. Chen, when you go back, take this with you and have it analyzed. Did we get any lab data back on the other two pieces of white cloth?" the Inspector asked.

"Yes, sir. No prints but some female DNA, but we don't have a match in the database."

"Okay, keep looking. What else you got, Kelly?"

"I haven't had a chance to connect with Jerry McAlester, but I'll try and do that this afternoon. That's all I got."

"Anything on the White Witch? Anyone?"

"I have some new information," Chen said.

"Okay, I'm getting to you, Chen. Ladies, anything else?"

Both Kelly and Molly shook their heads. "No," they replied in unison.

"Okay, it's your turn, Chen. What'd you dig up in the database?"

"Some more surprises. To summarize, we know that Gavin Green's wealthy father, Cornelius Green, had been engaged to the missing Erin Stone. We think that Sam Hughes had an affair with Erin Stone and she became pregnant. Cornelius Green accused her of infidelity and publicly dissolved the engagement. Finally, we know that soon after giving birth to the child, a girl, Stone dropped out of college and disappeared. Molly, please ask Hughes about Stone and his relationship with her," Chen requested.

"I will. It's on my list," Molly replied.

"We also know that Hughes, Will Porter, Jerry McAlester, George Walker, who is Alvin's older brother, and Harry Schaffer were high school classmates and part of the Black Raven Club. George Walker and Harry Schaffer are both dead. Walker died in an automobile accident in Glen Ryan, as I mentioned before, and Schaffer went MIA in Bosnia, presumed dead. Here's the blown-up photo of the five of them that I sent you yesterday. I analyzed it, and, although it's hard to tell looking at the photo even at this scale, all five men appear to have some sort of tattoo on their right arm. I could not piece it together, but it may be a black raven tattoo, which would make sense, given the name of the club. Molly, that would match the tattoo you saw on Hughes, right?"

Molly studied the photograph. "Sure looks like it," she said.

"Also, I identified the young woman in the photo. She's in the same high school class with the others. They're all seniors in this picture. You'll never believe who she is. Take a guess, sir." Chen stopped and looked at the Inspector.

"I don't know. She's Hughes's girlfriend."

"Possibly. But who is she?"

"Erin Stone," Kelly let out.

"Give the girl a star! Yes. It's Erin Stone," Chen replied.

Molly passed the picture to Kelly.

"Very pretty," Kelly observed. "I can see why she had the boys fighting for her. So, she went to school with Hughes before she got involved with Cornelius Green."

"Correct. They may have been high school sweethearts, as you guessed, sir."

"This one's a puzzler. You have anything else, Chen, before we start our analysis?" the Inspector inquired.

"One other thing, sir. I found the location of Harry Schaffer's cabin, which he bought just before he went off to war. It exchanged hands twice since Schaffer went MIA. The last sale was twenty-eight months ago. It was bought by a woman named Ariella Bianca. She paid in cash. When I searched further, there's nothing on Ariella Bianca anywhere, except for the deed to this particular property."

"Why's this relevant, Chen?" Molly objected. "Why would Ariella Bianca be relevant?"

"I have an aerial photo of the cabin taken earlier this year. I love modern technology. Nothing's hidden anymore. Look right here. I'll blow it up on my pad," Chen said eagerly, pointing to the arial photo on his tablet. He was never without his electronic tablet. "That woman in the photo is wearing a long, flowing white dress. Could that be our White Witch? Could that be Ariella Bianca?"

"Or could Chen Lee have finally completely lost his mind?" Molly replied, rolling her eyes. "This is ridiculous, Chen. You're totally speculating. You don't know the identity of that woman, and I, for one, can't tell if she's wearing a white dress in your fuzzy photo, or if she's hanging up a white sheet on a clothesline. I can't even tell if it's a woman. Are we getting this desperate?"

"Look, I agree that Chen's hypothesis is out there, but..." the Inspector said.

"Out there? It's insane, like this entire valley," Molly interjected.

"It could be a stretch, since we know the legend of the White Witch relates to Eleanor Drake, who died 200 years ago and presumably haunts this bizarre place. But we need some direction, given the little we have on this case," Chen reasoned. "You know, I just thought of something. Could the name 'Lenore' in our mysterious poem simply imply Eleanor, the White Witch? It's the same letters scrambled into a different name."

"Except that 'Eleanor' has an extra 'a,' Chen," Molly replied.

"Okay, it's a stretch, but good work, Chen." The Inspector ignored Molly's objection. His head was spinning as he tried to make sense of random clues buried in an endless matrix of folklore and hearsay. *Chen's an incredibly talented analyst and data detective, but he seems to have an endless supply of random questions or observations, most of which are completely irrelevant to the case.* "Anything new on the Drake legend?" he added.

"As I told you earlier, the Drakes were among the first white settlers in the valley around 200 years ago, and Arthur Drake was rumored to be a retired privateer."

"Aren't privateers pirates?" Kelly asked.

"Yes."

"He was a retired pirate? I didn't know pirates retired," she said and chuckled. "Did he get a pension?"

"Yeah, he got rich through his pillages. Drake owned most of the land around here, which he bought from William Penn's holdings. He died a cruel death at the hands of men searching for his rumored pirate plunder. Apparently, he got disemboweled. It's not clear if his wife, Eleanor, who was a German immigrant from Philadelphia, died at the hands of the perpetrators, or if she took her own life. Legend has it that the father and the son were both slaughtered in front of her eyes right up there at the old Drake place. The same legend claims that she was initially spared on account of her exceeding beauty, only to be raped, molested, and probably eventually killed by the attackers in that very house. Tragic story. I got all this detail from Professor Murray at the McLaren History Department, an expert on the history of this area. He has studied the legend and believes this to be the grisly truth," Chen summarized.

"Does he believe in ghosts, as well?" Molly asked.

"No. We talked about the legend of the White Witch, and he thinks it's simply folklore. However, he did admit that there was a growing number of locals who have reached out to him in recent months to report mysterious White Witch sightings. All believed these sightings to be of the legendary Eleanor Drake ghost," Chen replied.

"I don't buy it. I don't believe in that supernatural stuff," Kelly proclaimed. "No way."

"I thought that you were 'Miss Intuition,' able to sense things," Molly teased.

"Yeah, but that's different. We don't know much about the mind. I think some level of telepathy is real. Heck, if you stare intently enough at someone in a car next to you, or at the back of the head of someone in front of you, they'll often turn and look at you. Haven't you ever felt someone looking at you, even if you had your back to them? It may be our subconscious, but there's something to it. So, I'm all over that, and I can sense it better than most. But ghosts…no way! It's all crap if you ask me."

"Well, I believe in ghosts. I think," Molly admitted.

"That was reassuring," Chen snickered.

"Shut up, Chen. You may think you're so smart, but you're a pain in my…"

"As soon as you children stop squabbling," the Inspector interjected, "we'll move on to our analysis of the two deaths. We have a lot of work to do in a short amount of time. If these two deaths are related, we could have a serial killer on our hands, and he or she may have already decided on the next victim," the Inspector observed.

"Boss, on that note, shouldn't we call in the Feds? What if someone else gets killed on our watch?" Molly asked the question that the Inspector dreaded the most. If the FBI got involved, they would take over. He and his team would become nothing more than lackeys, if they remained involved at all. Furthermore, he needed to solve another case, like this one, to appease his own boss, who still regarded the Inspector as a loose cannon he could not trust.

"Molly, if we do not crack this case in the next four days, that means by Monday, I'll call in the FBI. I promise. Likewise, if another victim appears, or if the Green death was at the hands of the same person who killed Will Porter, I'll also call in the Feds. You have my word on it. But, given that this isn't a serial murder case, they won't touch it, even if I did call them. It's all in one state and it seems to be one overdose and one homicide. I'll grant you that the timing and the locations make the two deaths appear to be related, but right now we don't have any hard evidence to that effect. By the way, I don't consider hard evidence the white cotton cloths that Alvin Walker seems to be finding everywhere, as if he were on an Easter egg hunt. I swear he's planting evidence, but I can't prove it or find a motive for him. Kelly, you really need to press him harder. Molly, the same goes for Sam Hughes. Stop playing around with these guys, ladies. This isn't *The Dating Game*.

"What's *The Dating Game?*" Kelly seemed puzzled by the analogy.

"It was a silly old TV show long before your time," the Inspector snarled.

"Okay, no *Dating Game*, boss," Kelly replied, flashing a big smile.

"I don't have my cork board, but here are the suspects, as I see it," the Inspector continued.

"Sir, sorry to interrupt, but something's happening up at Drakes Plot. Maybe we'd better check it out," Chen suggested.

"Hell, just what I need, more drama," the Inspector said at the sight of Alvin Walker running down the hill towards them. He was waving the team up the hill and shouting something about "new evidence." The Inspector and Chen quickly headed up the hill to see what was the matter.

"Cabot's having a hard time with this case, isn't he?" Kelly observed, as she left the gazebo with Molly. The two women strolled up the hill at a leisurely pace.

"Yeah, but he's got a lot going on at home. Living with talkative Ms. Allen mustn't be easy. And he really doesn't want the FBI involved. I know him. He sees that as a defeat."

"What do you think the commotion's about?"

"Probably Alvin up to no good. I swear he's trying to drive Cabot insane," Molly concluded.

"I think he's succeeding. Look!"

The two looked up at the crest of the hill, and there was the Inspector waving them up. He was barely audible, except for the word "Walker."

CHAPTER 50

A Powerful Menace

The girls of the Eden Sisterhood had remained awake all night after their encounter with the mysterious man who tried to break into the house. Every sound posed a potential threat. At last, morning came without future incident.

"That was the longest night of my life," Marie proclaimed as she stretched her arms and legs. The girls had all huddled together on the two fold-out couches in the living room, three to a couch.

"Thank God for sunshine. Everything seems better in the light," Sarah said. "I've got first dibs on the shower." Of all the girls, she seemed the least frightened by the night's events and the only one that got some solid sleep.

"How could ya sleep, Sarah? Didn't that scare ya?" Marie asked.

"Yeah, but I can sleep through anything. Give me a cot and a pillow, and I'm out, regardless of any lunatic trying to break in," she replied. "I grew up around lunatics."

"You're crazy. Just for that, I'm gonna beat ya to the shower," Marie replied, and they raced off together.

"Kids!" Rebecca said with a sigh. She could not dismiss the thought of the night's intruder.

Agnes began to slice bread for the morning meal and Hazel set the table, while Rebecca and Rachel decided to see if last night's visitor left any clues outside the cabin. Carefully, they opened the front door and were greeted by a blast of crisp fall air, the kind that invigorates even the most tired soul. "It's beautiful out here after that rain. What a day!" Rachel said.

Of all the young women, Rachel was the biggest nature girl. Unlike Rebecca and Lenore, she lacked Amish roots. Unlike Sarah and Marie, she was a farm girl. Unlike Agnes and Hazel, she was not a local girl. Rachel was an enigma. She was a scientist and an artist, who should have gone to college had she had the means. Yet, she was also the most sensitive to the spiritual lessons and hard-earned wisdoms that Ariella infused into these young women at every opportunity. Thus, she formed a blend of two seemingly opposing forces, science and spirituality, catalyzed by her strong affinity for the outdoors. If there was a renaissance soul in the group, it was Rachel.

"Rebecca, do you feel that or is it just me?" Rachel asked. "I'm gettin' a strange vibe out here."

"No, but I feel like we were miraculously spared last night. I guess you were right. He couldn't enter unless we let him. Do you think Ariella protected us somehow?"

"With her, anything's possible. I wouldn't put it past her. Not much surprises me about her, anymore. She's more powerful than she appears. I wonder if he dared not enter for fear of her. I guess we'll never know."

"Look at the door." Rebecca pointed back at the front door.

"Oh, my God! It looks scorched. Who was that guy? How did that happen?"

"I have no idea. Blow torch, maybe? Look at the handle! It looks like it was heated to a high temperature. The metal seems discolored. Very odd."

"Maybe we'd better get back inside, just in case he's still out here." Rachel looked about nervously.

"Maybe we'd better, but I want to walk around the cabin to make sure everything's fine."

"Always the brave, Becky! Okay, I'll go with you, but let's make it quick. This glorious day isn't so inviting anymore."

The two young women walked around to the back of the cabin. They stopped at the back door, which also had signs of the potential intruder's determination.

Rebecca signaled her friend. "Come look at this, Rachel."

"A pentagram. That's what it's called, right? Charred into the door like the one on the front door. Weird," Rachel observed.

"It must've been a torch. I doubt we had a wandering pyrotechnical wizard visiting us last night—more like a bizarre lunatic."

"Are there any other kind?" Rachel asked.

"Maybe we should call the police," Rebecca suggested.

"Right, so most of us can end up either arrested, in foster homes, or sent back to our lovely families. I bet your Amish family'd love to see you, Becky."

"Enough. Let's check the east side of the house."

The two women walked around the last side of the cabin, the one closest to the woods. There were no signs of any entry attempts on the side that housed most of the bedrooms.

"Look over there in the woods." Rachel pointed at the tree line. "That looks like two sets of footprints. Let's check it out."

"Now who's being foolishly brave? What if our visitor's still hiding in there?" Rebecca sounded concerned.

"Then he'd have run after us by now," Rachel replied, while walking toward the tree line.

"You're pushin' it, Rachel."

"Oh, stop. Look at this—there were two of them, not one. Our bizarre friend had an accomplice."

"You're right. One set of prints is larger than the other. Here, they're next to each other, as if they walked away together," Rebecca observed.

"Maybe we should follow these tracks?" Rachel's scientific side was extremely curious.

"No. Let's get back in the house before they decide to come back. We appear to be safe in there. Come on."

"Wait, I hear something!" Rachel fell silent and listened.

"So do I! Someone's coming. Run for it!"

The two women ran around the log cabin toward the front door. They no sooner slammed it shut, when they heard the clear sound of someone running toward the house. To their terror, soon the door started to vibrate as the handle turned.

CHAPTER 51

The Outburst

Molly and Kelly ran up the hill toward Drakes Plot to meet up with Chen and the Inspector. They were greeted by an anxious Alvin Walker and his not so anxious boss, Gus Morgan. Alvin was holding an evidence bag with a small vial in it. He handed it to the Inspector, who seemed less than enthused.

"I'm telling ya, Inspector. This entire thing's drug related," Alvin said. "I've said it from the start. Green died of an overdose and so did this one."

"Gus," the Inspector addressed the police chief. He had no time for Alvin, the meddling deputy. "What drugs did you suspect Porter of dealing?"

"I can't remember."

"He was suspected of dealing heroin and cocaine, sir," Chen piped up.

"And, you know this how, Chen?"

"The DEA files I pulled yesterday at your request, sir."

"What's with all the 'sir'?" Kelly whispered to Molly.

"Chen's a brownnose. He can't help it," Molly whispered back.

"I'll be damned if I call the boss 'sir,'" Kelly whispered.

"Just know that Cabot likes it. It's not my thing, but he does eat that up," Molly replied softly.

"Chen, please have this analyzed and fingerprinted," the Inspector ordered, as he passed the crack vial in the sample bag to Chen.

"So, how did this crack vial get up here, and why didn't we notice it sooner?" the Inspector asked those present.

Alvin spoke up as expected. "Well, sir, our men found it within Eleanor Drake's old casket."

"Walker, are you telling me that Eleanor Drake had a crack vial hidden in her casket?" the Inspector asked with a strong acidic tone.

Molly chuckled but quickly controlled herself. She loved when the old man got on his high horse, and, in her opinion, there was no better fool who deserved his tongue lashing than the current recipient. Kelly covered her mouth with her right hand, so as not to burst into laughter.

"Sir, yes, but..." Alvin tried to defend his logic, but was cut short.

"Walker, the woman's been dead for 200 years. That could be a problem in your deductions," the Inspector replied. "Or are you insinuating that the casket was a drop off for the drugs?"

"No, sir."

"No. I got it. It's as you said—Will Porter was high on crack, and he decided to bury himself alive in Eleanor Drake's grave as a drug-induced suicide. Is that it?"

"Well, it could be, sir, or he..."

"Walker, this is the stupidest thing I've ever heard. First, based on the test results I just received from Frank....You remember Frank, our Chief Coroner?"

"Yes, but..."

"Well, guess what? Frank concluded that Mr. Porter was totally clean when he died—no drugs and no alcohol. On that basis alone, you're wrong. I'll give you the benefit of the fact that you weren't privy to this information. However, your idea's still ridiculous 'cause if you'd bothered to compare the soil sequence around Porter's body with the surrounding native soil sequence, you would have discovered that most of it was in the same order.

"Why is this important? Because if Porter's death resulted from the steep hole collapsing inward, as in an accidental death, the topsoil would be near his feet, not over his head. Furthermore, the grave would have been a collapsed hole, not a mounded dirt pile. He was buried alive by someone who wanted him dead. That someone used the same pile of soil that Porter excavated from the hole to bury him. The last soil out, the deepest soil, was the first one back in the hole. He was purposely buried. The evidence on the body further substantiates this. He was frantically trying to dig himself out just before he suffocated. No suicide!" The Inspector was on a roll. He disliked Alvin Walker, considering him at best a meddling fool and at worst an accomplice to the killings.

"By the way, the white cloths that seem to be mysteriously popping up everywhere are of the same garment and appear to be torn from that garment in sequence. In other words, the fibers of one sample fit the tear pattern of the other. What's most curious is that these 'clues,' and I use the word loosely, were torn in sequence such that the first one torn off was the first one found. The second one torn off the source material was the second one found. The third one torn away was the third one found. Catch my drift? Coincidence? I don't think so! Obviously, someone's leaving them behind as calling cards. So, Mr. Walker, I admire your enthusiasm, but your clues and your deductions fall far short of the mark." The Inspector walked away.

Ouch! That was a bit harsh even for Cabot, Chen thought, but did not say anything.

Walker was deflated. His boss had not stepped in to support him, a further indication that the two men were drifting apart.

As if the Inspector had not done enough damage, he turned toward Alvin and gave him one more salvo from his merciless howitzer of hate.

"Oh, and Walker, in case you're wondering about the monogrammed shovels at the scene, which appear to have once belonged to Linus Miller, they too are planted to throw us off. They appear to have been purchased at a yard sale a month ago. Sounds like this was all premeditated. So, where do the drugs come in? Maybe they fell out of Porter's pocket and into the grave, or maybe they're another item to throw us off the killer's track. Which is it? Start investigating that if you want to add value and stop hypothesizing nonsensical theories. Good day." The Inspector walked away with an angry gait.

Molly caught up to him on the way down the hill. Kelly and Chen followed at a few paces. They had never seen their boss be so publicly upset with anyone. Even privately, he seemed to retain more composure than he had done today. Was the pressure of the case getting to him? Who won in that dispute? Was the victor Alvin because he had finally managed to undermine the Inspector's sanity?

"Boss, are you okay?" Molly asked as they rushed down the hill.

"Never been better."

"That was harsh."

"Hopefully harsh enough to have an effect."

"What're you up to?"

"Trying to smoke out a rat. We need a solid break in this case, and we need it fast. Walker knows something. I suspect he's the one planting these bogus clues or may know who is. Either way, he may know the killer. So, maybe if I get him angry enough, it may shake something out." He winked at Molly and smiled.

"It may also get you in trouble or even killed. Did you think of that?"

"Sure. That's why I have you guys to protect me. Right?"

"I guess. You really think he's planting false clues?" Molly asked.

"I don't know, but it seems a little too coincidental that he keeps finding them, even after the professionals have combed the scene for evidence. We need to huddle and start analyzing this case. We need a few strong hypotheses that we can follow. But, before we do that, run over to that Amish Market and try to talk to your friend Lenore. I thought about it, and you might be on to something. I never thought she was a real person, but maybe she is. Go check it out, but hurry back.

"By the way, Chen has set up a little private field office for us in the neighboring village of Kiradale. I'll ask him to text you the address. Team meeting's at one o'clock at the new field office. Don't be late. Oh, and what I told you is between us. I want Kelly and Chen to think that I can be hard-nosed. Might as well get the most play out of this, right?" He looked at her with a twinkle in his eye.

"Sure, boss. I don't know why you would want them to think you're a complete jackass, but if that's what you wish, you go, boy. Your secret's safe with me. See you at one," Molly replied and ran down the hill toward the car.

He chuckled at her frankness. Only Molly could get away with such remarks. By the time Chen and Kelly caught up to him, the Inspector reinstated his gruff demeanor.

CHAPTER 52

An Amish Market

Every Thursday, the Amish Market was held in the old Kamerynville town square. It had been there as long as anyone could remember. People from all around the region would come to buy fresh produce, hand-made crafts and furniture, baked goods, and other Amish wares and specialties. The Lapp family had had a stand at the Kamerynville Amish Market for over fifteen years. They had developed a regular clientele and never missed a Thursday. Josef had taken over from his father as the key family member in charge of anything related to the Amish Market. As the oldest son, this had become his responsibility. In return, his parents let him keep a portion of the proceeds as income. He saved all of it, for he knew that someday he would have his own farm.

Today was a special day for Josef. He was with his older sister, who would help him run the Lapp Family stand. Lenore did not share his enthusiasm, for she felt exposed by the public scene. Though she had begun to remember some of her past, including most of her siblings, running the family stand at the market posed a frightening novelty. She remained cautious of crowds. After recently realizing that some of the Amish were upset with her regarding her mysterious disappearance and re-emergence, she withdrew into herself and trusted only her immediate family.

Her other fear concerned money. She had no concept of it, even though Josef had spent most of the journey to the market explaining the different coins and how it all worked. It still scared her. Surprisingly, her encounter with Molly early that morning did not faze her at all, probably because she had no concept of its potential implications. Conversely, her brother knew all too well what could follow, and he now wished that he had the counsel of his father.

As he pondered the potential negative repercussions of a police investigation into Lenore's affairs, he became aware of someone staring at his sister. Looking up, he recognized Amos Miller. Josef was a great fan of Amos Miller, and Amos thought the world of Lenore's entire family, especially her oldest brother. As soon as Josef saw Amos, he waved him toward the stand.

"How're ya, ol' man?" Josef asked. He had always called Lenore's suitor "old man," emphasizing the word "old." Amos was four years older than Lenore, but the age difference was not perceivable. "Haw'z it goin' at yur farm? Ya're the talk of the community. I can't believe what'z happened at Drakes Plot. Are the police gone, or is yur place still a parking lot for the English? I don't know how ya do it, Amos. Ol' Abel Snyder talked to yur brother Linus und came over last evenin' to tell us all 'bout it. What a shame. Was it an accident? Then there's the other fella in the river, in the same place as we found ya know who." Josef looked over at Lenore to make sure that she did not hear.

The two men caught up on recent events, while Josef continued to sell his farm produce. Finally, they got on the subject of Lenore, and both lowered their voices. "She asked me about ya, this morning. I guess she talked to *Mem* after the barn raising. Maybe she's rememberin' ya," Josef observed.

"Then why's she ignorin' me all the time und stayin' on the far side of the stand?" Amos replied. "She don't even look at me. Ah!" Amos sighed a heavy-hearted sigh. "She don't care 'bout no one but that snake, Ben Stoltzfus. I can't believe she's into 'im. Ah... Josef! This is as hard as losin' Elizabeth. My farm, Drakes Plot, and the English police all together don't add up to this."

"She's just shy, that's all. Why don't ya go over there an' talk to 'er." Josef nudged Amos while he weighed pumpkins for a family of four.

"Why bother? She ignores me every chance she gets," Amos lamented.

"What's got into ya, Amos? Ya chased 'er down when Ben tried courtin' 'er the first time. Go do it again! Since when're ya a quitter?"

"I'm no quitter, but I ain't a fool, either. I know when a woman's not interested. Believe me, I know," Amos replied.

Josef looked up to Amos as a big-brother figure. Amos was kind, smart, strong, handsome, and on the mind of just about every single local Amish girl over the age of fifteen. He could not comprehend why Amos was shy around his sister. It did not make sense, but then, the little he knew about love confirmed that love and sense were not related in the least.

"Well, ya're wrong, Amos. She asked about ya twice. If she weren't interested, she wouldn't have asked."

"What'd she ask?"

"She asked *Mem* if ya had been her boyfriend."

"No! Really? How'd she figure that out? Maybe she's rememberin'. What'd ya *mem* say?"

"That ya were friends. She wanted to let Lenore do the rememberin', I guess. Lenore heard of ya from one of the Styler girls, in a not so pleasant way, either. She told her about the shunnin'. Lenore couldn't remember any of it, so it took *Mem* a good hour to break it to her gently. She's been awfully quiet since. She told me she can remember things up to her seventh birthday, but nothin' more. Abel Snyder swears her memory'll come back, but he ain't sure that'll be a good thing."

"What does he know? But I agree that some things're better off forgotten. What else did she ask about me?"

"If ya're worth marryin'?"

"Get out!"

Josef laughed as he counted out apples for an English woman wearing large sunglasses who kept playing with her BMW keys.

"Seriously, she asked if I's worth marryin'?" Amos pushed the question.

"Yes. The seconds 're half price," Josef addressed the woman with the large sunglasses, who inquired about discounted apples.

Amos misunderstood. "What kinda comment's that?"

"Some of us work on Thursdays," Josef answered, looking over at Amos after the woman walked to a nearby stand of baked goods. "Ya thought I's referrin' to ya as seconds? That's funny." Josef laughed until his belly ached.

"I'm glad ya're enjoyin' yurself. What else did she ask?" Amos looked over at Lenore, who was working the far side of the Lapp farm stand. "Come on, Josef, tell me," he pressed. "I don't believe ya. All this time, she hasn't looked at me once," Amos added in a disappointed tone.

"If ya have to know, she asked me if I liked ya. And the reason she ain't lookin' over 'ere is 'cause she's workin' the other cash register, und she's very nervous 'bout it. I'd better go check if she's all right. Ya comin' along, or're ya too shy?" Josef laughed again.

"Okay, I'll come over. What'd ya tell her about whether ya liked me?"

"What do ya think I said? I told her yuz an old sow, und to stay away from ya. Stop worryin', Amos," Josef chastised his friend.

As the two young men neared Lenore, she looked up at Josef and said, "Thank goodness, ya're back. I need more ones."

"Okay, I'll get 'em, but I wanted to introduce ya to an old friend of mine. Lenore, this is Amos Miller."

There was a long pause, as Lenore looked at and through Amos. He felt her dark brown eyes scanning all his features to the greatest detail, as if she were trying to remember him. He felt a knot in his stomach and his throat dried up. She was so beautiful that it took his breath away. He sighed and thought, *How could I have let her go? Never again. I'd go with her anywhere.* In that moment, he realized how deeply he had always loved this amazing young woman named Lenore.

In that same moment, Lenore realized that despite all her best efforts, she had no recollection of the man standing before her. He was handsome, but he wasn't her type. If she had had any relationship with this stranger, it must have been forgettable since she had no recollection of it. Besides, if he had really cared, where was he all this time? *Probably courting other girls. Well, they can have 'im, 'cause I'm not interested,* she concluded. After nodding her head in a silent greeting, she turned toward her brother and away from Amos.

"Nice to meet ya, Lenore," Amos said in a timid voice.

"Likewise," she finally replied, while sending a strong signal of disinterest by looking past him toward the next customer. "May I help ya?" she addressed a large man who was picking through the fresh pears.

The moment was gone. Amos's greatest fear had materialized. He felt crushed by the invisible blow that struck his heart with a force that made him weak at the knees. *She knows of me but isn't interested*, he concluded silently. Walking away from Lenore, he caught up with Josef, who was weighing more pumpkins at the other end of the stand.

"Sorry, I couldn't stay there. It's getting busy. How'd it go? Did ya guys set up a date?" Josef asked.

"I love ya like a brother, Josef, und I always will, but yur sister ain't interested in me — not in the least. I need to go. Thanks for trying." Amos hung his head and shuffled away, completely deflated.

"Ya wait, Amos. She'll remember. Ya need to believe!" Josef shouted after him.

Amos turned around and replied. "She knows of me, und don't want to know more. I need to let 'er go. I need to go. I got a farm to deal with, und all them police. I need to go." Amos left, completely crushed.

On his way out of the market, Amos passed an energetic woman with large brown eyes and flowing chestnut hair. With his head hung low, he never noticed her. She too missed him as she walked with a purpose toward the Lapp's market stand.

As soon as Josef saw her, he froze. He knew trouble when he saw it. He pretended not to notice her as she walked straight up to him.

"Josef, I don't know if you remember me from the foggy bridge this morning? It was hard to see, and I was wearing my sweats." She addressed him with confidence. "I'm Molly Dvorak with the State Police. Can I talk to you for a few minutes?"

"Miss, right now's a very busy time. Can this wait 'til things slow down?"

"Sure, I can wait," Molly replied. "How long you think?"

"Usually it slows down after lunchtime, so about a half hour," Josef replied.

"I'll be back in half an hour," Molly replied, and walked away with an intention to explore the market.

For the next half hour, Josef pondered what he should or should not say to the inquisitive policewoman. Should he tell her about Lenore's disappearance and reappearance? If he did, there would be more questions and more trouble. His father might get in trouble for not going to the police. Lenore would surely be questioned and maybe even taken away. He could not say anything. Luckily Lenore did not remember anything, so that should work in their favor.

As he silently pondered, he realized that the foolish Styler girl had told Lenore about how she ran away and that she came back after a mysterious accident. But she didn't tell her about the river. That was good. *It'll all be fine. I just need to keep my mouth shut. I don't know anything. I need to stay with Lenore if that woman wants to talk to her. Lenore would insist on it anyway, but I better insist, as well,* he concluded. He was finally ready for Molly and just in time, for she was headed toward him once more.

After some small talk, Molly began asking Josef questions about Lenore and Gavin Green. To his amazement, this seemingly normal woman even asked about ghostly White Witches and mysterious Black Ravens. The entire time, he claimed to know nothing, and, for the most part, he managed not to lie. He artfully avoided the truth. Only on the subject of local folklore did he share his insights and engage in a meaningful conversation. Molly came away frustratingly empty.

Next, she had a chance to interview Lenore, who seemed like the most innocent person in the world. She could not remember much and Molly wondered if she suffered from a mental disorder. This made little sense given the complexity of the poem that bore her name. She knew nothing about White Witches, Ravens, or White Doves. Nor had she ever seen the poem or heard of Gavin Green. After years of interrogations, Molly could tell when most people were lying. Clearly, Lenore told the truth. Something did not fit. Did she have the wrong Lenore?

Something was clearly wrong with this girl, but what? She acted completely normal, except that she had no recollection of anything substantial. Furthermore, the deep but nearly healed cut on her upper forehead was unexplainable, although Josef insisted she fell and hit her head on a stall. Lenore could not remember any of it. Was that injury the source of her apparent amnesia? Was her brother hiding something else that even Lenore did not know? It seemed more probable as the interview continued.

Something was very wrong here, but Molly could not get anywhere with these two Amish siblings. Reluctantly, she wished them well and walked away. On her way out, she did not notice the young woman watching her from behind an adjacent market stand.

CHAPTER 53

An Old Nemesis

Rebecca approached the front door of the log cabin that provided a haven to the small group of young women. Once again, an intruder was trying to enter.

"Don't open it, Becky! You'll let in the evil," Agnes warned. The rest of the girls were huddled in the back of the room. Suddenly, Hazel rose and ran past Rebecca. Before anyone had a chance to stop her, she began to open the front door.

"Oh my God, Hazel! What're you doing?" Marie let out, as Rebecca rushed toward the partially open door in a desperate attempt to close it.

"It's Ariella!" Hazel proclaimed in complete confidence. Without further hesitation, she opened the door and greeted their leader.

"Ariella!" All the young women shouted in unison as they rushed to meet their mentor. As they got closer, they stopped. They could see that she was exhausted, and Sarah and Rebecca had to help her into the cabin.

"What happened? Where's Anna?" Rebecca asked on behalf of all the young women as they helped Ariella onto the couch.

"Get her some water and a blanket," Rebecca instructed the younger girls. "Maybe we need to call a doctor," she reasoned aloud.

This remark forced Ariella to respond, which she did in an adamant whisper. "No. No doctor."

"Okay, but you seem ill," Rebecca replied, still concerned.

Hazel placed her hand on Ariella's forehead. Calmly she leaned closer toward her, sensing that the latter was struggling to speak, yet wished to communicate something important.

"She says we're lucky he hadn't entered." Hazel verbalized Ariella's faint whisper.

"Thanks to her protection spell," Rebecca replied. All the girls were seated in a semicircle around the couch. Some sat in nearby chairs and some sat on the floor.

"There was no protection spell," Hazel replied, after hearing Ariella's whisper.

"What? Then why couldn't he enter? Was it a he or a they?" Rebecca asked.

Hazel once again listened to the faint reply. "'They, but he's in charge. He didn't want to enter because he knew I wasn't here. He's after me." Ariella finally regained her voice. "He was simply trying to frighten you and send me a message that nothing is off limits."

"Who is he? Or who are they?" Marie asked the obvious.

"You don't know him. It doesn't matter. Simply know that he's now my nemesis in this world, where good and evil struggle in equal proportions," Ariella replied, more audible now.

"So, you know who he is… who they are?"

"I know who he is, but not who they are," Ariella replied softly.

"I don't understand that," Sarah replied.

Ariella let out a soft chuckle. She seemed to slowly regain her strength. Straightening herself up on the couch, she continued her explanation. "As I've told you, all is connected. Even good and evil are closely connected. They seem opposites, but they're not. They're extensions of each other, like a spectrum. They're inherent to the ways of nature and to our physical being—to our humanity."

"What does that have to do with this villain?" Sarah asked.

"He's evil because he lost control of his mind and surrendered to his fears and hates. He's trapped in his own illusion of reality, which he's desperately trying to validate and solidify. Unfortunately, he's partially my creation."

"What do you mean?" Sarah was still confused, as were the rest of the girls.

"I've known him for a long time. His mind's warped and polarized. He needs help. But first, I need to get Anna back," Ariella replied.

"He has Anna?" Sarah asked.

"Yes, Sarah. He does."

"Is she okay?"

"So far, but I need to get to her."

"Where is she?"

"I don't know. I need to change and eat, and then resume my search."

"We should go to the police, Ariella," Rebecca insisted.

"No. They're not going to help us. I need to do this," Ariella responded.

"I'll go with ya," Rebecca replied.

"No. You must stay here. I need you here."

"Then I'll go," Rachel replied.

"No. You all need to stay here. He will not enter here if I'm away."

"How will he know that you're away?"

"He knows. He's been watching me. It's only a matter of time until we clash. We've been on that convergence for a long, long time. I thought I could change him, but I was wrong," Ariella confessed, while remaining vague about the identity of her arch-rival.

"So, you know his name?"

"Yes."

"What is it?"

"I don't wish to utter it here. It's better that you don't know. Just trust me on that."

"What about the other person? You said there were two. Becky and I saw two sets of footprints," Rachel recalled.

"I don't know anything about his accomplice, except that he has one," Ariella replied.

"Where were you all this time?" Marie asked.

"I went to try and find him. It's a long story, but I failed. He outfoxed me. I was pretty far from here when I had a strong feeling you girls were in trouble, so I ran here as fast as I could. That's why I'm so exhausted," she replied. She refused to admit that she had run into him just beyond Devils Bridge, and that the resultant struggle had weakened her. Although, she had won for now, the game had only begun. Deep down, she knew she had to exchange herself for Anna's freedom. She was sure of that.

CHAPTER 54

Wilson's Bar

It was ten minutes past one o'clock in the afternoon when Molly found the Inspector's new field office in the neighboring village of Kiradale. The village was tiny, about the size of Eden Crossing, which was little more than an old crossroads. A large, weathered wooden sign greeted all newcomers as they entered the village. The sign had a positive but odd message that seemed to echo the feeling Molly had as she looked about the quiet hollow.

WELCOME TO KIRADALE
Rain or Shine, Snow or Ice
Kiradale is a Sunny Place

Cute. I guess it rhymes in the local accent, Molly chuckled. *I wish this saying applied to our grumpy boss.* Lately, it seemed like the Inspector had lost his lighter side. He seemed stressed and concerned for his position. Molly realized that more than anyone. Often she looked to James Cabot as a father figure, but since she started dating Jack Fulton a distance had grown between them.

She reflected on this as she double-checked the address of the old clapboard house that appeared to be the team's new field office. It was squeezed in a short row of similar structures. The entire street front looked like a time warp to the 1930s. *This place looks more like a speakeasy*, she thought as she approached the dilapidated building. A sign outside the door read, "Wilson's Bar." The remainder of the sign was broken off by an unknown prankster or had simply weathered away with time.

As Molly entered cautiously, it became clear that the long, narrow, one-room establishment was not a bar at all. Rather, it had been an old barbershop, now abandoned. Apparently, the previous owner left town in a hurry for the place looked exactly as it would have when it was fully functional, right down to the razors, brushes, and combs. It contained two worn leather barber chairs, each facing a faded mirror. A long wooden bench stretched along the wall opposite the barber stations and the faded mirrors. This bench had been worn by countless customers who waited their turn or simply stayed to pass the time.

Above the bench were dozens of old pictures and framed news clippings that captured the history of Kiradale and the neighboring Eden Valley. These included group photographs of long-disbanded baseball teams and long-departed patrons. Among them were yellowed postcards of covered bridges, Amish buggies, and farm silos as well as dog-eared snapshots of tractor-pull contest winners, local beauty pageant contestants, and pie-eating champions.

But most prominent of all, besides the tattered American flag and a large rusty election sign that read, "I like Ike," was a large, centrally-placed picture of the Kamerynville High School football team, circa 1992. Above the 16- by 24-inch, framed picture was a faded banner that proclaimed the pride of the valley: "Eden Valley Ravens, State Champions, 1991-1992."

This picture seemed to go unnoticed by the Inspector and his team as they settled near the back of the barbershop at a small oak table with six rickety chairs. Beyond the table were two peeling brown doors—one led to an unsightly bathroom and the other seemed to be an exit to the back of the structure. To the left of the table, at the end of the long wall that contained the worn bench, sat an easel with a large white board that Chen had purchased at the Inspector's request.

The Inspector was holding court in this small enclave. He was in the process of setting up the whiteboard when Molly entered the barber shop, ringing the rusty bell attached to the back of the front door.

"Finally, a customer!" Chen proclaimed, as Molly entered. "But she's in need of more than a haircut."

Kelly chuckled, while the Inspector frowned.

"Nice of you to show up, Molly," he grumbled.

"Nice place, boss. You thinkin' of changing careers?" Molly replied, ignoring the initial remarks of both men while looking around her. "This place suits you, boss—it's vintage," she added, causing Kelly and Chen to burst into laughter.

"Let's cut the crap. We've got a lot of work to do." The Inspector was in a bad mood.

Molly did not let this stop her. She had to make one more verbal assault on Chen. After all, it was tradition. "Before we start, there's one thing I'd like to say, boss," she said as she sat down on one of the flimsy chairs at the end of the table.

"What is it?" the Inspector growled.

"Chen, my dear, you outdid yourself with the decor. Thanks for finding this gem for us to enjoy. I particularly like the poster above your head. It's so classy." She pointed to the yellowed pinup poster hanging behind Chen. It was a late 1940s advertisement with a drawing of a very leggy blond holding a bottle of aftershave as if it were precious perfume. The slogan read, "Lure Her with Spice. She'll Love You for It."

"That's enough, kids!" The Inspector cut off the banter, but in the process looked at the poster. "Chen, see if we can take that down. Molly's right. That's inappropriate in a working environment. Besides, we'll need the wall space."

"That's right, Chen," Molly added. "It clashes with the other pinups." She pointed to a plethora of smaller pinups on a far cork board.

"I said that's enough." The Inspector was not in the mood for banter.

What followed had Molly and Kelly silently snickering. Chen, who always obeyed the Inspector's every wish, proceeded to try to take down the large, risqué aftershave poster. As he fumbled with the task, the Inspector stormed in to assist. From Molly and Kelly's vantage point, the two men appeared to be pulling at the pinup model, each tugging at a leg.

"She's too much for them," Molly whispered to Kelly. They both tried not to laugh aloud.

"Chen, try loosening the top," Kelly suggested. That was when Molly lost it and started laughing aloud.

"Send a couple boys to do a man's job," Molly added in a whisper, so that only Kelly could hear. Now, both were in stitches.

"Damn this thing!" the Inspector said. "It's nailed to the wall. Like some fool would want to steal it. Just leave it! I can tape my notes over it."

"I can only imagine the faces of our suspects posted on this vintage classic. It's certainly an upgrade to your boring cork board, boss," Molly said in a serious tone. Kelly was about to burst into laughter again but stopped instantly at the sight of the Inspector's frown.

"Enough!" the Inspector chastised the two women. "Let's get started. We've got a lot to do and we're running out of time. We're lucky. We got some privacy here. Chen, anything new on your end?"

Chen had the place of honor and was asked to go first. In response, he inflated a little before beginning.

"After more digging into old files, I found this little gem." He handed the Inspector a piece of paper. "It's George Walker's last will. Apparently, he made one before his car accident four years ago. In it, he bestowed all the contents of a safe deposit box at the Kamerynville First National Bank to our mysterious Erin Stone. I found this odd, since there was never any evidence that George Walker and Erin Stone were anything more than friends.

"But it had one positive effect. It made Erin resurface. Walker's girlfriend at the time, Linda Stanley, sued Stone for the contents of the safe deposit box, which was described as a coin collection, but she lost. When I contacted the bank, they said that Ms. Stone took out the contents of the box on September 19, 2009, after winning the lawsuit. They would not confirm a coin collection and insisted that we would have to have a warrant or a subpoena to get more information."

"Chen, please get a warrant from Judge Andrews. Tell him Erin Stone is an official suspect in the Porter homicide," the Inspector instructed. "We need to talk to Stone, and we need to know the contents of that safe deposit box. Where's Stone, now?"

"Well, she seems to have disappeared again."

"That's impossible. People don't simply disappear these days."

"Well, Ms. Stone did, safe deposit box contents and all. I checked the address provided in the lawsuit, and she left soon after, leaving no forwarding address."

"Did you get anything new on Harry Schaffer?"

"Like I said, he went MIA in 1995 in Bosnia. I managed to track down his mother, who still lives outside of Kamerynville. I talked to her on the phone this morning. Although she seemed very cooperative, she did not add anything new to what we know already, except that Harry was never found and is presumed dead. She claimed not to know Porter, Hughes, Stone, or McAlester.

She did mention that her son was best friends with George Walker, and she lamented George's tragic death. I guess he used to come over to the house and visit her before he died. According to her, he was a real gentleman. She never heard of a Black Raven Club but did say that her son had a raven tattoo that he got in high school. She wasn't fond of it, as you can imagine. That's all I got."

"Good work. Kelly, what do you have?"

"This morning, I heard from a server at The Raven Inn that there was an attack on one of the maids at the inn the day before we found Green's body, and that Gavin was suspected to be the attacker, although it was never proven. We need to investigate this further," Kelly shared.

"Which server told you? And do we have the name of the maid who was attacked?" The Inspector was intrigued.

"Elaine Roberts told me. She said the maid's name was Agnes Wright. Strangely, Agnes disappeared later that day and hasn't been seen since. Elaine suspects that she's with 'the Sisterhood,' as she put it."

"What sisterhood?"

"They're known as the Eden Sisterhood and appear to be in a remote cabin north of Eden Crossing. She didn't know the address but gave me a rough location."

"What else do we know about this sisterhood?"

"Elaine knew little, but she did say that it seems to be a place for runaway women. That's why she suspected Agnes ended up there. I got Agnes's cell phone number off Elaine, but when I tried to call it, it came up disconnected. Chen ran the information Elaine gave me about the location of the sisterhood, and there are about three cabins in the area that fit the description. As luck would have it, one of them is Harry Schaffer's old cabin. Coincidence?"

"Okay, Kelly. Tomorrow, you are going to transform into a runaway and head up to Harry Schaffer's old cabin. Let's see if we can locate this sisterhood and penetrate it. Chen, you'll get her the exact location, right?"

"Already have it," Chen replied.

"Okay, boss. I can be a runaway, said Kelly. The other thing I have is that your favorite cop, Alvin Walker, has a raven tattoo, just like the boys in the photo. Coincidence? I don't think so. He must be in the Black Raven Club, as well."

"We need to keep digging. These guys must all be in the same club, which could have connections to drugs based on Porter's activity. We'll have to drag each one of them in for an official interview," the Inspector concluded aloud.

"Excuse me, boss, but are you going to drag each one of those guys into this creepy barbershop for an interview?" Molly asked in a deadpan face.

"Maybe. By the way, I like this place. How long do we have this place, Chen?"

"For a month. It was dirt cheap."

"I can see why. It's precious," Molly added.

"There's a lot of history here. It's a guy's kind of place," the Inspector added. "Good job finding it, Chen."

Molly stood up and walked around. "There's a lot of dust and mice turds around here if you haven't noticed. It's disgusting. Right, Kelly?"

"It is that, but I agree that it has a lot of charm," Kelly replied.

"Whose side are you on, little sister?" Molly made reference to the server at The Dead End Restaurant who thought Molly and Kelly were the Inspector's two daughters.

"I'm simply saying that with all these trophies and photographs, this place's like a local museum."

"No, it's a creepy, dusty barbershop," Molly objected.

"Please sit down, Molly. We have a long afternoon ahead of us," the Inspector replied. "Kelly, do you have anything else to report?"

"No. That's it."

"Okay, it's your turn, Molly. What did you find out about Lenore when you went to the Amish Market?"

"I think it's her, but something's not right. It's as if her brother, Josef, knows more than she does. She seems to have some form of undiagnosed amnesia. She had a cut on her head that was nearly healed, but at the time it must have been quite a gash. I couldn't help but wonder if she had recent head trauma. I know it's a stretch, but I can usually tell if someone's lying. Her brother was lying, but she's either the best liar I ever encountered or she has something wrong with her memory. I need to investigate her further," Molly concluded.

"Okay, you can take the lead on that. Anything on Hughes or McAlester?"

"I haven't had a chance to talk to Jerry McAlester. I thought Kelly was covering him."

"I am. I just haven't been able to catch up to him. He was out this morning, but he's at the top of my list," Kelly replied.

"Molly, you take him. Kelly, you focus on Alvin," the Inspector ordered. "Molly, anything new on Hughes? He's still my number one suspect."

"I didn't have any recent conversations with Sam, except the one I described at yesterday's meeting. But it sounds like you'll be dragging them both in here for official interviews. Is that right?"

"Yes."

"He'll strap 'em in a barber chair and force 'em to tell the truth, or else," Kelly interjected.

"Else he'll shave their heads," Molly added.

"Something like that. You have anything else, Molly?" The Inspector was finally lightening up. It seemed that the raven tattoo clue made him more hopeful.

"No, that's it."

"Okay, my turn. I interviewed the Miller brothers," the Inspector began. "I found that Linus owned the shovels we found at Drakes Plot, but gave them to his neighbor, who sold them at her yard sale. She claims to have sold them to a young woman. I got her description, but it's vague. I think Linus is telling the truth, but Amos is hiding something. I just can't put my finger on it. I thought the Amish didn't lie." The Inspector played with his large black mustache.

"They're not supposed to, but they sure skirt the truth. One thing's for certain, they're pacifists," Kelly clarified. "There's no way they're guilty of this."

"I'm not totally convinced, Kelly, but I know they're hidin' something. Right, Molly?"

"Absolutely. They don't trust us. I got that sense already. By the way, I'm going to go interview Lenore's family, tomorrow. You wanna come along?" Molly asked.

"I would," the Inspector replied, "but I need to go back to the Green Estate and check on a hunch. Let's take a quick break before we list our suspects and hypotheses."

During the break, Molly and Kelly went out the back door of the old barbershop and were pleasantly surprised by what they discovered.

"Wow, check this out!" Molly exclaimed to Kelly. "It's a perfect English garden, complete with manicured lawns and trimmed boxwood hedges. That's incredible! Who keeps this up?" The two women walked around the tranquil setting.

"I love the arbor," Kelly added, sitting down in one of the wrought iron chairs that surrounded a matching table. These were set in the middle of a flagstone patio, which was covered with an arbor hewn of old oak and overgrown with a flowering, purple wisteria. The entire garden was surrounded by an eight-foot stucco wall covered with ivy. It was a sanctuary of sorts, but for whom?

"Look, there's a gate in the back. Let's check out where it leads." Molly pointed to the old wooden gate.

"Sure. We should have the rest of our meeting on the patio," Kelly suggested, reluctantly rising from her seat.

"Not sure that's such a good idea. You never know who could be listenin' out here. By the way, I bet whoever tends this garden enters it through this gate," Molly concluded as she reached the gate.

Molly opened the old wooden gate and discovered a second manicured garden that appeared to be an extension of the first. In the far corner of this garden, at a distance of about eighty-yards, stood a woman in a long, white dress. Upon their entrance, she took flight along the garden path that hugged the stone wall beyond, never revealing her face. There was an otherworldly appearance to the figure, accentuated by the low, late afternoon light. Her ghostly, white gown and raven hair flowed behind her as if caressed by a supernatural breeze.

Molly and Kelly stopped at the sight of the unearthly form—neither trusting her senses.

"Do you see that?" Kelly whispered, trying not to breathe for fear of disturbing what appeared to be an apparition.

"Yeah," Molly replied, still motionless, her hand frozen to the iron handle of the old garden gate.

"No one will ever believe us," Kelly slowly whispered.

Both women gave pursuit to the mysterious woman, only to see her vanish without a seeming trace through the stone archway at the center of the distant garden wall.

CHAPTER 55

Never Again

Finally, the invasion of English authorities had subsided at Amos Miller's farm. For the first time in days, he had the place to himself without any interruptions. The crime scene at Drakes Plot remained restricted and guarded by a security guard, but except for that intrusion, all was quiet.

On this quiet afternoon that threatened rain, Amos was in his shed sharpening the blades of his plow. In the corner of the cluttered room lay Otto, his faithful dog, unalarmed by the red tail of sparks cascading off the sharpening stone. The latter was connected to a small generator. Although the Amish were forbidden the use of tractors, automobiles, and electricity, gasoline-powered generators were permitted and frequently used.

Amos sharpened his fourth blade when Otto suddenly stood up and ran toward the shed door. He did not bark, but simply wagged his tail. Amos had to finish filing the blade and did not dare to interrupt his task although he felt a presence enter the room. Having his back to the door, he could not see the identity of the visitor. But based on Otto's reaction, he knew it was a friend, not a stranger.

Finishing the task, he shut off the grinder and turned to face the doorway. To his surprise, the woman of his dreams stood before him. She looked angelic and radiant. Like a schoolboy with a crush, he could feel his heart race as she approached him. For a moment, he forgot to breathe. Had his endless prayers been answered or was he losing his mind? In that fleeting instant, he was not sure.

Seeing his questioning stare, she stopped before him and broke the silence with her soft voice. "Amos, it's all come back to me. I remember everything. I remember us."

Stepping closer, she gently reached out her hand to touch his arm—never breaking her eye contact. As if time had stopped, he savored the moment, hoping it was not a dream. She stood so close now. All that had separated them seemed to have vanished. Lost in her rich, brown eyes, he could not speak. There was no need for words; her loving gaze communicated so much more. Finally, he found his voice and heard his words, stating the obvious: "I love you."

Without a word, she placed her arms around his waist—slowly, purposefully, passionately. The Amish are not known for passion, but that is not to say that all are reserved. Lenore was not reserved. She had never been reserved. That was not her defining trait. A passionate woman, she had been constrained by religious walls which she had dared to scale.

God, she's beautiful, he silently acknowledged with his entire being.

"You," she said softly. Her lips pulled at his heart. "It was you all along. Wasn't it?"

She was so incredibly fervid that he could not utter another word. When he finally opened his lips, she silenced him with a sultry "shhhh…"

Her eyes were so mesmerizing, so alive, so piercingly ardent. He could not break her gaze. To do so might be to lose this dream of reality.

"I'm sorry I didn't remember," she said slowly, moving closer still until he felt her chest press against his, and then her lips. Lenore was fervent, and her kiss was the only means of sexual expression within the limits of what was allowed by her religion.

That kiss seemed to last a lifetime, and it expressed a longing that stretched further still. Amos touched heaven, for there was no place he'd rather be and no one he'd rather be with than this amazing woman. *How could I have released her? Never again*, he thought. "Never again will I release you," he whispered to her as they came up for air.

"Never again will I leave you," she whispered in a soft, seductive voice. Again they kissed, and this time he released the pins in her cap with his right hand, never breaking the amorous connection. Her cap fell to the ground, as an endless flood of thick, amber hair poured down her back.

"You're so beautiful," he whispered as they finally broke their kiss.

"You're so mine," she whispered with a giggle, her brown eyes sparkling in delight.

"Stay right there and don't move," he beckoned in a gentle, loving tone.

She eagerly submitted. Quickly, he walked over to the shed door and ordered Otto into the barnyard. The dog reluctantly obeyed. The shed door closed behind him, leaving the confused canine standing in the cloudburst that followed.

CHAPTER 56

Cane

riella was on a mission. She had to find Anna, and she had to do it quickly. Sensing this urgency, she spent a short time with her flock before setting out once more. Although some of the girls wanted to join her, she knew that she had to hunt this dangerous foe alone.

After a brief rest and a hearty lunch, she disappeared into the woods in the light rain that had begun to fall across Eden Valley. This time she headed northwest, away from the river and deeper into the extensive forest. Her quest was clear, and there was no time to waste. Soaked by the time she reached the large clearing, she did not even notice the rain.

Quickly she found the large oak tree that guarded the cave entrance, the home of the one person who could help her—the elusive hermit. Knowing his fragile mental state, she did not try to enter, but waited for him under the large oak tree. Since their last encounter, she had often wandered to this secluded meadow to observe him and to try to make him remember. Unfortunately, all such attempts had failed. Her only success was his growing familiarity with her presence. Although at times he confused her with one of his imaginary friends and fellow soldiers, she no longer presented a threat.

She sat and waited, determined to succeed, needing to discover something that only this shell of a man possessed somewhere deep inside his delusional mind. The dark clouds passed and the rain ceased. Soon, the sun emerged, long enough to start its descent toward the horizon, as the late afternoon shadows grew until they converged into dusk. Patiently, she rested against the mighty tree. There, in its peaceful presence, she found slumber at last.

In her odd dream, she felt a presence staring at her. Startled awake, she looked up and discovered a large gray wolf sitting before her. Had he come to see his master? Almost instantly, the hermit appeared as if summoned. He stopped and stared at her.

"What have we here, Wolf?" the hermit asked. "Looks like the Lady of the Woods. Maybe she's a nymph—but too large for a nymph," he mumbled to the patient animal sitting before Ariella. "Ya like her, don't ya. She must have magic to tame the likes of you."

Ariella was always surprised that although the hermit had grown accustomed to her, he never consciously recognized her from one visit to the next. In every encounter, she took on a new description in his fragmented mind.

"Harry, I need to talk to you," she said softly, deciding to try and stir some recollection of the past by using his given name.

"He looked at her as if for the first time, and a deep frown emerged upon his face. "What does this strange nymph want, Wolf? Who's Harry?" he asked the wolf, as if the animal were human and Ariella was not. "You don't know. Well, I don't know either," he concluded aloud.

"Oh, Harry! How'd you end up like this?" She spoke openly and firmly. There was no time to be sensitive with the truth, as she had been in past visits.

"Wolf, this one's very odd—stranger than the last one. Where're all these wood nymphs coming from? There must be a flock of 'em. Go away, nymph!" the hermit shouted.

"Harry, look at me. Look in my eyes. You know who I am. Harry, I need you to come back to me." Her tone portrayed her care and desperation.

He stared at her with a blank expression on his face. This, more than any words that he could have uttered, crushed her inside. He had no idea of her identity. She could not reach him. Unable to hold back her tears any longer, she let them stream down her cheeks, unabated.

The sight of Ariella crying triggered a memory in the disheveled woodsman. For a moment, Harry recognized her and smiled.

"I know you," he said in a calm voice that sounded as distant as the memory itself. He struggled in his confused mind, but those three words spelled hope.

"Harry!" she proclaimed. "It's me!"

She stopped crying and ran to embrace him. But before she could reach him, the memory was gone and he sprang back like a wild animal.

"Wolf, she's attacking me!" He screamed and reached down to pick up a large stick with which to defend himself. "Go away, crazy nymph!"

Ariella's heart and step stopped in an instant. Harry vanished, replaced once more by the fearful hermit. But there was hope. Maybe this was the breakthrough. Maybe he would remember her the next time.

"Goodbye, Harry," she replied softly to his continuing screams. She knew that there was no way to help him in this state. Reluctantly, she turned away and began retracing her steps across the wet meadow.

As she did, the gray wolf followed her at two paces. Turning to the faithful beast, she said, "Cane, you still need to stay here and guard him like we agreed." The wolf understood, but his eyes portrayed his desire to once more walk with his true master. She embraced him, for he had been her trusted companion for so many years. To her, he personified the great shaman who had been her teacher—the one who seemed to protect her still. That thought added to her flow of tears.

"Thank you, Cane, my faithful friend," she said and disappeared into the woods. The wolf returned to the hermit and sat by his side. As the wind shifted, he picked up the scent of an intruder and was about to investigate. But the hermit fervently beckoned him and together they withdrew from the meadow into the depths of the cave. The scene was clear of all, except for a silent observer, hidden in the deep shadows of the surrounding woods.

CHAPTER 57

A Long Night

A steady drizzle had begun to fall just as Molly and Kelly returned to the team's makeshift war room. After a quick search of the second garden and the thick woods beyond its walls, they had found no evidence of the mysterious woman, except some questionable impressions in the long grass outside the stone archway. If she were someone spying on them, she did an exceptional job of covering her tracks. Upon further discussion, neither Molly nor Kelly thought the strange encounter added any value to the investigation, so they decided not to raise the issue. The price of certain ridicule from their boss and endless teasing from Chen did not seem worth it.

As they entered the old barbershop, the Inspector eagerly awaited them. Their ten-minute break had turned into a twenty-minute absence.

"Where were you two? I was about to send Chen to look for you. We've got a lot to do and no time to waste. Okay, where were we? Ah… yes, the suspect list." He grabbed a marker and began writing on the whiteboard. "The suspects are Sam Hughes, Jerry McAlester, Alvin Walker, and Erin Stone. Any others?" He had the four names written on the board.

"What about Cheryl, the mysterious server at The Raven Inn?" Molly suggested.

"Okay, let's add her. Any others?"

"Elaine Roberts, the young server who seems to have a romantic relationship with Hughes," Kelly replied.

"She doesn't," Molly corrected, as all eyes fell upon her. "But she may be a suspect," she added, feeling herself blush.

"Okay, we'll add Ms. Roberts." The Inspector added her name to the whiteboard. "Any others?"

"Ariella Bianca, who bought the old Schaffer cabin."

"That's a stretch. I'll put her on the list of folks we need to interview," the Inspector replied.

"What about the Miller brothers, Amos and Linus?" Chen asked.

"I'm starting to agree with Kelly that they're innocent," the Inspector replied.

"Agreed, but Amos is hiding something," Molly chimed into the conversation.

"Okay, we'll add Amos to the list of folks we need to interview again. Anyone else?" the Inspector asked.

"Lenore," Molly suggested. "Put her on the list of folks we need to interview again, along with her brother, Josef."

"Okay, and you've got that task. Right, Molly?"

"Right."

"Any others?"

There were no further suggestions until Chen suddenly perked up. "How about the Amish couple that found Green's body? What were their names?"

"Abel Snyder and Esther Fischer," Kelly replied. Her memory still amazed the rest of her teammates.

"Good point, Chen. I'll add them to the interview list. Anyone else?"

"What about the Eden Sisterhood?" Kelly asked.

"I'll group them with Ariella Bianca."

"What about the White Witch and the Black Raven references in Lenore's poem?" Chen asked.

"Let's not get ridiculous. They're clearly disguises. Anyone else?"

There was a general silence. "What about Gus, the police chief?" Molly suggested.

"I'll vouch for Gus. He's innocent," the Inspector replied. "Is that it?"

"I think so," Molly replied.

"Okay, then let's talk about each of the suspects and any possible motives."

"That's going to be a short conversation," Molly replied.

"Let's review what we know. We know Gavin Green overdosed on heroin, but Porter's death was clearly a homicide. Yet to date, we don't have a legitimate link between the two. We also know of a high school club called 'The Black Ravens' that was started by Porter, Hughes, McAlester, Schaffer, and George Walker, Alvin's deceased older brother, but we don't know if the club's connected to the case.

"However, the members of this club appear to all possess raven tattoos, like the one on Porter's body. Unfortunately, the only reference to this Black Raven Club is the one yearbook photo that Chen discovered in the high school files. There's nothing more. Molly, you need to investigate this further with Hughes and McAlester," the Inspector requested. "Kelly, you need to push on Alvin Walker to see what he might know."

"I've got it on my list," Molly replied. Kelly did not reply; she simply nodded.

"Damn, we have so little. It's a stretch, but this club may be linked to some sort of drug activity since Porter was certainly involved with the use and possibly sale of drugs. For all we know, the Black Ravens are a drug gang," the Inspector said.

"A white-collar drug gang in Eden Valley? That doesn't sound right, boss. Are you agreeing with Alvin that the two deaths were related to drug dealing?" Molly asked.

"Well, it's one hypothesis. We know Green died of an overdose and Porter probably dealt drugs, so there's some merit to it." He wrote it on the lower half of the whiteboard as hypothesis number one.

"Did it occur to you that under that scenario, the killer might not be on our suspect list?" Molly reasoned.

"Yes, it could be someone associated with a drug deal gone bad, or it could be Hughes, McAlester, or our buddy, Alvin Walker. All are closely associated with the two victims," the Inspector countered. "But you make a good point, Molly. I guess I better add that uncertainty to our list. That reminds me. Chen, we need to reconnect with Drug Enforcement on general drug activity in the area. I hate to admit it, but I'm starting to think that drug dealing's the most plausible explanation for the two deaths," the Inspector reasoned.

Molly pushed back. "You're caving, boss. I disagree with you and Alvin."

"I'm not agreeing with crazy Alvin. Let's be clear. I'm just suggesting that drugs and drug dealing were potential motives, which is hard to dismiss given the evidence," the Inspector objected.

"Okay, but hear me out," Molly replied. "In the drug motive, where do Lenore and that poem fit into the picture, or all the White Witch stuff? And why was Agnes Wright attacked, as per Elaine's testimony? By the way, we need to add Agnes to your interviewee wish list. We still need to find her, since she may know the identity of her attacker."

"Damn it! There are still too many loose ends," the Inspector admitted in a frustrated tone, as he wrote Agnes's name on the whiteboard.

"Sure are. For instance, why would Will Porter be digging up the 200-year-old grave of Eleanor Drake, the legendary White Witch, and die in the process? That doesn't tie into the drug motive at all," Kelly observed. "I think there's something to the Drake legend. As weird as it sounds, what if he was looking for Drake's treasure?"

"Okay, hypothesis number two surrounds the Drake legend and treasure. This one ties in the White Witch. To your point, Kelly, it gives us some explanation as to why Porter died at Drakes Plot and why someone subsequently disturbed Arthur Drake's grave. But it does not explain Green's death or his connection to Porter's death. That motive leaves the two deaths unlinked," the Inspector pushed back. "I have found that the simplest explanation is usually the correct one, and the drug dealing motive is simpler than this treasure idea. We haven't found any evidence of a treasure. Even Dr. Murray, the authority on the Drake history and legend, thinks there's no treasure."

"I can tell this'll be a long night," Molly sighed.

"Actually, boss, both deaths could be linked to the treasure. Remember the White Witch drawings in Green's farmhouse and the holes dug in his earthen basement? They could be linked," Kelly reasoned.

"Again, we need more evidence. Any other hypotheses?" The Inspector dismissed the conversation, wishing to create his list before exploring the potential scenarios.

"There's the Erin Stone and Sam Hughes scandal in the Green family, and her mysterious disappearance," Chen replied.

"Yes, but what's the motive?"

"I don't know—marriage scandal. But that doesn't fit, does it?"

"No, not really. It's simply an odd fact. Any other hypotheses on motive?" the Inspector waited, marker in hand.

"Random serial killer," Kelly replied.

"A violent psychopath. That's number three." The Inspector added it to the list. "Any others?"

"What if it's all of them?" Molly suggested.

"Then we've got our hands full."

The team meeting continued into the evening. After some pizza, it continued into the night. In the end, there were no clear solutions, only more questions.

Eden Valley, Pennsylvania

CHAPTER 58

A White Witch and a Blue Truck

It was half past six in the morning when Kelly and Molly left The Raven Inn. They headed north, along the Eden River. Kelly was dressed in sweats, her hair disheveled, her clothes purposely soiled, and her only possession being a small, well-worn backpack. She was going undercover to discover the secrets of the Eden Sisterhood. The plan was for Molly to drive her within a short walk of the old Schaffer cabin. Kelly would hike to the cabin and pretend to be a runaway seeking refuge. Hopefully, the cabin was the home of the sisterhood.

"You look too clean, Kelly. Put some dirt on your face," Molly advised.

"I don't need to look like I've rolled around in a puddle," Kelly objected.

"Yes, you do. You're supposed to look like you've been sleeping in the woods for a week. I bet your packed clothes are all clean and folded. Right?"

"Yeah. I'm not a slob."

"Whatever. You have your cell phone?"

"Yes, Mom, I do. Anything else?"

"No. Call me later today or tonight."

"Are you worried about me?"

"No. It's protocol."

"Right. And packing me a lunch was protocol as well?" Kelly laughed.

"I didn't pack your lunch."

"You stuck all these healthy snacks in my backpack. You're so ready to be a mom, Molly."

"Okay, enough. This is your stop, you ungrateful sister. By the way, you don't smell like a lost stray either."

"How do they smell, all-knowing one?"

"Not like Coco Chanel."

"Oh, just wish me luck! I'll call you when I get a chance. And don't worry. It's not like these girls are dangerous. I'm crashing a sorority, for God's sake. Besides, I know self-defense." Kelly stepped out of the car and slung her pack on her back.

"Try to figure out what happened to Agnes Wright and who attacked her. That's the main point."

"I will! You're such a mom!"

The two parted as Molly drove away, leaving Kelly on the gravel road leading to Ariella's cabin. Twenty minutes later, Kelly reached the front door of the sleepy abode. She was surprised to see a large pentagram charred into the rough pine door. *That's bizarre. Maybe Molly's concerns aren't so ridiculous*, she thought.

Softly, she knocked on the door. Since there was no answer, she knocked again, harder. The door did not open, but a young female voice inquired timidly, "Who is it?"

"My name's Kelly. Is this the Eden Sisterhood?"

"What brings you here?" the young woman asked.

"I ran away from home, and I heard this was a safe place to stay. It'd only be for a day or two," Kelly replied, trying to sound desperate.

There was a long pause before the door opened a crack, revealing a safety chain. A young woman peered through the crack. "How do we know you're not with him?"

Kelly was confused. "Who?"

"The crazy, tattooed guy that attacked the cabin a couple nights ago and made the pentagrams. How do we know you're not with him?" The young woman behind the door sounded fearful.

So that explains it, Kelly thought. She was about to ask whether the tattoo was that of a raven but decided to hold off and not seem like she knew the man in question. "I assure you; I didn't have anything to do with that."

The young woman behind the door took a hard look at Kelly and closed the door. Kelly could hear whispers. Now, she could hear a new, more confident voice ask the young girl, "Who's at the door?" There was a short discussion within the cabin, and soon the door opened wide.

Standing in it was a woman in a flowing white gown and numerous beads made of turquoise and jasper. Striking bright eyes dominated her soft features. Her hair was raven black and flowed down to her waist. She was shadowed by several young women, one of whom was the one who questioned Kelly after she knocked on the front door.

Kelly was taken aback. The woman had a striking resemblance to the mysterious woman in the Kiradale garden, as well as the mural of the White Witch that was depicted in Gavin Green's bedroom, but her face was that of Erin Stone.

* * * * *

That same morning, the Inspector returned to the old Green Estate to further investigate the old, abandoned farmhouse and its surrounding property. Previous detailed forensics of the scene yielded no new breakthroughs in the case, and the police had no explanation for the numerous holes in the dirt-filled basement. They remained an enigma. Drug abuse paraphernalia was found everywhere, including evidence of cocaine and heroin abuse. The odd mural of the White Witch appeared to be recently painted by the occupant or one of his guests. Gavin's infatuation with the White Witch figure was further confirmed by several books on witchcraft and the occult and a worn copy of Dr. Murray's paper on the Drake legend.

The only new piece of evidence was that Gavin Green had had numerous visitors, confirming that the three mattresses in the second bedroom and the sofa in the living room got extensive use by various individuals. DNA analyses of organic material, such as strands of hair, indicated that several male and female visitors had occupied the quarters in the recent past.

Oddly, based on the DNA profile gathered from Gavin Green's body, he had not slept in the bedroom with the White Witch mural. Rather, he appeared to have slept in the second room, the one with the three dingy mattresses. Another male slept in the master bedroom. Furthermore, several different women had occupied one or both rooms. Unfortunately, none of the DNA evidence matched police files and records. Who were these visitors and where did they go? These were the loose ends that the Inspector had come to investigate.

During his visit the day before, the Inspector had noticed an old logging road at the far end of the large grounds that surrounded the old farmhouse. Distant from the residence, this road seemed to have been missed or considered unimportant during the initial investigations. His purpose this morning was to investigate that road. As he walked deeper into the woods, he felt a chill pass right through him. It felt eerie, like the woods themselves.

Deeper he went, until he reached a sharp bend in the road. Walking around the bend, he spotted a blue pickup truck several hundred feet ahead. Drawing his gun, he approached the vehicle, keenly alert to any sound or motion. All was quiet, too quiet—deathly quiet. Slowly, he advanced trying not to make a sound. With only thirty feet to go before reaching the truck, he could not see anyone inside. He was nearly there when something burst out of the woods. Turning to fire his gun, he spotted a doe who ran past the truck and disappeared down an overgrown path beyond the vehicle.

Damn. He spit on the ground, recovering his heart from his throat. *If that didn't stir any potential occupant, nothing will,* he concluded. Picking up the pace, he reached the truck. It was empty and the license plate had been removed. *What the hell's a new truck doing down here with no tags on it?* Looking closer at the truck, he saw that it was unlocked. He checked the interior, including the glove box, but all was empty. As he continued to search the truck, he noticed a small piece of paper wedged between the passenger seat and the central console. He pulled it out carefully and placed it in an evidence bag for future analysis, if needed. Once it was in the plastic bag, he read it. *It's a receipt for new tires. This repair place is up the road. I got to check it out.* After taking numerous pictures of the truck, he walked back to his car, which had been parked in front of Green's farmhouse.

Before long, the Inspector arrived at Ken's Auto Repair, on the outskirts of Kamerynville. Ken himself came out to greet him. After a short, friendly chat, the Inspector flashed his badge and showed Ken the pictures of the blue pickup truck.

"Sure, I know that truck. I've worked on it, myself. Nice truck. What's goin' on?"

"Do you know the owner?"

"Hell, yeah! That's Andy Taylor's truck. He used to live up the road, just out o' town, but not sure where he is now. Haven't seen 'im in a while. Weird guy, if ya ask me. He's always sniffing like he's got a cold. Odd thing that. Is he in trouble?"

"Not sure, but I found his truck in the woods behind the old Green place."

"That place's been empty for over ten years. Creepy place. What's the truck doing there?"

"Not sure. When was the last time you saw Mr. Taylor?"

"About a month ago, when he got them new tires. His old lady left 'im, and he was goin' around lookin' for 'er."

"What's her name?"

"Lynn, Lucy, Laura… Hell, I don't know. All I know's she left him for some other guy. Andy was wandering aimlessly lookin' for her. Poor bastard. Maybe he found her, and they ran off."

"On foot?"

"Now that don't make no sense, fella. You ain't getting far around here on foot. That don't make no sense, at all. I suppose they'd drive, no?"

"Without a truck? Anything else you can tell me about Andrew Taylor or his wife?"

"Never met his wife. I told ya that. But, like I said, he was odd, like he was on somethin'. Strange guy that one, but he paid cash. Seemed to have plenty of it."

"Why do you say that?"

"Because he'd buy all sorts of fancy things for that truck. He'd pull out a roll of hundreds and drop a couple like he was payin' for coffee.

He'd go and give me good business, though. All cash, too. Mind ya, it don't matter none to me. Cash or not, I pay my taxes."

"Any idea what happened to him, or who might know?"

"No idea. No, sir. I better get back to fixin' that old Jeep. They're pickin' it up in two hours."

"If you see Mr. Taylor or if you remember anything else of importance, please call me at this number," the Inspector asked, giving Ken a business card.

"Sure will."

After the Inspector left, Ken picked up his cellphone and dialed. Soon, a female voice answered. "The cops found Andy's truck in the woods," he said without saying 'hello' to the mysterious woman on the other end of the line. "What's goin' on?...Hell, I don't care, but where's my money?....Screw you, Linda. Just be warned that the cops are lookin' for both of ya....No, I didn't tell them a thing. I ain't stupid, like some people. Why was the truck there?....Fine. I don't need to know."

Ken hung up the phone and chuckled. "Them cops'll get their asses soon enough," he huffed, and returned to changing the brake pads on the old Jeep.

CHAPTER 59

Shoo-Fly Pie

Earlier that same morning, Molly headed to the Lapp residence in search of Lenore. As she pulled up the gravel driveway, she was struck by the complete lack of modernization. There were no cars, no electrical wires leading to the home, no tractors, no curtains, but there were plenty of monochrome clothes hanging on a line stretched from the house to the barn. The place looked well run, but in need of minor repairs and repainting. She was surprised by the size of the home, which seemed much too small to house a large family.

As she pulled up to the house, she was greeted by two dogs, a flock of geese and countless chickens. The dogs were friendly, but the geese were not while the chickens were apathetic. Stepping out of the car, she petted the dogs, dodged the geese, and ignored the chickens. Once at the front door, she searched fruitlessly for a doorbell before finally knocking. By the third knock, a teenage girl opened the door.

"May I help ya?" she asked.

After a brief discussion, Molly was welcomed into the home of John and Mary Lapp. Immediately, they offered her coffee and shoo-fly pie, a molasses-based Amish treat. "The pie's fresh out of the oven," Mary tempted. "If ya don't try some, it'll be gone before ya know it. These kids can eat," she said with a chuckle. She seemed incredibly sincere and very direct, which was a pleasant surprise for Molly, who had expected to encounter a quiet, submissive Amish wife.

"Well, then, I'd better try a piece. It smells amazin'." Molly smiled. She felt cheerful. The entire house had a positive, loving energy.

"I'll have one too, Mary," John added. He sat opposite Mary at the wooden table masterfully crafted by his own hands. The room looked plain, with no wallpaper or any decorative pictures on the walls, except a small drawing of Jesus.

Mary served up two generous slices of shoo-fly pie while her daughter, Eve, poured the coffee. Several young children sat on a long wooden bench along the length of the far wall. They silently observed the odd English woman who sat at the table. Molly could feel their wide eyes fixed on her. Under the children's gazes, she felt like an explorer entering a foreign land. *What a different world*, she thought, as she thanked her generous hosts for the pie and coffee.

The conversation flowed easily. John and Mary seemed very open and extremely kind, yet she did not learn anything new. Somehow they masterfully dodged her questions or answered them in a sincere, yet vague fashion. Furthermore, Josef and Lenore were both visibly absent. When Molly inquired about their whereabouts, John looked over at Mary, who seemed to be the one with the better answers. She spoke up immediately. "They're off shoppin' at Glen Ryan. We needed some chicken feed und some house supplies. I don't expect 'em 'til nightfall. It's a long trip by buggy."

Molly decided to be a little more forceful. She had introduced herself and the purpose of her visit when she first sat down, but she had downplayed the Porter homicide and did not mention the White Witch. She had been unsure of how it would affect the children, who were attentively listening to the conversation. Now, it was time to be more forward. Looking over at the children, she decided to appeal to Mary. "Mrs. Lapp," she began.

"Call me, Mary, dear."

"Yes, well, I need to speak with you about certain topics that might not be appropriate for the children."

"Children, go do yar chores," John ordered, looking at his children, and his command was instantly fulfilled.

Wow. These kids really listen, Molly thought to herself.

"What is it, dear?" Mary asked.

Before she began, Molly looked around to validate that the children had all departed. "Have you ever heard of the White Witch legend?"

"Sure… the old ghost legend. Some of the folks 'round 'ere swear they've seen 'er more than once, but I don't believe in no ghosts," Mary said sincerely.

"Nor do I," John echoed.

"Well, I don't either, but there seems to be a lot of talk about her back at The Raven Inn," Molly replied.

"There's always been talk. People need to feed their imaginations, whether they're Amish or English," John proclaimed.

"That's true. I have another question." Molly paused and sighed. She knew she was getting to the hard part. "Does your daughter, Lenore, write poems?"

Mary and John looked each other in surprise. "Not that we're aware. Why?" John asked.

"We found this poem at the old Green farmhouse near the covered bridge. Could it be written by your daughter? We think it may be a clue to the death of the young man that had lived there. But we don't understand the references in the poem. Does that look like your daughter's handwriting?"

Mary looked at it, and immediately answered for both parents. "How could it be? Our daughter, like all Amish children, only got schooled to eighth grade. She'd hardly be able to write a poem. Besides, she wouldn't have been in that old, abandoned house. She's here." Mary skirted the truth, leaving out just enough not to lie, but simply imply.

"Does she leave the house alone?"

"No. She travels with her brother, like today."

"Is that normal?"

"Yes, young women don't travel alone. They either travel with friends or spouses und family. Lenore never travels alone; none of my girls do," Mary clarified.

"I see. So, you're sure that Lenore didn't write this poem?"

There was a slight silence, as both Mary and John tried to reply without lying or plunging their daughter into a police investigation. "Yes. I'm sure she didn't write a note like that," Mary answered. John gave her a quick look, which went undetected by Molly.

"One final question. Do you know anything about either the death of Gavin Green or Will Porter?"

"All's we know is what ya told us, und what we heard through friends. It's horrible. This is a quiet valley. Now folks're all worried there's a killer on the loose. I'll tell ya that much. We're more careful with the children, especially the girls. It's awful. But be assured the Amish had nothing do with it. We're a peaceful, God-loving people."

"Mary's right. The Amish're innocent. I hope ya solve this soon, und let us know how we can help," John offered.

Molly wanted to say, *Telling me the complete truth would help*, but she refrained.

Realizing that she would not get any useful information from the Lapps, she thanked them for the delicious pie and departed, still convinced that Lenore Lapp was somehow connected to Gavin Green's death. *The rumor that Green had been seen with a former Amish girl before his demise doesn't seem to fit their story, unless Lenore had left the Amish and come back, or unless there's another Lenore. If she had left, they would've shunned her, which is obviously not the case. Something's not right*, Molly silently reasoned, as she drove away from the Lapp farm.

"That waz close," Mary whispered to John before the children returned.

"Mary, ya lied," John whispered back, with a shocked expression on his face.

"John Lapp, I've never lied in my life, und I'm not about to start."

"Ya said Lenore didn't write that note. Did ya see the handwriting? That waz Lenore's. She must've written it while she waz living away. I haven't got any idea what all that meant, do you? What waz our girl up to while she waz gone?"

"We may never know, und it may be best that we don't. The Lord must have a good reason for keeping it from us und from Lenore. I'm not sure I want to know."

"I agree, but ya lied, Mary. Ya knew the note waz Lenore's."

"Yes, I did know that, but I didn't lie. I said Lenore didn't write a note LIKE that one, not that particular one." Mary winked at John.

"Ya should be ashamed of yourself, Mary."

CHAPTER 60

Raven's Nest

S ince Molly had little luck with the Lapps and the morning was still young, she decided to return to The Raven Inn in the hope of talking to Jerry McAlester and Sam Hughes. As she pulled into the parking lot, she noticed a local police cruiser. *Wonder if that's Gus or Alvin. They're probably here for breakfast.* As she entered the lobby, she saw Alvin sitting on one of the couches, talking with Sam. She chuckled. *Two suspects on one couch. Maybe my luck's changing.*

"Good morning."

"Morning, Molly," the two said in unison.

"Out early today," Sam observed.

"Yes. I am. By the way, I need to talk to both of you."

"Well, sit down," Sam replied.

"I need to talk to each of you, separately. Alvin, may I talk to you first? It's about the case. Sam, may I get a few minutes of your time once Alvin and I are done?"

"Sure. No worries. I need to get back to the front desk, anyway. Ya know where to find me, Molly." Sam got up and walked to the other side of the large lobby, resuming his post at the reception desk.

"What's up?" Alvin asked, in his usual cocky tone. The only time he seemed to change that tone was when Kelly happened to be present. With Molly, he was terse.

"Let's go somewhere more private," Molly suggested.

After finding an empty conference room, they sat facing each other across a large table. "Alvin, the Inspector asked me to interview you about the case. I'll need to record the conversation since it's official testimony. Is that okay with you?"

"And what if it's not?"

"You have the right to refuse or to have legal counsel present."

"Are ya serious? This is ridiculous! Are ya implying that I'm a suspect? Does Morgan know about this?"

"I'm not implying that at all, and I don't know what the chief knows. I'm simply here to get your testimony about certain parts of the case."

"My testimony? I'm a cop, remember? I'm one of the good guys. This is such crap! Your boss can go screw himself—and feel free to record that."

"Alvin, I suggest you comply; otherwise, this could get complicated. It's regarding the death of Gavin Green. I simply need to know for the record what exactly transpired before we arrived at the scene."

"Why? Ya don't trust me? Morgan was there. He knows everything that I know. Are ya officially interviewing him, as well?"

"No."

"Just as I figured. That boss of yours has had it out for me from the minute he arrived here. He's embarrassed me and harassed me once too often. If I wanted to I could've raised a big stink, but I chose to let it go. Now I'm the bad guy? You guys are so screwed up. Look, if ya don't solve this case by Monday, Gus and I are calling the FBI for help and kicking you guys out. I think ya don't have a clue how to solve this case. This conversation only confirms it.

"I wrote down and gave ya exactly what transpired with the Green investigation before you arrived. I gave ya copies of all my notes from the interviews with Will Porter and the Amish couple. I'm not the one hiding anything, unlike your boss. I don't have time for this crap. Ya want an official deposition from me, go through the proper channels. I'm disappointed in you implying that I'm involved." He got up and walked away.

"We're not implying anything. What about the Black Raven Club and your raven tattoo?"

He stopped near the door and turned slowly in his tracks. "Never heard of a club like that and what about my tattoo?"

"Will Porter had one. Sam Hughes has one. Are they linked to that Black Raven Club? Is it a drug gang?"

"Are you accusing me of being in a drug gang?" he said slowly, weighing each word for added emphasis.

"No, but what's the link, Alvin? What's the link between the tattoos, that club and the two deaths? What do you think? Your brother George was involved in the club. He had the same tattoo."

"You leave George out of this. He was a better person than you or I'll ever be. That's a cheap shot."

"I didn't take a shot at anyone. I'm simply asking relevant questions of a fellow officer. Your brother and Porter had the same exact tattoo as you and Sam. That's not a coincidence. We know that Porter, Sam, Jerry, your brother, and a guy named Harry Schaffer started the Black Raven Club. What was its purpose? How's it linked?"

"Hell, you're proving my point that you guys are so screwed up that ya don't know your head from your backside, to put it politely. What you just said is all crap."

"Is it? You're in the know. You have a raven tattoo, right?"

"Yes, I have a raven tattoo. See!" He rolled up his right sleeve. But that doesn't prove a thing. There never was a Black Raven Club. Not sure where you got that idea."

"From your high school yearbook."

"Oh, and that's a trustworthy source. Half of those picture labels were a joke. You guys are barking up the wrong tree. You're right that we all have the same tattoo, but it's not related to any fictitious club or drug gang. It's meaningless, as you would know if ya did your homework."

"What does that mean?"

"Go figure it out, but I assure you it's not what you think. I'm going to have a conversation with Morgan. Your short, pompous boss is gonna give me a formal apology and by Monday you guys are out of here! You're a joke and the biggest joker is your arrogant boss!" Alvin walked out of the inn and drove away.

That went well, Molly thought and chuckled. *I don't trust that guy. Okay, let's hope the other "Ravens" are more cooperative.* She walked toward the lobby to find Sam Hughes.

Sam was still working at the desk. As she appeared, he smiled and looked at her a little too long, his eyes focused completely on her. "So, what can I do for ya, Miss Molly? Is your stay comfortable? Are you getting the VIP chocolates every night? I told the evening staff to give you a little extra," he said with a smile.

Molly had a strong attraction to this man, but she had learned her lesson with Jack and did not want to get involved with another potential homicide suspect. Besides, she had Jack. She was tempted, but her loyalty to Jack and to her job prevailed, at least for now.

Sam, on the other hand, was determined to succeed with this striking brunette. He knew that the attraction was mutual, yet he had no idea how to win her over. His usual style appeared to fall flat. To ask her out in the middle of an investigation seemed inappropriate. Equally inappropriate would be to knock on the door of her room some night and test if she would let him enter. Besides, there was Elaine. That relationship was equally innocent and equally frustrating. To make things worse, of late Elaine had grown more distant. Sam's prospects with the young server were dwindling by the day. His interest in Molly grew in equal proportion.

"Thank you. I do get them," she replied with a smile that made Sam more hopeful. "But I don't deserve that treatment. I thought everyone got them. If it's special just for me, I'd rather not have it."

Sam's ego deflated. "It's our usual service," he lied.

"Well, I need to talk to you about the case. Can we find somewhere private?"

"Sure. Give me a second to finish this reservation, and I'll get someone to cover for me. We can use the room over there." He pointed back to the small conference room where Molly had her discussion with Alvin.

Soon the two were sitting at the same table that she had occupied earlier. By contrast, Sam seemed more cooperative than Alvin.

"So, Mr. Hughes..." she began.

"Still Mr. Hughes, huh?" he interrupted with a smile.

"Yes. Still Mr. Hughes," she brushed it off without blushing this time. She focused on her mission. There was too much at stake.

"So, Mr. Hughes," she tried again, "can you tell me about Erin Stone?"

Sam was shocked. He was unprepared for that question. A long uncomfortable pause ensued before he replied. "What about Erin?"

"Can you tell me of your involvement with her?"

"We were friends in high school. There's nothing more to tell. I have no idea what happened to her. She disappeared soon after we graduated. I never heard from her since. Why do you ask?"

"Let me be blunt. Did you have an affair with Erin Stone while you were both freshman at McLaren University?"

"What? Where are you guys getting this stuff? No. I didn't. We were simply friends."

"Are you aware she became pregnant that year?"

"Yes."

"What can you tell me about that?"

"Only that she left school before completing her first year. I heard she had a daughter, but I have no idea what happened to either of 'em."

"You mean to tell me that the two of you were close friends, but when she became pregnant you abandoned her?"

"No. That's not what I said. When she became pregnant, I helped her. She was my friend but she had other help, too. Then one day, she simply disappeared and I never heard from her again. Back then, it was easy to disappear."

"What other help did she have? Cornelius Green?"

Sam appeared visibly uncomfortable. It was the first time that Molly saw him become angry. "Look, that guy's a bastard from what Gavin told me. He was his father. You know that, I'm sure. Why isn't he here, given his son's dead? Because he doesn't care. All he ever cared about was power and prestige."

"What's his connection to Erin?" she asked.

"Erin was simply a pretty box to check off on his greedy wish list. When it didn't work out, he crushed her like he crushed Gavin. If you're lookin' for someone to blame, find that bastard! As for Erin, I tried to be the best friend I could to her, but it wasn't enough. I have no idea what happened to her."

"You loved her, didn't you?"

"That's got nothin' to do with this case."

"I'll take that as a 'yes.'"

"My, aren't we aggressive today, Miss Molly."

"I was about to say that about you, Mr. Hughes. Obviously, I hit a nerve."

"You hit a dead end. You want answers, go find that bastard, Cornelius Green."

Sam took a deep breath and appeared to calm down again. It was as if the old Sam returned. "I'm sorry I got so upset. It's a sensitive subject. Yes, I did care for Erin, but we were only friends—nothing more. Trust me on that. I wish I could've protected her, but she wouldn't have it. Are we done? I need to get back to work."

"We're almost done. Let's change the subject—what's with the raven tattoo? It seems like half of you guys have one, as did Will Porter."

"These things?" He rolled up his sleeve to reveal an identical tattoo to the one that Alvin possessed. "That's a secret. If I told ya, I'd have to kill you," he replied, transforming back to his jovial self.

His sudden transformation, combined with the "killing" reference, startled her.

"I'm just kidding, Molly." Sam chuckled and turned on his charm.

Molly felt flustered by this man. He had a power over her that was both exhilarating and frightening. *Which is the real Sam?* For a minute, she was absorbed in self-reflection. *Be honest, Molly, you're attracted to him. I always fall for this type. Is it a curse, or is it just part of being a woman?*

She was roused from her thoughts by Elaine's voice. The young server, who had been covering the front desk for Sam, stood in the doorway. She sized up Molly without saying a word. "You've got a call on line one. It's urgent, and Jerry needs you in the kitchen. Sorry." Elaine glanced back at Molly before leaving the room.

"I must run. I hope that explanation helped and sorry I lost my cool." He smiled at her and disappeared.

What explanation? she thought. Then, she remembered the question. *Damn, I missed the most important part.* She got up to go to the front desk, but Sam was already gone. *I guess I'll go find Jerry. Maybe he can help me.*

She found Jerry McAlester running around the kitchen quelling a lunch rush. He was in a particularly poor mood when he physically ran into her.

"Sorry, but you need to leave. We're too busy right now," he proclaimed on his way to the fry vat.

"Mr. McAlester, it will just take a minute."

"Can't you see I have a dining room full of hungry customers? I can't talk to you. It'll have to wait," he snapped at her and ran off.

The kitchen was a madhouse, forcing Molly to postpone her attempts for an interview. She decided to head upstairs and compile her notes. When she returned to the kitchen two hours later, there was no sign of Jerry. Apparently, he had left for Kamerynville minutes earlier.

"When do you expect him back?" she asked one of the kitchen staff.

The young man seemed caught off guard. "You better ask Sam," he replied and sheepishly turned away.

Perplexed and annoyed, Molly searched for Sam. He too was nowhere to be found. In the lobby, she ran into Elaine. "Elaine, where are Sam and Jerry?"

"Didn't you hear the fight?"

"What fight? I was in my room."

"Sam and Jerry had a big fight. It's been brewing all day. Jerry took off and Sam ran after him. Boys'll be boys, you know. By the way, if you want Sam, go for it. You have my blessing. He's all yours. Good luck with that," she replied, and returned to the front desk.

Crazy place. Damn, I'd better head out to Kiradale, Molly concluded, after looking at her watch. *I guess I'll be late to another team meeting. At least some things never change.* She chuckled to herself as she left the inn.

* * * * *

Molly pulled up to the team's temporary office, the former barbershop in Kiradale, fifteen minutes after the start of the team meeting. Entering in a hurry, she was greeted by the Inspector and Chen, who were seated at the old table at the far end of the furnished barbershop.

"This place's creepy, boss. I feel like we've been transported back to the 1940s," Molly reflected, as she rushed to her chair. It became apparent to her that humans were creatures of habit. Everyone occupied the same seats as the night before except Kelly, who remained undercover with the Eden Sisterhood.

"Nice of you to join us, Molly. You're timely, as usual. Thank you for your valued opinion. I know how much you love this place, so I hope you enjoy our meeting," the Inspector replied, turning up the sarcasm.

Chen chuckled, while Molly tossed her long brown hair in defiance. She had had a frustrating day and didn't appreciate the ribbing. "I hate this place," she mumbled.

The Inspector wisely decided to ignore her. Rather, he shifted his attention to the case. "Okay, it sounds like we all had a very productive day. As you know, Kelly has infiltrated Ariella Bianca's sisterhood. She sent a couple quick texts summarizing her day. So far, it looks like Ariella has accepted her. There are six other young women at the house—all in their teens. Apparently, they're all very frightened because someone tried to break into the cabin last night and burned large pentagrams onto the front and back doors. Finally and most importantly, Ariella Bianca is our missing Erin Stone. Pretty amazing, huh?"

"Why would Erin Stone change her name and run a sisterhood for runaway teenage girls?" Molly asked.

"We don't know the answer to that. Hopefully, Kelly can get us some more information. Any other questions regarding Kelly's findings?" There was silence. "Okay. Then I'll share my discovery at the Green Estate." The Inspector discussed the abandoned blue pickup truck. "It belongs to Andrew Taylor, who had a falling-out with his wife, Linda, about a month ago. We're trying to find the whereabouts of both."

"Boss, after you told me about the Taylors, I did some searching on the web and found this on social media. Gavin Green appears to have been friends with both Linda and Andrew. I found an address for the Taylors but didn't have time to investigate. Linda remained very friendly with Gavin, even after she left Andrew. There might have been a love triangle there. What if Andrew killed Gavin out of jealousy?" Chen was on a roll.

"Great work, Chen. You're really making points on this case," the Inspector noted. "We need to add Andrew Taylor to our prime suspect list. Let's pay the Taylors a visit."

"Boss, why would Andrew Taylor leave his truck behind Green's place? That doesn't make sense. Was it broken down?" Molly asked.

"No. Works fine. In fact, it was unlocked and we found the keys under the driver's floor mat. I have forensics combing over it. There're plenty of prints and hair samples. But it's not clear why the truck's there."

"I simply can't imagine why Taylor would leave it there. If he were the killer, he'd use it to flee, wouldn't he?" Molly questioned.

"Not if he wanted to ditch the truck for some reason. I checked, and there was a car stolen near Kamerynville the morning after Porter's death. He could have walked or hitched a ride to Kamerynville, which is only about ten miles away, and stole that car. By now, he could be in Mexico."

"But why hide the truck there and not simply leave it in Kamerynville? That doesn't make sense to me," Molly objected.

"We have no idea, Molly. By the way, Chen, let's put an APB on that stolen car as a potential getaway vehicle in a pending murder investigation," the Inspector instructed.

"Are we officially classifying Green's death as murder?" Chen inquired.

"No. I meant Porter's death. That's an official homicide, while Green's death remains a drug overdose."

"Molly, did you get anywhere with the Lapps?"

"No. They're a great family, but I couldn't get anything out of them that was of any use to us. Neither Lenore nor Josef were there. It was a waste of time."

"Did Lenore Lapp write that poem?"

"Her parents deny it and claim she was with them the entire time. I suppose it could be a different person, but how many Lenores can this little town have? I tried researching that, but Amish records are very limited."

"What about Sam and Jerry, and the tattoos?" the Inspector asked.

"I got nothing. It was such a frustrating day. Jerry apparently got in a fight with Sam and threatened to quit. This is according to Elaine Roberts. Sam chased after him, but neither returned before I had to get out here for this meeting. I waited as long as I could. That's why I was late." She decided not to mention her discussion with Sam. The fact that Sam told her the meaning of the raven tattoos but she did not hear his response because she was daydreaming over him would not have gone over well.

"But I did confront Alvin and he lost it," Molly added. "He acted very suspiciously and very defensively. He also threatened to call in the FBI by Monday. Don't be surprised if you get a call from Gus regarding Alvin's complaints."

"Hell, if I care. Gus would side with me, anyway. Alvin's trouble regardless of his previous track record. I hope he calls. Did you ask him about the tattoo? He has one, right?"

"He has one, all right. He showed it to me. But he wouldn't tell me what it meant. He denied the Black Raven Club, dismissing it as a yearbook joke."

"Of course he denied it. I still think he's guilty. It's no coincidence he keeps finding staged clues. He's probably planting them." The Inspector's tone always soured when he spoke of Alvin Walker. "Anything else, Molly?"

"One last thing. I asked Elaine about Agnes Wright. Agnes apparently did get attacked in the old stables behind The Raven Inn. But no one knows who did it. Elaine suspects Gavin Green, although Jerry McAlester was apparently not at work that morning. Did Agnes end up in Ariella's sisterhood?" Molly asked.

"Yes. She's there and Kelly plans to talk to her. I forgot to mention that," the Inspector added. "All right, it's your turn, Chen. What'd you find regarding the bank deposit box with the coin collection that George Walker, Alvin's deceased brother, bestowed upon Erin Stone—or should I say Ariella Bianca?"

"Well, thanks to your help, we got a warrant to access the bank information. What I found was that the coin collection was a sizable amount of gold coins. The estimated value of the coins is unclear since they were never insured or inventoried. But the bank records indicate forty-five gold Spanish doubloons, which at today's market would be worth about half-a-million dollars."

"What?! Does Alvin know this?" Molly was shocked.

"I'm not sure, and I doubt he would tell us if he did. I doubt he knew at the time of his brother's death, since there was never a recorded dispute over the deposit box or any other item in the will. At least there was nothing official that I could find. It's most likely that the content of the box went unnoticed, since the coin collection was valued at two hundred dollars in the inventory of the will.

"Wow, that's a twist. You suppose it had anything to do with the legend of the Drake treasure?" Molly asked.

"Hard to say, but the coins could date to the time Arthur Drake was a suspected privateer," Chen replied. "You might be onto something, Molly."

"Wow! This case keeps getting more and more bizarre. What're your thoughts, boss?" Molly asked.

"It's a big stretch to think that George Walker somehow managed to find Drake's treasure, if there ever was one, hide it in a bank deposit box, and will it to Erin Stone," the Inspector said. "But I guess we need to explore all angles. Chen, you've got more data mining to do, and Kelly has got a lot of questions to ask our friend Ariella. Molly, you need to get back to Sam Hughes and Jerry McAlester. If you want to pull them in as suspects, do it. We need to learn more about their relationship with Erin Stone and about that Black Raven Club.

"We also need to know about Erin's relationship with George Walker and Harry Schaffer. She received a sizable amount of money from George Walker, and her present property once belonged to Harry Schaffer. She's in the middle of it all. We need to work all our hypotheses. We know there're drugs involved. Now we know there's money involved. And we know Erin Stone is Ariella Bianca, who appears very involved," the Inspector summarized.

"Okay, but I'm tired. I need to get some sleep. I've been up since five, and it's been a very frustrating day," Molly objected. "I need to pass on dinner."

"That's fine. We're done for now," the Inspector replied.

Molly got up to leave, when she caught her purse on the large, framed picture of a high school football team. The picture was entitled "Eden Valley Ravens, State Champions, 1991–1992." She nearly pulled it off the wall as she tried to rush by it. Upon righting the picture, she froze.

"Guys, come here. It's been in front of us all this time. Look at this picture."

The three huddled around the old, framed picture. In the photograph were Sam Hughes, Jerry McAlester, George and Alvin Walker, Harry Schaffer, and Will Porter. Besides the state championship trophy that they won as members of the Raven's high school football team, they all proudly displayed their newly-begotten raven tattoos.

"So much for the Black Raven Club idea," the Inspector added.

"Alvin was right. That club idea was a red herring," Molly observed.

The comment soured the Inspector's face, as he let out a loud, "Humph!"

As if in response, the large picture slipped off the wall and crashed to the floor.

Eden Valley, Pennsylvania

CHAPTER 61

Crossing Eden

Kelly awoke to the smell of breakfast. Everyone slept, except Ariella.

"Good morning, Kelly. I'm sorry I woke you. How'd you sleep?" Ariella asked.

"Fine. I slept fine."

"That couch's pretty comfy. I've fallen asleep on it many times."

"What time is it?"

"A little before six. I'm an early riser. Sorry, I won't be able to spend much time with you today. I need to go out to take care of something. It's rather urgent but make yourself at home. If you have any questions, one of the girls can help you. I made you some breakfast." Ariella served up some eggs and toast.

"Thank you," Kelly replied, as she sat down on one of the bar stools at the kitchen island. Ariella sat next to her and began eating her usual bowl of oatmeal. "Where're you headed?" Kelly asked, trying to probe for information.

"Not sure, yet," Ariella replied with a smile. "I won't know until I get there."

The reply made no sense to the logical Kelly. "I don't understand," she observed.

"Well, I'm looking for someone, but he's very elusive. It's a long story. Safe to say, he's more likely to find me. Although I have my own ways of searching." She chuckled before taking another spoonful of oatmeal. "How're the eggs? They're fresh from our chickens out back."

"They're wonderful. Thanks again for letting me stay here."

"Stay as long as you like. But right now all we have is the couch. I need to expand this place."

Kelly wanted to ask how Ariella could afford to feed all these runaway girls and think about expanding her house, but she decided that question seemed too personal. Rather, she needed to figure out where Ariella was going and whom she was seeking.

"Who are you trying to find?" Kelly asked.

"A man who was once like family to me. It's a long story, but he's in trouble, as is a dear friend of mine. Well, I'd better run before I waste the day. Morning's the best time to connect."

"Connect?"

Ariella laughed. "I'll explain it to you when it's time. I assume you'll be staying for a while? Since you're one of the older girls, please help Rebecca look out for the younger ones. Hazel, in particular, needs a lot of love. She's had it very rough and is still so young."

"I'll do my best."

"Good. Well, goodbye. Gotta run." Ariella disappeared before Kelly had a chance to ask any more questions.

She's in a hurry. Wonder what's going on? Kelly thought, as she finished her breakfast.

She was putting away the dishes when Rachel walked up to the kitchen counter with sleep in her eyes.

"You snuck up on me," Kelly teased.

"I do that. The others call me 'the ghost' 'cause I can sneak up on anyone," Rachel said and giggled. She was a happy soul since she found the sisterhood.

"I see. Do you want some breakfast? I'll make it for you," Kelly offered. The two women had become instant friends. They seemed to be made of the same mold. Each felt that she had known the other for years, not hours.

"I can get it. I like my cereal," Rachel replied and fixed herself breakfast. Kelly observed that all of the young women of the sisterhood appeared to be very self-sufficient. Life had taught them to fend for themselves.

"Ariella left a few minutes ago. She seemed to be in a hurry and didn't say where she was going." Kelly started a conversation of interest.

"She's trying to find Anna," Rachel replied, as she sat down behind the kitchen island with her big bowl of cereal.

"Who's Anna?"

"Her full name's Annabel Lee. She's one of us. She's Becky's age. Everyone loves Anna, but she disappeared a couple days ago without a word. We're all worried. I think Ariella thinks she was kidnapped, but she won't admit it. I've never seen her this worried. It's scary. I'm sure you saw the markings on the door. Someone attacked this place the night after Anna disappeared—a strange guy with a raven tattoo on his arm. Becky saw his face through the window—pretty scary. I try not to think about it. I wish I could do something, but I don't know what."

"A guy with a raven tattoo?"

"Yeah. I think there was more than one guy. The next morning, Becky and I went out to investigate. That's when we found those markings on the doors. We also saw two sets of footprints leading into the woods. That's how I know there were two of them. I hope Anna's okay. I hope she doesn't end up like Lenore."

"Lenore?" Kelly had hit a gold mine.

"Yeah. Lenore was another one of us, and she disappeared about two months ago, just like Anna. It's like someone's stalking us. We're all afraid to go outside without Ariella. When she's here, no one messes with the place 'cause she's too powerful. No one can harm her. She's a shaman. Her Native American name means the White Dove, but she's more like a white witch, if you ask me." Rachel was on a roll, fueled by her bowl of Lucky Charms.

"White witch?" Kelly asked.

"Haven't you heard of the legend of the White Witch? If I didn't know better, I'd say Ariella was just like that legend. Mysterious. She seems to be able to blend into the woods like a ghost. I've seen her simply vanish, as if she were a ghost. But her greatest power is that she can cross over," Rachel added nonchalantly, as if she were talking about the weather.

"Cross over?"

"Yeah. She's so powerful that she can cross over to the other side."

"Other side of where?"

"If you asked her, she'd say 'the other side of Eden.' I don't understand it, but somehow she can go into a deep trance. She claims to leave her form and reach beyond it. It's fascinating, but I'm not sure I believe it. I wouldn't tell her that. But there's something to it, 'cause she knows things that she couldn't possibly know otherwise. It's as if she gets her information from an all-knowing source. Like I said, I don't understand it, nor does anyone else around here. We just go with it."

Kelly was confused. "I still don't understand."

"Like I said, neither do I."

"What is Eden?"

"Heaven, or whatever exists beyond this world."

Kelly was completely baffled. "So, she crossed over to heaven? Are you serious?"

"I suppose it sounds crazy, but that's how I understand it. My advice is that you don't ponder it, 'cause logically it's nonsense. You simply must either accept it or let it go. I'm not sure where I stand on it, but I do believe her. Like I said, she knows things that people normally don't know."

"Like what?"

"Like she knew you were coming. She told us the day before you showed up that we were going to get a new sister and that her name would be Kelly. She said that you would show up the next day, and you did. Did you plan that with her? Was that a trick? I was meaning to ask you that."

"Are you teasing me, Rachel?"

"No. Ask any of the other girls. She knew when Agnes was coming, too. She was expecting her. It's as if she can see into the future. But it doesn't end there. She sees into your heart, too. She already knows all about you and why you're here."

"I doubt that."

"Well, let's test it. The night before you showed up, she told us that you wouldn't be a runaway. She called you 'a seeker of justice,' and said that you were coming to protect us. Is that true? Is it true that you're not a runaway and that you're here to protect us?"

Kelly was shocked, nearly dropping her cup of coffee. "Well, I'm not a runaway. I'm just traveling about. So, I guess that's true. But I don't know about protecting anyone. I'll do my best," Kelly stuttered.

"See. She knew that. Like I said, she also knew your name would be Kelly. Pretty cool, huh? I think she can cast spells, as well. That's why she's like a witch. I swear she can disappear. I asked her about that, and she just laughed. She denied it, but I've seen her disappear into the woods without a trace. It's not like a person walking into the woods. It's like a ghost or something. Not that she's a ghost, but you know what I mean. I'm not making sense, am I? You'd have to see it. Ask the other girls. But she says that she can't do that and laughs when we ask her."

"How long have you lived here, Rachel?"

"About five months. Rebecca, Hazel, Marie, and Sarah have been here longer. Anna arrived a month after me and Lenore came a month later, but stayed for only about a month and a half. Agnes came last week. She's new."

"Why did Lenore leave? What happened to her?" Kelly returned to the subject of most interest. Rachel was an incredible wealth of information, which she wanted to mine before any of the other girls awakened.

"I don't know, exactly. Apparently, she left here and got attacked at Devils Bridge by a mysterious evil that Ariella won't discuss. She claims Lenore's fine and back with her Amish family. But knowing Lenore, she wouldn't have run away from here without saying good-bye to me. Ariella says Lenore left a note, but I've never seen it. We were close. I think someone kidnapped her. I think it was the same guy that has Anna and attacked our cabin."

"Why didn't you call the police?"

"The police around here don't do much. Besides, most of us are runaways and the police would take us away, especially the ones under eighteen, like Hazel, Sarah, Marie, and me. We can't call the police. They're the enemy."

"Did Ariella say anything about the guy she thinks kidnapped Anna? She told me he was once like family. What does that mean?"

"She knows him. She said so, but she won't tell us who he is. She says as long as we don't know, he won't harm us. I don't get it, but I must trust her. We can't do much else. I'm not about to try and find this guy. Besides, he's probably the one that attacked Agnes, as well. She says that guy had a raven tattoo."

"Agnes was attacked?"

"Yeah. Before she came here, she was a maid at The Raven Inn. The guy with the raven tattoo attacked her in the old stables behind the inn, but she never saw his face. She was lucky the owner got to her before the guy could harm her. I guess he got away. He had a mask and a dark hood."

"And she never reported it to the police? Why?"

"Because Agnes thinks the police are somehow involved. I don't know, but she thinks the local police are in on it."

"How'd she know about this place?"

"Apparently one of the servers at the inn told her."

"Who?"

"You'd have to ask her. I don't know. But Ariella was expecting her."

"Expecting her?"

"Yeah, like I said, she had one of her premonitions that Agnes was coming. Crazy, huh?" Rachel laughed.

"Crazy is right," Kelly agreed. "Wow. There's a lot going on around here. You said you knew Lenore very well. What was her story before she got here?"

"Lenore, like Becky, was an Amish runaway. Once you leave the Amish, they shun you. There's no more contact. None. Well, unless you come back willingly and repent. It's just the way it is. Everyone avoids you, even your family avoids you. It's as if you died, or worse, never existed. I guess that's how they keep people from leaving. Well, Lenore left and was shunned. She wandered about until she ran into Ariella deep in the North Woods. She was the sweetest person you could ever meet. We were close. Anyway, she was in love with one of the Amish men and she really missed him. Sometimes I think she regretted leaving, but she didn't want to be Amish anymore, so she stayed away. It made me sad. She seemed sad at times, too. I guess that's why she liked to write poetry. She wrote great poems."

"I see. That makes sense."

"What do ya mean?"

"Nothing. Do you really think Anna has been kidnapped?" Kelly changed the subject to the pressing issue of the missing girl.

"Yes. I know it, 'cause I've never seen Ariella afraid — not until now."

Just then, Sarah, Marie, and Hazel poured into the room. The three youngest girls had such energy that the entire mood changed, and Rachel's insights ceased. Kelly greeted them but quickly excused herself. "I need to get my morning walk," she confessed.

"It's too dangerous out there," Hazel said.

"I'll be fine. I promise," Kelly replied. As soon as she got away from the cabin, she called Inspector Cabot and informed him of all that she had learned.

CHAPTER 62

The Proposal

On this crisp morning, Amos Miller had never felt more alive. Months of remorse had been transformed to joy by the one person capable of creating such magic—his beloved Lenore. To say that he walked on clouds would be an understatement, for he felt lighter than that. His heart soared to heights rarely visited by mortals.

God, thank you, he repeated over and over in his mind. *She loves me. She knows me. Lenore's back. God, thank you.* He whispered his gratitude to the restless chickens as he spread the feed and to the sluggish cows as he refilled the troughs with silage. "She loves me!" he shouted at his dog, Otto, who jumped in joy, sensing his master's euphoria. "God, thank you for this miracle!" He gazed at the vast blue sky. Youth awakened within him as he ran to get hay for the horses and the mules. "Lenore! My dearest Lenore. Thank you for coming back to me!" he screamed aloud to the apathetic mules, before shouting it to the rest of the world around him.

On this brisk morning, Amos Miller appeared to be the happiest man alive. Rarely has one soul so dearly loved another as Amos loved Lenore. He had surrendered her once, but never again. No, never again would they part. He would surrender anything and everything to be with her.

Meanwhile, the subject of his euphoria returned to her parents' home. She had finished her morning chores and was helping her mother with breakfast when she noticed the open buggy coming up the long, gravel drive. She strained to see if it was Amos, but, to her surprise, it was Ben Stoltzfus. Her heart sank, for she remembered her blossoming courtship with her other suitor. She did not know what to do or what to say to him. No one except Amos knew of her most recent memory gain. Nor did anyone know of her rekindled love, except Amos himself.

Although she still did not remember how she had lost her memory, or how or why she ran away, she remembered her love for Amos, and that was all that mattered. Unfortunately for Ben, her reawakened love had extinguished any sparks of attraction that she had for him. It felt as if a tidal wave washed away a budding rose. The latter never stood a chance. She would have to tell Ben that she no longer felt the way he felt. Dreading that conversation, she ran to her room, hoping to hide.

"Lenore, get back 'ere!" Her mother insisted. "Ben's 'ere. He's not 'ere fur me."

Safe upstairs, she pretended not to hear her mother.

"Oh, John, she's a stubborn one," Mary said to her husband, who had just come into the kitchen for a cup of coffee.

"Like 'er mother," he answered.

To the surprise of John and Mary, Ben had come to talk to John. The two went out on the porch and a lengthy conversation ensued. Mary observed them through the kitchen window. She could tell that her husband was not excited, but he seemed to agree with what Ben had to say. Soon, the two men entered the kitchen.

"Ben, how're yur parents?" Mary asked. "Please tell yur mother I'm praying fur 'er und 'er father. It must be hard. If she needs anythin', ya must let me know."

"Thank ya, ma'am. I will. Grandpa's not doing well, as ya know. Thank ya fur your prayers und the kind offer."

"Would ya like a piece of pie? It's apple. I made it this morning."

"No, thank ya, ma'am."

"Well, suit yourself, but it's one of my better ones. Have a seat. Lenore'll be down in a minute."

"Mary, Ben asked me if he could marry our Lenore, und I agreed." John dropped the news without warning.

Mary braced herself against the kitchen counter. "I see," she replied, trying to force a smile. She was not very fond of Ben and his family. They were fine as acquaintances, but she wanted better for her precious daughter. She did not find them genuine. "That's quite a surprise, Ben. Does Lenore know? Call me odd, but I feel it's her decision." She glared at John.

"I haven't asked her yet. I wanted to ask Mr. Lapp, first."

"I see. When were ya planning to ask Lenore?"

"Today, if he agreed."

"John, may I talk to ya for a minute?"

John and Mary walked onto the porch to be out of earshot. "John Lapp, how could ya agree to this? Don't I get a say? More importantly, doesn't our daughter get a say? This is very presumptuous of ya. Frankly, I'm shocked! What were ya thinking? Lenore's still recovering from her accident. She can't take this on right now. She's not in her right mind. I won't allow it. John Lapp, I insist that ya talk to that boy und tell 'im it's not all right—not at all." Mary was furious, which was an extremely rare sight.

"Mary. Why're ya upset? Ben's a good man. He's the best choice fur 'er. He has the means to comfortably support 'er. Besides, she's fond of 'im, as ya observed yarself. She needs to get married before she ends up an old maid. She's nearly twenty."

"She's eighteen! I'm not allowing this und that's final. Do I need to tell 'im myself?"

John sighed audibly. He loved his wife and admired her strong will, a trait rarely encouraged among the women of the community. It was one of the main reasons why he loved and respected her so much. But, in this case, he disagreed. Sure, Lenore was recovering from an injury, but it was obvious that she and Ben were attracted to each other. To go back on his word, or to have his wife overturn it, felt unacceptable. *What would the other men say?* "I stand by my word, but I agree that Lenore needs to have a say. Ya right about that. She needs to heal first."

"So, you'll tell 'im ya changed yur mind?"

"No. I'll do no such thing. But I'll ask 'im to slow it down."

"John, that's not good enough."

"Well, that's the way it's gonna be, Mary." Mary knew that her gentle husband had a limit to his flexibility. Once he dug in, there was no way of budging him. Reluctantly, she accepted the terms and walked back into the kitchen. John followed.

What awaited them was unexpected. Lenore had returned to the kitchen to greet Ben. However, Ben did not waste time on formalities. As John and Mary entered the kitchen, they saw Ben on one knee proposing to their oldest daughter, who had an expression of shock mirrored by her mother. Although Ben had prepared a lovely proposal, Lenore did not hear anything except "will ya marry me?" Her head began to spin and she felt like she needed to throw up. Sensing this, her mother rushed to her rescue.

"Lenore, please sit down. Ya're still not well after yur fall. Ben, I'm so sorry I interrupted yur beautiful proposal, but Lenore's not feelin' well. That's why she waz in her room. Didn't she tell ya?" Mary put her hand on Lenore's forehead. "Oh dear, ya're runnin' a fever."

Lenore was too shocked by all that had transpired to say a word. She simply sat in the chair looking pale and faint.

"Oh, I didn't realize. I'm so sorry," Ben muttered. His crowning moment had deflated into an embarrassing apology. He was crushed. Lenore's reaction and that of her mother were completely unexpected. With his confidence deflated, he stared at Lenore in a hope that she would utter the magic word, but no "yes" materialized. Instead, Mary hurriedly accompanied Lenore up to her room, leaving John and Ben alone in the kitchen.

"I guess this wasn't a good time," Ben admitted sheepishly.

"It'll wait, son," John replied, relieved not to have to revisit his decision.

"Is she okay?"

"Sure. Ya wanna cup of coffee?"

"No. I better get going."

"We'll see ya tomorrow at service, then."

Ben did not reply. He was too deep in thought. Walking out the screen door, he proceeded down the long, gravel drive.

"Ben!" John shouted after him. "Ya forgot yur horse und buggy!"

CHAPTER 63

Anna's Hourglass

Anna knew she was underground. Although her captor bound her and muffled her voice with a rag, he did not bother to conceal himself from her, nor did he care if she knew where he had taken her. Like a soldier on a mission, he considered Anna as collateral in a much larger battle of supremacy, revenge, and greed. As the captain of her destiny, she belonged to him, not unlike a live toy. He portrayed a perverse apathy toward life and suffering that scared the brave young woman. Like a spider, he had stung his prey with a mild narcotic that calmed her, before he spun her in strips of cloth that bound her hands and feet. Seated on the dirt floor in the dim cavernous cell, she had lost track of time. The narcotic dulled her senses, robbed her of her bearing, and drowned her fears.

He leered at her. "Ya're a pretty one, ya are. Just like Lenore."

She felt half awake and half intoxicated by his potion. Suddenly, he rose and pulled the cloth out of her mouth. In the process, he touched her lips with his dirty fingers, just because he could. Then, he touched them again. Just because he desired it. She was powerless, maybe too powerless. Silently, he cursed himself for drugging her too much. In that state, she wouldn't provide the satisfaction that he craved. She wouldn't fight.

"Say something! Beg me to release ya. Scream for help or mercy. Don't just sit there!" he yelled at her like a madman. His alter-ego was evil and predatory. "Damn you! Ya're a bore. But I've got time. Ya'll come around. Here's some water and some grub." He checked the leather straps that bound her arms and feet to assure himself that his prize could not flee. "I've had my eyes on ya for a while. Ya're quite a catch," he snarled, while salivating like a ravished wolf. To him, Anna was not a person, she was simply a pawn in a larger game—a pawn that happened to excite his perverse delight.

After reassuring himself that his prize remained secure, he turned to leave. "I've got things to do and places to be. I'm important, ya know. No one will ever find ya because they'll never catch me. Ha, ha, ha," he cackled in a sick, self-absorbed laugh. "I'll enjoy ya later. Yur time's ticking, pretty thing. I'll be back tonight when ya're more in the mood." He laughed again.

He was about to leave when he decided to walk up to her once more and caress her. She excited him. She flinched, pulling back as he caressed her face and then her lips. "That's better. I see you're getting excited. Yes. This'll be most enjoyable. I'm hungry like a wolf."

He drifted into madness now, revealing his true nature—that of a merciless animal hidden from the world in a cloak of his own creation. What had once been a trusting, caring child had slowly turned into the vile monster that now haunted this valley, trying to feed the ever-increasing appetite of a mind trapped in its own downward spiral of self-satisfaction. He resembled a black spider entangled in a web of his own creation, pulling his victims into it in a lost sense of salvation. The perverse mental web had become the master, and he too had become its senseless slave.

"Ha, ha, ha. No one'll ever catch me, for no one'll ever know my identity. I'm not what I seem to be. Right, my little dove? Let me touch ya again, just to get ya excited and just because I can. This time lower."

As he reached out to touch her breast, Anna thrashed at him. She was a woman of great strength and vitality. Being a victim was an unacceptable role—not now, not ever. The pathetic shadow he cast upon her seemed terrifying, but empty of any substance. She, by contrast, encompassed all that he could never achieve, nor ever truly touch, for she possessed a purity of heart and a nobleness of character far beyond his comprehension. Although in this horrific scene she was the victim and he was her cruel oppressor, in a broader, timeless reality, she cast the eternal light and he diminished into a helpless shadow. In the school of illusions and opposites that is this physical life, he drowned—intoxicated in his own cowardly emptiness, while she silently suffered, only to grow stronger as a result.

"I like it. I like that ya're resisting. Good. That damn drug's wearing off. Ya'll be ready soon, and I'll be back for my reward. I deserve you. Yes, I deserve you. I have always deserved you, and many more like you. Did you know that she's the one collecting my little delights for me? Isn't she kind? I control her. You know who I mean. Ariella's not who she pretends to be, my little dove. Don't be fooled by her. She collects you delightful runaway treats and feeds them to me.

The first delight, your little friend Lenore, tried to escape, but I caught her. Unfortunately, I had to strike her down before I got to enjoy her. My mistake, but I won't make that mistake with you. Ha, ha, ha! Ya see, no one escapes me, little dove. No one escapes me.

Remember that. So this time, and in the future, I'll enjoy every morsel until there's nothing left but an empty plate. Ha, ha, ha. Yes. Every morsel of you, my beauty." He touched her breast because he wanted to and because he could, for she could not stop him. She flinched back, her large brown eyes glaring. Yet, life was not fully in them. He had robbed her of that with his narcotic venom.

"Didn't ya figure it out, yet? They won't figure it out either. They're stupid cops. It's right in front of their eyes, and they can't see it. Ha, ha, ha. Your precious mistress is preparing my meals. Yes, she's harvesting you tasty treats, charming ya with her magic. Why? The answer's so simple. It's to feed ya to me, for I'm her true master. She's a devil in angelic white. I know, for I created her. The RAVEN RULES the DOVE! Remember that my dear, my dove."

Laughing, he picked up his dark cloak and covered himself in it, hiding all, even the large black raven tattoo inked on his right forearm. Still laughing an empty sinister laugh, he disappeared through the cave opening into the mist that permeated the surrounding woods. He knew that the sand in Annabel Lee's hourglass would soon run out. He knew because he owned every grain.

CHAPTER 64

The Search for Annabel Lee

Upon receiving Kelly's information, the Inspector immediately roused his remaining team to action. It was clear that a young life was on the line, and that a probable serial killer was on the loose. Finally, he set aside his biases and called his contact at the FBI for manpower support. He did not bother to consult with the local police, as he no longer trusted them. Time was critical now. The FBI would review the request and promised to make a rapid decision, but even that would take too long.

As a father of two daughters and the mentor to his team, James Cabot was a man of great heart and natural paternal instincts. Although he did not know this young woman named Annabel Lee, he treated the situation as if his own daughter was now at the mercy of a dangerous madman.

With that passion and steel determination, he plunged himself into the case. All potential suspects would be grilled and grilled again, if needed, until they lawyered up. The evidence would be scrutinized with his and Chen's eye for minute details and meaningful patterns. All sleep would be suspended until Annabel Lee was safe. That is the kind of man who was hidden behind the unassuming exterior of this small, middle-aged detective, who had a large mustache and an even larger heart.

He met Molly and Chen outside The Raven Inn in the large white gazebo, central to the western garden. They decided to meet outside because he did not trust Sam Hughes or Jerry McAlester. For that matter, he did not trust anyone associated with the inn. Molly and Chen were already waiting for him when he reached the gazebo. Kelly was not present since she remained undercover within the Eden Sisterhood.

"Okay, team, we need to kick this case into high gear. My gut tells me we have a serial killer on our hands. I decided to contact the FBI. They're evaluating the case versus available manpower, but I expect them to be involved soon."

"Why'd you contact the Feds, sir? We'll have to take a backseat once they arrive," Chen protested.

"It's not about who's in charge anymore. It's about saving a young woman. Kelly's doing a great job gathering inside intelligence, which indicates that a missing girl is in grave danger. As I texted you earlier, it appears that Lenore may have been this guy's first victim, but apparently she survived the ordeal. For all I know, Green and Porter got in his way and paid the price. Not sure how drugs, money, or even a crazy treasure fit into all this, if they do at all, but we are going to workday and night to find this girl. Understood?"

"Yes, sir," Molly and Chen answered in unison.

"Good. Molly, we need to get more information out of Lenore Lapp. Your hunch was right. She knows more and may know our person of interest. Chances are she does. Go back there and be more insistent. Track Lenore down and talk to her. I have a feeling, based on that poem, that she knows her attacker or attackers. It may be Taylor or any one of these tattooed clowns." The Inspector looked over at Molly.

She nodded in agreement. "I'm on it." She liked when he kicked into overdrive, even if it took a while at times. "But Lenore appears to have memory issues, so it may be a dead end."

"Do your best but don't waste time if it's going nowhere. Time's critical." He paused to catch his train of thought. "I suspect Gavin

Green was most likely the second victim. But I'm not sure since that death appeared to be a drug overdose. Then, the killer struck again, burying Will Porter alive at Drakes Plot. Now, he appears to have Annabel Lee. He's escalating his violence and shortening the time between attacks. That's not unusual for serial killers.

"Let's summarize what we know about him. As mentioned, drugs may be involved, as well as money or some kind of a treasure. Although the latter's a far shot. What's clear is that the killer has a large raven tattoo on his right forearm. As we've discovered, several members of the 1992 Eden Valley Ravens football team possess the same tattoo. The home office ran some more intelligence regarding the members of that team. That information, combined with a close analysis of the photo from Kiradale, has yielded this short list of tattooed suspects.

"We have Sam Hughes, Jerry McAlester, Alvin Walker. The others, Harry Schaffer, Will Porter, and George Walker, Alvin's older brother, are all deceased or presumed deceased, in the case of Schaffer. According to school records, Andrew Taylor was also on that team, and may or may not have a tattoo. He's not pictured in the infamous team photograph. He was a sophomore, Alvin was a junior and the rest were seniors when the football team won the state title in '92."

"To summarize, our suspect list grows short. Assuming that Schaffer's dead, since there's no evidence to the contrary, our suspects are Sam, Jerry, Alvin, and Andrew Taylor, who may be on the run in a stolen vehicle with Anna in it. We have an APB out on that stolen car, right Chen?"

"Yes, sir. I've got every cop in central and western PA looking for him."

"Good. Now, for the twist—the killer may have an assistant, whose identity's a total mystery. But that theory is solely based on hearsay evidence from a recent attack on the Eden Sisterhood cabin. So I'm not sure how much I trust it. I wouldn't rule out Erin Stone as a suspect and an accomplice, despite her seeming efforts to find Ms. Annabel Lee."

Just then, Inspector Cabot's cell phone rang. Apparently, Gus Morgan possessed new information regarding the case. He seemed pleasantly surprised that the Inspector had asked for FBI involvement.

The two had a brief discussion before the Inspector hung up and turned his attention back to the team.

"That was Gus. He has Linda Taylor in his office. Apparently, she came in distressed about her missing husband. I'll run down there and talk to her. At the same time, I'll put pressure on Alvin Walker. If he's in on this, I'll crack him," the Inspector threatened. "Molly, I need you to really put some pressure on Hughes and McAlester. Come on! These two guys are at the top of the suspect list. We need to make at least one of them sing."

"I'll get right on it," Molly replied.

"Chen, go with her in case there's trouble," the Inspector ordered.

"Yes, sir."

"All right, team, let's get this done. There's an innocent girl's life at stake. We've got no time to lose. If I hear anything new from Kelly or anyone else, I'll text you. You do the same if you get a break. We'll meet in Kiradale at noon. If you're going to be late, Molly, let me know, okay?" He smiled at the perpetually tardy detective.

"Yes, boss," she replied. "I'm with Chen. He'll call you if we're even a minute late. Right, Chen?"

"Very funny, Molly. At least I don't fall asleep at team meetings."

"I never fell asleep at a meeting. You're lying. You're like the little brother I'm glad I never had," she barked back.

"I'm your worst nightmare, Dvorak," Chen replied.

"Okay, enough. We have work to do. This is serious. I expect results."

"Yes, sir," they replied in unison, while Molly frowned at Chen. He stuck his tongue out at her when the Inspector turned his head.

"Very mature of you. Hail, the prodigal son," she whispered, so the Inspector could not hear.

Soon, the team split up. The Inspector drove to the local police station in Kamerynville, and Molly, along with Chen, headed back inside The Raven Inn to find Sam and Jerry.

Upon entering the lobby of the inn, they spotted Sam Hughes behind the front desk. He had just finished with a customer and was about to head upstairs to his office.

"Mr. Hughes," Molly called out. "We need to talk in private."

Sam had met Chen the day before, so he was aware of his role. Chen's presence signaled an official police meeting, rather than the informal social interaction that Sam hoped to have with the charming detective. "Sure. Shall we go up to my office?" he suggested.

"That'd be great. This is Chen Lee. He's my partner on the force."

"Yes. Hello again, Chen."

"Hello. We met yesterday," Chen replied.

"Oh, I didn't realize," Molly said.

"Nice to see you both," Sam lied. He had no desire to sit through yet another police interrogation.

"All business today, Molly?" Sam tried to flirt a little as they ascended the wide, central staircase that dominated the lobby.

Molly did not take the bait. She was in police mode. The three walked in silence the remainder of the way to Sam's office, where they quickly began the interview.

"Chen, can you close the door, please?" Molly asked.

"This is official, isn't it?" Sam tried to lighten the situation, but to no avail.

"Mr. Hughes, may we have your permission to record this session?"

"Should I have a lawyer present? You're very intimidating, Molly."

"You have the right to legal counsel, if you so desire. Do you?"

"Are you arresting me or something?" Sam asked in bewilderment.

"Should I be arresting you?" Molly asked. Chen remained silent, awaiting permission to record the interview.

"No, 'cause I didn't do anything."

"Sounds like a guilty conscience. We're not here to make any arrests. We simply need more information regarding the recent deaths of Green and Porter."

"I'm always willing to help the police, as you well know. You've interviewed me enough times. So, yes, you can record whatever you like. I've got nothing to hide," Sam replied as he sat down in his large leather chair.

Once again, Molly proceeded to grill Sam about his past involvement with Erin Stone. But she did not learn anything new. Then she switched to the subject of the 1992 Eden Valley football team and the associated raven tattoos. The topic of the Drake treasure was fully explored, along with the legend of the White Witch. No stone was left unturned in the intense interrogation. Molly retained fine form, fueled by the knowledge that a young woman's life depended on her abilities to uncover the truth. She spared him nothing of her intensity and offered little empathy, except the occasional drink of water. Two long hours later, Sam felt exhausted and glad to see Molly and Chen leave his office. "This is crazy," he concluded aloud. "You guys have it all wrong," he echoed down the hall.

Molly and Chen had returned to the lobby before they exchanged a word. The Sam Hughes interrogation had been long and difficult, but it had begun to answer some of the key questions about the case. They had much to review with the rest of the team that afternoon, but now they had to find Jerry McAlester, the inn's head chef and Sam's high school friend. Upon reaching the kitchen, they learned that Jerry had left minutes earlier. It appeared odd, given that lunch preparations would soon begin. The kitchen staff had no idea why he left or where he had gone. Molly and Chen decided to pay Sam another visit in his office.

"Back for more?" He looked up from his desk. Although he was visibly tired, he had a popular inn to run.

"Sam, we do appreciate your cooperation," Molly replied.

"It sure didn't feel like it a few minutes ago."

"It's part of the job."

"Right. What else you need?"

"Jerry seemed to have left unexpectedly before we had a chance to talk to him. Do you have any idea where he went?"

"He's runnin' away from you, Molly," Sam said with a chuckle.

"Seriously?"

"I don't know. I have no idea what that guy does. If he weren't such a damn good chef, I'd have parted ways with him long ago. I don't trust him anymore," Sam confessed.

"Why?"

"We're old friends, but lately the guy's been acting strange. He disappears at times and he never has a straight answer. He's getting very sneaky in his old age. I don't know what he's up to, but all this runnin' off is getting old. So, good luck finding him, 'cause I sure as hell don't have a clue. This is between us, so don't leak it out, please. I've finally found a replacement for 'im. I haven't told 'im, yet, but I'm plannin' to on Monday."

"So, you have no idea why he left or where he went?"

"No, I don't. He's a free spirit."

"Okay, thanks."

Once Molly returned to the lobby, she and Chen called the Inspector. Unfortunately, he could not answer. He, too, had his hands full.

* * * * *

Linda Taylor possessed an undeniable charm and a sharp wit. A tall brunette in her mid-twenties, she appeared younger. Her natural intelligence trumped her lack of a formal college education. Although she appeared confident, she hid a huge void in her heart—an abyss of formidable proportions.

As the Inspector entered Gus Morgan's office, he found Linda seated in a corner chair playing on her smartphone. Gus briefed the Inspector in the foyer of the station, sharing with him that Linda appeared desperate to find her lost husband, the missing Andrew Taylor.

"Ms. Taylor, my name's Inspector Cabot. I'm with the State Police. The Chief informed me of your situation. I'm sorry to hear about your missing husband. Do you know why he left?"

"I have no idea," she replied and began to cry. "We were very close. He lost his job a few weeks ago. That put a strain on us, but we managed. Then, two days ago, Andy went to Kamerynville for a job interview for a construction job. I'm not sure where. He's an electrical contractor. Anyway, he left early in the morning in his truck and never came back. I spent the past few nights awake, waiting, calling, and texting. I tried reaching him countless times, but there's no reply."

"I see. Did you have an argument?"

"No. We were perfectly happy. He's my little teddy bear. I always call him that because he is so…oh, what am I going to do? He might be in trouble."

"Why would you say that?"

"Well, after Gavin's death….What a tragedy! We were close friends, you know…all three of us. Well, after Gavin died, Andrew wasn't the same. He wasn't himself even before Gavin died. Come to think of it, he seemed almost glad that Gavin was gone. I must confess, we did have one argument. It was right after Gavin's death. I thought it was terribly cold of Andrew to say what he said." She paused for effect.

"What was that, Ms. Taylor?"

"He said that Gavin deserved to die." She looked up at the Inspector, and locked eyes with him.

I've seen this woman before, the Inspector thought. *Where have I seen her? I know those eyes, but the hair's different.* He pondered silently. "Why would he say that?" the Inspector asked.

"He seemed jealous of Gavin. I don't know why. Andrew and I were close. There was no reason to be jealous. It was an odd reaction. But we worked it out, if you know what I mean?"

"What do you mean?"

Linda laughed and tossed her head. "Now, now, Inspector, you shouldn't ask me such personal questions. Shame on you!"

"I see. I get it. Right."

"Anyway, we were happy again, but he continued to act odd."

"What do you mean, Ms. Taylor?"

"Well, he would disappear in the middle of the night, several nights in a row. When I confronted him about it and about the mud on his shoes, he got very defensive. He said it was none of my business."

"I see. Ms. Taylor, we found your husband's truck down a logging trail behind the old Green farmhouse. It appeared abandoned. Do you have any knowledge of that?"

"What! Are you sure? That's not possible. He took that truck with him when he left."

"Do you have any idea why your husband would abandon his truck in the woods like that?"

"No. That makes no sense! He loved that truck."

"Here's a picture of the vehicle." The Inspector showed her one of the photographs he had taken with his smartphone. "Is that his truck?"

"Yes. That's it. You found it where?" she asked in disbelief.

"Behind the old Green estate on a logging trail near the rear of the property. There were no signs of forced entry or vandalism to the vehicle. It appears to have been simply abandoned. We're running tests on it to see if we can get any clues to your husband's whereabouts. Once we're done, you can have the vehicle back."

"Oh, I don't care about no truck," she replied in a southern accent previously undistinguishable. "I just wanna find my husband. Please find 'im. I'm so worried." She started to cry once again.

"We'll do our best, Miss. Anything else you can share to help us find him?"

"No, except I heard him talkin' to some woman named Ariella. When I asked him about her, he said she was a business partner. He wouldn't tell me more."

"Did you overhear anything else, Ms. Taylor?"

"I heard a lot of yellin' about money owed for some kilos. What're kilos? He wouldn't tell me. I'm scared 'cause he's been actin' odd, lately. I hope he's not mixed up with anything bad. Is he?"

"Not sure, Miss. Anything else of interest?"

"No. Wait, he called her the White Witch. Is that important?"

"Not sure, but we'll check it out. But this doesn't explain the abandoned truck in the woods," the Inspector replied.

"Maybe he met her there instead of goin' to a job interview, and she….Oh, my God! You need to find 'im. He seemed scared of her. What if she threatened 'im?"

"We'll check her out, Ms. Taylor. By the way, where were you on the nights of September 21st and September 24th?"

Linda seemed surprised by this question, but she quickly recovered. "What day was the 21st?"

"It was a Friday, a week ago?"

"I was with my husband."

"Are you sure? That was the night of Gavin Green's death."

"Yes, I'm sure. I was with Andrew. We had gone to bed early that night after watching TV. Why would you ask me that? Am I a suspect?"

"No. I'm simply asking because it's my job. How about the night of the 24th, the following Monday night?"

"I was home, but that was the second night Andrew snuck out. He did the same thing on Tuesday night. I was going to follow him on Wednesday, but he stayed home after that, until he disappeared on Thursday morning and never came back."

"I see."

"We have several witnesses who claim that about a month ago your husband drove around the valley looking for you because you left him for another man. I hate to be so blunt, but is that true?"

"What! That's preposterous! I love my husband. How dare anyone say that about me. Who said it?"

"We can't reveal our sources, but are you saying that you did not leave your husband about a month ago?"

"Yes. I mean 'No.' I did not leave him. He left me."

"A month ago he left you?"

"Yes. He left me for that little sleaze at The Raven Inn."

"Who is that?"

"Elaine's her name. They were together, and the rest was a cover-up to make himself look better."

"But, Ms. Taylor, you just claimed that you and your husband were perfectly happy."

"We are. He apologized, broke up his affair with that bitch and I forgave 'im. We're very happy. He's a good man. But lately, he's been acting odd again. Maybe that hussy is tempting 'im back. I wouldn't put it past her. Maybe she knows where he is. I bet she does. I bet they ran off together. Did you check that?"

"We will check that, I assure you. Any questions for me?"

"Inspector, do you have any suspects in regard to the two deaths?"

"Unfortunately, I can't share that information. Oh, one last question. Have you ever heard of Lenore?"

This question took Linda by surprise. She paused before answering, as if she was weighing her options. "No. Never heard of her," she replied at last. "Anything else, Inspector?"

"No. That's it. How can we best reach you if we have any further questions?"

"My cell," she replied and gave him the number. "I'll be at home. I'm not planning on going anywhere."

She got up and left, leaving the Inspector wondering where he had seen her before.

Molly finally reached the Inspector. He was still pondering the Linda Taylor interview when his cell phone rang. Something about that woman felt oddly familiar, but he could not place her. Frustrated, he finally gave up the futile mental exercise.

"What do you mean McAlester's missing? We need to find him. I'll talk to the Chief and get his help. Do we have a make on his car?"

"Yes. I'll text you the information. But Hughes seems innocent," Molly said.

"I'm not so sure, but let's discuss it this afternoon. Damn it, two of our key suspects are missing, McAlester and Taylor. Maybe they're working together. That may be why Taylor ditched the truck. He was counting on a ride from McAlester."

"What're you talking about, boss?"

"Ah, nothing. We'll review it this afternoon. I still need to talk to Alvin Walker."

"Have fun with that. Any word from Kelly?"

"No. I don't want to call her and risk blowing her cover. By the way, is Elaine at the Inn?"

"Yes. I just saw her few minutes ago. Why?"

"Nothing."

There was a pause on the line before Molly spoke in an excited tone. "Boss, call off the dogs on McAlester. He just pulled up to the inn. Gotta run. Bye."

Before Molly hung up the phone, Chen approached Jerry McAlester, who had just gotten out of his '69 Mustang convertible. "Mr. McAlester, my name's Chen Lee and I'm with the State Police." Chen flashed his badge. "We have a few questions to ask you."

Molly rushed up and joined the conversation. The three walked onto the wide front porch of the inn and sat in a cluster of white wicker chairs. It was ten-thirty, and Jerry was getting nervous about lunch preparations. "Can we make this quick? I've got to get ready for lunch," he said in an eager tone, before reluctantly taking a seat in front of the two detectives.

"We'll try, but this is an official homicide investigation," Molly replied. "We need your time or we will have to take you in."

"Okay. I get it. It's ruled a homicide, now?"

"Yes. We are treating Will Porter's death as a homicide."

"Man, that poor bastard. He was an old friend, you know. What a shame," Jerry replied. He seemed a little nervous, but it wasn't clear how much of that anxiety stemmed from the delayed lunch preparations versus a guilty conscience.

After getting permission to record the interview, Chen set up his recorder while Molly began asking tough questions. "Where were you just now, Mr. McAlester?"

"I ran to the bank. I just realized my rent's due. Last thing I need is that miserable old landlady to kick me out. I had to get money out so I could pay her tonight on my way home. Why do you ask?"

Molly could tell Jerry was a smooth operator. He would be a difficult nut to crack. The interview lasted a total of forty minutes, at the end of which Jerry rushed off to the kitchen as if it were on fire. "I need to get in there or lunch'll be a disaster," he shouted as he ran off.

"Do you think he's telling the truth?" Molly asked Chen, after Jerry departed.

"No. I think he's lying about something. He wouldn't keep eye contact. Did you notice when you asked about the drug dealing, he kept looking at his shoes."

"Yeah. I noticed that. He did the same thing when I discussed Erin Stone and the Gavin Green death. The only time he didn't do that was when we talked about Will Porter's death. This case is going to drive me insane. We can't seem to get a break."

"I know, but he's very suspicious. He claimed that he didn't know Gavin Green was on drugs. Yet later, he slipped and said that Green used drugs frequently. Remember?"

"Yeah, and when I asked him to clarify, he denied he said it and claimed he had no knowledge that Green was on drugs."

"Did you notice how he reacted to the Drake treasure question? First he denied it and then he agreed with Sam's testimony. He's hiding something."

"Well, let's get over to Kiradale. Should I call Cabot to tell him we'll be a few minutes late?"

Molly sighed. "I need to teach you to stop sucking up to the boss. What's gotten into you lately?"

"I'm not sucking up," Chen objected.

"Yes, you are. Ever since you got married this spring, you've been suckin' up."

"Screw you, Molly. That's not true."

"Fine. Go ask Kelly when she gets back. She noticed it, too. What's with that?"

"I'm not sucking up, but I do need a raise. We're trying to start a family on one income," Chen confessed.

"Well, after we crack this case, go ask the boss for a raise. I'll back you up on it. But stop the sucking up. It's getting old, Chen. It's not like you. Where's the easygoing, fun-loving guy who teases me all the time? I miss that guy. You're not a brownnose. Kelly hasn't even gotten to know the real you, 'cause you've morphed into this butt wipe."

"Butt wipe? That's a bit harsh."

"Well, what else would you call it?"

"You really miss the old me? I thought you hated when Bob and I teased you?"

"I didn't. By the way, have you heard from Bob? I need to call him. He left me a message a couple weeks ago, and I forgot to call him back," Molly confessed.

"Big Bob's doing great. He called to tell you that he and Suzy are getting married. The wedding's next May in Brennantown. It's going to be huge. Bob said that his soon-to-be father-in-law is sparing no expense. He asked me to be the best man."

"No way! That's great news! Crap, I need to call him. I miss that guy."

"So do I. But he's making it big, Molly. The new blues album's shaping up to be even bigger than the first one. He told me that old Chesterfield stopped drinking. I guess the band ganged up on him after he showed up drunk at a couple of the shows. That guy's something else. I hate to say it, but he's the one who put them on the map. What a sax player, huh?"

"He's amazing. But I think that together they're even more amazing. Suzy's vocals are out of this world, and Bob's a great trumpet player. What a band! Are they coming to town anytime soon? I guess they've outgrown us," Molly replied.

"Bob said they'll all be in town for Christmas. Don't be surprised if they make a few appearances at the local clubs."

"We've got to go see them."

"Definitely. Plus, I'm sure Bob will come by the station. He says he misses working with us. Can you believe that? He's rich and famous, and he misses working with us on crazy cases like this one, where we get no sleep for days straight. I'd switch with him, anytime."

"I'm sure a few days on this case would straighten him out," Molly concluded.

She was driving to Kiradale while they reminisced about their old friend and former colleague, Bob Braxton. When they finally reached the field office, it was ten minutes past noon. "He's the one who's late. His car's not here."

They were about to enter when Molly's phone rang. It was the Inspector.

"There's a break in the case," the Inspector began. "Meet me at Gus's office in Kamerynville. Bring Chen," he ordered, and hung up the phone before Molly had a chance to ask any questions.

CHAPTER 65

A Witch Hunt

"**B**oss, what's going on?" Molly blurted out as she entered the local police station and saw Inspector Cabot seated in the front lobby.

"Walker was right all along. I hate to give him credit, but he called it," the Inspector replied.

"What? You and Alvin Walker are buddies now? I thought he was a key suspect?" Molly looked around and whispered.

"Remember the white scraps of cloth at both crime scenes? I thought Walker was planting them, but he wasn't. Fred, one of the local officers, found the last one, not Walker. Well, we got the lab results back. Two of the three cloth fragments had strands of hair on them. The DNA results are a match for Ariella Bianca. Apparently, she was at both crime scenes, probably impersonating the White Witch. That begins to explain what Amos Miller saw at Drakes Plot. It also ties back to the murals in Gavin Green's room. He was obsessed with the legend, but the recent ghost sightings were nothing more than Ariella Bianca dressed up as a white witch."

"Slow down, boss. That makes no sense. Our main suspect is a male with a raven tattoo."

"What if it's the other way around. What if the killer is Ariella Bianca, aka Erin Stone, and her accomplice is the man with the raven tattoo, which is most likely Hughes, given their past relationship?"

"You matched Ariella's DNA? Where'd you get her DNA?" Molly did not like the new development. Then she remembered the mysterious woman in the gardens at Kiradale and Kelly's first impression of Ariella. Kelly told Molly that Ariella looked like that phantom woman and like the White Witch depicted on the Gavin Green's mural.

"It appears that Ariella had a small run in with our local authorities. Alvin brought her in earlier this summer on indecent exposure charges. Apparently, she went swimming naked in the Eden River one morning and Gavin Green reported her to the police. Alvin brought her in and took a DNA sample for the record, with her permission, of course."

"Convenient. I guess you're right that the local police had it figured out all along. Funny how that works," Molly replied.

"The DNA is solid evidence. We need to bring her in for questioning."

"So, I guess you don't need to know what Chen and I got out of Hughes and McAlester, right? After all, Alvin already solved the case," Molly replied.

"Molly, don't do this. Look, the Feds have agreed to come in if we need help. Gus is convinced that Ariella's our killer. We need to let him have a chance. If the FBI comes in here, we're out, and it'll be up to them and Gus. If he doesn't get a shot at this, the FBI'll be here as fast as you can say 'see ya.' Do you understand, Molly?"

"I get it. It's political. No pun intended, but this is turning into a witch hunt."

Chen started laughing at Molly's pun. "That was great," he proclaimed. "This is a true witch hunt!" He laughed some more.

"What's with him?" the Inspector asked, seeing the change in Chen's behavior.

"He's done kissing up to you. I straightened him out. You'd be proud of me," Molly replied. She had no tolerance for politics, especially when a young woman's life was on the line. She was disappointed that the Inspector had caved to the opinions and whims of the local police, whom she considered useless, at best.

Chen overheard the conversation and began laughing again. "Sorry, sir," he added out of habit.

"Molly, go calm down," the Inspector instructed. "Chen, try and reach Kelly. We need to find Ariella's whereabouts."

"Sir, in all due respect, if we call Kelly we'll risk blowing her cover," Chen objected.

"It's a risk we have to take."

"By the way, for what it's worth, Sam Hughes did not have an affair with Erin Stone," Molly interjected.

"What does that have to do with anything? Who cares?" The Inspector was getting annoyed with Molly's persistent and vocal opposition to his plan.

"He has no motive, so he's not the tattooed killer. McAlester, maybe, but not Hughes. I'm convinced of it."

"Oh, like you were with Jack Fulton? You get blinded by the strong, masculine types, Molly. Don't mix business with pleasure again. Haven't you learned your lesson?" The Inspector chastised her.

"That was a real cheap shot!" Molly snapped back and stormed out of the local police barracks. Chen followed her out. He was no longer laughing.

"What the hell got into him?" Molly vented to Chen, as they walked away from the barracks.

"Who knows? He's probably got his boss breathing down on him and got reamed out for calling in the FBI without checking with the brass. Morgan took advantage of it and the DNA provided an excuse."

"It's a wild-goose chase. Meanwhile, that poor girl, Anna, could die at the hands of some tattooed lunatic. I still think it's either McAlester or Taylor that did this, not Ariella, despite what the local cops think. When you provide a shelter for homeless young women, you don't go around killing people. It doesn't fit. Besides, I trust Kelly's judgment. She would have sensed Ariella's dark side by now."

"What if Ariella's really good at hiding it? Maybe she has a dual personality. This place is full of lunatics—what's one more? What if she's using that sisterhood to draw in easy victims with no families to report them missing? It's the perfect scenario, like serial killers targeting prostitutes."

"That's crazy, Chen. It's not that at all. These girls aren't prostitutes! They're young women who have had it tough and are trying to make something of themselves. She's not using them. She's helping them and empowering them," Molly objected. She was angry at the Inspector and the local police. *Alvin and Gus are scoundrels,* she thought. *I'll be damned if I let them get away with this.*

"Look, Molly, we need to let this one play itself out. Don't do anything stupid," Chen advised.

"To let an innocent young woman die because of police politics is the stupidest outcome of all. I'll do anything in my power to prevent that from happening, even if it costs me my job. Are you with me, or are you still sucking up to the boss?"

"Well, if you put it that way, I'm in. What's the plan?" asked Chen.

"We need to reach Kelly."

* * * * *

Rachel was showing Kelly the farmyard, tucked away on the north side of the cabin. It consisted of an old barn with two cows, a pasture full of goats, and a grassy pen with a henhouse and a couple dozen chickens. Rachel loved to tend the animals and shared these chores with Rebecca. This morning, Rebecca stayed behind to look after the younger girls, especially Hazel. It was Hazel and Agnes who seemed the most frightened by the recent events. Rachel, on the other hand, appeared surprisingly unfazed.

Kelly was about to try to milk a cow when she was startled by the buzzing of her cell phone. "Excuse me, Rachel, but it's a dear friend calling. I really need to take this," Kelly explained, as she reached for her phone.

"No worries. You can try later. I'll go feed the goats. They're always hungry," Rachel replied.

Kelly rushed out of the barn, answering the call in a whisper. "What's going on? I thought we'd talk after three. You can't just call here randomly, you know," she chastised Chen.

"It's the Inspector's orders. He and the local police want to bring Ariella into the local station for questioning. It appears that she's become the prime suspect in the case," Chen shared.

"What? That makes no sense. She didn't do it."

"She may be an accomplice."

"Whatever. What do you want me to do?"

"Is Ariella there?"

"No. She's off looking for Anna, as we all should be doing. This is ridiculous! What's with Cabot? We need to find Anna."

"He thinks she's with Ariella or that Ariella knows her whereabouts. He wants you to tail Ariella. Molly and I can help."

"Chen, I'm not with Ariella. She left this morning. I have no idea where she went. Tell Cabot he's looking in the wrong place. When's the FBI getting here? We need help finding Anna."

"Molly's got a plan. Here, I'll let you talk to her." Chen passed the phone to Molly.

"Hey, Kelly. Sorry for the surprise call. It wasn't our idea," Molly began.

"No worries. What's up?" Kelly cut to the chase. She knew that she could be overheard by Rachel if she stayed on the phone too long.

"Cabot has lost it. He's got his political cap on this morning. All we can guess is that the commissioner chewed him out. Anyway, he's playing a game of witch hunt with Morgan and Walker. I can't believe it, but it's not important right now. We need to find Anna," Molly proclaimed.

"I couldn't agree more."

"So, here's my plan. We go along with the orders and look for Ariella, not to arrest her, but to follow her. She's probably closer to finding Anna than we are right now. We didn't get much out of the interviews with Hughes and McAlester, except that I did manage to convince Cabot to put a tail on McAlester. He's got one of the local deputies following him in an unmarked car. He then insisted on putting a tail on Hughes, although I think it's a waste of time. He's innocent and never leaves the inn.

"I'll be quick. I think our two main suspects are Jerry McAlester and Andrew Taylor, who's still missing. His wife, Linda, described him as behaving oddly. My gut tells me that Taylor's somehow involved. How? I don't know."

"Okay, Molly. That's all fine, but what's the plan? I can't be on the phone much longer." Kelly looked around, expecting to see Rachel at any moment.

"It's pretty simple. Chen and I'll head out to meet you. We'll make sure we're not detected, but we'll provide you some cover at a distance. You need to figure out how to find Ariella. Does she have a cell phone?"

"Are you serious, Molly? That's not a plan! You want me to call Ariella and ask her to tell me her location, so I can go and meet her? Are you kidding me? Please tell me you're kidding and you really have a plan."

"Does she have a cell phone?"

"Molly, I'm not calling her."

"Look, we're not asking you to call her. We simply want to track her cell signal. Does she have a cell phone?"

"I don't know."

"Can you ask someone and text me back with her cell number? Please hurry."

Kelly hung up the phone and went to look for Rachel. She found her cleaning out the goat pens. "Rachel, does Ariella have a cell phone? I wanted to see if I could help her look for Anna," Kelly explained.

"Yes, but she rarely uses it. I bet it's still in the house."

"Oh, too bad. I feel that she's in trouble of some sort and needs help," Kelly confessed one of her motives.

"I could be wrong about the phone. She might have it with her. Let's check."

Kelly followed Rachel into the house. Rachel soon found Ariella's cell phone. It was still on her writing desk.

Kelly was visibly disappointed.

"Let's talk to Becky. She might know where Ariella went. I have my own idea, but let's talk to her. I want to look for Anna, as well."

The two women found Rebecca hanging laundry on the line. Hazel was helping her. After Kelly expressed her concerns and eagerness to help Ariella, Rebecca bought into the idea of the search. "She could be long gone, but I'd look in one of two places, either the reflection pool by the big waterfall or the wildflower meadow in the North Woods. I'd go with you, but I really need to stay here and look after the other girls." She glanced over at Hazel, who was busy hanging laundry.

"I know where to go. I'll take you, Kelly," Rachel said eagerly. She was always ready for an adventure. "Let's grab a little gear and some water before we go."

While Rachel packed the gear, Kelly managed to text Molly that Ariella did not have her cell phone, but that she and Rachel would start looking for her. Molly replied that, if need be, she would try and track Kelly using Kelly's phone signal. "Hopefully, you'll have a signal in those woods. We're on our way. Can you wait for us at the cabin?" Molly asked.

"No. We need to leave. I'll have the cell phone on. You can't just show up here, guns blazing, and blow my cover. What're you thinking?" Kelly replied.

"Who're you texting?" Rachel asked as she walked up to Kelly. She had a large backpack slung over her shoulders.

"One of my friends. It's a bad habit. I'm surprised we have a signal out here," Kelly replied in an attempt to change the subject.

"It's 'cause we're so close to the river and there's a tower on the opposite ridge. Where we're going, there's no signal. We'll lose it soon. That's one of the reasons why Ariella rarely takes her phone."

"I see. Well, let's go."

The last text that Molly received from Kelly contained the following message:

No signal where I'm going. No worries, Mom. I'm a big girl now!

CHAPTER 66

The Scream

achel was a seasoned hiker. Not only did she know her way around these woods, but she moved with stealth and speed. Kelly had a hard time keeping the pace, but she had no desire to slow Rachel. Time was of the essence, for a life was at stake. The two women reached the deep pool at the base of the large waterfall. The afternoon sun played with the gentle ripples on its surface, creating hundreds of small light beams that transformed the surrounding woods into a canvas for the multicolored light show.

"This place's amazing!" Kelly proclaimed. "What great energy!"

"This is Ariella's portal. The root of her power lies here. Careful you don't disturb it."

"I guess she's not here."

"Let's hurry toward the wildflower meadow."

"Is it far?" Kelly asked.

"It's about thirty minutes north, but, if we run, we can make it in half that time."

"Run? Okay." Kelly answered in a dull tone. She was starting to appreciate the need for regular exercise. She noticed that somewhere between the cabin and the waterfall, she had lost the cell signal. *I guess we're on our own now.*

Rachel broke into a full run. To her, the rugged, narrow path provided a comfortable racetrack. Unfortunately for Kelly, it was a strenuous ordeal. It wasn't long before Rachel disappeared out of sight. *Great. She's gone*, Kelly concluded, and stopped running to catch her breath. Soon, she resumed her jog along the narrow trail, driven by the need to find Anna.

Ten minutes passed and still no sign of Rachel. Kelly started to feel abandoned. *What's with that girl? She wouldn't leave me here, would she?*

Suddenly, her thoughts were derailed by a loud scream. It sounded like a howl. No, it was a scream that ended with a howl. It was clearly male. *Or was it a wolf?* she thought and began to dash down the path. About eighty paces further, she ran straight into Rachel, who stood frozen in fear.

"Are you okay?" Kelly demanded.

"What was that? It sounded like a werewolf," Rachel mumbled.

"Werewolf? You've been reading too many fantasy novels. That was a man."

"It sounded like a wolf and a man."

Kelly agreed, but did not wish to voice her agreement, so as not to frighten Rachel any further. Kelly took the lead as they approached the woodland meadow. The scene before them looked enchanting. The deep, dark woods made of old oak and beech trees had given way to a large, oval opening. The setting sun illuminated the meadow, turning thousands of yellow wildflowers into gold. The regal color was enhanced by the countless purple blossoms of wild flax.

Wow. That's what I call a wildflower meadow, Kelly reflected. "The scream seemed to have come from this meadow," she said to Rachel.

"There's no one there. I'm telling you—it's a werewolf. We need to go back. These woods are strange and full of ghosts. It's a werewolf. Look! There he is, over there!" Rachel pointed to the far side of the meadow. The two women stood two hundred yards from the edge of the clearing. From the shadowy woods, they could see the light illuminating a large wolf. Fortunately, the breeze blew in their faces and the large animal was not aware of their presence — not yet.

"I told you, it's a werewolf," Rachel whispered.

As all fell silent and still, the large animal turned his head and stared straight at them. Its large, yellowish eyes seemed to know everything. A cold chill passed over Kelly, as if the beast had looked straight through her. She and Rachel froze in fear.

* * * * *

Earlier that morning, Ariella had gone to her sacred waterfall and reflecting pool. She had entered her hidden sanctuary, where she once more crossed over to Eden. At first, she dared not enter too deeply into her meditative trance, for she feared the previous disturbing revelation. Yet something urged her to go further. As fear held her back, this insatiable curiosity urged her forward. In an internal tug-of-war, curiosity prevailed.

Finally, Ariella entered deeper into her trance, deeper into Eden. Once more, she encountered the image of the legendary ghost, the White Witch. Once more, she saw her own face within the flowing white veil of this mysterious creature. This time, however, she did not retract in fear. This time, she accepted this image as natural and crossed past it, moving through the translucent figure. Her meditative trance became dream-like. "Reality" was bending to her will, for now she could see through the eyes of this specter, this White Witch. It was as if she had become one with this ghostly being. Was it her imagination? To doubt was to lose the power—she had to believe.

In a flash of revelation, she achieved that which only her great Shaman Master had the ability to attain. He described it and tried to teach her, but she could never embrace it. At that moment, which seemed like eternity, she attained duality. She fully embodied the ghost of Evelyn Drake, the White Witch.

Presently, the witch was moving freely through the woods like the wind itself. It was clear that she, too, was searching, searching for something. *Could she be searching for Anna?* Ariella thought. *How could that be?* Her mind momentarily doubted and the images ceased.

Regaining her composure, she once more passed through the image of the White Witch, and, in crossing over, she seemed to possess the phantom's might, at least her ability to "see." Ariella had stumbled upon a curious power. In this deep meditative state, through the rumored specter herself, she could somehow see quickly, simultaneously, fragments of what appeared to be reality. Thus, she could rapidly hunt for Anna's whereabouts and for the evil that imprisoned her.

In this state, she quickly found the hermit and realized that he held the key to the gates of hell that imprisoned her precious Anna. Within that same instant, she understood that she could free them both—Harry and Anna. They were held by the same shadow, a shadow of fear. This experience was too much to sustain, even for Ariella's powers. She had to let go, for to remain was to become permanently one with the ghost of the White Witch. Was this specter real, or was she Ariella's creation or simply her imagination?

Real is what we perceive—nothing less, nothing more.

With that thought, she had one quick glimpse of her nemesis before all went black. She awoke on the cold, wet ground that confirmed her only reality. Gasping for air, she knew exactly what had to be done having discovered Anna's captor. But she had to hurry, for Anna's hourglass was almost empty.

Quickly, she ran down the narrow trail from the waterfall to the wildflower meadow for there was no time to lose. The sun had passed its apex. When she reached the meadow, she headed straight toward the large oak tree that marked the entrance to Harry's cavernous dwelling.

"I know you're in there, Harry!" she screamed.

Soon, the large wolf emerged. "Hello, Cane. Where's Harry? What's he up to? Never mind, I know all about it. I'm coming in, Harry!" she screamed, rushing past the wolf, who did not oppose her will. After all, she was his true master.

Without further hesitation, Ariella entered Harry's cave. She had to free Anna. That was all that mattered. "Where are you, Harry?" she bellowed, as she made her way into the main chamber.

There, slumped in the corner, was the target of her quest. A moment of fear entered her mind, as she realized the slouched form could be lifeless.

"Oh, my God!" she exclaimed running to the back of the cave, where she encountered the body of Harry Schaffer, the hermit. He was fast asleep with a large pad of dried moss under his head, his body covered in deer skins.

"Wake up, Harry. I need your help."

The hermit opened his eyes and stared at Ariella with a blank expression, for he had no idea as to her identity. Only the large, gray wolf seemed to remember this woman, for he stayed near her, as if he were protecting her.

"Who're you? What're ya doin' in my house?" The hermit sat up and growled like a bear. He was about to strike at her when the gray wolf stepped forward and challenged him. "What's gotten into you, Wolf? Ya ought to keep strangers out of our cave. Who're you?" the Hermit asked once more, looking at Ariella with a bewildered stare.

"I'm Erin Stone. You must remember, Harry. I need your help. Remember where we first kissed in high school? You took me there, blindfolded. I trusted you. You said you found it. Remember? You said you found the treasure. That's when you gave me this," she pulled an old Spanish doubloon out of her pocket.

He sat there, staring at her and the gold coin. There was something familiar about both.

"Harry, he has our daughter. He has Anna. He figured it out. He says he'll kill her if I don't tell him where the treasure's hidden. But I don't know, Harry. I don't know where it's hidden. Only you know. I need you to remember. Her life's at stake. He thinks I know, but I don't. That knowledge is locked up in the most impenetrable safe of all—your lost mind, Harry. Please remember me. PLEASE!!!"

Kneeling before him, she kissed him all over his furrowed face. It did not matter that he was covered with weeks, if not months, of grime. She did not care for she loved this man more than life itself. He was the only man she had ever loved, or that she could ever love. As the father of her only child, Annabel Lee, she needed him back. The war had stolen him from her, and with it she lost everything of any true value. Now that she had found him alive, she him— she needed his help. Together they could take on this evil, but divided they risked losing the one soul that bound them forever.

"Harry, I love you! I have always loved you!" She continued to kiss him all over his face. As he sat there bewildered, her passionate kisses flooded him for what seemed like eternity. With her genuine love, she projected a power that seemed omnipotent, filling him with a strange sensation of which he had no recollection, but one. As she continued to shower him with affection, she touched his heart. Once his heart ignited, the mind quickly followed, and the shroud began to dissolve. He was Harry Schaffer, and this was his beloved wife, Erin Stone. The revelation felt so powerful that he let out a primordial scream of equal measure.

Not wishing to be outdone, the large, gray wolf finished the eternal proclamation with his own powerful howl, sending all the surrounding creatures, including Kelly and Rachel, into a frozen moment of genuine fear. That scream receded into history, forever changing its creator.

* * * * *

Anna regained her full senses after being drugged by her captor, only to awaken to a horrific nightmare. In a dark underground chamber, her feet and arms were bound tightly with strips of leather. One end of a thick rope was tied about her waist with the other end attached to a huge boulder at the far side of the damp cavern. A faint light penetrated through a distant entrance, which remained out of sight, blocked by a scree of fallen rocks.

Where am I? she thought, feeling tired even though she had been sleeping for most of the ordeal. With her senses fully functional, Anna began piecing together fragments of her memory—his face and the large raven tattoo on his right forearm. Although she had never seen him before, she could sense his merciless cruelty and insatiable desire. A feeling of dread crept into her mind, filling her with a sickening sensation. The feeling was terrifying. She felt like a living meal for an insatiable ravenous beast. The devil himself could not possess less mercy.

Presently, she could do little except wait to see if he returned to untie her. Then the final struggle would begin. To scream now would be like ringing a dinner bell for a meal in which she served as the main course. To escape seemed futile. She had tested the rope and the leather straps several times, attempting to loosen the rope or chew through the straps, to no avail. Having tried to rip her hands free to the point that they bled, she failed to free herself. Mercy had not come. *Help me, God! Please help me, God!* she prayed, for that was her sole option now. It was a silent prayer of desperation—a plea for mercy from an unseen power whose existence she still doubted. No mercy came. The light from the mouth of the cave fell into darkness, and into that shadow stepped a lustful beast that commanded the hollow shell of a deranged man.

CHAPTER 67

Bloody Hallows

"Oh, my God! Frank, are you sure? I need to find my team. Thanks, Frank!" Inspector Cabot seemed completely baffled. The news from the chief coroner had changed the case and the suspect list. Alvin Walker was wrong. The Inspector had suspected it until recent politics clouded his judgment.

"Screw these guys," he said to himself, referring to the local police, and left the station without a word. By the time he reached his car, he dialed Molly. He called three times before she picked up the phone.

"Where are you? Any leads on Ariella? Is Kelly okay?"

He had a plethora of questions and self-critique. *How could I have done this to my team? That's the last time I let my boss intimidate me to do something against my better judgment. The safety of my team and the public are first and foremost,* he thought. *We need to find Anna and fast,* he assured himself. Molly was filling him in on the situation. *She was right to take over, but now Kelly's missing. Damn it! This is what fear and inaction get you.* He silently chastised himself.

"Molly, we need to keep trying to reach Kelly. Is there any type of enhanced signal tracking that we could use to pick up her cell phone?"

"There's a type of targeted satellite triangulation out there, or so Chen assures me, but short of a presidential order, we can't get to it. It's classified and solely military."

"Damn. That won't help. Okay, back to good old detective work. Where are you now?"

"We're nearly at the location where we lost her signal. There're two main paths ahead. One leads along the creek, and the other heads deeper into the woods."

"Okay, each of you take one and see if you can find her."

"That was our plan, boss. As you know, we'll lose the signal soon. For the record, I'm heading deeper into the woods and Chen's taking the path along the creek. Over and out."

Suddenly, the Inspector got a knot in his stomach. *Ah, that was stupid. They shouldn't separate. I need to call her back.* He tried three more times, but to no avail. *Okay, keep focused, Cabot. With this new development, I need to find Ms. Taylor. She needs to know,* he thought. Jumping in his car, he drove off to the Taylors' apartment. When he arrived, no one was there.

It is odd how our memory works. We can force ourselves to try and remember a name, or a person, or a fact, and, often, the more we try the less we succeed. Yet at other times, a recollection is placed before us when we seek it the least. That was the case with Inspector Cabot, as he rang the Taylors' doorbell one last time. "Now I know who she is!" he said aloud for no one to hear. "She's Cheryl, the mysterious waitress from The Raven Inn. Linda Taylor is Cheryl. What the hell's going on here?" He jumped in his car and headed to The Raven Inn to push Sam Hughes for more answers.

When he arrived at the inn, he stormed into Sam's upstairs office. "What do you know about a woman named Linda Taylor?" he asked without any attempts at cordial greetings.

"No, 'Hello,' Inspector? Where are your manners?" Sam chuckled as he looked up from his paperwork.

"Cut the crap, Hughes. Tell me all you know about Linda Taylor."

"Well, there's not much to tell. She was hitting on me weeks ago. Then, she claimed that one of my servers broke up her marriage. Odd girl. Really odd. Why do you ask?"

"Never mind that, it's police business. Are you telling me that she and her husband were broken up weeks ago?"

"It was about a month ago. I ran into her husband when he was driving around here in his pickup truck looking for her. He claimed she ran away from him. I think he suspected she ran off with another guy. Sure looked like it. A few nights later, she shows up here in the bar, all smug and flirty. When I ignored her, she started making up a story about Elaine breaking up her marriage. I asked Elaine about it, and she said it's a lie. I believe Elaine. Linda's an unstable weirdo, if you ask me."

"Interesting. I need to talk to Elaine. That's the young server, right? Is she here?"

"She should be. She lives down the hall. Is she in trouble?" Sam felt very protective of Elaine, even though of late they had become distant. Deep down, he really fancied the young server, who reminded him of the love of his life, his deceased wife, Sandra.

Sam and the Inspector walked down the hall and knocked on Elaine's door. She soon answered, wiping the sleep out of her eyes. "Sam. What's up? I took a nap. Those late-night shifts do me in." She looked surprised to see the Inspector standing behind Sam.

"Elaine, this is Inspector Cabot of the State Police."

"I know who he is. What's up?" Elaine was not only strikingly attractive, but she also had a presence that exuded confidence and a strong character not typically evident in a young woman her age. Just seeing her standing there in nothing but a long T-shirt that reached down to her knees, Sam couldn't help but feel a strong attraction toward her.

"Well, Miss, I need to know about Linda Taylor, and your involvement with her and her husband, Andrew Taylor."

"There's not much to tell. I met Andrew in Kamerynville at a place where I was a server. It was about four months ago, just before I moved here. He would come in for lunch and always flirted with me. It was ridiculous. The guy wore a wedding band, and he acted like he had never seen a woman before. He tipped very well, so I put up with it for a while. Until one day, he came up to me and said that he wanted to go out with me. He even told me that he was ready to leave his wife. I told him he was nuts, and my manager asked him to leave. He stalked me for weeks, until I moved here. Then, he started showing up here. He'd drive around looking for me. I saw him do that on several occasions. He's a creepy guy."

"He seemed creepy," Sam reiterated. Like I said, when I saw him riding around about a month ago, he was looking for his wife, Linda. He told me she left him."

"Yeah, he said that to you 'cause he knew you were my boss. Sam, you can be so naive. He wasn't looking for Linda. He was looking for me. He showed my picture to several people in this place. He was creepy. Then, one day, he stopped coming around. I thought it was because you had said something to him. Did you tell him to leave me alone?" Linda asked Sam.

"No, I didn't 'cause I didn't know he was stalking you. I would've done a lot more than that if you had told me about him."

"I was gonna, but then he stopped showing up. He was looking for me, and for a way to get past you. Why do you think I was getting so nervous? Then, the other creep started hitting on me. You know, Gavin Green. He was even creepier. That guy had no conscience. He was after sex and nothing else. I didn't tell you this, but he attacked me in the wine cellar the night you fired him. I fought him off, but I know what he was after. I'm sorry I didn't tell you, Sam. I didn't want to upset you."

"You should've told me. As your boss, it's my job to protect you."

"I'm sorry. But he's gone now and so is Andrew, right? Andrew's gone, right? Right, Inspector?" she asked.

"Yes, Miss."

"Thanks, Elaine. I'll come by and talk in a few minutes, if that's okay?" Sam asked.

"That'd be fine," she replied. "I really am sorry."

After Elaine closed the door, the two men walked down the hall toward Sam's office.

"Well, that solves that. Now, if you could solve my bigger problem," Sam told the Inspector in passing.

"What problem is that?"

"My chef is missing, again. He keeps mysteriously disappearing."

"Really? Where does he go?" The Inspector's ears perked up.

"I have no idea."

*　*　*　*　*

"It's not a werewolf, Rachel. But it is a wolf, and a big one." Kelly was perplexed. She had no desire to take on this large wild animal. But what was it guarding? "Maybe he's guarding Anna," she whispered.

"You know, Ariella mentioned that she used to have a large wolf as a pet, and I swear I saw that same wolf waiting for her at the edge of the woods a couple weeks ago. Kelly, I think she's nearby."

"I guess we'd better investigate."

"Great. We have to walk up to a huge, wild wolf, and hope that it doesn't kill us or maim us. That doesn't sound like a great plan, Kelly," Rachel objected. She had barely finished her sentence when they heard a noise behind them. "What was that?"

"Get behind that tree!" Kelly ordered. She, too, hid behind a large oak. The noise came closer. It was nearly upon them. Kelly reached into her pocket and fingered the small gun she had smuggled with her. She was about to pull it out when Molly appeared around the bend in the path, closely followed by Chen.

"What're you two doing here?" Kelly whispered, as she stepped out from behind the tree onto the path.

"Kelly! We found you! I told you she'd be down this path, Chen. Aren't you glad you came along?"

Both Molly and Chen gave Kelly a hug before she could stop them. At the sight of Rachel standing next to a large tree, Molly tapped Chen on the shoulder, for he was still embracing the reluctant Kelly. "I think we just blew her cover," she whispered.

Kelly tried to smooth over the confusion. "Rachel, you can come out now. These are my friends, Molly and Chen. Guys, this is Rachel. She's been my brave guide."

"Who are you guys, really?" Rachel asked, after all the introductions.

"Well, it appears that you're onto us, Rachel. But we need you to keep this our secret. Will you promise to keep a secret from the other girls, especially from Ariella?" Kelly asked.

"Sure. You're the police, aren't you?"

The three detectives looked at each other. "Yes. How'd you guess?"

"You look like a cop." Rachel pointed at Chen.

"Great," Chen mumbled, as he fixed his baseball cap. "I look like a cop even in this outfit."

"Especially in that outfit," Rachel replied and laughed. She had a great sense of humor, and her laughter was addictive. Soon, they were all laughing, forgetting the large wolf that watched them from the far edge of the meadow. Their presence was well known to him now.

"Glad you're here, but we've got a wolf problem." Kelly pointed at the large animal staring at them from a distance.

"Yikes! He's a big boy. I hope he doesn't come this way!" Chen exclaimed.

"Well, at least now we have numbers on our side, and I know I can outrun you, Chen." Kelly laughed.

Just, then, two figures materialized from behind the large oak tree that dominated the far end of the meadow. The wolf appeared to obey the woman in the flowing, white dress. Without looking up, the two figures disappeared into the woods beyond the clearing. They appeared to be in a hurry.

"That's Ariella, but someone new is with her," Kelly observed.

"Why are you after Ariella? She's the nicest person in the world." Rachel spoke her mind.

"We know that, Rachel," Kelly consoled her. "We're not going to hurt her. We're trying to find Anna, and Ariella might know where she is. Do you know the other person?"

"I think he's the hermit that lives around here."

"Hermit?" the team looked at each other. This was a new player that had not appeared on any previous radar screens. "Are they friends?"

"I don't know. She never mentioned 'im," Rachel replied.

"Well, we better not lose them," Molly said, as she ran down the path.

Ariella and Harry, the aforementioned hermit, had an advantage over the team. They knew the woods so well they could walk through them blindfolded. In addition, they had a very large wolf as a companion. It became a strenuous effort to keep up with them.

"They're heading toward the river, toward Devils Bridge," Rachel said.

"Good, we may get our cell signal back," Molly observed.

Chen checked his phone. "No signal yet," he replied.

"If you're trying to help Ariella, why didn't you let her know you were here when you had a chance back at the meadow?" Rachel asked Molly. The two had taken the lead.

"We don't want to slow them down or distract her. We'll be her backup if she needs it," Molly replied, trying to quell Rachel's concerns for her mentor.

"I see. You realize Ariella knows you're following her anyway," Rachel observed.

"Probably."

"Can we slow down?" Chen asked, taking up the rear.

"No. We can't lose 'em," Molly replied. They were jogging down the wooded path toward Devils Bridge. Rachel was leading since she knew the way.

Chen was puffing. He and Kelly were starting to fall behind.

"She knows exactly where she's going. She's on a mission," Molly concluded. "Do you suppose she knows where Anna's hidden?"

"She knows," Rachel answered.

"I'm getting a signal. I need to call Cabot," Chen proclaimed. "Can we please slow down?"

"You can fall behind, if you want, Chen, but we're not slowing down." Molly was clearly in charge and her laser focus was indisputable.

Chen did not want to lose the team, so he postponed the call. "There's the river." He pointed to the ribbon of water that had come into view below them. Presently, they came upon the steep ridge that created the west side of the Eden Valley.

"And there's Devils Bridge," Molly replied. *This may end where it started*, she thought. *I just hope it doesn't end with another death.* "Let's pick up the pace, guys! They're pulling away!" She broke into a run.

"Damn, where do you get your energy, Molly?" Chen yelled from the rear. His legs were aching and his lungs were burning.

"I love to run."

"Great, and I love to sit. What about you, Kelly?" Chen asked Kelly, who was just ahead of him.

"I like to party," she replied, visibly out of wind.

Rachel took up the lead with Molly close behind her. The faster pace began to cleave the small group in two as Kelly and Chen fell farther and farther behind. "Come on, you two! The bridge is down this steep slope, and we can't lose 'em. It looks like they're already crossing it," Molly yelled back at Kelly and Chen.

"How're those old people kicking our butt?" Chen huffed.

"Old? They're in their thirties," Kelly said between gasps.

"Like I said, how're those old people kicking our butt?"

"You're killing me, Chen. I need to stop. Yell up to Molly that we're slowing down," Kelly insisted and slowed to a walk. Chen did the same, after yelling up to Molly, who did not change her pace. "At least we have a good view from the top of this ridge," Kelly concluded.

They could see that Ariella and her two odd companions, a hermit and a large wolf, had already crossed the bridge and were headed down the road toward The Raven Inn. Molly and Rachel were halfway down the steep hill, in hot pursuit.

"You know Rachel will make a fine detective someday," Chen observed, as he and Kelly cautiously began to scramble down the steep wooded incline toward the bridge. "We're never going to catch them. Maybe we'd better see where Ariella's headed while we have a vantage point."

"That sounds like a great excuse to sit down," Kelly replied and laughed.

"Exactly. Let's observe before we strike."

"It's more like we're going to miss the party at this rate."

They caught their breath, while Chen called the Inspector. He did not reach him but left him an urgent message.

"Look. From up here you can see Ariella's headed toward the Green Estate. There she goes into the property. What a view from here! There's Molly. She's at the bridge. We'd better get down there, Chen," Kelly proclaimed and began her descent toward Devils Bridge. Chen reluctantly followed.

* * * * *

"Harry, are you sure those caves are back here?" Ariella asked, as Harry took over the lead, for he knew these woods better than anyone. His memory of the past was still very clouded, but he understood the urgency of Ariella's task.

They had begun to follow the old logging road that led deep into the eastern wooded portion of the expansive Green Estate. Although these woods were closer to Kamerynville and civilization than the North Woods, they were much darker and thicker with undergrowth. The only clear access was the old logging trail, the very trail on which the Inspector had discovered Andrew Taylor's abandoned blue truck, now in police custody.

This primordial forest, called Bloody Hallows by the early settlers, had a violent history, as the nickname implied. Here, in this deep maze of dolomite caverns and weathered fissures that took the form of steep walled passages, a bloody skirmish occurred between the early settlers and the native tribes. That history predated the later settlers, such as the Greens and the Drakes. It was over three hundred years ago that this soil and this stone were drenched in the blood of the nameless victims of western progression.

The name of this natural labyrinth dated back to that event. Although it was of geological and historical interest, the Bloody Hallows were largely forgotten because they were entirely encompassed by the privately-owned and long-neglected Green Estate.

"I'm sure I can find that cave," Harry replied, "but are you sure she's in it?"

In what amounted to a mental avalanche, Harry's prolonged, battle-induced shroud had rapidly lifted. Unlike Lenore's memory loss, which had been physically induced and took time for the physical trauma to heal, Harry's was a subconscious choice brought on by extreme physical and mental suffering. As a result, it returned much faster, like a dam that had suddenly broken.

"I'm sure. Remember I told you years ago that I had a strange power inherited from my mother?" she asked.

"You mean the ability to connect with 'Spirit,' as you use to call it? Wow, it's all coming back so fast!"

"Yes, what a miracle! Anyway, over the years that we were apart I worked hard to improve that gift and it's pretty powerful now," she replied and chuckled.

"So, you 'saw' this cave and Anna in it?"

"Yes. I also saw her captor. Tragically, I created him, Harry."

"You didn't create him, Erin. He created himself." He liked to call her Erin. He wasn't used to her new name, which she selected at the end of her shamanic transformation.

"We can debate that later, but right now we must save Anna. I'm sure she's there. Let's keep running. You sure this is the way, Harry?"

"Yes. I'm certain." He pointed to the wall of dolomite that loomed in the foreground.

They headed into a narrow passage formed by a large, eroded fracture. Here, the forest transformed into a natural maze carved out of the native dolomite. The fractures in the rock had been eroded by water over millennia. This erosive force, combined with tectonic uplift that continually pushed these soft rock formations to the surface, created a labyrinth of steep-walled passages, some of which were over twenty feet deep. It was like a huge English maze made of stone, instead of holly or boxwood.

Deep inside the maze was a set of caves that, unlike the passages that led toward them, had a ceiling of more resistant quartz sandstone. It was as if the passages had a natural roof at the far end of the maze. Farther still, some of these caves plunged deeper into the earth, beyond the level of the natural groundwater, as they followed the gently dipping strata of ancient dolomite. Thus, many were flooded in the deepest sections.

In the modern era, only two men had ever explored this labyrinth to the degree that they knew every passage. One of those men now returned. The other had died four years ago. Harry Schaffer and George Walker were best friends until war tore them apart. Together, they had found a clue to a treasure that had spurred legends—the fabled Drake's treasure. It had been moved here by Drake himself before his murder by fellow privateers.

Wisely, Drake had not buried it in soil, like most treasure. Rather, it was buried by water. It lay in one of the flooded passages in the deepest cave. There, in pitch black cave water, rested a pirate's treasure stolen from a Spanish galleon over 200 years ago. It was so inaccessible that they had only recovered a small portion. They were sworn to secrecy, but one of them broke his promise.

George, a virtuous man like his father, Rev. James Walker, kept the secret until he died. When Harry had to go to war, he left his portion of the treasure with George, who had never sold the coins for fear of starting a crazed treasure hunt. Rather, after Harry disappeared, he placed them in a safe deposit box, which he later willed to Erin Stone, Harry's wife. That is how the money ended up with Erin, aka Ariella.

However, Harry, in his youthful eagerness, had told his girlfriend, Erin, about the discovery. That exchange had been overheard by one other soul, Jerry McAlester, Harry's old grammar school friend. Fortunately, Harry had not revealed the location, never mentioning the Bloody Hallows to Erin or anyone else. But he had revealed the discovery of the treasure, which spurred a group of his fellow classmates to go on a futile treasure hunt. These included Jerry, Sam Hughes, and Will Porter.

Molly was surprised that Ariella led them back to the mysterious Green Estate. She was even more surprised when Ariella and Harry passed the farmhouse and headed down the old logging trail. *I can't drag this young woman into this,* she reflected silently. Conversely, Rachel seemed eager to be part of a police investigation, which she perceived to be geared toward helping Ariella.

"Rachel, thank you for all your help, but I need you to stay here and tell the others where I went; otherwise, they may never find me. It's really important. I need you to stay back at the old gate, and, when Kelly and Chen arrive, tell them to head down the old logging road." She pointed toward the far end of the large, grassy meadow that stretched beyond the dilapidated farmhouse.

"But I want to follow Ariella and make sure she's okay."

"She'll be fine. I'll make sure of that. I really need you to stay here. Please. It's important. You can help Ariella the most by sending the rest of the team after me. I will need them."

Rachel reluctantly agreed and stayed behind to wait for Kelly and Chen. Molly quickened her pace, plunging into the woods along the old logging trail. She ran the entire way, hoping to catch up to Ariella and Harry. The road narrowed after about a mile and a half, transforming into a walking trail. Despite her quickened pace, she had lost track of the fleeing couple. Soon, she found herself in the bizarre stone maze. *I've never seen anything like this,* she thought. *It's a natural labyrinth. How the heck am I supposed to find them in this place?*

As she entered the maze, she kept listening for movements ahead of her, but failed to notice the dark figure that had crept behind her—trapping her in the maze.

CHAPTER 68

Recollection

Amos Miller, the young Amish farmer, harvested corn with a team of four mules. He did not mind the hard work, for this was a time of reward. His crop grew better than the past two years, which had been plagued by drought. This year the corn was plentiful, with multiple large ears on every stalk.

The late afternoon sun plummeted toward the horizon, turning everything a precious shade of gold as Amos approached his barn with another wagon full of corn. As he neared the silos, he saw an open buggy coming up the driveway. Pulling his mules to a stop in front of the barn, he ran to meet the visitor pulling up to the front of the farmhouse. Before long, he enjoyed a warm embrace from his welcomed guest.

"I missed ya so much," she whispered into his ear as he reluctantly let her go.

"Can ya stay for a while?" he asked.

"For about an hour, then mother needs me for supper," Lenore replied.

"Come sit on the porch. Can I get ya anything?"

"No. I have all I need right here."

Another passionate embrace followed. This one ended with a fervent kiss. It took three such embraces before the couple finally reached the porch and settled onto a large, bench swing. Amos placed his arm around her, while she rested her head on his shoulder. Looking up at him, she finally spoke. "I had to tell ya first."

"What? What do ya have to tell me?"

"I remembered everything, und it's so scary," she revealed in a sad voice.

"Ya can tell me." He tried to console her.

"Ya might feel differently about me after ya hear it." She looked at him sincerely, her brown eyes mesmerizing. In that moment, Lenore could have told Amos anything and he could not love her any more or any less. She could see the love in his eyes, which gave her assurance to continue.

"Well, I remember that after I ran away, I wandered about Kamerynville. No one seemed to want to hire me, und there waz so little I knew about the ways of the English. I slept in the park the first night, wondering what I had done."

"Ya poor thing. I shouldn't have let ya go. I'm so sorry. It's all my fault." Amos squeezed her tighter.

"It waz my decision, Amos. Don't be sorry. Anyway, I waz desperate that night. But, the next morning waz market day in the same park. I awoke to people setting up stands all around me. It waz then that I realized that *Dat* would be there for the Amish Market." She paused to compose herself.

"Yes?"

"I waz torn. Here waz my chance to go back. Part of me wanted to go back to see ya und my family, but part of me waz scared of the embarrassment in front of the entire community. Besides, I wazn't sure if *Dat* would shun me. He waz supposed to shun me. What if I tried to go to 'im, und he pretended I did not exist? That would've killed me inside. Anyway, I waz scared to stay und scared to leave, so I simply sat there on the park bench while all around me people, including Amish folks that I knew, started putting up stands und tents. The Amish folks who knew me ignored me, except for a few children. But soon their mothers pulled them away. I guess the word spread quickly that I had left for good. I'll never forget what one mother told her children. It was Janet Stoltzfus. God bless her. She waz simply following the rules, but it hurt me to hear it."

"What did she say?"

"She told them, 'That's not Lenore. There's no Lenore, anymore.' The oldest child, her daughter Judith, objected, but she corrected her by insisting, 'Lenore's shunned. She's no more.' I remember Judith asking if I waz a ghost. I guess Janet ran out of patience because she simply replied, 'yes.' After that, the children were all scared of me. It waz then that I knew I couldn't go back. I cried my eyes out on that bench for an hour or more. In that time, I saw Josef und my dad setting up their stand, but if they saw me, they did not acknowledge me. I began to feel like a ghost." She teared up as she told her story.

"I'm so sorry," Amos replied and hugged her tight.

She took a few moments to regain her composure, before continuing. "Well, as I sat there lost und alone, this beautiful woman in a white, flowing dress appeared seemingly out of nowhere. At first, I thought I waz seeing things. I thought she waz an angel. That sounds silly, doesn't it?"

"No, not at all." Amos comforted her.

"Ya're the sweetest man in the world," she replied and they kissed once more.

"Well, it turns out she waz very real. She told me of a place for runaways. It turns out that it waz her place. Her name waz Ariella. She ran a shelter up in the North Woods, up along the river about four miles north of The Raven Inn. She offered me shelter but I did not know who to trust, so I refused. To make a long story short, I wandered about the valley for another week or so but couldn't find a job. I waz getting hungry and desperate."

"I should not have let you go," Amos replied. He felt a sense of heavy guilt.

"Hush, it waz my choice. Anyway, I wandered up into the North Woods. They're beautiful but scary. I got lost for several days. Until, one morning, I awoke and there she stood, angelic as before. She did not say a word. She already seemed to know all. There waz kindness in her eyes. They spoke for her. She simply took me by the hand und led me out of those dark woods right into her home. It turned out she did run a place for runaway girls like me. It was a happy place und I waz blessed to find her. I guess I should say I waz blessed that she found me, or more like never gave up on me, for I don't think she ever lost sight of me. I lived with her und several other girls who had no place else to go. The group called themselves the Eden Sisterhood, but really they were just a group of friends. I lived there for seven weeks, und it was a very happy time in my life. They're a great group. They're very caring." She paused to organize her thoughts. Although her memory appeared to have completely returned, her acceptance of those memories felt difficult at times. Some did not feel like they belonged to her.

"So what happened next? How'd you end up in the river? Do you remember that?"

"That's where things got pretty weird, und I have to trust that I am recalling everything the way it really happened."

"I'm sure ya are, Lenore."

"Well, here goes. One morning, I followed Ariella into the woods. She always rose before dawn und seemed to disappear across the wide meadow behind her cabin. She'd simply vanish for a few hours into the woods, leaving me und the other girls until nine o'clock or so. Then, she'd return refreshed und joyful. It waz as if she needed to transform every morning. I know it's odd. She'd say it waz her recharge. When I asked her about it, she seemed guarded, providing simple answers about walking in the woods und meditating. Well, ya know me, I'm so darn curious. Anyway, one morning, in early August, I followed her at a distance, managing to keep out of sight without losing her. It helps that Pa und I used to sneak up on groundhogs to clear them out of the fields," she said and chuckled.

Amos was all ears. "So, what'd ya see? Wait 'til I tell ya about what's been happening at Drakes Plot. But we'll leave that for another day."

"Okay. I'd love to hear it. We've got so much to catch up on, Amos."

"Yes, we do. So, what happened next?"

"Ya're cute the way ya asked that," she replied.

He could not help himself and kissed her once more. They were not a reserved Amish couple. After all that they had endured, neither had much respect for religious roadblocks as far as their relationship was concerned.

"I could kiss ya all evening, but ya need to go in a half hour. So, what happened?" Amos asked after finally prying himself from her lips.

"Well, ya'll just have to trust me here, 'cause even I doubt what I saw," Lenore whispered.

"I believe every word. I promise."

"So I followed her but I think she knew I waz there. I think she wanted me to see what I saw. That sounded funny, 'see what I saw.' Sorry. I get so easily distracted these days."

"It's part of the recovery."

"If ya say so. Well, Ariella ended up at this beautiful crystal-clear pool that waz fed by a waterfall. It's an amazing place that somehow seems largely undiscovered by everyone but Ariella. Maybe she has some sort of spell around it. Anyway, it waz her sanctuary." Lenore paused to regain her thoughts once more. She seemed to struggle to clearly remember what happened next. Amos waited patiently this time, trying not to divert the conversation. He was very eager to know more.

Lenore became very still as she recalled what happened next. Then, she began in a soft voice that was no louder than a whisper. "She walked up to the pool, which waz illuminated by beams of morning sunlight. She disrobed und plunged into the pool."

"The English love swimming naked," said Amos.

"Why would ya say that? Ya have a lot of experience in that area that I don't know about?" Lenore asked.

Amos turned red. "No. I just based that on what ya said."

"Sure. Ya're blushing, Amos Miller. Have ya been skinny dipping with English girls?"

"Stop, go on." He was glad to have her back in full form. "Seriously, what happened next?"

"Okay, okay… she dove under the waterfall und disappeared."

"Disappeared?"

"Yes. But it gets stranger. Soon after she disappeared…This is the crazy part. Ya sure ya want to hear this?"

"Yes! Ya can't leave me hanging."

"Sure I can. Oh, my goodness, look at the time. I need to go."

"Lenore, that's mean. That's really mean. Ya still have twenty minutes."

"Okay, I'll stay. But, no more interruptions, young man."

"Not even for a kiss?"

"No more interruptions, except for a kiss." She giggled again.

He loved her giggle. It seemed to light up the world and paint it in warm, glowing colors that never faded, not even after the sun had set. He knew that he would fall asleep tonight with that giggle in his memory. To him, she was everything. As he reflected on this, he missed the next part of her story. "Can ya say that again?"

"Weren't ya paying attention?"

"Yes, but ya have a way of distracting me."

"Is that a good thing?"

"Very much a good thing. In fact, it's a great thing. I can't wait for a lifetime of yar distractions. Ya can distract me forever, Lenore Lapp."

She smiled, realizing that this was the first time he admitted a "forever" with her.

"Okay, I'll say it again. After Ariella disappeared beneath the surface of the pool for over five minutes, I saw what looked like a ghost in the same flowing, white dress that Ariella wore. I remember rubbing my eyes to make sure I wazn't imagining it, but I wazn't. There she waz floating over the pool toward the waterfall. I thought I waz going crazy. I didn't dare to breathe. I simply stayed hidden in the thicket. The odd phantom simply remained floating in thin air near the waterfall, while the light of the sun passed right through her. I swear it did. Amos waz I going crazy?"

Amos had let go of Lenore and stared at her before smiling. "If ya're crazy, then so am I."

"What do ya mean?"

"I saw the same ghost a week ago up here at Drakes Plot. Otto waz with me und saw her too. I could tell by the way he reacted. There's been a lot of talk about a ghost lately. It's the ghost of Evelyn Drake. I'm sure of it."

"Ya saw her too? Really? Ya not just saying that to be nice?"

"No. I did, but I'll tell ya about that later. Before ya have to leave, please tell me what else happened?"

"The ghost disappeared about ten minutes later und Ariella appeared out of the water soon after that. She got dressed und headed back home. I tried to follow her, except that she saw me. We talked und I told her what I saw. She didn't seem fazed by it, although she didn't seem convinced about the ghost. But she did tell me that there's a small cave behind the waterfall, und that's where she often goes to meditate und recharge. I guess the only way to get to it is to enter underwater. Since I don't know how to swim, I wazn't about to look for the cave. But the ghost thing scared me."

"It scared me too," Amos reflected. "What happened next? We still have fifteen minutes."

"I stayed with the sisterhood for a couple more weeks, und although I waz happy, I missed ya und I missed my family. One morning, I finally got the courage to come back to ya. But I can't bear tearful partings, so I simply slipped away, leaving nothing behind but a farewell note for Ariella."

"But ya didn't come back to me. Did ya change ya mind? Ya were always welcomed back. Ya know if ya repent, ya can come back. Besides, I'd never shun ya, Lenore. Not for anything. I would've taken ya back regardless. I really would've. Why didn't ya come?"

"I tried. I really did, but I never made it here."

"What happened?"

"I'd better make this quick. I really need to get back home."

"Would ya rather tell me another time?"

"No, I just need to tell ya quickly. Ya need to know everything," she insisted, before resuming her story. "I walked along the footpath that heads by the river, und when I got to Devils Bridge I ran into him."

"Him?"

"Yes, the odd English. He seemed very sweet. He convinced me not to go back right away, but to wait a while. He convinced me that ya'd all shunned me, und I couldn't come back just like that. I believed him 'cause I recalled how Janet Stoltzfus proclaimed me for dead."

"Since when does Janet Stoltzfus decide anything? I would've taken ya back, Lenore. Ya're back, aren't ya?" Amos insisted.

"I know, my love, but at the time, I didn't trust myself. Anyway, he offered me a place to stay, at least until I figured it out. He gave me shelter in the old farmhouse by Devils Bridge."

"The old Green place? I thought that place was abandoned?"

"Well, it is, und it's not."

"What do you mean?"

"This Englishman lived there. His family owned the farm, but he didn't keep it up or anything. He waz an odd one. His name waz Gavin Green."

"Gavin Green!" Amos pulled away again and looked at her as if she were the ghost now.

"What's the matter? Do ya know him?" she asked, startled by his reaction.

"Gavin Green's dead. Abel Snyder found his body under Devils Bridge a few weeks ago, not far from where Josef found you."

"Dead? Are ya sure?"

"Yes. Gavin Green's dead. Ya stayed with him?"

"I stayed at his house for only about a week. He started to get really creepy und I got scared." She looked Amos straight in the eyes to reassure him.

"Oh, Lenore. That sounds awful."

"It gets worse," she warned. "Can I ask ya a favor, Amos?"

"Sure. What?"

"Can ya put yur arms around me again und hold me tight as I tell this part? It frightens me to speak of it."

"Gladly. What happened?" He placed his right arm around her waist and held her tight, while holding her hands with his left. They were intertwined once more, giving Lenore the courage to proceed with her confession.

She let out a heavy sigh before resuming her tale. "Well, the place waz horrible. It waz completely rundown und full of odd books und candles. I had a small room with a mattress on the floor. He slept in an old bed in another room. The kitchen had no running water, und everything waz old und dusty, even the plates und cabinets. There waz an old dug well und an outhouse. The entire place felt gloomy, und there waz an odd smell about it, like sweet-smelling smoke. Later, I discovered that it waz marijuana smoke.

Even the books were creepy. They were about witchcraft und devils. When I questioned him, he told me odd things about an evil Raven und his war with the White Witch. It waz all very odd. He seemed obsessed with this White Witch. Then, he started to threaten me if I said anything to anyone. He didn't trust me. He even tried coming on to me, but I managed to fend him off. After that, he locked me in the attic." She was visibly upset and paused.

"Ya can tell me the rest later. It's okay."

"No, I want to tell ya now, while I have the courage," she replied. "Where waz I? Yes, that attic waz very creepy. It waz full of dusty old clothing, und cobweb-covered odds und ends. The scariest of all waz a large stuffed raven with yellow eyes that sat above an old wardrobe und stared down at me. It waz a terrible place. I wrote a poem to pass the time. Ya know how I need to write when I get scared.

"The next night, I saw a few of his friends coming over. Some never seemed to leave. The party lasted all night und people were passed out all over the lawn. I could see them in the morning from my window. They were doing drugs und acting very strange. It waz the worst time in my life. I waz so scared.

"A few nights later, I managed to sneak out 'cause Gavin forgot to lock the attic door. I started running, determined to come here. At first, I got disoriented by the thick fog, but eventually I found the road to Devils Bridge. When I got halfway across the bridge, some-one waz waiting there for me in the shadows. He stepped out, but I could not see his face. He wore a dark black hood. He appeared like an image of death, itself. I turned to run away, but there waz another hooded figure standing behind me. They must have been hiding in the shadows of the bridge timbers. 'Oh, no ya don't. Ya're not going anywhere,' the first one said. He laughed a most sinister laugh, like he waz enjoying himself." She stopped, sighed, and pressed her face into Amos's shoulder. He eagerly comforted her.

"I need to tell ya the rest before I leave." She pulled away a little but did not let go. "As the two surrounded me, the leader said something I wish I could forget. He said it in the coldest voice that chilled me to the core. He said, 'Foolish Lenore. Too bad ya didn't join us. Now, ya need to pay the price.'

"I noticed the long iron bar he waz holding in his right hand. As he raised his arm to strike me, I saw the raven tattoo on his right arm. It looked like that dreadful bird in the attic. That awful image waz the last thing I remember. Mercifully, I awoke hours later to find dear Josef hunched over me. Ya know the rest. Thank God, I'm back, Amos. I don't ever want to leave the Amish, again. I waz wrong. I waz wrong to leave. But I'm scared that Raven guy will find me und kill me."

He hugged her in his arms and whispered in her ear. "I'll never leave ya, und nothing'll harm ya again 'cause it'd never get past me. Nothing'll harm ya again, Lenore. No, nevermore, my dear. Nevermore."

CHAPTER 69

The Lone Wolf

Rachel sat patiently by the old gate at the overgrown entrance to the Green Estate. Within minutes, she saw Kelly and Chen headed toward her as they crossed Devils Bridge. With her focus on them, she did not notice the car coming toward her from the opposite direction, the direction of The Raven Inn. It drove quickly. As she turned to face it, the black SUV passed her and headed toward the bridge. She saw it stop in the distance, and, to her surprise, both Kelly and Chen got into it. *Who's that?* she wondered. Her question was soon answered, as the vehicle turned around and headed back, pulling up in front of her. When it stopped, Kelly sprang out of the passenger seat.

"Rachel, where's Molly?" she asked.

"She headed down the logging trail after Ariella. She told me to come back here and wait for you, so I did. Can I come along?"

"You did the right thing." Kelly dodged the question, pondering what to do with the brave young woman. To take her along was dangerous. To leave her here was irresponsible. She decided that Rachel would be safer with her, rather than roaming about the Green Estate on her own.

"Sure, get in."

The Inspector was not happy to have a civilian passenger along on a police mission, but Kelly adamantly replied, "She's my responsibility. Can we leave it at that?" and opened the passenger-side rear door for Rachel, who sat down next to Chen. Introductions were brief since there was no time to waste. The Inspector accelerated the unmarked police SUV down the logging road in pursuit of Molly and Ariella.

"There's a new development, but I'll tell you later," the Inspector added, looking over at Kelly, as if to say, "Foolish girl, I can't tell you in front of our civilian guest."

As they reached the end of the logging road, it became clear that the rest of the journey would have to be on foot. "Kelly, stay here with the girl," the Inspector ordered. "Chen, let's go. Make sure your safety's off," he instructed. "It's hard to say what we'll find. Kelly, I'll call you if I need you. Don't call me unless it's an emergency and make sure your friend's safe at all times," he insisted, before he and Chen jogged down the trail, leaving Kelly and Rachel in the car alone.

* * * * *

"Harry, are you sure the cave's back here?" Ariella asked, as the two penetrated deeper and deeper into the narrowing fissures of the maze. The wolf was just ahead of them, paving the trail.

"Wolf's picked up a scent. This is the right way."

"Harry, his name isn't Wolf. His name's Cane, and he was looking after you for me. Cane and I go back many years, but that's a long story," she replied.

"I can't wait to hear all your stories, Erin. But right now we need to find Anna. The sad thing is that I don't even know what she looks like," Harry sighed. The war and its aftermath had robbed him of being a father.

"She's tall, beautiful, and smart. But, most of all, she's so innocent, and she's always seeking to learn. You'll love her."

"I already do. Look! Cane stopped."

The wolf waited, staring at a small opening approximately twenty yards ahead. It formed the terminus of the tight, steep-walled canyon that surrounded them. As they penetrated further into the maze of eroded fractures, surrounded by sheer walls of dark gray dolomite, the crevices grew deeper and narrower until they stopped. At that seeming dead end, the dark opening presented a passage to the underground network before them. That labyrinth of caverns formed over millions of years by the same geological uplift and water runoff that had eroded these fractures, except that from here on, the system dove underground into a dark, formidable fortress of intertwined caves and natural shafts.

"That's it, and by Wolf's, I mean Cane's, reaction, someone's in there," Harry observed.

"He has Anna in there. I know it. I can feel his evil. It's like an energy scent. Cane smells him and I feel him. His stench is undeniable. He's in there. We better be careful. This is one of those times I wish I had a gun," Ariella confessed.

"You mean you don't?"

"No, I don't believe in them. But we have a wolf. That counts for something."

"Not against a gun, Erin. We better be silent. Wolf, Cane…silence!"

The three crept through the cave entrance. It was pitch black inside. "We can't see a thing in here," Ariella objected. "I didn't count on that and I always forget my cell phone. I just can't get used to it."

"I got us covered." Harry produced a small flashlight.

"How'd you end up with that? That's my flashlight," Ariella objected.

"I know. I found it near your waterfall weeks ago. I might've lost my mind, but I've always been resourceful," he replied with a chuckle. Like Lenore, Harry struggled with his regained memory. In that respect, they both seemed to travel parallel paths, except he had lost years, while she lost only weeks. Thus, for Harry, the transition to present reality seemed even greater. But he had no time to ponder himself or his challenges. His focus was on saving the daughter he had never known.

"Yes. You were always resourceful, Harry."

"This is for when we get deeper," he referred to the flashlight. "For now, we go without a light. Follow me. Once your eyes adjust, you'll see the way for a while. We don't want to give ourselves away with the light if we don't have to."

"Harry, let Cane go first. He can follow the scent."

They plunged into the dark passage with the wolf leading them. Soon, it became pitch-black as the cave narrowed to a tight tunnel. Silent, barely breathing, Harry refused to use the light for fear of warning their enemy. His army training had returned and provided the edge he needed. Besides, he knew this cave from his youth, having explored it with his best friend, George Walker. He knew that soon the passage would open, and they would enter a large room full of stalactites and stalagmites. This was the first of three large chambers that comprised the heart of this subterranean fortress. As they neared the end of the tunnel, they could see a glimmering light in the distance. In the darkness, the small light seemed as bright as the sun. Here, the tunnel widened.

Harry beckoned Cane to stop and pressed past him to take the lead. For the next twenty feet, they had to crawl until they came to the edge of the tunnel. Before them was a beautiful room, the size of a large barn. In the dim light, the stalactites and stalagmites cast shadows that transformed into thin forms. A flickering light made the shadows dance like ghosts of an ancient past, when Native Americans and their ancestors used these grounds as a sacred shelter from a world of strange predators. The room was vented at its ceiling through an unseen crevice. This allowed the air to stream into it and allowed the small fire at the back of the room to consume the dry wood in hungry orange flames. A sole woman sat by the fire with her back to them. She seemed to be warming herself.

"Is that her?" Harry whispered.

Ariella moved past him toward the entrance to the cavernous hall. She strained her eyes to recognize the lone woman before them. As she moved a bit closer, she slipped, pushing a small stone out of the mouth of the tunnel to the cave floor two feet below. Although the sound of the small, falling stone was subtle, in the silence of the surroundings, it was like ringing the front doorbell of a hellish hall. Now, the form turned toward them, revealing a face that made Ariella cringe.

* * * * *

Molly had become so focused on her quest that she did not notice the man following her into the maze of fissures and crevices. He stalked her for a while, knowing that she remained oblivious to his presence. The game of cat and mouse would have played out longer had it not been for the crows. These vile creatures descended upon a nearby tree that hung over the edge of the fissure walls. Their ruckus made Molly look about her. Instinctively, she drew her gun at the shadowy form that stood no more than twenty paces behind her.

"Don't shoot. You'll warn them we're here," the man instructed her, little fazed by the turn of events. She recognized the voice. As he stepped out of the shadows, his features confirmed her suspicions.

"So, it was you all along. My bet was on you," Molly replied. She kept her gun pointed at the man who stood before her.

"Then, you lost your bet, Molly," he replied calmly.

"I don't think so. Where is she? What have you done with her?"

"Anna, I assume. Or are you looking for Linda?"

"Linda? No, Anna. Where is she?"

"I'm pretty sure she's straight ahead, but in this place, it's hard to tell. I got lost in here the other day. It took me most of the afternoon to find my way out of this maze, and I didn't find the cave entrance."

"What cave entrance? Cut the bullshit, McAlester. Where're you holding her, you drug-dealing murderer."

"Wow. You sure think highly of me." He chuckled and began to walk toward her.

"Stop, or I'll shoot you!"

"I'd advise against that."

"Don't tempt me."

"Shooting a man in cold blood would not look good on your resume," he replied, but he stopped in his tracks just in case she really meant it.

"Shooting a cold-blooded killer in self-defense would look just fine."

"Until the truth came out, for this isn't self-defense and I'm not a killer."

"I've had enough. Lie down on the ground, hands behind your back," she ordered, pointing the gun.

"Molly. We don't have time to waste. We're after the same guy. I'm with Drug Enforcement."

"Very funny, McAlester."

"Here." He tossed his badge at her.

She carefully picked it up, keeping her eyes and her gun pointed straight at him. Glancing down at the badge, it became clear that Jerry McAlester doubled as an undercover narcotics agent.

"Can you put the gun down, please?"

Molly finally lowered her gun. "What are you doing posing as a chef?"

"It's a long story. But I'm a damn good chef." He laughed. "I'll tell you later. Right now we need to find them. He's got Anna in there. I'm sure of it. A man and a woman disappeared down here a few minutes ago."

"That was probably Ariella and the hobo."

"Ariella and the hobo? What're you talking about?"

"Long story."

"I hear ya."

"No time for stories. Let's hurry. Why didn't you tell me you were a narc?"

"I couldn't blow my cover, could I?"

"Which way now?" Molly asked as they came to a fork in the labyrinth of tight passages.

"I don't know. I've never seen this part. You go down one and I'll take the other," he suggested. "I'll take the wider one and don't make any jokes," he added.

Molly started to like Jerry McAlester. He had a good sense of humor and a fearless mentality. "Scream if you need me," she replied.

"Very funny. By the way, falling for Sam's a very bad idea," he added and disappeared before Molly had a chance to comment.

* * * * *

The Inspector and Chen entered Bloody Hallows and its maze of dolomite fissures. They had no time to admire the little-known natural phenomena. They had to find Molly and Anna.

"This place gives me the creeps. I'm claustrophobic," Chen admitted. They walked single file, with the Inspector keeping several paces ahead.

"So why do you drive a pint-size Fiat?"

"That's different. Wait, did you hear that?"

"What?"

"I thought I heard Molly's voice."

"I didn't hear a thing," the Inspector replied. They both stopped to listen.

"I swear I heard her up ahead."

"Let's quicken the pace and no talking." The Inspector broke into a jog, while trying to remain stealthy.

Soon, they had reached the same crossroads that Molly and Jerry had encountered minutes earlier. "Now what?" Chen asked.

"You take one and I'll take the other," the Inspector instructed.

"I'm taking the wider one. This place feels like it's going to cave in on me," Chen said nervously.

"Fine. I'll take the narrow one," the Inspector replied, choosing the same passage as Molly.

CHAPTER 70

Of Good and Evil

"Who's there?" the woman by the fire asked in a frightened tone. She could not see into the far shadows of the cave, momentarily blinded by the light of the fire.

"I know her," Ariella whispered to Harry. "She came to see me two months ago. Strange girl. Why's she here?"

"Come out of there. I can see you," the woman lied.

"She's unarmed or she'd have drawn a gun," Harry whispered. "I say we let Cane scare her a bit."

"What if she's got a gun? We can't risk it."

"Put your hands up where we can see them!" Harry suddenly bellowed to everyone's surprise. He turned to Ariella and whispered, "Now we'll know for sure."

The woman became visibly frightened and ran toward the left side of the cavern hall, towards a second passage that led deeper into the series of chambers. "Cane, go get her!" Ariella ordered the wolf, who immediately sprang to action.

Cane covered the distance between the cave entrance and the fleeing woman in a matter of seconds. The sight of the large wolf barreling toward her made the woman scream in fear. Before she knew it, she was cornered while still screaming. Ariella and Harry ran toward her, ordering the wolf not to attack, and warning the woman to stop screaming and not to move. She did as ordered and stood pressed against the cave wall, while the large wolf stood before her, ready to pounce.

"Good boy, Cane," Ariella replied. She petted the wolf once she and Harry reached the petrified woman, who continued to cower before the beast. Cane was a formidable creature more than twice the size of a normal wolf—all teeth and muscle covered with a silver-gray coat that evoked a ghostly appearance. His growl made a deep guttural sound that was nothing short of terrifying. He seemed to be far more than a wolf. Cane was "the Wild" incarnate.

"Get him away from me! What is that thing? That's the f—kin' largest wolf I've ever seen," the woman objected.

"He's not budging until you tell us where we can find Anna," Harry said.

"She's probably dead by now."

Cane sensed Ariella's increased tension and growled before she could reply.

"I wouldn't anger him if I were you," Harry warned.

"Where is she?" Ariella asked in a calm but intense voice.

"He's got her. You know who I mean." The woman chuckled nervously.

"Where is he, then?" Harry asked.

The woman instinctively looked toward her left, to a passage that led from the far side of the cave deeper into its sister chambers. "I don't know."

"Cane," Ariella addressed the wolf. The large wolf growled and moved closer to the woman.

"Stop, please! I beg you! Stop him!" the woman pleaded, while pressing herself against the wet cavern wall.

"I know you. You're Linda Taylor, aren't you? You came to see me a while back. Who did that to you, Linda?" Ariella asked, as she walked up to Cane and calmed him.

"What does it matter?" Linda answered. "He does whatever he wants."

"We can help you, Linda," Ariella replied. "Let us help you."

"No thanks, you stupid witch or whoever you think you are. You're powerless against him. And your precious Anna is dead. Don't you know you created her for him to enjoy? That's exactly what he does. There were more, you know. That precious sisterhood's for him, right? You find them and feed them, and he enjoys them. At first, I thought the two of you worked together, but now I see you found yourself this scraggly loser." She looked over at Harry, who was still dressed as a hermit and hadn't shaved in years.

"You watch your mouth," Harry warned.

"Or what, you'll kill me with your stench, you pathetic bum? No, let me guess, you'll sic this beast on me like the coward that you've always been. I know who you are, and so does he. You're Harry Schaffer, and you've got the treasure. That's all that he's after, you know. That's why he asked you to be here. I suppose you thought it was your idea. Well, it's all his idea. You're the pawns and he's the master."

Linda Taylor spoke bravely, no longer fearful. The reason for her newfound courage was standing in the shadows to the left of Harry and Ariella. Linda could see him, and Ariella suddenly felt the pang in her heart that surfaced every time she encountered her nemesis.

"He's here, isn't he?" Harry asked, for he saw Cane's reaction. The wolf began to growl, staring past Harry toward the far passage of the cave.

"Yes, my dear visitors. Welcome. I've been expecting you. Welcome, Erin. Welcome, Harry. Did the mindless scarecrow miraculously find his brain? How useful. Erin, I can't get used to that pretentious name you call yourself these days. No, to me you're the same old whore that you have always been. But, for once, I'm grateful to you. First, you found your daughter for me to enjoy. And now, you've brought me the man I seek, and you healed 'im for me, as I expected, given your predictable sense of misguided loyalty. Bravo, Erin. Bravo."

All eyes turned toward the dark, far corner of the cave. There, in the deepest shadows, stood the form of a man who addressed them.

"Don't try siccing that pathetic beast on me, Erin. I'll kill him without hesitation. I might just for sport." He laughed a sinister laugh. "I've waited for this revenge for much too long. Ah, the pleasure to crush you! That's why I returned here. I came to steal everything from you, bit by bit, like you did from me. It's the day of reckoning. Right here where you and this pathetic hobo first proclaimed your love for each other. Oh, I know. I know everything." He laughed his sinister laugh, once more. He was a man with a dual personality. He could charm and hide his true self, or he could revel in the narcissistic evil that he had chosen to become.

Ariella stood unmoved and silent, with the wolf on her left and Harry on her right. She was trying to read the situation, knowing that only her calmness held the solution.

"Say something, you witch! The White Witch, isn't it? Or what other pretentious name or image do you claim these days? My personal favorite is the White Dove. What shamanic bullshit! It defines your lunacy, Erin. Your endless illusion and refusal to see yourself for who you really are—nothing but a poor farm girl who became a money-hungry harlot. That's what you are. Look in the mirror! You're not the White Witch, or even some powerful White Dove shaman. You're a fraud!

"Oh, and then there's you, Harry. The stench precedes you. You're nothing but a fool, and her next meal ticket. But I'm gonna change all that. I'm gonna give you both a chance to tell me where you hid Drake's treasure. I know you have it. Answer me, you pathetic fool! Answer me, you presumptuous whore!" He was waving his gun about as he stepped into the light. Linda, whose face was black and blue from his recent rage, ran toward him like a loyal cur. He ignored her, for she was nothing to him but a means to this end.

Ariella remained silent, trying to listen for the sounds of her precious Anna. She cared little for this egocentric showmanship. He sensed that in her and became angry. His calm confidence morphed to violent loathing.

"Let's see. I can't shoot him before he tells me where the treasure's hidden. Which is close by, isn't it, Harry? I'm finally close. It's hidden somewhere in Bloody Hallows. I thought it could be in the basement of the old farmhouse or in the graves at Drakes Plot, but then I remembered the odd riddle written on the bottom of poor George Walker's tombstone. It's so pathetic. I heard it was specified in his will. It must have been a sorry message for you, Erin. You had so many pitiful lovers. Let's see, it goes something like this:

In Memory of ES:

*The light of day never again shall see
a gentler soul than was she.
Seek with pure heart and all is found,
Eden's treasure on hallowed ground.*

"It makes me gag. What a pathetic epitaph for a sorry fool. But his clue was right there, all the time. It was left for you, Erin, and you never got it. Stupid, Erin."

Ariella spoke calmly, "George Walker was a living saint—beware of defaming him."

"Ahhh, she speaks. George Walker was just another one of your misguided love-sick dogs, like these two curs." He laughed a hollow laugh. "He left you a sorry clue on his tombstone, and you were too stupid to find it. Why didn't he just tell you? Oh, wait, I know—because you were running about the country like the floozie that you really are. 'Gentler soul'—what crap! Anyway, Anna and I finally figured it out. She's smart, you know. She knew all along. I guess she had done a lot of research on Erin Stone, her deadbeat mother who left her to go find herself.

"You never fooled her, Erin. She found you. I bet you thought you found her. Your ego always gets in the way. She knew you were her mother before she met you. She told me. I had befriended her first. I can be charming. You know that. And she told me she just wasn't sure if she wanted a mother like you. Smart girl. Too bad she didn't want to join me. I offered. She would have been much better than this useless loser." He kicked Linda as she huddled next to him.

"Too bad Anna had to leave so soon. I grew quite fond of her. But let's resume our little revenge play that I have taken so much trouble to orchestrate. I've got the stage and I've got the gun." He laughed, betraying his lunacy. "So, I won't shoot Harry—not yet. I could certainly shoot that overgrown dog of yours, Erin. It's just like you to hang out with two mangy mongrels." He laughed. "Why, you got one on your left and one on your right. Yes, that's what I'll do. I'll start there. Then if Harry refuses to cough up what I need, I'll shoot you. That'll be a pleasure greater than the one Anna gave before she died. Yes, she's dead, and I loved every moment of it!"

Pointing the gun at the large wolf, he was about to press the trigger when Ariella stepped in front of the animal, completely blocking the shot.

"Now, what did you do that for, Erin? Hmmm…I guess I'll have to shoot you first." He aimed the gun at her and was about to pull the trigger when Harry jumped forward.

"You kill her and you'll never know where that treasure's hidden 'cause she's the only one who knows," he lied. "She hid it while I was gone."

"Nice try, Harry. But if Erin knew, she wouldn't be with you. You fool. You really think she loves you? She wants the money like I do. Nice try. Prepare to die and become a true ghost, Erin." He laughed aloud.

"You fear that ghost, don't you?" Ariella asked calmly. Her words rang like a church bell through the cavernous hall that was his heart. "Well, I control her, and if you've harmed Anna in any way that ghost'll haunt you forever."

He stopped for a second processing that statement. *Could she control a ghost?* he wondered. *Could it be true that she and that ghost were one and the same?* His thoughts turned to words. "There's no ghost. There's just your endless crap, Erin. Well, I'm about to put an end to it. Unless dirty Harry, here…" He paused and laughed at his own pun. "No, it's smelly Harry. Yes, dirty Harry is much too mild and noble. Anyway, unless smelly Harry tells me right now where that treasure's buried, you'll die in about one minute, and then, I'll kill that wolf with the second shot. Smelly Harry, where'd ya stash the loot?"

"Okay, I'll tell you, but don't shoot her," Harry pleaded.

"Don't tell 'im, Harry. He'll shoot me anyway. He's nothing but a greedy coward, and that's all he'll ever be," Ariella calmly proclaimed. She did not fear death, for she knew it was nothing more than a powerless curtain.

"Shut your hole!" he demanded. Linda cowered behind him, giggling nervously.

"Where's my daughter, you coward?" Ariella used a stern voice for the first time.

"Dead, like her mother's about to be," he answered and took aim.

"Stop! I'll tell you," Harry pleaded.

"Don't tell him anything, Harry," Ariella demanded.

"It's not far. It's in this set of caves." Harry let out the secret to save the love of his life.

"I thought so. Tell you what, I'll only wound her, and if you can find it before she bleeds to death, then you can be the hero, smelly Harry. Maybe you can save her. How's that for a deal, old rotting one?"

"Please don't hurt her," Harry pleaded out of love.

"Too late for that, hobo," he replied, as he took aim at Ariella.

What happened next occurred so quickly that the sequence was hard to determine. Linda screamed, for she saw something on the other side of the cave. This caused a distraction and the wolf instinctively sprang into action, lunging at Ariella's nemesis. The latter shot at the charging animal, grazing him. But the beast ignored the wound and leapt at his attacker. Before another shot was fired, the wolf was upon him and in one swift bite he tore away the gun, including the trigger finger. He might have killed the man, for he had his teeth around his throat, had Ariella not ordered him to stop. Once released, the villain screamed in terror. As Ariella came to his aid, Harry grabbed the gun while the wolf fled into the shadows at the far end of the cave, disappearing like the free spirit of karmic justice that he personified. Linda scurried away in fear, despite Ariella's pleas for her to stop and tell her Anna's whereabouts.

By the time Molly entered the hall with her gun drawn, she found the man with the raven tattoo in shock with a bloody hand wound that had been hastily wrapped with a white cotton cloth that Ariella had torn from the hem of her dress. A tranquil fire burned in the far corner of the cave, creating haunting shadows that danced the length of the eerie chamber. All was silent, except the man's moaning. Like the large, gray wolf, Ariella and Harry had disappeared.

The Inspector arrived next. "What's going on?" he asked Molly.

"It's our man, as you predicted," she replied. "Boss, if you watch him, I'll try and find Anna. She must be farther down these caves. He won't tell me where. By the way, how did you know it was him?"

"It's not my first bizarre case, Molly, and with my luck, it won't be my last. Maybe it's time to retire."

"And miss all this fun? You'd be bored." She laughed and ran down the far passage toward the second cave chamber, leaving the Inspector wondering who was really the boss of his team. The thought made him smile inside. "Wait up. This guy's okay and not going anywhere." He had handcuffed him and called Chen on his shortwave radio. The latter was already headed into the entrance of the cave.

* * * *

"We need to catch up to Cane," Ariella proclaimed to Harry. "He's been my guardian since my mentor died. I'm sure Cane'll find her."

Ariella and Harry ran after Cane into the far passage of the cavern. It was another tunnel that led deeper into the grotto. This one was large enough that they could run through it, though they had to be careful. The floor and walls of the dolomite passage were wet and slippery, coated with slick deposits of travertine. Harry led the way, using the light of the flashlight to guide them. Without it, they would have been completely blinded by the pitch black.

"I know this place. That fool was a lot closer to the treasure than he realized. It's buried in the flooded corner of the third chamber. It has always been there since Drake put it there over two hundred years ago. George Walker and I found a part of it by accident when we were kids. Later, I found more, but I know there's still more. That fool was in the right spot," Harry confessed to Ariella.

"Harry, right now, the only treasure of any true worth in this cave is our daughter."

"Cane ran through here, all right. Those are his tracks." Harry pointed at the large wolf tracks.

"He's probably already found her."

"He wouldn't harm her, would he?" Harry wondered, after seeing what the wolf was capable of doing.

"No. Back there, he was only protecting us."

Suddenly, they froze. A chilling sound echoed through the entire cavern system. Molly and the Inspector heard it as they entered the same passage that Harry and Ariella were navigating. Jerry and Chen heard it as they entered the first cave. After an encounter like the one he had with Molly, Jerry convinced Chen that he was one of the good guys. Even Linda heard it, as she scrambled out of the cave through a tight and muddy side entrance. The cry was primeval and eternal in its power and intonation. It was the sound of a mighty wolf howling.

"He found her," Ariella said.

A few minutes later, Ariella and Harry entered the second great room of the cave system. This one was smaller, and there were collapsed walls of rock on the far end. In the dim light of Harry's dying flashlight, they saw the wolf standing guard next to the body of a young woman.

"Oh, my God, it's Anna!" Ariella said, as they ran toward the fallen girl. The wolf was licking Anna's face. She began to awaken, having fainted at the hands of her captor. She had gashes on parts of her body and her clothes were nearly torn off, as if she had been attacked by a beast far more ferocious than the wolf that guarded her. Ariella quickly examined her, while Harry kept the light. She began to apply ointments to the wounds. She always carried these ointments within her white sash. "She'll be okay. She's alive and she'll be okay," Ariella concluded with a deep, thankful sigh. Anna was shocked by the vision of the large wolf and the hairy hermit. She came to her senses with a fearful retraction. Seeing Ariella, she finally calmed herself.

"How'd you find me?" she asked.

"Cane and Harry did." Ariella nodded toward the wolf and the hermit. "Are you all right?"

"I think so. I tried to fight him off, but I was tied up. He was about to…well, something distracted him, just in time. I guess he got scared. Last thing I know is he hit me so hard I passed out. What's with the giant wolf? He's scary. And, who's he?" She looked over at the hermit.

It was clear that Anna would soon be back to her inquisitive self. Ariella gladly answered all her questions, while tending to her wounds. When Molly and the Inspector finally entered the second chamber of the vast grotto, the Inspector could not believe his eyes. "Look at the size of that wolf!" he exclaimed, drawing his gun.

"Perfect timing—the batteries are about to run out." Harry greeted the two detectives as if they had been called to do nothing more than bring a working flashlight.

"Who the hell are you?" the Inspector asked Harry, while still holding his gun.

"I'm Dirty Harry and she's the White Witch." Harry pointed at Ariella and chuckled.

"Right, and I'm Peter Pan and that's Tinker Bell," the Inspector replied, glancing at Molly.

Molly began helping Ariella tend to Anna, fearlessly disregarding the gray wolf, who quickly disappeared into the shadows, never to be seen again by the stunned Inspector.

* * * *

Meanwhile, Kelly was having a hard time trying to stay awake. She questioned her decision of bringing Rachel along. Her promise to guard the young girl had forced her to miss all the action. It had been well over an hour since the team had disappeared down the trail beyond the logging road. Even Rachel was bored. She decided to wander down the wooded path.

"Wait, Rachel. You need to stay here." Kelly jumped out of the car to catch up to her.

"This is boring. Let's find out what's going on down there. We're not helping at all out here."

"Inspector's orders. If I cross my boss, I could get fired," Kelly replied.

"Wait. I hear something," Rachel placed her finger on her lips to signal Kelly to be silent. The two young women were becoming good friends.

Before they had a chance to react, Linda Taylor ran by them, not noticing their presence. She appeared terrified. Kelly immediately recognized her as a person of interest and gave pursuit. Within minutes, Linda was in custody. So it was that Anna was saved; Linda, an accomplice to the crimes, was captured; and the mysterious serial killer was subdued by an unlikely foe, a large, equally mysterious wolf. All appeared to be resolved, except that the villain in this case seemed to have risen from the dead.

Brennanville and Eden Crossing, Pennsylvania

CHAPTER 71

The Revelations Number Nine

"Finally!" Molly looked at her watch. It was ten minutes past seven on Halloween night. She had decided to accept her boyfriend's invitation to spend the night at his new house handing out candy to local trick-or-treaters. "I thought you said this neighborhood gets a ton of trick-or-treaters. It's past seven and we finally got one."

"Hey, that's what the neighbor lady told me."

"Let's hope she's right or you're going to be living on candy. You never do anything small, do ya, Jack?"

Before he had a chance to defend himself, Molly opened the door. "Trick or treat!" screamed several young children dressed in Halloween costumes. Molly handed out the treats and was about to close the door when a figure emerged out of the darkness. She was dressed in a white witch outfit.

"Trick or treat!" she said, as she stepped into the light on the front porch of Jack Fulton's new home.

"Not again!" Molly sighed and laughed. "No more white witches, but you're welcome to come in, unless you're plannin' on hittin' all the houses in the neighborhood."

More children in costumes approached the door. They paused at the sight of the white witch standing on the porch. "Wow! That's a great costume," said one of the girls, who was also dressed as a witch, with a black pointed hat and a black cape.

"Come on up," Molly invited. "She won't bite."

The children overcame their fear, collected their treats, and quickly disappeared back into the night. "Come on in, Kelly. Nice outfit." Molly laughed.

"Wow!" Jack proclaimed, as Kelly entered the living room. "You look great. Where'd you get it?"

"From a good friend of mine." She looked over at Molly.

"It's very realistic," Jack replied.

"Ariella gave it to me. She's amazing. By the way, Rachel convinced me to officially join the Eden Sisterhood. I'm having such a great time and learning so much. It's a great place for young women who need shelter—a place for them to find their inner strength. She's so good at relating to these often-mistreated girls. Anyway, I try to go over there every weekend and help her out. It's my new charity. Molly, you should go with me, sometime. By the way, they're expanding to the Brennantown area and guess who's going to run that shelter?"

"Our boss!" Molly said.

"That's funny!" Kelly laughed. "No! Anna's going to run it, and Rachel and I are going to help her. There's a greater need in the area than I would've thought," Kelly added, as she sat down. "They're starting an Eden Brotherhood for boys, as well. You could help too, Jack."

"I'll look into it. Do I get to work with the great Inspector Cabot?"

"That I would like to see." Kelly laughed a hearty laugh.

"Can I offer the white witch some white wine?" Jack asked.

"Sure."

The number of trick-or-treaters increased for about another hour, which made serious conversations difficult. Instead, the three friends focused on small talk and enjoyed the roaring fire in Jack's slate fireplace. After the Halloween activity subsided, the conversation turned to the Eden Crossing case. Jack was sworn to secrecy, and as the wine flowed, so did the revelations. It was clear that Kelly would be testing out Jack's guest bedroom that night. It wouldn't be the last time. She and Molly were becoming like sisters beyond the workplace.

"Can you believe that case? Are they all like that?" Kelly asked, being new to the team.

"No. That was a particularly odd one."

"I know you gals can't talk about too many details, given its police work, but I'm really curious," Jack said. "What happened with the White Witch? Was it a legend or a ghost or Ariella dressed up in an outfit like yours, Kelly?"

Molly looked over at Kelly before answering. "It depends on who you ask. One thing's for sure. Linda Taylor, one of the folks on trial, admitted to having dressed up as the White Witch on numerous occasions to perpetuate the White Witch legend she and others seemed to obsess over. If you ask me, there was never a ghost. It was simply Linda Taylor. Some still suspect Ariella, aka Erin Stone, of being the White Witch, but there's no evidence for that. It was a rumor that probably started because she nearly always dresses in the white, flowing robes of a Sioux shaman and likes to hike around the woods on early mornings. What do you think, Kelly? You know her a lot better than me."

"I think Ariella is more powerful than one might think, but I don't know about her involvement with the White Witch legend. She refuses to talk about that. Linda was probably the only White Witch out there. But it's curious that the Evelyn Drake legend turned out to be more accurate than anyone ever suspected. There was a crazy treasure hunt, after all. Will Porter searched for the treasure at Drakes Plot and paid the ultimate price, while Erin had the treasure all along. It was the mysterious coin collection in the sizable safe deposit box that she inherited from her old friend George Walker. George and Harry Schaffer apparently discovered the treasure when they were kids. Crazy, huh?" Kelly concluded.

"I read in the paper that the murders were drug related. Is that true?" Jack asked. He and Molly never talked about her work, so he was eager to learn more, now that the two women were willing to share some insights into one of the most bizarre cases on record.

"Yeah, it was drug related. Sort of," Molly replied.

"I still can't believe Jerry McAlester was an undercover narcotics agent. He's good. Oops, forget I said that, Jack. I don't want to blow his cover. That investigation into the local drug gang is still ongoing. Apparently, Will Porter was very active in the gang and used his bartender job to set up deals. Linda and Andrew Taylor, as well as Gavin Green, were all involved, including others. It's a local gang tied to connections in Pittsburgh," Kelly said.

"I didn't realize that opioids, like heroin, were so prevalent in rural communities across the state. I always thought they were inner city issues, but the trend is a rapid expansion into rural communities," she added.

"I know. It's crazy! Turns out that Will Porter was the main local drug dealer and Gavin Green was trying to take over. Linda testified that Agnes stumbled upon the drug activity at the Green Estate and was going to turn Gavin in to the police, so he tried to kill her," Molly explained.

"What about Sam Hughes? He must have suspected all the drug activity around him?" Jack asked. "The papers were pretty critical of him 'cause Green and Porter were both employees at The Raven Inn."

"I heard he was helping McAlister keep his cover over the last three months. So he probably knew part of the story but McAlister swore him to secrecy. We may never know the details. But he's a good guy. He really is. You'd like him, Jack. We should go over there some time for dinner," Molly added. She still fancied the rugged innkeeper.

"I don't know. It's quite a drive," Jack replied.

"Oh, Kelly, I forgot to tell you. Sam sent me an e-mail yesterday. He's engaged. Can you believe it?" Molly added.

"Good for him. Is it that server?"

"Yeah, Elaine Roberts. He sounded so happy."

"Congratulate him for me."

"I will."

"Speaking of weddings, do you remember that young Amish farmer?"

"Amos Miller?"

"Yeah. Get this, he and the infamous Lenore are getting married as well. I heard it from one of the sisterhood girls. Lenore keeps in touch with several of them. They're getting married next spring. I guess Lenore decided to remain Amish," Kelly explained.

"I don't blame her. If I could marry an Amish guy, it'd be Amos Miller," Molly proclaimed.

"Are you leaving me for an Amish guy?" Jack asked.

"If you don't behave, I might." Molly put her arms around Jack as they sat on the couch. They were stronger than ever. She was even considering accepting Jack's standing marriage proposal, but something inside her still resisted.

"I can't believe Alvin Walker turned out to be innocent. He seemed so guilty. I guess he and Gus Morgan were simply finding clues that Linda had planted at the two crime scenes," Molly reflected.

"You mean the scraps of white cotton cloth?"

"Yeah. She planted them to frame Ariella as the White Witch and the killer. I still don't know how Ariella's DNA got on them unless it was one of her old dresses. But those fake clues were too obvious, as the Inspector insisted," Molly reflected. "Kelly, you mentioned the safe deposit box full of the Drake coins. Isn't it odd that George Walker, Alvin's deceased brother, left the coins to Ariella and not his brother?"

"You haven't been reading the boss's memos, have you? Shame on you!" Kelly replied.

"You mean the long, wordy summaries?"

"Yes, those lovely things."

"I got a little behind. Please fill me in—o wise witch."

"Well, as you know, George Walker was with his best friend, Harry Schaffer, when they found the treasure as kids. At first they hid it in an undisclosed location, but after Harry went to war George placed the old Spanish doubloons in a safe deposit box in both their names."

"You mean the two teenage boys found a gold treasure and managed to keep it a secret until now?"

"Yes. I guess they were good at keeping secrets. I know you couldn't keep a secret like that, Molly. You'd own too many Gucci bags. That would give it away."

"Very funny, Kelly. But why did George will his half of the coins to Ariella instead of Alvin?"

"I asked Ariella about that. It was bugging me, so one night I asked her," Kelly replied.

"What did she say?"

"She said that she, Harry, and George were the closest of friends in high school. Apparently, the two boys let her in on the discovery, and in exchange for her secrecy the three made a pact that if either George or Harry did not want the coins or could not possess them for any reason, they'd leave their share to Ariella, who went by her real name of Erin Stone at that time. I suspect that both boys were in love with her. Anyway, George simply fulfilled that promise in his will. I guess he had no desire to cash in the coins. But when I talked to Ariella recently, she mentioned that she had offered to share the coins with Alvin now that the case was over, but apparently he's wealthy on his own and wanted her to use that money to start an Eden Brotherhood charity in memory of his brother, George. She thinks very highly of Alvin Walker," Kelly explained.

"What! You're pulling my leg," Molly replied.

"No. It's true. I swear. It seems that Alvin, for all his egocentric ways, has a good heart. Ariella said that George always claimed that his younger brother took it hard when their mother died. I guess Alvin was pretty young when she died. It seems that when Alvin went to college in Texas, he had a bad breakdown and drank a lot. I guess the case brought out the ego and the insecurity in him, as well as some instability. I sure didn't like that guy and the way he treated us. But as the sole heir to The Walker Estate, he doesn't need to work at all. He does it simply because he enjoys being a part-time cop."

"And a royal pain in the butt!" Molly proclaimed.

"Agreed. He was the one who initially screwed things up and threw us off track. When the mistake first came out, I thought he was an accomplice and did it on purpose," Kelly said.

"What mistake?" Jack asked.

"He believed Will Porter," Molly replied but did not expand on her answer.

The two women looked at each other, realizing that maybe they were sharing too much. After all, it was not public knowledge that the department, including the coroner's office, misidentified the initial victim in the case as Gavin Green when in fact it was the body of Andrew Taylor that surfaced under Devils Bridge. Fortunately, the mistake had not leaked to the media as the body was simply reported at the time as a John Doe. Apparently, Alvin Walker made the mistake based on witness identifications, and no one challenged it given that Gavin's only relative, his estranged father, refused to cooperate.

Molly decided not to share any more information and Kelly quickly switched the subject.

"I swear that Ariella seems to have an odd power to see through things. She still hasn't let me in on the secret, but I've heard from the other girls that it's her shamanic powers. She seems to connect to a 'higher source of inspiration,' as she calls it. I know that you don't buy into that, Molly."

"You're right. I don't buy into all that supernatural spiritual nonsense. Yet, it seems to continually pursue me—even in my relationships." She nudged Jack, who chuckled.

"I'm working on her, Kelly, but Miss Logical is a hard nut to crack."

"Look, I admit that there are many things that are inexplicable, but I'm a detective first. I don't care if you and Jack believe in all this mystical stuff. Great! I'm open-minded, but I need proof. Take that ghost idea, for instance. In the end, it was Linda Taylor, but everyone got all excited about a ghost. I don't believe in ghosts and I'm still on the fence about all the stuff that you two buy into, like mediums and channels. Not even your favorite case convinced me, right, Jack?"

"Like I said, she's a hard nut to crack. She's referring to the Mary Collins case," Jack clarified.

"I know. I heard all about how you guys met. Hey, what ever happened to Mary Collins?" Kelly poked the bear.

Jack played along. "She's doing great and Molly has even stopped being jealous of her."

"I was never jealous of her. She's a child. Plus, we're so different. If you had the hots for Mary Collins, you'd never be with me. I'd make sure of that," Molly proclaimed.

"I can tell you're no longer jealous," Kelly answered with a touch of sarcasm.

"I'm not! I never was jealous. Should I be?" She turned to Jack. Kelly smiled, for she had succeeded in fanning the flames.

Jack decided to throw water on them. "Of course not! To answer your question, Kelly, Mary's seeing a very nice guy. Her friend, Jennifer, fixed her up with a fellow student at McLaren Medical School. They seem like a great match."

"Speaking of great matches, I forgot to tell you that we're all invited to Bob Braxton's wedding. He and Suzy are tying the knot next summer. It's going to be a big wedding, right here in town. Isn't that exciting?" Molly reminded them, glad to be off the subject of Mary Collins.

"For a second there, Molly, I thought you were going to announce that the Inspector was tying the knot," Jack replied.

"That's funny. I love Cabot, but he's beyond hope. I forgot to tell you. He and Ms. Allen broke up two weeks ago. All he said was, 'Thank God.'"

Laughter ensued.

"Love's a mysterious thing," Jack concluded.

"Well said, professor." Kelly chuckled.

"Not a professor, yet," Jack corrected her.

"Stick with me and you'll get there, honey," Molly replied and winked at him.

"I guess I'd better leave you two lovebirds alone," Kelly said and got up to leave.

"You're not going anywhere except the guest room," Jack insisted.

"Okay, but I have one question for Miss Logical. Since you don't believe in the spiritual, Molly, how do you explain what we saw in the gardens of Kiradale? That sure looked like a ghost to me."

"That was probably Linda dressed up as the White Witch—spying on us," Molly replied.

"It looked more like a ghost to me," Kelly said.

"Next, you'll claim that big wolf was a spirit, as well. Just because he disappeared and we never found him, doesn't mean he wasn't real. It just means that animal control's useless. For all we know, he could still be roaming about Eden Valley scaring others."

"He's not," Kelly replied with certainty.

"How do you know?"

"Don't tell anyone outside this room, but he's very tame. He's Ariella's pet."

"What!"

"I think she held that back from the police because she didn't want animal control to force her to put him down. He's harmless. I see him with her all the time."

"Whatever. But it proves my point that there was a logical explanation behind it, as there is behind everything," Molly concluded.

"Except when our minds can't fully grasp the magnitude or complexity of that reality, and its seeming lack of logic, right?" Jack added.

"See! You're a born professor 'cause I didn't understand a word of that. I'm just a simple girl dating a big-brained bruiser," Molly replied.

"You guys need to get a room, and I need to get some sleep. I'll take you up on the guest room offer," Kelly replied. Molly showed her the room and helped her get settled.

As Jack and Molly prepared to head upstairs to his bedroom, he returned to the question that Molly had ignored. "Hon, what mistake did Alvin Walker commit? You said he believed Will Porter. I thought Porter died."

"He did die."

"Well, I don't get it. I have a lot of questions for you, but I know you shouldn't discuss these cases."

"I didn't realize you didn't know the outcome of the case, Jack. You can ask me about cases, anytime. If I can't tell you the answer, I'll let you know. This point is very sensitive, so please never repeat it. But I will tell you, okay?"

"You have my word," Jack replied.

"Alvin made a critical mistake and none of us caught it for a long time, which threw us off course for most of the investigation. We all believed his police report and witness confirmations as they related to the identity of the first victim. But no one, not even the coroner, had verified that identity, which did not look good for the department, especially for Frank Dunn, the chief coroner. The error exposed key gaps in our victim identification process that we have since fixed."

"What happened?" he asked, for he did not fully understand.

"Will Porter, who appeared first at the crime scene, purposely misidentified the body as that of Gavin Green. Linda Taylor, who appeared shortly after him at the scene, confirmed that identification. Thus, Alvin had two seemingly independent positive identifications and assumed they were correct. The coroner showed up and Alvin rightfully restricted further access to the crime scene to non-official personnel. After his initial field investigation, the coroner had the victim placed in a body bag and the misidentification stuck as the truth.

Apparently, the identity switch was part of the plan. Linda admitted that the night Andrew Taylor died, she and Will played a trick on Gavin Green. She dressed up as the White Witch earlier that night and together with Will they scared the heck out of Green. Apparently, Gavin Green believed the White Witch was real, so it wasn't that hard to do. Also, he was high at the time, so the trick worked exceptionally well. In fact, it worked so well that Green ran out of his house onto the nearby bridge where Linda was waiting in her full witch costume. He panicked and jumped off Devils Bridge. Scared to death, he landed in the river and Linda claims he would probably have drowned had she and Will not pulled him out.

"Anyway, that's how they got the idea to get rid of Andrew Taylor, who was becoming a liability because he found out about Linda's affair with Gavin and threatened to expose them and Will's drug gang. According to her testimony, while Gavin recovered from his 'White Witch' encounter and midnight swim, Linda headed to The Raven Inn and talked to Sam Hughes to have an alibi to protect her from what came next.

"In the wee hours of the morning, Linda called Andrew in a panic pretending she was in trouble, telling him that Gavin had gone crazy and that he was going to hurt her. Andrew jumped in his truck and drove to The Green Estate, where she was staying since their separation. When he got there, he found the front gate locked, so he left the truck and ran across the yard toward the house, cutting his bare feet in the process because he had jumped in the truck with no shoes. Once in the house, Gavin and Linda, who had returned from the inn, ambushed him, knocked him out and drove him to the bridge where Gavin shot him full of heroin, creating the overdose. Together, they dressed him in Gavin's monogramed pajamas and threw him off the bridge.

"They called Will later that morning, and he agreed to go down to the river to 'discover' and identify the body to the police as that of Gavin Green. Linda also waited at the scene to make sure no one who knew Andrew or Gavin got near the body. When Alvin arrived, she was there to confirm the body as that of Gavin Green but lied about her name as listed on Alvin's police report, introducing herself as Cheryl Girard. The Amish couple that discovered the body just before Will arrived were an unexpected twist in the plan. However, since they did not know either Andrew or Gavin, they did not impact the identity swap other than to help give it an added level of validity.

"That swap worked mostly because none of us confirmed Linda's and Will's statements or questioned Alvin's police report. Besides, the body fit the profile of Green and was dressed in Green's monogramed pajamas. Additionally, there was no police record for either Gavin or Andrew, nor any fingerprints or DNA on file. We never checked photos once the body went with the coroner. We simply assumed that Gavin Green was dead and the first victim, when, in fact, Andrew Taylor was the first victim and Gavin Green was the killer. According to Linda's testimony, when Will started demanding money from Gavin to maintain the secret, Gavin told him about the Drake treasure. Will bought the story and went to Drakes Plot to dig up Evelyn Drake's grave, unaware that Gavin followed him. Once the grave was dug and no treasure was found, Gavin made his appearance and killed him. Yet Gavin still believed that the treasure was buried somewhere in Drakes Plot, so the following night, he took a big risk and dug up Arthur Drake's grave, only to find it empty as well.

"By the way, before the Andrew Taylor killing, Gavin Green was already growing more and more aggressive. Linda confessed that she was there when Green tried to kill Lenore Lapp, striking her on the head with an iron bar and pushing her body into the Eden River off Devils Bridge. Then, he got brazen and attacked Agnes Wright in the barn behind The Raven Inn. He was trying to frame Sam Hughes, whom he loathed. He even got a black raven tattooed on his arm and made sure that Agnes saw it, so as to implicate Hughes.

"The attempt backfired because Agnes managed to resist and screamed loudly enough to attract the attention of Hughes, who arrived at the scene to save her. It appears that she was simply a pawn in Green's game. Linda testified that Green had confided in her that he was planning to frame Sam Hughes for the Lenore incident, if it ever surfaced."

"Wow, that's a complicated case," Jack replied, wishing he hadn't asked his initial question. "So, the killer and attacker in all the instances was Gavin Green. He wasn't dead after all. He just made it look like he died so he wouldn't be a suspect. Crazy case. I'm glad I don't have your job, Molly." It was past midnight and his mind was too tired to keep up with Molly's explanations.

"Yes. But that's not all. Linda admitted that Gavin became increasingly obsessed with the Drake treasure. Before Andrew's death, Gavin, Andrew, and Will Porter, who were all in on the treasure hunt, dug holes in the basement of the Green farmhouse because Gavin initially thought the treasure was buried there, for reasons unclear to anyone but him. His greed turned into desperation.

"That is when he decided not only to try and frame Erin Stone, aka Ariella Bianca, for his own staged death, portraying her as the White Witch, but also to try and get the mystery of the treasure out of her. Given that he had failed to find it either at the Green Estate or at Drakes Plot, he suspected that Ariella knew its whereabouts. Thus, he and Linda decided to raid the Eden Sisterhood cabin to frighten Ariella into revealing her secret, but they didn't succeed. Frustrated, Gavin decided to take Anna hostage and leverage her for the Drake treasure.

"However, Ariella somehow figured out Anna's location. She told me in the final debrief I had with her that she knew in her heart that Gavin hated her so much that the chance of him releasing Anna alive was very slim. That is why she took on the risk of finding him herself. She believed that police intervention would delay her and further risk Anna's life. Besides, she knew that she was a suspect in the case and didn't want Gus to stop her. In the end, she succeeded, although I'm still not sure how Harry Schaffer, aka the Hermit, played into it all, except that she somehow got him to help her."

Jack was tired and desperately wished that he had not asked about the case. However, Molly was on a roll that could not be stopped.

"The other odd thing was that if young Erin Stone, who was briefly engaged to the much older Cornelius Green, had married him, she would have become Gavin Green's stepmother. Apparently, Gavin's mother blamed Erin for the divorce and wanted her dead. Instead she died a year later. Gavin blamed Erin Stone for his mother's death. I guess that fueled his hatred for Erin, aka Ariella. It didn't help her cause when she got pregnant with Harry Schaffer's baby while engaged to Cornelius. I think Harry and Erin got married before he left for Bosnia, but I'm not sure. Like many of these cases, part of the root cause was an unsettled family score. Weird stuff, but, in the end, justice seemingly prevailed in the form of a strange, large wolf.

"Like I said, it's all too bizarre to think about. The scariest thing left is that that huge wolf is still roaming around. I don't care if Kelly claims that he's a pet. He's a huge wild beast, if you ask me. I'll tell you what, now that I know that he's running about, Kelly's never getting me near that Schaffer cabin—charity or no charity."

Molly stopped her explanation at last. She too was tired, and this was not how she had hoped to spend the evening. There were good reasons she never discussed her cases with Jack, and this was one of them. It was a mood killer. "Did you follow all that?"

"No. All I wanted to follow was you up to bed," Jack replied. "You know, I'm glad I'm a geologist, not a detective. Geology's much easier to comprehend than a case like that," Jack concluded and headed toward the stairs. "By the way, in case you had any doubts, I'm going up to bed and straight to sleep."

"Too bad. I bet Amos Miller has more stamina than that," she said with a chuckle.

"Who's Amos Miller?" He could not remember all the names she and Kelly had tossed around that night.

"The hot Amish guy, of course," she replied and smiled.

"Yes, of course, but if that's supposed to make me jealous and change my mind, it's not working."

"Too bad. I guess I won't give you your present, then?"

"What're you talking about?" He stopped and stared at her. She had his full attention.

In silent response, she pulled out a straw Amish hat and placed it on her head, while letting her robe slip off her bare figure and sprinting past him up the stairs.

CHAPTER 72

Forevermore

The full moon danced on the dark pool at midnight, courting the subtle waves in a tranquil tempo. A gentle, westerly wind swept over the bare torso of a sole bather, creating a chill that aroused her. Ripples disturbed the haunting serenity of black water, full of mystery.

The lone bather seemed fearless as if she knew all, caring little for what lurked in the shadows. Intrepid, she disappeared below the dark surface to emerge moments later, triumphant and cleansed. The moonlight played with her silken hair, turning her face into a reflection of itself. She was Diana of old, risen once more. The goddess of the moon felt at home in her royal bath. Nothing could threaten her.

At the base of the tranquil pool, a waterfall announced its presence to the silent night. In harmony with the wind, it played a timeless tune forever faintly familiar.

"It's a chilly night for a swim, Erin." Harry always referred to Ariella by her given name. As she stepped out of the dark pool, he wrapped a towel around her shoulders. "Even Cane thinks ya're crazy." He chuckled, while looking at the gray wolf that sat on a nearby rock, staring at the fickle moon.

"I needed that swim. I hadn't done that in weeks. Besides, you know we're all a little crazy, Harry. That's what makes us human. Cane's the only sane one." She smiled, as the wolf came down from his pedestal and nuzzled against her. Suddenly, they all stopped and fell silent.

In the blue light of the moon, there appeared a translucent specter of a woman in a white, flowing gown. She stopped before them for a moment before drifting across the enchanted pool that Ariella enjoyed moments earlier. A large, black raven followed, beckoned by his timeless mistress.

"She and I are one, you know," Ariella whispered.

"I know, and neither of you entertains imposters."

"You're learning, Harry. You're learning."

Embracing, they walked slowly down the wooded path that led to the old cabin. Before they disappeared into the distant mist, the wolf stopped and howled to pay homage to the rising moon and to the White Witch that ruled the night, forevermore.

David Stockar is a fiction writer with an appreciation for classic literature and creative storytelling. In his work, he explores the complexities
of relationships and motivations, often taking the reader beyond the
foreground of daily existence into deeper eternal mysteries. He enjoys
multi-layered plots that juxtapose complex characters and ethereal
elements. His favorite genres are mystery and adventure novels. Born
in Prague, he lives in Pennsylvania with his wife and children.

Please visit www.davidstockar.com for information on David's other
books and writings.

Your reviews are greatly appreciated on Amazon and Goodreads, or
wherever you purchased this book.

The colorful and creative images that adorn the covers of David's
books are works by his mother, Helena Stockar. Please visit
www.helenastockar.com to learn more about her life and her art.